UNTOUCHED

BOOK ONE

JEN ATKINSON

𝒥𝒜
books

Printed and bound in the USA.
First Paperback Edition: 2018

- Content Editor: Maggie Dallen
- Line Editor: Heidi Shuler, Eric Kenley
- Cover Design: Heidi Shuler

ISBN-13: 978-1985134003

ISBN-10: 1985134004

1. Fantasy—Fiction 2. High Schools—Fiction 3. Wyoming (State)—Fiction 4. Romance—Fiction

For Sydney
Who knows that a trial can be a blessing in disguise.

1

WHISPERS AND GLARES

W hispers are hard to ignore. Especially when I can hear my name, *Thankful,* mixed in with the murmurs. I'm pretty sure no one is expressing their gratitude this early September morning.

I grew up in this small town. I'm not new to Glenrock. Seventeen years, same place, same people, but none of them know me. Not really. Clutching the book bag my mother made me buy for this day, I walk through the school hallway. People pass by me with whispers, but no one smiles, no one says hello. I stare at the ground, wishing I were home, at my desk, with my mother, my instructor in all things scholastic, spiritual, and moral.

Another *Thankful* floats into the air like a balloon on a string without a hand to hold it. I walk and let it float to the ceiling without a glance back.

Navy blue lockers line the narrow hall. I find number 212 and drop my bag to the ground. Twisting the knob to the correct numbers: twenty-one, thirteen, eleven, I pull at the lever, but the locker refuses to open. Trying again, blood rushes to my face, burning it to an uncomfortable warmth. *Just open. Open!* It doesn't.

"Can I help?"

Looking over my shoulder, I see a girl there. Her rectangular glasses are rimmed in black, but clear and wide enough I can still see her dark eyes behind them. Smiling, she blinks, and her eyelashes almost hit the edge of her eyebrows. I turn just a little to face her, my heart beating faster with the direct communication. "Uh, sure. I think it's stuck." I rest one hand on my stomach, hoping my breakfast will stay put.

"I'm Chelsea," she says, pulling the slip of paper with my locker combination from my hand. She twists the knob, not careful like I did, but fast, like this is her locker and she's opened it a hundred times. Lifting the latch, the door releases. "You have to pass the second number—spin it around once more."

"Thanks," I say, taking the paper back from her outstretched hand. Breathing in through my nose and out through my mouth, I try to smile. "I'm Thankful."

"Yeah, the homeschooled girl, right?" With the back of her hand Chelsea brushes the edge of her glasses, pushing them up on her nose.

I bite my lip. "Yeah." This is how I'll be known for the rest of the year, until college. It wasn't as if I was the only one in Glenrock who had been homeschooled, but they'd all gone to public school at some point. My point was the last possible point, senior year. And I wouldn't be here still if it weren't for Mom.

"My mom *never* could have homeschooled me," Chelsea says and her tone is familiar, like she's known me forever, not a mere sixty seconds. "No way is she smart enough. I mean, she maybe could have handled English, but I'm in calculus—Linda would have given up way back in pre-algebra."

I took calculus last year, but I don't say as much. I don't say anything, because I can't figure out how to respond to Chelsea's accusation that her mother isn't very smart, or smart enough. To agree seems insulting; to disagree would mean correcting someone I don't know on a subject I really know nothing about.

"Who do you have here, Chels?" another girl I've never seen before asks. She's with a girl I recognize, though. Friends are few in my life. It's not as if I had classes with… well, anyone. But Errica and I used to play when we were kids. She lived on my block until her dad got a promotion and they moved to the upscale part of town.

"Yeah, yeah," Errica says. Her low-lights of red and dark brown mix into her blonde with perfection. She's taller than the last time I saw her, maybe an inch shorter than my five-foot-seven. I guess a decade will do that. Her grown-up teeth have all come in and they're straight—braces straight. "Who's the new blood?" She bounces over behind the other girl and squeezes her way in. I can see her recollection, but she still asks the question. I don't know if I should say hello and call her bluff or just play along. As she said, *I'm* the new blood.

I stay silent.

I glance down at my Jimi Hendrix T-shirt and fold my left arm behind my back, tugging at the ends of my dirty blonde braid. I wish I could blend in with the lockers, become invisible.

"Hi, girls." Chelsea's laugh lines crease and she points to me. "This is Thankful. Thankful, the girls."

Errica links arms with Chelsea. I flash back to being seven years old. I wanted to play with Errica's Fashion Place Barbie, with its long blonde hair and its pink-and-white striped miniskirt. But she wouldn't let me.

"I'm Sonia," says the first girl. Her hair is striking red, like a strawberry or the fingernail polish I painted on Mom's toes last night. And unlike Errica's, I think it's her real color. "This is Errica."

"Hey," Errica says, not meeting my eyes.

I say hello, but pass the awkward moment by pulling out my schedule. "Where's Hunt's class?"

"Let me see your list," Chelsea says, again taking the paper from my hand. I get the feeling she's the leader of this little posse. At least she acts like the leader. Still, I like her. She's blunt, no whispering, and so far she's friendly. "What the—you only have five classes listed." Errica and Sonia crowd around her to look at my list.

"We have seven periods a day," Errica says, one eyebrow raised high on her head. She looks at me like I'm too stupid to realize how public school works.

"I know," I say, my voice mimicking her *why-are-you here* tone. "I have one religious release period I go home for. And I have enough credits I don't need the full seven class periods to graduate." I wish I didn't need any credits. If I weren't so close to graduating, I wouldn't be here at all. It's not where I should be. I'm not with Mom.

"Impressive," Chelsea says, and Errica snaps her mouth closed.

I'm not sure what brought on the hostility. When Errica and I parted ways at seven years old, things were fine. In fact, I'd missed her. I'd missed having any friend at all. I didn't realize just how much until now. But as I watch Errica's linked arm with Chelsea's, I feel a pang of jealousy, like I did all those years ago for that Fashion Place Barbie.

"I've got Hunt for English too," Chelsea says, pulling her arm from Errica's. "I'll show you."

Hanging my jacket in the locker, I close it up. Chelsea says goodbye to her friends and we walk down the hall together, passing more ogling eyes and *Thankful Tenys* whispers. Chelsea hears them too. She rolls her eyes and makes a gagging motion with her index finger and mouth.

"Agh! This school, all three hundred and eighteen students, psha, no, this whole town, they're idiots. They'll get over it." She points to the classroom on our right. "I did *not* grow up here," she says, defending herself. "Anything new, any change, and this town goes loco. You know?"

I shrug. I like Glenrock. I always have. The winters are cold and the wind is harsh, but I've always thought the people were nice. Still, I can't deny what Chelsea says about change. I've never heard my name on so many lips before. "How do they know who I am, anyway?" I only know a few of them. Errica, a couple of others, but most of them are strangers to me.

Grinning, Chelsea shakes her head. "I heard about you when we moved here a few years ago. They called you all kinds of things: the shut-in, the girl locked away by her evil step-mother, the girl too afraid to come to *real* school. And then there were others, I'm guessing the less dramatic, more truthful tales: the homeschooled girl who doesn't come out of her house."

Turning for the classroom, I laugh, finding the whole thing funny. Of course I left my house. "Evil stepmother?" I say, widening my eyes at Chelsea. "Yeah, and I have mice friends and a couple of stepsisters, too."

Chelsea laughs with me. It's all so ridiculous and I'm glad she realizes it. "Is that so?" she says, feigning shock. "And I hear your mother is so deathly ill, you can finally escape her evil clutches! Maybe for the first time in years you can step outside." Chelsea laughs again, but I can't join her.

Her words pinch my heart until I'm certain it must be bleeding on the inside. My mother is an angel. There isn't an evil bone in her body. But she is sick—so sick she couldn't teach me anymore. Sick enough that our lessons have turned into me cleaning up her vomit and giving her sponge baths. So sick I spend my days taking care of her and my nights trying my best to sleep in the crook of Grandpa's old recliner, right next to where she lays on the couch, waking at every sound she makes.

Chelsea doesn't notice I'm not laughing. She keeps smiling,

keeps chuckling, and then turns to wave to a boy in a letterman jacket just outside the class we've entered. Turning back to me, she swings her body around, bumping into another boy walking toward the exit. With his head down, he never saw her coming, but with the hit, his face lifts, red and angry.

Jerking back, Chelsea holds up her hands. "Chill, Liam," she says before he can speak.

Liam runs a hand through his dark hair, closes his eyes, and blows out a puff of air; a rumble escapes his throat. His hands clench into fists and he storms out of the classroom, turning sideways through the door so not to bump into a girl just coming in.

Taking a seat at a desk next to Chelsea, I stare at her, my eyes wide for real this time. "What was that?"

"Psha! *That* is Liam Gregor. He's got more stories attached to his name than you. Only, unlike you, I'm pretty sure all of his are true." Chelsea slaps the desk with her hands. "Arrhh," she growls, shaking her wrists and hands like she might have cooties or something.

I can't even guess what kind of stories trail behind Liam and I don't get the chance to ask Chelsea with Mr. Hunt standing in front of the class. He clears his throat and waits for attention. His whole being calls for it. He's tall, and though his biceps show definite muscle, his stomach is round and falls over the buckle of his belt. His bald head is bowed, looking at the names on his list. He stands with his feet apart and looks nothing like what I think a high school English teacher should resemble. He should be coaching wrestling, not teaching Shakespeare.

My knees beneath the table begin to shake. Mr. Hunt is halfway through the class list; he hasn't gotten to me yet. I feel like I might vomit. I don't want to be here. I don't want to do this. Forget friends. Who needs them, or a diploma for that matter? My breaths stagger, like I can't quite take in the oxygen. I can't do this. I can't.

Springing to my feet, I suck in another useless breath. "I'm going to the restroom!"

Mr. Hunt goes quiet for a second. With his hands behind his back, he looks up from the list on his desk, his eyes boring into me. "Sit," he says, and continues down the list.

But I don't listen. I can't breathe in this room. Too many bodies. Too many whispers. Too many stares. I run, afraid he'll chase after me. Out in the hallway, I search for a bathroom and see one just a few classrooms away. Looking back, I don't see anyone following me. Still, I race toward the restroom as if I'm being hunted down.

The bathroom doesn't have a door, just an open entrance that turns a corner to provide privacy. I screech to a halt, so not to hit the dark figure blocking the doorway. His back is to me. At least I think it's a he. It must be a *he*. He's too tall and broad to be a girl, any girl I've met, anyway. I check the sign next to the entrance again. *Women*.

"Hey," I say, trying to be brave, but it's difficult, as I was just a coward who ran from my English teacher. "You can't go in there."

"I know that." He spits the words and turns in a careful motion to face me. *Liam*.

I'm afraid, but with no one around to save me, I try not to show it. I stand tall, my shoulders squared. "Then could you move?" I try to imitate the authoritative way Errica spoke to me when she told me there were seven class periods.

The same growling sound he made when Chelsea spoke to him rumbles from his throat. His eyebrows are furrowed, low and dark, and his mouth is in what seems to be a permanent scowl. But he moves over. I scurry through to the safety of the bathroom, but I'm not alone.

I hear the sobbing before I see anyone. One of the five stall doors is closed. The sobs come from it. "Are…are you okay?" I ask. There's no answer. I bite my lip and look at my reflection in the mirror. I look like any other senior girl at Glenrock High, but I'm not, and everyone knows it. Bending down, I turn on the sink. Filling my cupped hands with water, I splash the liquid onto my face. The sobbing behind me continues. "Do you need anything?"

The stall door is thrown open, slamming into the wall behind it. "I could use a little privacy!" the small girl yells. She storms past me, bumping into Chelsea at the entrance. "Argh! Move!"

"Wow, people today," Chelsea says, her tone light and airy. Raising an eyebrow to me, she points at the doorway. "What's wrong with her?"

I shrug. "I asked. You saw my answer."

"Yeah, well, hormones. You know." She walks over, standing next to me, and looks at herself in the mirror. Lifting her glasses, she wipes under her eye, removing the tiniest speck of strayed mascara. "So, what's your deal?"

"Oh, ah…" I'd planned a whole breakdown once I reached the bathroom, but with the crying girl already a mess and now Chelsea here…. "I just need to go to the bathroom."

Chelsea turns to look at me. "Yeah, right, let's go with that story."

Blowing out a sigh, my eyes skirt the ground. "Okay, I got a little overwhelmed is all. So many people and that teacher—he's… he's huge." I can hear myself proving everyone's wrong theories right, and I hate it. Maybe I am the girl too afraid to go to school. I'd never thought of myself that way. Mom started out teaching me at home and I liked it that way. We both did.

"I get it," Chelsea says, back to admiring herself. "First year. You're like the *untouched*. Like a fresh, new kindergartener."

"Kindergarten?" That was going a little far. I open my mouth to complain, but Chelsea starts to laugh and I realize she's joking. "That wasn't funny," I say, but I'm already settling down.

"Sure it was. You'll learn quick. Don't stress. It's not *that* terrible. Not all of the time, anyway." Chelsea leans her backside against the porcelain sink and looks me in the eye. "Besides, I've got your back. I'll clue you in right now. I'm funny, everyone knows it. Sonia is sweet. Errica is moody, and more often than not, pretty witchy." She points to the door. "And Holly, well you saw, she's hormonal."

"So, you know everyone by their one-word-description?" I ask, thinking *hormonal* could cover every single teenage girl in the building.

"Yep." Chelsea pops the word. Peeking back at herself in the mirror, she rubs her lips together, her pink lip gloss blending unnecessarily. Turning back, she points at me. Bouncing her eyebrows, she says, "You're untouched."

I raise my brows in return and look at myself in the mirror. My dark blonde hair is pulled away from my face, running down my back in a braid. Chelsea doesn't know how right she is. No friends, nothing even close to a *boy*friend or much experience with anything. "Awesome," I say. "Just what I need, *another* nickname."

"Hey," she says, shoving my shoulder. "I'm kidding. Besides, everyone knows you shouldn't call Holly hormonal, at least not to her face. She'll punch you, and that isn't a joke."

My brows knit together, remembering Holly's sobs. "Well, at least she had her friend waiting for her. Maybe she can talk to him."

Scrunching her face, Chelsea asks, "Who?"

"Liam," I say. "He was blocking my path into the bathroom. He must have been waiting for her."

Chelsea's eyes go wide and she shakes her head. "Liam does not have friends here. No wonder Holly was crying. If Liam was around, she's probably cursed." She grabs my hand, no more joking in her voice. "Come on, Thankful, Mr. Hunt is waiting."

I WALK INTO GOVERNMENT FIVE MINUTES LATE. IT'S MY LAST CLASS of the day. After English, things went on the semi-decent side until now—five whole minutes late. I went to another class with Chelsea, then a class with Sonia and then Sonia had her boyfriend, Brice, lead me to P.E. Brice didn't see the need to find me an escort like Chelsea and Sonia had. If I weren't clear across the building in the gym, I might have been fine searching on my own.

Miss Jackson nods me into the class, telling me without words to find a seat. There's one desk left and it's in the back, right next to Liam Gregor. I sigh, *glares on top of the whispers. Great.* Liam doesn't glare at me though. He doesn't even look at me. Sure, he scoots his desk-chair combo along the carpet until he's a good three feet away from me, but he doesn't glare. Shouldn't I be the one scooting away from him? He's the scary one, after all.

Miss Jackson hands us information sheets and leaves us to fill them out. I don't know where she's gone, but the whispers and chatters begin the minute she's out the door. Only two people in the room aren't talking, me and Liam. I hear a whisper in front of us; again my name, *Thankful Tenys.*

"It's Ten-is," I say, emphasizing the pronunciation of my last name.

The class goes quiet and the girl in front of me turns in her desk, looking back at me with eyes as big as headlights. She's caught.

Her startled stare fuels my courage. "Ten-is, you know, like the sport? If you're going to talk about me, you might as well get *something* right." Turning my head away from her, I find myself looking right at Liam. He still doesn't look at me, but a small grin plays at his lips, softening his face and all its features. And I am stunned.

Liam Gregor is exquisite. At least when he isn't glaring.

2

DAY 3

Like I'm rewinding a movie, I ignore the instructor in front of me and replay a conversation with Mom from more than two months ago, trying to remind myself why I'm doing this again.

"*Friends*, Thankful. Real, live, unrelated-to-you friends!" Mom had said, trying to convince me to go to public school. It was difficult, as she sounded so strong that day. Which made me ask the question: Why do I have to go? Why can't I take online classes? Or get my GED?

In the beginning I'm not sure why Mom and Dad decided to homeschool me, but after a few years it became my choice. And as strange as it may sound, I loved learning from home and from Mom. So, I stayed. After Dad left it was like a lifeline for both Mom and me. We had each other every day, all day, as well as a small child support check from Dad to pay for our means.

"I don't need friends," I'd told her, "I have you."

"That isn't enough. You need more. It's time, Thankful." Now, I realize it was the safe way of saying *I won't always be here for you.*

"Get out. Have fun. Live a little." Translation: *You shouldn't have to nurse your sick mother all day.*

Her whole body pled with me. It wasn't until I concurred that she smiled for the first time in three days. I'd agree to just about anything to make Mom happy.

Which is why I'm here.

Again.

Day three.

The hallway bustles with people, even with our small school of just over a few hundred. It feels as if all three hundred eighteen students buzz in this one hall at the same time. Sonia and I walk to lunch, side by side, but we don't say much. Chelsea seems to be the buffer between me and... the rest of the school. We're polite, we're calm, but neither of us knows what to say to the other.

"Hola!" Errica squeezes in between us, fresh from Spanish class. Somehow I fall behind and she takes my place. She loops her arm with Sonia's and gives me a half-second glance. "Did you hear about Holly?" she says to Sonia.

Hormonal Holly?

I speed up just a little, curious, and make my way around to Sonia's opposite side.

Sonia slows until I've caught pace with her. "Yeah. Poor Holly."

"What happened to her?" I ask, remembering her sobs, Chelsea's one word description of her, and Liam waiting outside the bathroom.

Errica sighs out a long, heavy breath as if explaining things to me is exhausting, even though she just asked Sonia if she'd heard.

Sonia purses her lips, her eyes darting from side to side. "She touched Liam Gregor."

"Not just touched." Errica stops walking and holds out her hand, fingers spread for all of us to look at, "full hand-on-hand contact. They reached for the front door handle at the same time."

I snort, just a little. I can't help it, she sounds so ridiculous, so second-grade-cootie-ish. *They both reached for the door...* give me a break.

"Laugh all you want," Errica says, "but not fifteen minutes later she was cut from the volleyball team. GHS hasn't cut anyone from the team in ten years."

"And how many other people did she touch in between that time?" Could they really be this illogical over one boy? Could they really believe Liam is cursed?

"But it wasn't *other* people who sat outside the bathroom listening to her cry, now was it? You're the one who told us that." Errica adjusts the pack on her back, and her lip curls with annoyance at my obstinate tone.

I can't decide if I'm grateful not to be the main topic of the day or if I want to run as far from this place as possible. I can only imagine the rumors about me. I feel for Liam. If Mom only knew the superstitious gossip that goes on here, she may not be so enthusiastic for me to *make friends*. I clear my throat to speak. I don't want to be friends with Errica anyway. "And you really think it's because she touched Liam? That it's his fault?" I let the ridiculousness of what she's saying ring in my voice.

Errica glares at me, but it's sweet Sonia who says, "We know it's Liam's fault."

Two Weeks Later

A SMALL MOAN, LIKE THE CRY OF AN INFANT, FILLS MY EARS. I KEEP my eyes closed, but reach out for Mom's hand. It's burning hot, like someone just warmed it up in the microwave. Opening my eyes, I stand, leaving Grandpa's recliner to rock back and forth on its own. "Mom," I say, touching her head; it warms my hand like a heating pad.

She doesn't hear me. She's still asleep. But she's on fire. Her hair and nightgown are soaked in sweat. She groans again. I stifle a cry. I can't cry.

"Thankful, go find a bed. Please." Aunt Phoebe's voice commands me. Moving in front of me, she lays cold rags on Mom's body, her head, her hands, her feet.

"But Mom—"

"Is being taken care of," she says, picking up a cup of ice chips. She rubs each little cube over Mom's lips until it has dissolved. "This is why I'm here, Thankful." It is, and she's good at it. She's been here less than a month and already Phoebe seems to know what Mom needs before she does. Like the rags and ice—I would have heard her if she'd come in beforehand to check Mom's temperature.

Still, I don't move, but I don't know what to do to help.

"Thankful," she says my name with a sigh. "You can help me by going to bed, getting rested for school tomorrow."

I'm not surprised when Phoebe answers my unasked question. She's very perceptive. "I am not going to stupid school with Mom like this."

She throws her head back, her long, coral hair falling backward. "Ha!" she says. "Yes, you are. You've tried to get out of school every *single* day for two weeks. You—"

"I'm not trying to *get out* of anything. I will not leave Mom when—"

"Thankful." Mom puffs through a lack of air.

I rush over, moving Phoebe out of the way with my body. "What, Momma? What do you need?" See? She needs *me*. For years it's been just me and her. She needs me.

Mom's hair, a lighter blonde than my own, a prettier blonde, mats to her head and cheeks with sweat. Her thin hand pats around on the blanket covering her until I take it. She squeezes my fingers with almost no pressure. I can hardly feel her touch except for the heat she radiates. "Go to bed, baby. Go to school."

Feeling as though someone punched me in the gut, I nod. Leaning down, I kiss her hot cheek. Then I hurry off to her room and crawl into her vacant bed. She hasn't slept here for weeks. But, it still smells like her, lavender and generic dryer sheets. Lying on my stomach, I press my face into her pillow to muffle my sobs and screams.

———————

"HOLY MARY!" CHELSEA SAYS WHEN SHE SEES ME. "WHAT happened to you last night?"

I'm glad it's just the two of us in her car. By whatever miracle, she hasn't picked up Sonia or Errica yet. They're usually on the route before I am. "Where are the girls?" I ask.

"They went in early. Science project." She's still staring at me like I'm from another planet. "Are you going to answer my question?"

I should have told Chelsea I didn't need a ride. It would have been easy. I could have told her I couldn't wait for them to finish the last two class periods of the day. I normally do homework in the library until my friends are done with the school day, but we don't ride together every day. It's only been a week since we started the routine. Why didn't I cancel? Why didn't I see my swollen eyes and blotchy cheeks in the mirror and realize I couldn't face my new friends, not like this. Not meeting her eyes, I wring my hands together. "Rough night."

"I'll say." She doesn't put the car into drive. We sit in front of my house, not moving. "You can't go into school looking like that, people will think the Liam curse has gotten to you." Digging into her purse, she pulls out a green bottle. Pulling off the cap, she squeezes some of the tan goop onto her finger and starts to rub it into my face. "Maybe it has." She stops her work and gives me a pointed look.

I don't say anything. I don't believe in Liam's so-called curse, and besides, it's not as if I've ever touched him or spoken to him—not really. I can still hear Errica's voice, the nasty tone she used when she spoke about him that first week. She'd caught me peeking over at him during lunch one day and felt it her duty to give me the lowdown. "He's an outcast," she said, "anyone who knows anything stays away from Liam Gregor. Sure, some have tried to be nice, but what do they get? Broken arms, or" she flung a pointed finger toward Sonia, "failed tests, or lost personal items." Looking at Chelsea, Errica had added, "I still think he took my mother's necklace." Chelsea had agreed, Sonia just listened, her stone face telling me she knew all this already—she believed all this. And I... I couldn't have faith in any of the words, not from Errica's lips, not with her cruelty, even with Chelsea and Sonia concurring.

Chelsea covers my swollen eyes and red-freckled cheeks and then moves down to my neck. She takes more jars and bottles from her bag and in five minutes I've been made over. "There," she says. "At least it's less noticeable."

And she's right, it is. I look away from the overhead mirror. "Thanks, Chels."

"You need to be careful," she says, joking, "or someone will think your evil stepmom is getting better."

I choke on any words, any joking comebacks I should say. None of them are funny. I would rather have the "Liam curse" hit me. Covering my new face with my hands, the sobs begin again.

"I—Oh... I—"

"It's okay," I say, even though it's not. She doesn't know any better. No one does. At least she's kidding. I meet her eyes and try to smile. "My mom," I say, hating the words even before they come. "She *is* sick." And I can see in her eyes that she understands, she knows the word *sick* doesn't mean a cold or the flu—at least not in this case.

3

HAPHEPHOBIC

Walking into Mr. Hunt's English class, I am grateful for Chelsea. Grateful she chose to rescue me that first day of school and grateful for the bag of tricks she carries around—as well as my second makeover of the morning.

"Good morning, Miss Tenys," Mr. Hunt says, his lips turning up just a touch at the corners.

"What was that?" Chelsea asks when we take our seats. ·

I shrug, but she can tell I'm withholding. I don't feel like telling her my Aunt Phoebe came to school last Friday to talk to each of my teachers about Mom. I don't feel like resembling an eight-year-old at the moment.

Mr. Hunt's wrestling coach persona seemed to melt away when my tall, thin, thirty-something aunt walked through his door. With her hands flattened on his desk, she leaned into him, smiling and winking, their movements like a synchronized swimming routine. He excused my first day flight on the spot, as well as any future ones I may need to have. Sure, I looked like a child, but it's handy having Phoebe for an aunt. As a kid I saw Phoebe maybe twice a year. Even so, we were close; she was just always off on some adventure. She'd send me packages though, something expensive and unneeded from Hong Kong, Sydney, or New York. Living with her the past month has been different, but having someone to protect me, to take care of me for the first time in a long time, it's been nice—strange, but nice.

Chelsea squints her eyes, but doesn't press the issue.

With ten minutes left in the class period, Mr. Hunt tells us to discuss with our neighbor the main differences of the two antagonists in the book we've been reading, *Lord of the Flies*.

Chelsea shuts her book and turns toward me, her eyebrows raised. "So, how ya doing?"

"Fine." I clear my throat, remembering she witnessed my meltdown. "Better." It's obvious we aren't talking *character differences* so I shut my book, too. I don't feel like being the subject topic, and without Errica or Sonia around I find my bravery. Chelsea didn't judge me, not like everyone else had that first week of school. So I ask. "What's really going on with Liam Gregor? You don't really think he's..." I lower my voice, even though I'm already whispering, "cursed. Do you?"

"Liam? Why are you thinking about him?" Her lips pucker as if she's just put something sour into her mouth.

In truth I hadn't stopped thinking about him—not since his almost-smile in government class that first day. Sure, Errica had plenty to say the two times she talked about him, but her low opinion of him only made me believe the curse to be even more of a farce. In the end all she'd accomplished was making him sound more interesting than anyone else I'd encountered at Glenrock High. I never spoke to him though; it was obvious that everyone avoided him *and* that he preferred it that way. Still, I peeked his way a few times in government, away from Errica's tongue lashing, waiting for another earth-shattering glimpse, but nothing even close to his semi-grin ever occurred again. "I have a class with him."

"Has he been a jerk to you? I can totally get a jock to—"

"No, Chels, no. Thank you, but no. He's just... confusing. No one speaks to him. No one sits with him." Even loners have one, sometimes two confidants, don't they?

"It's the curse," she says, like there's nothing else to talk about. When I wait for more, she sighs and holds out her fingers, touching each one as she makes her case. "He's bad luck. He's mean. He's a haphephobic. He growls at people, literally—"

"Haf—e—what?"

"Haphephobic, the fear of being touched or touching others," she says. "Only instead of screaming or running away or using a pint of hand sanitizer like a normal weirdo, he growls at you."

I do remember the rumble that escaped his throat when Chelsea bumped into him.

Chelsea holds out her finger list again. "He contorts his face like he's the most miserable person on earth, which leads me to self-absorbed. He only thinks of himself and making others unhappy. You will *never* see Liam Gregor make anyone happy—ever. If you aren't miserable and Liam Gregor stands next to you, you soon will be. And, he's ugly."

I chuckle at how passionate she speaks about this. Still, it's obvious that others feel the same as Chels. He's avoided like the plague. And it seems as if he likes it that way. "He isn't ugly." It's the only defense I can give him. I don't know him or if anything Chelsea says about him holds any truth. What reason would she have to lie, though? She defended me without knowing me. Still, that's a long list. It seems a little petty for Chelsea. So maybe it isn't petty, maybe it's true.

"Yeah, well, he should be. Someone so mean and cursed shouldn't get to be hot."

I'm curious, but I'm not a glutton for punishment, so I'm not sure why my curiosity leans the way of Liam Gregor. But it does, even with Chelsea's long list of negatives. Hours later, I walk into the lunchroom alone—no Chelsea or Sonia flanking my side, and I see him. I have no plan, no conversation starter, but I walk toward him anyway. I want to know for myself. I can't take Errica's cruelty or Chelsea's prejudice against him as truth. Not yet.

He sits alone at a table in the corner, *his* table, his back to me.

Tapping his shoulder with the tip of my finger, I wait for him to turn, to growl—to do something. But he doesn't. He has head-phones tucked into his ears, but I can't hear the music playing. I bite my lip, and with just my pointer finger, I tap the bare skin above his elbow. He jerks, and I back up just as his chair flares out, his glare full force on me. *Haphephobic.* The rumble starts in his throat. Silly that he doesn't scare me anymore just because he's beautiful.

"Ah, hey, Liam," I say, waving my hand and ignoring the stares of the neighboring tables. "Anyone sitting here?" I ask, pointing to the opposite side of his small round table.

"No," he growls, pinching his arm where I tapped.

"Oh, great," I say, my ridiculous bravery fueled by curiosity alone. I sit across from him, setting my bagged lunch on the table.

His furrowed brows somehow, amazingly, deepen their crease. "That wasn't an invitation," he says, staring at his lunch sack.

My heart thumps inside my chest and I'm not sure what to say. I feel as if I'm on stage in a play that I have no business being in. And yet I want to stay. I want to see if I can make his almost-smile reappear.

Chelsea walks in and spots me from across the room. Her eyes look like they may pop out of their sockets. Screeching the metal chair along the tiled floor, I stand, afraid of my friend more than Liam at the moment.

Shuffling over to Chelsea and the posse, I flush. "Hi."

"Are you trying to kill the day?" she asks, one hand on her hip. Her red floral top plays tricks on my eyes, making her brown, straightened hair look as if it might be auburn.

"Ahh—"

"You were sitting with Liam Gregor," Errica pipes in, explaining what an idiot like me couldn't possibly understand.

Sonia gives me a weak smile—it says *Thankful doesn't know any better*. But I do. I've been told. I've seen the way everyone shifts away from Liam, like the Red Sea parting as Moses walks through it. I've heard Errica's gripes and Chelsea's opinion. I just don't care at the moment.

"I know." I talk only to Chelsea, looking at Errica as little as possible. She has this way of leaving me feeling two inches tall and slapped. "I just wanted to talk to him."

"After everything I told you?"

I chew on my lip. I don't want to offend her but I won't lie, and as much as I like her, I won't kiss up. I won't be Errica. "People said a lot of things about me, too. I don't want to judge him off of what others say, but what I know—no offense." Sure, he wasn't exactly welcoming, but I still wish we'd had another minute before the girls came in. "It's just…" I say, biting my lip and hoping to help her understand, "people often get the story wrong. You know?" I tug on a strand of my long, dirty blonde hair and look at Chelsea. I'm guessing she's thinking about my sob story this morning—I know I am.

"I get it," she says, pushing up on the rim of her glasses. "But you'll want to be careful with Liam Gregor." She starts to walk, and I turn in step with her. We sit at an empty table on the opposite side of the room from Liam. "I don't want you to get hurt, T."

"I get it too," Errica says, widening her brown eyes. Her lunch tray dropping to the table, forcing me to remember she's still there. "But why would you pick Liam Gregor to *judge* and *know*? You could make your own call on some other guy and it wouldn't be social suicide."

"I'm not really worried about my social status," I say, looking past her, at the table behind her. I don't feel like meeting her wide-eyed, *we've already explained, why don't you understand these things* grimace.

"That's obvious." Errica's dark brows raise and she presses her glossed lips together. "But don't think you'll bring us down with you. You may need to look for another place to eat."

I haven't figured out the popularity poll at Glenrock High yet. I haven't tried. But it's clear Errica's sure she's in the running for first place, and my questionable choices are going to hurt her ranking.

"Err—" Sonia's green eyes stare at Errica like she's committed a crime. "We don't talk about it much. But things happen around Liam, Thankful. It's just the truth."

"Don't look like that," Errica points to my face.

I'm not sure how it's contorted, but apparently it makes her feel guilty or maybe just annoyed.

"Everyone in school knows it. It's not just us. Liam Gregor is invisible to all of us. We pretend he isn't there and in turn he leaves us be."

"That doesn't really sound like a gift, pretending he's invisible." I can feel my cheeks burn when I speak to her.

"Maybe if you'd been around more, you'd understand. You'd know that in elementary school when we were forced to hold hands with our neighbors little Liam Gregor would burst into tears and say things like 'Aaron bleeds' or 'Marc falls down' and sure enough later that day Aaron would get a bloody nose and Marc would fall down at recess." She narrows her eyes on me as if children falling down on a playground could be my fault. "How would you know anything? All you've done is hide in your house for the past seventeen years." She stands and picks up her tray.

"Shut up, Errica," Chelsea says while Sonia pats my hand.

Errica storms away and I'm glad to be rid of her.

"You coming over tonight?" Chelsea checks her makeup in the reflection of the window behind us. The subject change cools off the intensity of our previous conversation.

"Umm... I... I don't know," I say, thinking about Mom's night. I'd called Phoebe twice already. She said things were better. Still, I'm not sure I'm ready for a sleepover at Chelsea's. "I need to talk to my mom."

Chelsea nods, a celery stick hanging out of her mouth.

"Thankful, you have to come." Sonia's face lights up and her sweet voice sounds like a flute playing a happy tune.

Maybe I do have more than one friend.

I'M LATE TO GOVERNMENT, AGAIN, BUT THIS TIME I'M SMILING. Mrs. Lowe stopped me in the hallway. She handed me my family studies essay. I chose to write about the effects of being raised by a single parent, and in my case, a parent suffering from an illness. I titled it *The Thankful Mother*. It was honest and healing and *me*. And she liked it. She more than liked it. Mrs. Lowe said it was the best piece she'd seen written by any student in years. She wants it published in the paper—not the school paper, but the *paper* paper. I'm not sure about that. I'm not ready to expose myself in such a way. But the look on her face and the bright red *A* on top of my paper fills me with something I haven't felt for a while... pride, satisfaction maybe. Value? I've worked so hard to take care of my mother, only to watch Huntington's disease depreciate her, despite my efforts. It's nice to be graded again. It's nice to have someone say: you thought about it, you worked hard, you studied, and it's worth something. Mom did that, before, when she could.

I hand Miss Jackson my excuse note from Mrs. Lowe and take my seat in the back beside Liam. He doesn't look at me, of course, but I glance his way, softening my gaze. "Hi, Liam."

He says nothing, but I don't care.

My limbs seem lighter and my insides unburdened; I even answer a couple of questions instead of sticking to my quiet invisible back row. Getting up to leave, I wave, "Goodbye, Liam." He doesn't acknowledge me. But I don't mind. His rudeness sends a different vibe than Errica's. I don't take it personally. When I see Chelsea waiting for me outside of class, I hug her hello. "Hey, I need to talk to my mom and my aunt, but I'm sure I can make tonight work. I'll be there," I say, my mood improved one thousand percent.

"Yes!" Chelsea says, pumping her fist. I'm flattered that she cares so much if I'm there or not.

I laugh at her and she laughs too.

"Move," a gruff voice comes from behind us. "Other people need to get through here."

Turning, I see Liam. His dark hair, a deep brown cocoa, falls into his vision. Despite how it covers his forehead and eyes, I can see the scowl on his face. Chelsea tilts her head and sticks out her tongue at him. I giggle at her expression, but Liam just growls. "Sorry, Liam," I say through half a laugh.

He moves to pass by us, but the hallway crowds with people as the tardy bell is a minute away from ringing. He just bumps me, his arm touches mine for maybe half of a second, trying to get through the hall. "Move!" he yells. "Geez! I realize the worst thing that's happened to you today is an A for *The Thankful Mother*," his eyes are closed like I'm a infuriating child he's had to deal with all day, "but some people have problems. Some people have actual issues to worry about. Some people have places to go! Could you care about anyone other than your giggly self for one second, and move out of everyone's way?"

The hallway goes quiet at his rant, but no one looks at Liam. They peer at me. I squeeze past him, hurrying for the closest bathroom, hearing Chelsea as I do. "How dense are you, Gregor? The worst thing that has happened to her? Her mother is dying, you idiot."

Chelsea's voice seems to boom in the silent hall. Everyone

knows now. The rumors are true. At least that one is. But, now they will believe all the other ridiculous things said as well. My name will start floating in the air again with gossip, and worse, pity.

And even though I am horrified at the thought, my sole focus whirls around Liam's words. Reeling, I run a hand through my hair, my chest rising and falling with the unwanted attention and with the question: how does Liam know about my essay? The only other person to read it was Mrs. Lowe, and no one knows about my already graded *A*. No one but me, and somehow Liam Gregor. And I have no idea how.

4

POOR, POOR THANKFUL

I stir in my sleeping bag on Chelsea's bedroom floor, but I don't open my eyes. I'm *trying* to sleep, but it isn't coming. I'm so used to sitting halfway up in Grandpa's recliner that lying down flat is almost too comfortable to let my body relax, which makes no sense, but somehow that's the way my body works. I hear shuffling behind me and open my eyes, but otherwise keep still. The digital clock on Chelsea's dresser reads 3:00 a.m. in electric green. We stayed up watching movies I'd never heard of until almost two. I thought everyone else had fallen asleep by now.

"Did you find anything?" I hear Chelsea say.

I almost roll over to see if she's talking in her sleep, but then Errica responds to her in the dark. "I told you I would. I have my sources." Errica giggles.

"Okay... so?" Chelsea says, and she sounds more bored than exhausted like she should be.

"She's seventeen, a senior—"

"Holy, Errica, something we don't already know." Chelsea whispers her gripe.

"Yeah, okay. Her dad left town when she was pretty young, nine or something. No note, nothing, just gone. Rumor is her mom did something illegal or immoral—something."

My face flushes with warmth until I'm sure it's a bright red no one can see in this darkness.

"Her aunt lives with them now, since the mom is sick."

The mom… Errica says it like she never knew my mother, like she never sat on her lap or ate her peanut butter sandwiches. Errica I get, but how can Chelsea sit there and listen to this without a word in my defense, like I'm not even here? And I know it's me. Out of the three hundred eighteen students at Glen Rock High, seventy-eight are seniors—there's no way it isn't me. I'm guessing Eric's *source* is her memory or her own mother. She's full of gossip and misplaced facts.

"Where's her aunt from?" Chelsea asks.

"San Francisco, San Diego… San—something."

San Antonio, genius! Not even the right state. Besides, Phoebe hasn't lived there in years. The last year she's been in New York.

"Any reason she's so interested in Gregor?"

"Glutton for punishment?" Errica spits out. "Actually, I think she likes the attention. 'Oooh poor me, I have to go to school'," Errica says, mocking my voice as if I were a seven-year-old. "'Oh no, I don't have a daddy and my mommy—"

"Shut up," Chelsea says, but I can hear an airy laugh come from her throat at Errica's show.

I bite down on my fingers balled into a fist. I want to scream. I want to cry. But I won't do either of those things. Not here, not in front of them. I close my eyes, knowing I won't sleep one second.

At five a.m. I am up, stuffing my sleeping bag into its case. I pull my hair back, not bothering to comb through it, and bend over to tie my shoelaces. I am out of here. Slipping out Chelsea's door, I hear shuffling, but I don't stop.

"Hey! Hey, Thankful," Chelsea hisses at me. "Where are you going?"

Looking back, I see her standing at the door, one hand on her hip. Her T-shirt just covers her underwear and she hasn't bothered to grab her glasses.

"I need to go," I say, not meeting her eyes.

"Now? It's five in the morning." She crosses her arms over her chest. "No goodbye?"

"Sorry," I say, though I'm not. "I didn't want to wake you." Or see you…or talk to you…

"So, you're really going, now?"

Skirting my gaze to the floor, I'm losing patience with this act.

When I don't say anything, she grins. "Come on T, it's Saturday. Linda's going to make waffles with strawberries."

I should be quiet. I should just leave, but I'm so annoyed with her giggles and asking me to stay and even the way she calls her mother Linda; I can't stand it. "I would," I say, "but you know, poor, poor me, I need to go cry over my daddy."

The blood drains from her face and I can see she understands what I'm referring to. I give her my biggest, fakest smile and turn on my heels. Hustling out the door, I don't look back to see if she follows. Getting into Mom's 1981 Chevy Impala, I throw my things into the back seat. The Chevy's engine roars to life in the quiet of the morning. Pulling the car I affectionately refer to as "the boat" out onto the empty, silent road, I race home to my mother, probably to cry, to make a big fuss—poor, poor me.

"Maybe Errica's right," I say, stirring the eggs Phoebe made with my fork.

"Ha! Now you *are* feeling sorry for yourself." Phoebe grabs my hand and stops my stirring. "Just because she's a jerk doesn't mean you should start feeling insecure about yourself."

But what was there for me to feel secure about? I have no experience, no looks, now I could add no friends to that list.

"Hey," she says, leaning down until her orange hair falls over her shoulder and I can see the details of the freckles on her face. "You have more inside you, more going for you than that entire school. You *are* better than them."

I offer her half a smile, but I don't find her words all that comforting. I'm not better than the kids at school and I don't want to be. That sounds like something Errica would say. I know Phoebe isn't like her. She's my aunt, she loves me, and she sees greatness in me that doesn't exist. And I love her for it. Still, I won't start believing I'm better than anyone else, it isn't right.

Phoebe takes in my expression and says, "But it's true."

5

LUNCH DATE

I don't want to go to school, but Phoebe won't hear any of my excuses. Call me a coward, but how can I face Chelsea? I actually thought we were friends. I can't stand the thought of walking by her and Errica while they whisper my name.

Mom slumps on the couch in front of me. I'm cutting up her breakfast into tiny, toddler-size pieces. Pieces she won't choke on, now that she has difficulty chewing. She looks so uncomfortable with one shoulder up and the other drooping down. Her head falls to the side of her slouched shoulder.

Setting the plastic knife and fork down, I move the TV tray with her breakfast out of the way. "Momma, let me help you sit up." She doesn't say anything, but her eyes flicker toward me and I know she's heard me. It's going to be a bad day. I can tell by the way she's situated.

Standing behind her, I put my hands on either side of her, holding her bent arms by the elbows. I pull her upward and adjust her to a straighter position. Her arms start to jerk back and forth and I hold on to them. "You're okay," I say, holding her still.

Shaking her head in tune with her jerking arms, she tries to speak. "S-s-st-st-stop touch—stop-touch—"

"Stop touch?" I say, trying to make out what she wants. "You want me to stop touching you?"

Her head stops shaking and she frowns and nods, her arms still trying to jerk free of my touch.

I let go and back up, tears springing into my eyes. I move her breakfast next to her and keep the moisture in my eyes from falling. "Bye, Momma. I'll see you after school." I bend to kiss her good-bye, but stop myself. It will only make her angry.

Phoebe's at the front door, and she grabs my hand before I leave. Squeezing it, she says, "Just a bad day, honey. She doesn't mean it."

"I know," I say. My mother is an angel with a disease inside her that at times turns her into a monster.

Phoebe squints at me but doesn't say anything.

Entering English five minutes early, I'm the first one there. I planned it that way. I talk to Mr. Hunt for a minute about what Phoebe did this weekend. It puts him in a good mood, thinking about Phoebe. When a couple of kids sit down, I sit next them, making sure I'm blocked from Chelsea's regular seat. With my "free-to-go" pass from Mr. Hunt, I skip out of class five minutes early, too. I do the same thing in my next class and then avoid Sonia in family and consumer sciences, making my way to lunch without having to have an awkward encounter.

"Thankful!"

Or so I thought.

Glancing back, I see Chelsea running up behind me. I keep walking.

"T, come on. Let me explain."

"I think I got the gist," I say, trying to sound cool, but tears are close. So, I head to the one place I know she won't follow. "I have a lunch date, excuse me." I walk over to Liam's table. I can see

Chelsea in my peripheral, keeping her distance. She's far enough away she won't be able to hear me in the noisy lunch room.

"I'm sitting here today, got it?" I say, feigning a smile for Chelsea's sake, and without waiting for an answer, I sit across from Liam Gregor.

"What are you doing?" he asks, but without the usual malice.

"I'm eating lunch, that's what people do in here, right?" My insides tremor with anger, but I plaster a grin to my face for show and open my lunch sack. "I mean, I know I'm the freaky home-schooled girl, but I still need to eat lunch!" I pound my fist on the table, knowing my attempt at a bubbly tone is too high to be believable, but Liam doesn't seem to notice.

Shoving another bite of turkey-something-or-other into his mouth, he glances over at me. I expect him to growl, but he doesn't. Am I the only one who sees his appeal? The way his dark hair falls into his cocoa eyes, his skin the color of tanned leather, he's beautiful. If he were *just* incredibly good-looking, I would never be brave enough to sit here. If he were *just* an intimidating ogre, I would be terrified to face him. But somehow the combination… it's like they cancel each other out. And with everything weighing on my shoulders, growls and glares from Liam are the least of my worries.

"Bad day?" he says. And I'm surprised by his interest.

I don't know what to say. Is it different than any other day? Last week when life sucked, at least I thought I had friends. Today when life sucks, I know I don't. I slink down in my chair at the thought and pull a plain peanut butter, no jelly, sandwich from my bag. "Yeah, I guess it is."

"Then why are you here?" he asks, his tone low and menacing as he motions to his table.

I'm suddenly unsure how long beauty will cancel out fear. Raising my eyebrows at him, like I'm not afraid even a little, like I don't care that he could squish me like a bug, I clasp my hands together. "Why not?"

"People just stopped talking about you," Liam says, and though he isn't smiling, he isn't grimacing either. "Sit here, they're going to start again."

Throwing my head back, I laugh like Phoebe, though I know I don't look as sure of myself as she does. "Like I care what people say about me. Do you know what people say about *you*?" I can still hear the tremor in Chelsea's voice that first day when she so seriously told me that Liam was cursed.

"Of course I do."

"And?" I say, crossing my arms for dramatic effect.

"And they're right." He shrugs.

Dropping my arms to my sides, I look at him, my fear dissipating and my anger nearly gone. I soften my expression. "You really think you're cursed?"

Liam crosses his arms, leans back in his chair and peers at me. My disappearing nerves squirm to life inside my body. I'm not sure he's ever looked at me so pointedly until now. He's always skirted direct eye contact. "Tell me about your essay," he says.

I'm surprised. I can feel my eyes go wide and I try to make my face normal again. "Maybe you should tell me about *my* essay," I say, playing it cool. Why is it so hard?

Laughing, Liam sits up straight and returns his fork to his food, though none of it makes it to his mouth. "How would I know? I didn't write it."

"Oh, that I know," I say, my arms on the table, I lean toward him. "I wrote that essay, and I made sure no one but Mrs. Lowe saw it."

Liam stays calm and yet something appears off in his dark brown eyes. Panic? "If that were true, *Thankful*," he says, spitting my name out like it tastes bad. "How would I know about it?" Getting up from the table, he leaves his tray, pushing it towards me and walks away.

I watch him stalk out the cafeteria doors and wonder how I

offended him. He's the one lying about my essay. What did I do wrong? I'm so busy staring at the door, Liam long gone now, that I don't see her coming. Not until she's right in front of me.

Errica's hands are on her hips and she's glaring at me like I've just killed her cat, or maybe ripped all the hair out of her Fashion Place Barbie.

Clenching my jaw, I stare back at her. "What do y—"

"You've brought this on yourself, you know that, right?"

I search her face, trying to remember some stupid thing she must have said in the last week. I have no idea what she means. I see Chelsea in the distance, making her way toward us.

"Whatever happens, whatever it is, it's your own damn fault. We warned you—"

"Errica, back off," Chelsea says, her tone in posse boss mode.

Throwing her hands up into two stop signs, Errica bares her teeth, her cheek bones pronounced. "Backing off," she says and walks away, whipping her long hair in my face as she goes.

"Ignore her," Chelsea says. "She's just—"

"Being honest?" I get up from the table. "She doesn't like me. I get it. At least she's honest about it. She hasn't pretended to be my friend." I shove past her, leaving my untouched lunch next to Liam's.

Dropping myself into my desk in government, I am worn out. I need to go home. I need to see my mother, talk to Phoebe, get away from this school and these people and—

"Is your life really as messed up as Chelsea said?" Liam stares at me. Liam never looks at anyone. And here he's looked me in the eye twice in one day.

"Well, Chelsea lies," I say and a tired sigh falls from my chest. "And I don't know all she told you, but my guess would be yes, it is."

"That's… interesting," he says and he's smiling.

"Interesting?" Turning in my desk, I face him. What is wrong with him? Maybe the rumors about Liam are true. Maybe he does thrive on the misery of others. "My messed up life is *interesting* to you? You really are morbid, aren't you?"

I spin away from him. I don't want to see his stupid, beautiful face right now. I don't want to see the girl in front of me or Miss Jackson at the head of the class.

"Sorry," he says, but he doesn't look sorry, he looks amused. "What's wrong with your mom?"

I'm not sure what's happening here. When did Liam Gregor decide to notice me? More importantly, why, out of everyone in this school, have I become a person of interest? If this day weren't so miserable, I might be excited by his conversation. I had been trying to get to know him, after all. But today—"Why are you talking to me?"

Liam laughs, but it isn't like any laugh I've ever heard before. It's under his breath. It's quiet. No one else in the room has noticed. "You talk to me all the time."

I wouldn't call my one, maybe two attempts at friendliness *talking all the time*. And today I don't feel very friendly. He should know that after lunch. Sometimes with my mood swings, I think I'm the one with Huntington's. Even in my head the sarcasm isn't funny.

"So?" he says.

I shake my head. "You can't revel in my misery and then expect me to feel like sharing." Standing, I gather my books. I'm leaving. I don't care that Phoebe will ream me out later.

Pressure on my arm stops me and I glance back. Liam holds my wrist. I look up to his eyes and find his pupils dilating. Isn't he supposed to be haphephobic? But he's touching me. The foreign pressure warms my skin. I squint, examining the blackness of his eyes.

He shuts his lids for a second and then two. When he opens

them, his irises are back, the rich, coffee-like brown ever present again. "Where are you going?" he asks.

No one has noticed that Liam is talking, that he's touching me. We stand at the back. Still, I expect turned heads, gasps, and horrid faces. But they only see what's in front of them. Even Miss Jackson has her head in a book.

I pull my wrist from his grip and walk out of the classroom without a word, too miserable to be charmed even by the unlikely touch of Liam Gregor.

———

As much as I wanted out of class, I wait to go home. I stop at a gas station and go in for a drink. Then I sit in my car, doing my homework and sipping on my root beer. Bad day at home… bad day at school… maybe I could live in the boat. I don't make it home until long after I should have, even without skipping government.

"Where've you been?" Phoebe's folding towels and it's stupid, but it's not the way Mom folds them and it bugs me. She stops folding when I don't answer, and puts the doubled over towel down.

"Just stopped at the Loaf n' Jug. I got a drink and did my home-work." Well, it's mostly true. I leave out the skipping class part.

"Ah…" she says. "Well, you've had visitors. Guest number two is in the kitchen with your mother."

"Wha—" I stutter. "Number two? Who's in there?" And with my mother, today of all days. I couldn't remember the last time someone came to see me. The terrible truth would be seven-year-old Errica.

"Chelsea's here," Phoebe says as she picks up the half-folded towel. She shakes it open and folds it a different way this time.

"Chelsea?" I spit. How could she let her in the door?

"She seems sincere, Thankful. She's sorry. I think she just got caught up in stupid teenager crap. She didn't mean to hurt you."

"What happened to always being on my side?" I hush my voice and drop my bags in the living room. "And Mom—"

"I am on your side, but you need a friend, someone your age." She sounds like Mom now. "And Sall's doing better. The meds have helped today. Don't worry. Now go!" Phoebe waves her hands at me, shooing me toward the kitchen.

I start to go. If anything, I need to at least save my mother from Chelsea's evil clutches, but then I stop. "Wait, you said second visitor. Who else was here? And don't tell me you have them waiting in the attic for some Tenys family fun."

"Nope," she says, shaking out another already folded towel. "He left the second I told him you weren't here."

"He?"

Bouncing her eyebrows, Phoebe says, "Oh, yeah. Mr. Hottie, Liam-something-or-other."

I can feel my mouth drop open, but I can't seem to close it. Liam Gregor came to my house? I should feel scared, that seems the logical emotion right now, but I don't. I mean, the boy has a reputation. We've hardly talked, and yet he came to my house to see me?

"Don't act so surprised, Thankful. You're a pretty girl. You've got your momma's blue eyes and your grandma's thick hair with a splash of freckles from yours truly. It was only a matter of time before the boys came knocking."

I nod, still stunned, but I know that isn't true. I'm not Phoebe; boys don't *come knocking* for me. I make my feet move, remembering Mom and Chelsea.

They're both quiet, sitting at the table. Chelsea stares into her glass of water and Mom watches her. They both look over at my arrival.

"Thankful," Mom says. "Y-you're home." It's the clearest she's spoken in a week.

Kissing her cheek, I whisper in her ear. "Hi, Momma." Looking at Chelsea I say, "I am. I must have been quiet. What are you two doing?"

Biting her lip, Chelsea looks at me. And Phoebe's right, she does look sorry. She doesn't look like the confident, carefree Chelsea I met on my first day at GHS. But how can I trust her?

"Just visiting with your new friend," Mom says, but I can tell there hasn't been much visiting. At least Mom's jerks and stutters are gone and her mood has improved. "Honey, it's time to move."

"Okay," I say, taking her by the arm. I help her up and we walk together into the living room.

"Time to move?" Phoebe says, standing.

Helping her onto the couch, I cover her with a blanket. "Yep." She'll be there for the night now. Small efforts, but they wear her out.

Chelsea's behind us and, though I haven't forgotten about her, I haven't addressed her yet either. "We're going outside, okay, Mom?" Asking her is habit. She couldn't stop me even if she wanted to.

Mom doesn't answer. Her eyes are already closed. Phoebe's pulled her pajama pants up to her knees, rubbing Mom's legs with her moisturizing ointment. "There you go, Sall," she soothes.

Stepping onto the cement porch, I cross my arms, defenses up. The sun shines down, making Chelsea's chestnut hair sparkle in its light, somehow making her appear even more angelic. This only annoys me. Sure, she's a pretty girl and she may *look* sorry, but looks can be deceiving. I don't know if she's upset or if she's just manipulating me to find out more dirt on the Tenys family. Just the thought makes me angry.

"She looked tired. She doesn't sleep in her bed?" Chelsea shoves her hands into her pockets, her hips rocking nervously.

"She likes the couch," I say. "She wants to be out where we are, not shut up inside a bedroom. And moving is difficult."

Nodding, she says, "Makes sense."

"Is that information to share at your special sleepovers or just plain old curiosity?"

Dropping her head, she sighs. "I deserve that. You're good at holding a grudge, you know?"

"Is that your super special apology? Because it bites."

She flicks her gaze upward. "Man, T, I'm sorry. It's just, you really haven't made this easy."

"You say that like I should." I tighten my arms and look out at the boat parked in front of my house. I should have taken the long way home. Maybe she would have given up and gone home. Why would Phoebe let her in the door, anyway?

"Right, okay. Let me just say what I need to say, and then I will leave." She shuffles her feet. "It's obvious you don't want me here."

I don't disagree with her.

"It's just a dumb girl thing. Errica started it a couple years ago. She was bragging that she could find info on anyone. We kind of made it a game. Anyone new at school, anyone we didn't know already, got a 'background check'."

I laugh, short and curt, though I don't find anything about this humorous. "Fun," I say.

"I like you, Thankful. That's real. And for some strange reason, I want to make sure you have at least one friend."

And now I feel like a charity project.

"So, let me know when you're ready to put away the proud face." She slaps a piece of notebook paper into my hand and walks away.

Nice apology. I wait until she's gone. Unfolding the paper, I read.

The Info: Chelsea Harper

*My parents are divorced.

*I live with my dad and stepmom young enough to be my sister during the week. Linda on the weekends.

*I have lived in four different states—back and forth between parents. Somehow they both ended up in this place.
*I hate Wyoming wind.
*I can't wait to graduate and be on my own.
*I had never suffered the pain of losing someone, not even a pet, until I spoke to Liam Gregor. I didn't believe the warnings. But three words, one awkward handshake and not an hour later Dad broke the news. My favorite cousin, a year younger than me, dead.

I understand two things from Chelsea's note. One, maybe Chelsea is sorry, maybe she sincerely does want to be my friend—maybe. Two, she's serious about this Liam curse.

6

I DON'T KNOW WHAT THIS IS... BUT IT'S NOT A DATE

D espite Chelsea's note, I can't believe in the "Liam Curse." If Chelsea wants to be my friend, now that I've forgiven her, she can prove it by dealing with me talking to Liam. I had to find out why he'd shown up on my doorstep.

"Chels," I say, waving to her from my back row seat in English.

Her eyes go wide and she slides into the desk next to me. Sighing, she looks over at me. "Thank you," she says. "If I had to sit next to oogly eyes Peterson again, I was going to be pissed."

Laughing, I shake my head. I know she doesn't care about Leroy Peterson or think he has "oogly eyes," whatever that means. She's just being funny. She's just being normal. Chelsea isn't the kind of person who needs a "make-up" moment, and I'm glad.

"Oogly eyes?" I say. "That's two words, where have your skills gone? I thought we all had one word titles."

Chelsea laughs, and the last of the tension disappears.

Searching in my backpack for my English notebook, I set it on top of my desk and look up. Liam stands in the doorway, staring at me, his eyes like laser beams, directed only at me. He beckons me over with his finger.

Chit-chat, home visits, and now he's calling me out of class. Twirling a strand of my long hair around my finger, I raise my eyebrows at Chels and stand. She stares back, all the joking gone from her face. I am walking to my doom. At least I'm certain that's what Chelsea thinks. I don't look back at her as I walk away. I don't want her to think I'm worried or afraid. I'm not, and I don't want to see that she is.

"What's up?" I say out in the hallway. I'm trying to play it cool, *Phoebe cool*, even though I'm a jumble of nerves on the inside.

He squints at me and leans one shoulder against the wall. Biting his lip, he doesn't answer.

I cross my arms and stare at him. His dark russet hair is disheveled, and I follow the twist of a lock of hair down to his mouth. His lips are closed and just turned up into the smallest of grins. My eyes travel down to his black T-shirt, untucked over his flat stomach and snap of his jeans. "Uh, Liam?"

"I think…" He says each word slowly, like he isn't sure of what he's saying. And then he brushes a hair from my cheek, his finger tickling my skin.

My face warms as blood rushes into my cheeks. I stop myself from covering my blush with my two flat palms on my face. My heart races with the sensation he's left there.

Liam closes his eyes for a second, and then two… and I'm standing there, waiting for the boy to finish a sentence. Smiling, his face softens, and beautiful Liam is back. He opens his eyes and says, "Yeah, I think we should go out for breakfast."

My heart beats faster with his grin. How can anyone look like that? I will myself to stay strong despite Liam Gregor's pretty face. "Uh, you mean, skip class?" I'm not a class-skipping kind of a girl, and I'm also not a just-because-you're-a-boy-and-you-spoke-to-me-I'll-do-anything-you-ask kind of a girl. Yes, that grin might make my heart pump blood a little faster, but I'm not about to get grounded over breakfast. Where is this coming from, anyway?

Studying my face, he cocks his head. "You have a free pass, don't you? A get-out-of-jail free card?"

I bite my lip. I do, sort of. How does he know? Mr. Hunt, of all people, would never want to give bad news to Phoebe. Of all my teachers, he'd be the one to let it slide—ugh! What am I thinking? Am I actually considering this?

"I'll have you back before second period. Scout's honor." He squares his arm and holds up three fingers.

I lick my bottom lip, the curiosity beating me down. "Fine," I say. "Just once. Let me grab my things."

"No time." Taking my hand, he laces his fingers through mine, pulling me after him.

Seventeen years without one date allows calculating how many chances I've had to hold a boy's hand easy—like zero chances. I'm so very aware of the feel of his skin on mine. I realize it's for speed purposes, but it still makes my insides scramble. Like that section of my body sits under a magnifying glass in the sunshine.

We follow a trail next to Highway 26, a quarter of a mile or so, to one of the few cafés in town. But we're in Glenrock. We won't get away with anything, even with Mr. Hunt's efforts to please Phoebe working in our favor. If we sit down in this café, someone will see us. Someone has to serve us. Everyone in town will end up knowing about it. Liam doesn't seem concerned about any of that though.

He opens the door and waits for me to pass him into the restaurant.

"I can't get in trouble," I say. Phoebe has enough to worry about taking care of Mom, she doesn't need Thankful problems.

"You won't," Liam says, his eyes boring into me. Maybe there's a reason he avoids eye contact, he's so intense. "My family owns this place. They won't say a word."

I glance past him, feeling a wrinkle form between my eyes. Won't say a word? We're walking right up to the people that should be punishing him. And he's sure trouble isn't waiting inside? I bite the inside of my cheek and amble into the small eatery. It's empty.

"Sit down," Liam says, walking through a swinging door to the back area.

Picking a seat near a window with its blinds drawn, I lift a slat with my pointer finger and peek out at the quiet Glenrock street. Pulling back my hand, the single blind falls closed. Pressing my lips together I scan the diner, my heart drumming. I push my long hair off of my shoulder, its dull blonde such an average color. Looking down at my hands in my lap, I examine the flatness of my stomach. It isn't bulging, but it isn't muscular or tiny either; it's average. Leaning over, I look at my skewed reflection in the napkin dispenser; my eyes, my nose, my mouth- all average. Nothing horrible or beautiful about any of it. I tip the napkin case back, onto its side. I don't want to see my average face any longer. A noise at the kitchen door bolts me upright.

"Aw, Thankful Tenys," an older man with Liam's dark hair and protruding eyes speaks to me. He follows Liam over to the booth I've chosen and pulls a chair from another table along with him. Sitting on the chair at the end of the table, he peers at me.

Biting my lip, I wring my hands beneath the table top. I glance at Liam, and then back at the man, trying to make his eyes waver from my face. "Have we met?" Glenrock is small—it's small even for small, but I don't know everyone—in fact, I hardly know anyone. Maybe the rumors about me never leaving my house are more accurate than I thought.

Sliding in, Liam shakes his head, giving his eyes half a roll, the first teenagerish thing I've ever seen him do. "You have not," he says, giving the man a pointed look. "Thankful, this is Troy Gregor, my father."

"No, Liam's right, we haven't met," Troy says. "But I know

you, of course. Everyone in town knows about you and your first year at school."

And all at once I beg for average. I'd been ready to kill the word before, but now... ugh, why can't I just be like anyone else? Someone that no one knows or, for Glenrock, someone everyone knows, but no one cares about. "Right," I say. How dumb of me to think it would only be teenagers gossiping about me.

"Okay," Liam says. "You've met her. Now, eggs? Please? We want to make it to second period."

Troy stands up and, tipping his chair onto one leg, spins it around. Picking it up mid-spin, like a circus act, he sets it back in its place. "Eggs, coming up." Pointing at me, his russet eyes sparkle. "Scrambled?"

Nodding, I press my lips into a flat grin.

"And a muffin? Blueberry?"

"Sure. Thank you, Mr. Gregor."

"It's Troy. Not even Pops will let you call him Mr. Gregor," he says before disappearing into the back room.

"Sorry about that," Liam says, his hands falling into his lap. His shoulders relax and his face softens, losing a little of its intensity. This place... his dad... something changes and Liam doesn't seem terrifying at all, just normal. "What are dads good for, if not to embarrass you?"

I don't know why he's embarrassed. But then I don't know anything. Why are we here again? Looking down at the table, I clasp my hands together. "So... you came to my house?"

"I did."

"And you asked me to breakfast," I say, regretting my word choice. *You asked me to breakfast...* that sounds like I think we're on a date. And I know we aren't. I don't know what we're doing. Biting my lip, I shake my head, trying to erase the words. "Why?"

His eyes narrow and for the second time this morning, Liam studies me.

Squirming in my seat, I look back at him. "Your look is so scrutinizing. Do you know?" I comb my hair behind my ears. "You make me wish I were a mind reader."

His eyebrows furrow. Liam's normal angry face is back. If he doesn't like me accusing him of scrutinizing, he shouldn't look at me that way.

But then, softening his face, he gives me half a smile. "I think we should be friends."

"Oh—kay. You came to my house to say you'd like to be friends?"

"Yeah." Setting his arms onto the table, he leans in, his eyes roving over my face. I can tell he isn't finished speaking.

I lean in too, my face inches from his now, listening.

"I think… it could work," he says.

I'm not sure why his wacky offer feels so appealing to me. Who says *I think we should be friends*? Don't people just hang out and one day call each other friend? I'm pretty sure, even with my limited experience, that friendship isn't like asking someone out on a date.

"Are you willing to find out?"

"Sure." I sit back, feeling nervous. Will I have to sign a contract? "Are you always this formal?"

"What do you mean?"

Troy brings out our food: scrambled eggs, blueberry muffins, and juice.

"Thanks," I say, peeking up at him as he sets the food in front of us. Troy acts like the two of us sitting in his empty restaurant during school hours is a perfectly acceptable and normal occurrence. Does Liam have any rules whatsoever? I suppose as his new "friend" I could find something like that out.

"You were saying?" Liam's still looking at me.

Stalling, so Troy can leave, I shove a fork full of eggs into my mouth. Troy exits and I chew, thinking about how I should say this.

"Have you… I mean… do you always take people out for breakfast to negotiate friendship?"

Liam cracks a grin and it causes my heart to speed up. I breathe in and out, waiting for him to answer, trying to stop the race going on inside my body.

He folds his arms across his chest, covering the name of some 80s band on his T-shirt. "Thankful, how many *friends* have you seen me with?"

Biting my lip, my cheeks burn pink. "Uhh—"

Leaning toward me again, he whispers, "I'm Liam Gregor. I don't have friends."

And he didn't. Until now.

7

A CHANCE

"Thankful!" Chelsea's white face appears in front of me as she pounces on me in math. She pulls me in for a hug, not caring that we're surrounded by gawking peers. Chelsea doesn't hug. "Where have you been? Are you hurt?" Looking my body up and down like a mother would a small child who's fallen on the playground, her arms flail about. Covering her eyes, she shakes her head. "You left, you didn't come back and I thought—"

"Chels, I'm fine," I say. "We just went to breakfast. I didn't mean to—"

"Breakfast?" She spits out. "You went to breakfast with Liam Gregor? I thought you were dead somewhere in a ditch and you were having *breakfast?*" Huffing out a breath, she shoves the books I'd left in English into my arms and stomps toward the back wall. She sits between two boys, even though there are empty doubles of desks all around the classroom. She's offended, pissed off... something. Whatever the case, she won't be sitting by me this period.

Chasing her down in the hall after class, I pull her shoulder to a stop. "Chelsea, stop this."

Staring at me like I'm boring her to death, she swallows hard.

"I get it." I grit my teeth and ball my fists. "You're a *believer*. Well, I'm not."

"Didn't you read my note? I told you what—"

"I know. I know what happened. And I'm sorry for your loss," I say, hoping I don't hurt her feelings even more, but I have to continue, I have to get this out. "But I don't think it was Liam's fault. I just don't. You could have talked to anyone right before you got that horrible news. And I know you don't like the idea of me being friends with Liam. But we are. Friends, I mean. You made a great effort to convince me that you're *really* my friend." I cross my arms. "So, be my friend, Chels. Don't let something stupid like me having breakfast with Liam Gregor ruin things all over again."

By lunch Chelsea's normal again. My speech seems to have worked, for now. I walk into the cafeteria, the girls beside me, my eyes glancing over to where Liam should be. But he isn't there.

"What do you think, T?" Sonia says, but I haven't heard what she's asking my opinion on.

"Thankful."

The four of us, Chelsea, Sonia, Errica and I, turn at the gruff voice. Liam's leaning against the lunch room wall, waiting for me, it seems.

"Seriously?" Errica says. "You've decided to start speaking to people, now?"

Chelsea tries to look bored, but in the short time we've been friends I've come to learn the difference in her sarcastic *I'm bored* face and her *putting on a show for the world* face. Sonia gives Liam a weak smile.

"Go on ahead," I say to Chelsea and Sonia. I couldn't care less what Errica does. They walk away after a second of Chelsea giving

Liam a stare-down silent threat. "Hi," I say, turning back to him. I shove my hands into my pants pockets and wait for him to speak.

Narrowing his eyes, his lips part slightly. "Lunch? I have a table for us over—"

"I'm not sitting with you today, Liam." I pinch my bottom lip between my teeth, feeling guilty with each word. "I've been straight with the girls. They know we're friends, but it's an adjustment. And believe me when I tell you that I realize that isn't your fault." Shaking my head, my throat tightens. But even with my action I second guess myself. Isn't it partly his fault? Sure, the boy isn't cursed. I won't believe it. But is he so harsh with everyone because they think he's cursed? Or do they all think he's cursed because he's so harsh? I shake my head again, confusing myself. "Chelsea and I are just getting things worked out. I'm gonna sit with her today."

"Huh. I never pegged you for a lemming."

"I'm not a lemming." I twist my hands behind my back, balling the two into one tight fist, my nerves rising with the confrontation. "I'm not following anyone blindly. You of all people should know that." I don't care that I'm lecturing him. I expect the girls to play nice. He has to, too. "Chelsea was my first friend here. Unlike you, *she* was nice to me." I bite the inside of my cheek, feeling the tightrope I'm walking narrow. "You guys don't get along. You won't sit together. So, today, I'm sitting with them."

"Fine." He pops the knuckles on his right hand.

"Fine," I say, wondering when my social life got so complicated —oh, right, *this morning.*

"Tomorrow?"

Nodding, I tuck my fingers back into my pockets, feeling a twinge of excitement in my stomach. *Tomorrow.*

WALKING INTO MY HOME, I'M QUIET. MOM'S SOFT SNORE IS THE

only sound in the little house. Her meds have been working, I guess, no vomiting and no outbursts for a couple of days. So, they're calling that working. Sure, she sleeps more than half the day... I wonder what Mom would say about me skipping first hour to have breakfast with a boy. Would she be disappointed? Would she—

"Thankful Tenys!" The scolding whisper comes from the kitchen-living room doorway. I thought I'd been so quiet, but then it's Phoebe.

Walking toward the kitchen entrance, my light countenance disappears. Her hands are on her hips, pinching the sides of her jeans until she's clutching her hip bone. She *really* does look angry. Phoebe doesn't get angry. Why should she, she's tall and thin and gorgeous; she's healthy and smart and sexy. I'm easy and Mom is impossible to be angry with. Does she have a reason in the world to not be content?

Her eyes narrow on me. "You skipped class?"

"How—" Crap. We must have been seen. Someone must have driven by. I knew I'd get caught. Dang it! The one time I—

"Nothing, and I mean nothing," she says, closing in and looking down at me, "gets by me, miss. Noth—ing."

"Who told you?" Stupid question, but it still comes out. I want to know.

"You think I'd give away my informant?" And the word makes me wonder if it was more than a passing car, if Phoebe has someone *purposely* watching me. Phoebe laughs and the thought vanishes. An *informant*? Yeah, right. All of Glenrock could be called her informant, I would guess.

I cover my face with my hands, embarrassed by the behavior that is so unlike me.

"Thankful," she says, her voice kinder now. "Skipping school?"

"I know. It was stupid. Just a boy and English and... ugh. It won't happen again."

"That's right, it won't," she says, and part of me wants to

remind her that she isn't my mother. "So, a boy? Could this be the elusive Mr. Gregor?" And… she's back to Phoebe.

I bite my lip, trying to hide my smile, and resist the urge to cover my face again.

"It is!" she says, clapping her hands. "Tell, tell. I'm done lecturing. Dish."

"We're just friends," I say, walking away from her. "There's nothing to tell." But I can't shake my stupid grin. I open my bedroom door and walk inside, tossing my book bag to the ground.

Phoebe tags along behind me and falls onto my bed. Lying on her side, she props her head up with her hand. "*Uh-huh,*" she says in a tone that tells me she doesn't buy it.

"It's weird," I say, needing to talk to someone about this. Mom isn't an option and Chelsea is definitely out. And, well, Phoebe is kind of perfect. She's good with men, this is *her* area. She loves me, she won't judge me. So… "He has zero friends. He's never wanted any and, sadly, no one wants him either. For some crazy reason he wants to be friends with *me*."

"Crazy? He sounds brilliant." She adjusts her head onto a pillow and I sit on my blue bean bag across from her. "Why doesn't the kid have friends?"

"This town, people here, I don't know. It's weird. They're convinced he's cursed." I've never abused Glenrock. It's my home. But I do feel frustrated with it for Liam's sake.

"Bah." Phoebe throws her hand in the air. "Kids are mean, they don't always need a reason."

"He's kind of dark and brooding, but I don't think he wants to be. I think they've made him that way. You know?"

She nods, and I don't know if she really gets it, but it's nice to have someone on my side for once.

"Sounds sexy, like this book I read—"

My laugh comes out without permission. Phoebe would find

dark sexy, while everyone else in school, possibly in town, finds it frightening.

Sitting up, she shrugs, her lips pursing to a smirk.

"The thing is, people had all these preconceived notions about me, too, and almost none of them were true. I think the same thing has happened to Liam." Only, I had Chelsea willing to give me a chance, helping me get through the whispers until they were close to non-existent—Chelsea who refuses to give Liam anything close to a chance.

"Sounds like he needs you, kid. He needs someone to give *him* a chance."

8

HANG OUT

I t's Liam's day. I'm glad. He's grumpy when it isn't his day, more so than normal. It's been more than a week since I talked to Chelsea about my friendship with Liam, since I've been swapping lunch tables back and forth every other day. She doesn't like it, but she's handling it better than Liam.

"You've eaten lunch alone for how many years until now?" I ask him, my tone teasing. It won't offend him, it's fact.

He sets his fork down. "I was complaining again?"

I nod, though I don't mind too much. It's nice knowing how much he likes eating with me.

"If we did breakfast on my off days—"

This isn't the first time he's suggested breakfast on the days I eat lunch with the girls. Shaking my head, I remind him, "I'm not skipping school. Phoebe would freak, and I'm not killing my 4.0 for *breakfast*."

Crossing his arms, he leans back in his chair, tipping two of the four legs off of the ground. A growl rumbles in his throat. "Okay, then after school. We could study or… Hang. Out." The words sound strange on Liam's lips and he knows it. Liam has never *hung out*, not in his seventeen years of life. I think he has less experience in the department than I do.

"Sure," I say, trying to hide the thrill I feel in my stomach. It's just the unfamiliarity of it all. I keep telling myself I'll get used to it, to him.

"Good." Reaching out, he holds my wrist between his thumb and fingers, like he's pinching it, only it doesn't hurt. His soft touch reminds me of a feather tickling my skin. His eyes close and the smallest of grins appears on his lips. Weird—but then normal for Liam.

Chuckling a little, I ask, "Why do you do that?"

"What?" Letting go of me, he opens his eyes.

He rarely touches me or anyone. Chelsea was right about that. Liam doesn't like physical contact. Still, when he does touch me, on those rare occasions, he always shuts his eyes, like it's a difficult task, but he's making an effort. I chew on my thumbnail. Being friends isn't a free pass to interrogate, but he's waiting, so I say it. "You know," I say, laying my hands in my lap and biting at a piece of skin on my lip. "Whenever you touch me, you close your eyes."

Sitting straight in his seat, his eyes narrow. "No, I don't."

I raise an eyebrow at him. "Prove it." I hold a hand out to him, my palm upward. I expect him to just touch my fingertips, like a snowflake on my skin. Or to just ignore my childishness all together. But he folds his entire hand into mine. Looping our thumbs together, he wraps his fingers around mine. My entire hand and up to my elbow tingles and warms at the foreign contact. I'm so busy looking at our scooped hands that I don't notice if he's kept his eyes opened or not. Following his arm up to his chin, his lips, his nose... his eyes. They're open and again his pupils are dilated, blacking out any of the deep brown that should be there. That's right, he *did* keep them open once before. This same thing happened. "Liam, your—"

"Tonight." He nods. "Let's *hang out*, tonight."

I WATCH LIAM AS HE READS, SITTING ACROSS FROM ME IN A BOOTH at his family's café. It's a thick book with a title and author I've never heard of. I've done all my homework and drank three more colas than I normally drink in a week. I'm getting bored.

He looks angry when he reads, a normal expression for Liam, I guess. But I've become accustomed to Liam's rare I-don't-hate-the-world face. His thick brows are furrowed and his lips are turned in, making a flat line frown.

Looking down at my own book, the one Mr. Hunt assigned for English, *1984*, by George Orwell, I scan over the page I've been opened to for far too long. I've read this book already. Liam is much more interesting. I drum my fingers on the table, keeping my head down, but my eyes up, watching. He doesn't move. I let a small sigh fall from my chest and keep spying on him. Nothing, he doesn't even shift at my sound.

Reaching my hand across the table, slow and quiet, I poke one of Liam's fingers holding the cover of his novel. He closes his eyes, but just for a second, and then keeps reading.

So… like a four year old, I try again. I poke the same finger, pulling my hand back fast, like he might bite.

"Thankful, what are you doing?" he says, shutting his eyes and sighing like he is my overtired parent.

"Just an… experiment," I say, touching him quick and hard once more. This time he stares at me, glaring like I *am* that four-year-old and I'm in trouble. But my experiment works, for about three seconds Liam's pupils dilate. A quiet squeal leaves my lips at my discovery and, I reach for him again.

His hands clutch his book, but shoot up into the air, and I miss him altogether.

"Hey!" I say. But his glare has me apologizing. "Oh, ah, sorry." I clear my throat, but I can't leave it alone. "But Liam," I say biting my cheek and trying to be soft, "your eyes—"

"I know, Thankful."

Oh. He knows. Of course he knows... a weird birth defect or something.

Biting down on my fingernail, I look at him. "Would you mind? I mean, could I try something?"

He peers back at me.

Spying around the diner, he sees just one man at the counter. Troy is in the back with Liam's Pops, who I've now officially met. I guess he feels it's safe or private... something, because he nods.

Getting up from my seat at the booth, I step over to his side and slide in next to him. He turns, looking at me, his eyes narrow, not with anger, but curiosity. He is so close and my heart beats so loudly that I'm sure he can hear it. His arms are at his sides, his hands resting on the seat of the booth. Facing him the best I can in the compartment, I take his right hand with my left. "Keep them open," I whisper, and he does. I lace my fingers through his and squeeze. Without breaking our connection, I study his face. The brown goes black and I count... nine, ten, eleven... and then the color comes back. Eleven seconds. Eleven, with his pupils dilated and now, even though my hand still clutches to his, they're back to normal. Eleven seconds, it's not that long and yet it felt like an eternity as I sat, watched, and counted.

"Liam," I say, my heart drumming, "what just happened?"

9

TACO NIGHT

Studying me, as if I'm the one with changing eyes, he squeezes my fingers. The pressure feels intimate and blood rushes to my face, warming my cheeks. I look down at our books spread over the tabletop, not meeting his gaze.

"*Bambinis.*" Pops stands at our table.

I suck in a breath and peer up at him, startled by his sudden appearance.

His thick gray hair is as long as Liam's and stands out of control. There's something in his beard, lunch maybe. "What-a you doing out-a here?" Liam's grandfather still has an Italian accent. It isn't thick, but ever present. "Li? Your homework is done?"

Squirming my hand from Liam's, I fold it with my other on top of the table, less conspicuous. "Mine is," I say, showing too many teeth when I smile at him.

Pops doesn't return the gesture. I can see where Liam gets his dark brooding cynicism. "Li?" he says again.

"Yes, Pops, it's done."

Pops nods and leaves; his puckered glare making me feel he

disapproves of me. I don't know why he would. It doesn't get much less threatening than Thankful Tenys. I'm the one who won't let his grandson skip first period every other day.

"He likes you." Liam stares at me again.

"It looks like it," I say, my tone laced with sarcasm.

Liam may not care, but I don't want Pops to have anything to hold against me. I don't want to be accused of something that *isn't* happening, so I move back to my original seat across from him.

"He does," he says, sitting straighter. "He... well, he doesn't trust women. Six wives, single, and not once a widower."

"Uh-huh," I say, looking him in the eyes. The color is there, reminding me how I can make it disappear.

Crossing his arms, he stares back. It's almost like he's daring me to ask again. I may be inexperienced and "untouched," but I'm not a *complete* coward.

Or maybe his Pops talk was meant to distract me and I'll admit, I'm somewhat distracted by Pop's not-so-Glenrock life, but I'm not letting him off the hook that easy. I haven't forgotten what just happened. I clear my throat and sit taller. "You're changing the subject."

His lips disappear and his mouth flattens into a frown again. We sit in a staring match.

I huff out a breath and lay my elbows on the table, my forearms crossed in front of me. "Liam! Are you going to tell me?"

His lips reappear and he puckers them out, like he's thinking it over. "No," he says.

"No?"

"No."

"But that isn't fair." I pound my fist on the tabletop.

Liam's chuckle rumbles from his throat. "It's not what you think."

"What do I think?" I don't know what I think, so, how could he? He's so elusive and secretive, which only feeds my curiosity.

Leaning toward me, he takes one of my hands in his and keeps his eyes open, letting me watch the brown disappear. "You really want to know?"

Nodding, I hold my breath, and ignore my racing heart. And... wait... for him to speak.

"Fine," he says. "You answer three questions for me. *Honestly*. And I'll tell you. Deal?" He holds out his empty hand, ready to shake on it.

I take it. Easy breezy. I'm kind of an open book anyhow. "Deal," I say, shaking his hand. Eyeing the wall clock, I grit my teeth. "Shoot."

Looking at his watch, Liam's lips turn up at the corner just a touch. "It's already six. Phoebe will... how did you put it? *Obliterate* you if you aren't home in time for dinner."

"Six?" Crap. It's taco night. Phoebe does not like eating tacos alone. No doubt Mom's already asleep. So, she's... alone.

I really need to stop being so harsh with my judgment, verbal and nonverbal, of Phoebe. She'd never *obliterate* me. The most she's done is give me a haughty lecture. Still, somehow she commands respect, obedience, fear, not in a I'm-afraid-to-be-around-you way, but in a ooo-I-better-listen-to-this-lady way. It's a shame she isn't anyone's mother, she'd have the job down.

Releasing myself from Liam's soft grasp, I gather my things, shoving them into my backpack. Its dark denim already shows the wear from where my binder sits inside, heavy with my high school notes and papers. I sling it onto my back and point at Liam. "Tomorrow," I say. I won't forget.

He nods and opens his novel back up. "Tomorrow."

PHOEBE ROLLS UP HER FLOUR TORTILLA, STUFFED WITH MEAT, cheese, black beans, lettuce, salsa, sour cream, and anything else she felt like shoving into it. Mine is pretty plain, meat and sour cream. Black and white. Kind of like me. Average Thankful has never been very interesting or exciting.

"Why don't you try some salsa, señorita?" Phoebe asks. She's moving her hips to the beat of an old rock song. It isn't blaring, but it isn't quiet, that's for sure. I peek into the living room. My mother doesn't move.

Poor Momma. I didn't even get to talk to her today. I was selfish and went out with Liam and that equaled zero Mom time. I watch her. Is she upset with me? Is she happy she didn't have to put on a smile for me today? I hate when we don't talk. Neither of our days are right when that happens. Before I went to school, we spent all of our time together. Even when the sickness got worse and she couldn't teach me. It was awful, and I took care of her all day, but we were together.

She's so still... Did she wear herself out with—

"She had a good day. You can spend all of tomorrow with her," Phoebe says, looking over at me. "Come add some spice to your young life, *chica.*" Taco night is like giving Phoebe permission to use everything she learned back in Spanish One class. Dancing toward me, she grabs my hand, her long red hair swaying with her movements. Spinning me around like we're ballroom dancers, she pulls me in to her side and dips me.

I laugh and force myself upright. I haven't laughed in a long time. Not like that. Liam's fun, but not exactly funny. And Chelsea and the girls... well, the tension is gone, but I don't always find the girl group humor as funny as they do. This is just moving, no thinking, no stressing, no worrying. No sickness. No guilt.

Phoebe winks at me and pushes my hands with hers until they're stretched out tight. Swinging our hands to the rhythm, her green eyes gleam, and then she pulls me under her arm. Raising mine, she swings underneath it. I twist and turn and spin at her command. I know there's a name for this move, but I don't remember what it is. We do it again and again, until I'm breathing heavy and laughing so much, tears leak from my eyes.

"The Pretzel," she says.

Nodding, I lean against the counter and hold my chest. *Phoebe.* I'm glad she's here. I'm glad I'm not alone in this. I'm glad I have someone who loves *her* as much as I do. And then more tears leak from my eyes.

With her back toward me she finishes off our plates with a fruit salad she's made from everything about to expire in the refrigerator. The plates are in her hands, but then she puts them down and turns around to look at me. I'm sobbing. Silent and still, but the tears run down my cheeks without my permission or control. She doesn't say anything, but wraps her arms around me, letting my cry into her chest.

And I wish so much they were my mother's arms.

10

QUESTION #1

I brush Mom's hair, gently, so that I won't hurt her tender scalp. "What do you want to do today?"

She doesn't say anything, but I see her peek at me.

"We could watch a movie? I bet Phoebe hasn't seen everything in our chick-flick stash. Lived it, sure, but watched it on a screen, I'm doubting." I try to laugh, but it's hard without a reply from Mom. Before she would have laughed and had something great to add to that comment. But she doesn't say anything, not a sound. With her eyes at the corner, she peeks up at me again. Her mouth sits in the flat line it's been in all morning. "Or we could make ice cream sundaes and—" I stop, remembering the new diet Dr. Curtis started her on, hoping it would help decrease her side effects. "What about…" I say, trying to think of something she'd like.

Shaking, she holds her hand out. I'm not sure what she wants and then she shakes her hand at me.

"Umm…" I say, looking around. Her guessing games aren't always fun. They often end in an aggressive, angry fit. Shaking her open hand up toward me, I give her the only thing in my grasp, the brush.

She sighs.

That's it. I got it right.

Like I've done hundreds of times before, I walk around the couch and sit on the floor in front of her. Mom's hands tremble, but she runs the brush through my long hair. She doesn't sing like she used to, but it still feels right. Normal.

Closing my eyes, I start to hum a Dylan Bend song she used to sing to me, *The Wind, the Leaves, and Me*. It's her favorite. Grandma used to sing it to her. I pretend Mom's humming with me. I think about better days, different times, when the world was right and my mother was whole. Then different Dylan Bend lyrics seep into my consciousness. I hum the new song aloud, but keep Dylan's words to myself. *Remember the days when her head was true and her eyes were clear. Now her thoughts are backwards and her mind isn't hers.* The words croon in my head. I sing them for her. I hate them for her.

The brush on my head stops its steady movement. It jerks spastically, pulling my hair along with it. I reach back for the brush and her hand, but they jerk together and I can't catch them. My hair yanks back and forth from my scalp. I grunt with the pain. Stuck in my spot, I try to stop her, to release myself.

"Sall," Phoebe says, rushing into the room. "Sally, honey…" She hurries behind the couch. I can't see her with my head stuck to the brush and my butt on the floor. "Dang it, Thankful, grab the brush," she says like this is my fault.

And maybe it is. I'm the one who sat in front of her. I'm the one who gave her the brush.

"Shh-shh-shh." Phoebe hushes my mother as she spasms, holding her awkwardly from behind the couch, rocking her side to side.

My tear ducts sting. I grab the boat's keys sitting atop the end table and hurry out the door, coughing out a sob with my escape. Getting into the vehicle, I drive, not knowing where I'm going.

———

A TAP ON MY CAR WINDOW STARTLES ME. MY MUSIC IS TURNED UP and my seat laid back. I'm not asleep, but my eyes are closed. Blinking in the sunshine, I open my lids. Troy stares in at me. He makes a circling motion with his hand, telling me to roll down my window.

Sitting the seat back up, I brush my hands over my mussed hair before pushing the button to roll down my driver's side window a little.

"Liam's inside," Troy says, pointing to the café. "He's just in the back. He cooks on Saturdays. Come in." He grins at me and I need that smile. It's Liam's smile, the one he rarely gives, the one that makes him beautiful. And Troy is Liam's *father*. He's nice and happy and... fatherly.

I look at him, the longing to not be alone, to be normal screams inside of me. When I don't budge, Troy beckons me with his hand. That's all it takes and I'm up and moving.

I intertwine my fingers and squeeze them together again and again, shuffling my feet as I follow behind him.

Troy winks at me. "Come on," he says again.

"I don't want to interrupt work. I was just passing by and—"

"No interruption," Troy says and his eyes crease like moons. "Liam needs a girl like you. He needs a little fun in his life."

Is that what Liam and I have? Fun?

Sure. Okay. Fun. Liam is different. He is unexpected. And when I'm with him... well, there's a reason I drove here rather than Chelsea's house. But I don't know that either of us could be defined as... well, fun.

"Sit down," Troy says, pointing to an empty booth. They aren't all empty today. It's ten in the morning, but a couple Glenrockers are having breakfast at the diner.

Nervous, I wait for Liam. Maybe he won't be happy to see me. It's Saturday. We've never done a Saturday before. We've never even talked about Saturdays before. Maybe he won't appreciate my surprise visit. I wring my hands beneath the table and jump when the kitchen's swinging door opens. It isn't Liam, though. Troy comes out holding a drink and a straw.

"Coke, right?" he asks, remembering what I drank three glasses of last time I was here.

My sugar high that night took a while to die. I sort of vowed to myself not to have another cola for at least a week. I nod at him though. I don't want to be rude when he's never charged me for food or drink before. Biting my lip, I say, "Thanks."

"Liam's just finishing up." He sets the glass and paper wrapped straw in front of me.

Opening the straw I stick it into my drink and then tie the wrapper into knots until it's too small to tie again.

When Liam comes out, he doesn't look pleased. I *have* interrupted. His brows are furrowed and his mouth moons into a half frown. He wears a white stained apron at his waist and he smells like bacon. His eyes turn to slits, his wary stare boring into me. Crossing his arms over his chest, he says, "Thankful."

"Hey." This is a bad idea.

"What are you doing here?"

"Li," Troy says from behind the diner's counter. "Be nice. She's your friend."

Liam rolls his neck to one side and then the other. His neck makes a cracking sound and I feel like I'm in a gangster movie about to get popped or whatever they say for *murdered*. Only, I'm not afraid of Liam, I'm just uncomfortable, my emotional morning with Mom and the awkwardness of my non-invitation to the diner.

"What's wrong?" he asks, his voice lower so only I can hear him. "You don't look happy."

"You don't look too happy yourself," I say, annoyed. But I'm not irritated with Liam, just the situation, the day. I shake my head. "Sorry, I can go. I should have called or—"

Sitting down, he stops my words with his outstretched hand. "What's up?" He attempts a grin.

"Nothing." I press my lips together and decide to take a sip of Coke to occupy my mouth.

"Nothing? Then why do you look like your grandma just died."

I never looked in the mirror. I don't know what he's seeing, but I suppose it isn't pretty. I have been crying. I look down into my Coke glass, looking for a reflection that's too dark to see.

"Crap," Liam says, his tone unlike I've ever heard before. "She didn't, did she?"

"No, not today anyway," I say, and though I know the idea isn't even close to funny, a laugh bubbles from my lips.

A true smile reaches the corners of his mouth. "So, you aren't here to bear bad news."

Raising an eyebrow at him, I shake my head. "Were you afraid your favorite boy band had broken up?"

Narrowing his eyes at me he sets his elbows on the table, his arms crossed over one another and outstretched.

"What did you think I'd come here for?"

"Honestly?" he says sitting back.

I nod.

"That face, those eyes, I thought you'd come to break things off with me."

I laugh again. I can't help it. He's so dreary and dramatic.

"Shut up." His arms fold over his chest again.

Reaching out, I touch his arm. "Hey, I'm sorry," I say through another giggle. "No, I'm not here to end our friendship." And in some strange way his vulnerability in our friendship is comforting.

I'm someone he needs. I'm someone he wants. He can't lose me. And I need that from someone right now.

Liam's eyes are closed. I don't see the black I know is forming at my touch.

"Why would you even think that?" I don't know why my lips turn up with the question. Maybe it's because Mom was right, I do need school, I need someone outside the family to call my friend. And so does he.

Opening his eyes, he looks at me like I've just asked what the color of the sky is today. And I guess I can see his point. He doesn't exactly have a line of people asking him to hang out on Friday nights. "Are you going to tell me what happened? I'm not an idiot. I can see the wrong all over your face."

"Why don't you ask me a question instead?" I say. I haven't gone into the details of Mom with Liam and I'm not sure I'm ready to. I don't know how his crypticness will handle it. I can see him just shrugging his shoulders. And I'm pretty sure neither my heart nor my *face* could handle that right now.

"Why don't you just explain?" The fold in his arms tightens.

"Is that question number one?"

"Thankful," he says and his growl rumbles a little in his throat.

"Fine." I hold my hands up in surrender. "You want the girly drama, Liam, I'll give it to you." And I do. I tell him everything, from my dead-end longing for the way Mom and I used to be to my attempt at normalcy this morning.

He's looking at me, his brows in their normal furrowed state. I can't tell if he's pondering, bored, or angry. "So," he says after a minute. "This disease, it makes her act different."

Running a hand through my hair, I say, "Imagine Alzheimer's."

He nods.

"Imagine Parkinson's."

He nods.

"Now, mesh them together," I say, cramming my two hands together for effect. "That's Huntington's. Well, more or less."

"No," he says, and the word is just audible. His hushed tone tells me he comprehends how awful it is.

"Yes," I say in the same hushed tone. "Yes." I don't mention that it's hereditary, that I have a fifty-fifty chance of inheriting the neurodegenerative disease, that it's the reason my father left us.

We're so quiet, we can hear the couple two tables down talking. I don't know what he's thinking and I'm afraid, like my father, he'd just like to run.

On his feet, Liam goes over to the counter bar and lifts the lid on a glass case. Setting two muffins on a plate, he comes back and sets them in the middle of our table, along with a drink for himself.

"Okay," he says, pushing the plate toward me. "Question number one: What is your happiest moment in life?"

Good. New topic. Oh! And a question. That means I'll be one-third closer to Liam spilling his guts. "My happiest moment..." I repeat. Okay, this might be harder than I thought. I've never tried to narrow it down or even figure out which of my memories might be my favorite.

"And the truth," he says, pointing at me with the straw from his drink.

I'm still thinking when I see her in my peripheral. Phoebe stands in the doorway, her arms crossed, watching me. She leans against the doorframe and her sleek skinny jean legs and silky long hair look out of place in the small town diner. I can see in her face she isn't angry.

Clearing my throat, I look back at Liam. "Uh, my aunt is here. Just a minute."

Liam turns his head and peeks over at Phoebe.

"Mom—" I say when I'm close enough to speak only to her and not the entire diner.

"Is sleeping," she says. "Thankful, you can't run away every time—"

"I *did not* run away." The accusation heightens my defenses. "I needed space. I needed air. I have never run away. I have been there through the worst, worse than you've yet to see and I will be there—"

"Okay." Phoebe's eyes go wide. "I get it. You did not run away. But honey, you took off. I realize you're more of an adult than half the people who can vote in this country, but you're still seventeen. You do have a supervising adult living with you. It's common courtesy to tell me where you're going. Yeah?"

"Yeah," I say, unclenching my teeth from their gritted state. I'm annoyed by her lecture, and it doesn't help that Liam sits not far behind, watching us.

"So," Phoebe says, looking over my shoulder. "You came to see cutie pie, huh?"

"Phoebe!"

"Wha—at?" she says, drawing out the word. "He is cute. I can see why you like him."

"It isn't like that." My cheeks start to burn.

"Sure it is." Squinting in Liam's direction, she lifts her hand in a wave to him. I put my hands on her shoulders. "Oh, yeah... yep, he likes you," she says, watching him.

I push her body until she's walking backward out the restaurant doors. "Phoebe! It's not like that." I want her to leave. I don't want her analyzing. I don't want her guessing games that leave her the constant winner. I just want her gone.

"Okay, okay," she says, holding up her hands. "Get your stuff, let's go."

"But—"

Pointing to herself she says, "Supervising adult, remember? Let's go, babe. I love you. I like him. But we're going home."

I bite the inside of my cheek. I don't have an answer for Liam now anyhow. And Phoebe apparently needs to win this grown up vs. teenager battle. "Just let me say goodbye."

"See you at home," she says, and I'm glad she at least trusts me enough to leave and not wait around for me. She almost drew a line in our relationship today, one I don't want drawn. I love Phoebe. I can show her respect, I do, but I don't want a babysitter.

I watch her get into her Jeep and drive away before going back inside. Standing at the head of our booth, I shove my hands into my pockets. "I have to go."

Nodding, Liam stands up.

"I don't have an answer anyway. I'll think about it."

"That's okay," he says and walks me to the door.

I wave to Troy, who washes each bar stool with disinfectant. He waves back at me and gives me a big grin. "Bye," I say to Liam and turn toward the door.

"Thankful." His tone sounds urgent.

I let go of the door's push handle and turn back to him. My breath catches in my throat, both by the shock and the squeeze Liam has on me. I hadn't expected a hug, it's so un-Liam-like. But his arms are wrapped around me and it isn't awkward or small. His head is bent so we're cheek to cheek and his arms hold me close.

Letting me go, his now black eyes meet mine. "Bye."

11

IT'S CALLED A DATE

"So, you're telling me you've never, *ever* been kissed?" Chelsea says. "Like, never?"

I'm not ashamed of the fact, not until Errica sits down beside her at our lunch table and then I want to deny everything I've just told Chelsea. Providing Errica with ammunition just doesn't feel smart.

"Never what?" Errica says, her eyes like daggers in my direction.

Opening my mouth, a slow wheeze comes out.

"Been to a concert!" Chelsea interrupts my hiss and yells at Errica.

It's not as if I'm the only girl in the world to be seventeen and unkissed, but I can just imagine how Errica would use it against me. I'm grateful for Chelsea's quick thinking.

"And this surprises you?" she says to Chelsea, ignoring me. Leaning her head close to Chelsea's, she keeps her eyes on me but talks as if I'm not there. "*Untouched.*"

"Psh—I never should have—"

Standing to leave, I give Chelsea a small courtesy smile.

"T, wait. Geez Errica, you're such a jerk."

"It's okay," I say, looking at Chelsea. It doesn't shock me that she recited the funny conversation we had in the bathroom that first day of school. She likes making people laugh. How could she know that Errica would use it against me? "I need to talk to Liam, anyway."

Chelsea's lips press close and her eyes drop to the table. "Sure, okay," she says as Errica sticks a finger in her mouth, making a gagging motion.

Liam's eye narrow, watching me walk to him, like he knew I'd be coming. "Trouble in paradise?"

"Just the usual," I say, sitting across from him. "So, I have an answer for you."

"Yeah?" he says, his body straightening up. Glancing at his wristwatch he says, "Is it a three minute and thirty-two second answer?"

"Well—"

"Tell me after school. I don't want to rush."

"All right." I'm not sure why Liam wants to know my happiest moment in life. But trying to pinpoint one has made me do a lot contemplating. Life wasn't always as difficult as it is now. A time does exist when it was *perfect*. Not really perfect, but simple and happy and, to me, that unreachable once-upon-a-time reality seems pretty perfect.

The bell rings. Time for fifth period. He combs the hairs threatening to cover his eyes out of his face and we head for the door. "Pops is trying out online dating."

"What?" A laugh bursts from my lips at the absurd image in my head. "I thought he was done with women?"

"Oh, he is. But somehow he can't stay away either. He thinks this is a good compromise. He believes he won't get burned this way."

"How old is he, anyway?"

"Eighty-one." Liam offers me a smile. With his hair combed back and his lips turned up, my equilibrium feels off and my head light. I sway and stumble over my own feet. Reaching for my elbow, Liam catches me, keeping me upright and steady.

"Thanks," I say, feeling warmth move from my elbow to my chest. I'm such an idiot. "Stupid. Clumsy." I try to laugh again, but it's awkward.

"People trip, Thankful." He holds my arm and his eyes stare at his feet, his lids covering most of the black. When they're normal again, he peers back up to me. "It doesn't make you a klutz."

"T!" Chelsea yells, running through the hall toward us. She's smiling, which is odd since I'm standing with Liam.

"Hey, Chels," I say, and I can't help my bobbing head. Liam. Chelsea. Liam. Chelsea.

"I have a-maze-ing news!" she sings, without even a glance at Liam. I never realized how good she is at shutting someone out. I always feel so included by her.

"Yeah?" I say, my eyes still darting back and forth, so not to shut Liam out.

"Sadie Hawkins is this weekend." She grabs my arm, pulling me just out of Liam's grasp.

Staring at her, I move my head in a circle, trying to wrap my brain around her thought process. "Okay…" I'm pretty sure that's a dance. Yeah… a girl-ask-boy thing. I've never needed to know about stuff like that before.

"And I just got us *both* dates!"

Coughing on the saliva I just attempted to swallow, I cover my mouth. "You wha—"

Jumping in place, she yanks on my arm. "Kent Holmes for me and Marc Bailey for you!"

I don't know who either boy is. Still trying to catch my breath, I squeak out, "Who?"

"Marc Bailey. You know, the cute guy in English. He's tall and built and has a pair of luscious lips, if you know what I mean?" She winks at me and maybe it's my imagination but I swear she gives Liam a half second glance as well.

My coughing starts again. Ugh. Yes, I know what she means. "Chels, I don't know how to dance and—"

A small rumble comes from Liam's direction. I turn to look at him, but I just catch his backside as he walks away and into the classroom.

"Anyone can dance," she says to me. "And besides, I want to do this with *you*. We'll double and it will be amazing. This is your first dance, T. I am psyched. You should be too."

Nodding, I bite my lip. Oh, I'm feeling psyched, but I don't think it's the way Chelsea means. "You're sure he's okay going with *me*?" I'm not exactly Miss Popular.

"Yes! He's excited." Gasping in a breath, she claps her hands. "Maybe it will be a night of firsts," she says, bobbing her eyebrows and puckering her lips.

"Stop that," I say, laughing at her ridiculous face. "Or I will refuse to go with you."

Her face freezes and she links arms with me. "It will be a night you'll never forget. I promise."

I'm still trying to place Marc Bailey from our English class when Liam kicks my desk's leg with his foot. Looking up from my worksheet, I glance over at him. "What?" I mouth.

Leaning over, he whispers to me. "Are you actually going to this dance?"

Shrugging, I peek from our teacher at her desk back to Liam. "I guess. It's important to Chelsea."

"It's a zoo." His eyes bore into me—only the way Liam's can. "Just a parade to see what everyone is wearing and who everyone is with."

"Okay…" I shrug again. I already agreed to go and Chelsea will be there. It might be fun. "Call me a giraffe."

His brows furrow and he stares at me.

"You know, part of the zoo?"

"Yeah, I get it," he says, his Adam's apple bobbing.

"It's not a big deal, Liam. It's one night. Chelsea's my friend. I can do this for her." Sure, I'm not so confidant in the dating area, and maybe dancing kind of scares the pants off me, but I have one year of high school. Public school. One year. I might as well *do* something, *try* something. I don't want "Untouched" written under my name in the yearbook. Isn't this why Mom pled so hard for me to be here instead of in front of a computer? Besides, the distraction might be welcome.

Convincing myself is proving difficult, trying to convince Liam will be impossible.

"Phoebe!" I drop my book bag in the front entrance and yell through the house. "Phoebe!"

"Where's the fire?" she says, Mom's pill bottles in her hands. She must be separating them out for the week.

"I'm going to a dance," I say, and I don't know why my voice cracks and my eyes threaten tears. It's *just* a dance.

Shaking the bottles in her hands like they're maracas, she moves her hips.

"Sadie Hawkins. What do you wear to a Sadie Hawkins dance? I don't know how to dance and—"

"Whoa, slow down, Mr. Gonzales. You asked a boy out?" Her cheekbones push up with her annoyingly huge grin. Strands of red hair have fallen from her bun and line her face, framing her grin.

"Chelsea asked him for me." Covering my eyes with my hands,

I lean face first against the coat closet door. I am so humiliated saying those words out loud to *Phoebe* of all people.

"What? I didn't think Chelsea liked Liam."

"It's not Liam, it's a cute guy," though I can't remember what he looks like, "from our English class. Marc Bailey."

"Wha—? You little player." She laughs and pinches my sides until her tickling jerks me away from the closet.

Half laughing, half crying, I shake my head at her. "I am *not* a player. I don't even want to be a player. I wouldn't even know how to be—"

Smirking at me, she wraps an arm around my shoulders. "Honey, I know. I'm teasing. And I'm excited! Yes, we need to go shopping!" Elbowing my side, she says, "Ooo! Go tell your mom!"

Raising my brows at her, I press my lips together. That's exactly what I am dying to do. But—

"Good day," she says, smiling at me. "Really good day."

Biting my lip, I keep my grin minimal and nod at her. Hurrying into the living room, I see her, sitting up; her hair combed, holding a cup with clear bubbly liquid, she sips it through a striped straw.

"Thankful," she says with a grin. I can see she isn't completely out of discomfort, but she sounds just like *Mom,* just like she should.

"Hi, Momma," I say, trying to force the tears of joy to stay in my eye sockets.

"How was school, baby?"

Wiping my face like I'm tired, I rub away an escaping teardrop. "It was good." I grin and meet her eyes. "Mom, I have a *date*—with a *boy*—to a *dance.*"

Her face brightens and she sets her drink down. Taking my hand, she tugs until I'm sitting next to her and wrapped in a hug.

"Crazy, huh?"

Pulling back, she shakes her head. She smiles and, even with the illness affecting her entire body, she looks so pretty with her blonde hair tucked behind her ears, her blue eyes wet and bright. "Absolutely not crazy."

Laying my head on her shoulder, I flip through the channels on our small television set. This is my religious release class, my spiritual high. The one I've been so desperately in need of. Time 101, true, good, and right *time,* with Mom.

It's not until the credits roll across the screen and blend with Mom's soft snores that I realize the time. I am late meeting Liam at the diner. Phoebe has gone grocery shopping and could be gone for hours. We're out of... well, everything and with Mom having a good day, she felt she could go.

Standing, so not to disrupt her, I run into the kitchen. Picking up my cell, I dial the diner's number. "Troy? It's Thankful. Can I—"

"He left, Thankful," Troy says and then chuckles a little. "He's headed your way."

"Oh. Okay." Headed my way? Setting the phone aside, I look around my house. Bustling about, I clear away a pile of clean laundry from Grandpa's chair and dirty lunch dishes still sitting on the table. It looks as if Phoebe's been enjoying Mom's good day too and I'm glad.

Sitting outside on my porch step, I see him walking up the street.

He watches me as he approaches, his eyes brooding as normal. "Aren't you supposed to be somewhere?"

"Why?" I say, joking, my mood light. "When I knew you'd come to me."

He folds his arms over his chest and stands in front of me.

"Didn't I tell you? I'm psychic." Putting my hand to my temple, like I'm getting a vision, I watch him. One of his eyebrows quirks up at my strange mood.

"So, what really happened?"

"Mom's having a good day, a really good day," I say, squinting up at him. "I lost track of time. Phoebe's shopping now, so I couldn't leave. I did call the diner, but you were already on your way."

He nods and again I notice the time, this time in neon green on the face of Liam's wrist watch, 3:45. He didn't wait long before hunting me down. We meet at 3:30.

"I'll leave you, then."

"Hey." Standing up, I'm inches away from him. Tugging at the tails of my shirt, I look up at him, blinking in the sunlight. "No reason to go. Mom's asleep now. Stay."

"Yeah?"

"Yeah."

Walking to the wall of my house, he sits on the grass, leaning against the wooden siding. It's a pretty fall day. The sky is blue and the wind minimal. Nodding his head, he motions for me to sit next him. When I do, he sets his head back against the wall. "So," he says, looking over at me. "Your best day…"

12

MY BEST DAY

"I was eight years old. It was a Saturday, and my dad was home from work. He often traveled or went in on weekends, but this weekend he stayed home. He made waffles with little chunks of pineapple in them. I loved pineapple. He didn't. He made them for me. The three of us sat around the table eating and talking. I can't remember a thing anyone said, I just remember sitting there, together, the purest happiness filling me." I pull my knees up to my chest and look at Liam, waiting for the you're-a-weirdo vibe. He doesn't send it, so I keep going.

"Later we went to a matinee. It was at the dollar theater in Casper. We saw a reshowing of E.T. It terrified me. I hated it. I literally screamed out loud in the theater." I laugh at the memory.

Liam chuckles with me, but doesn't say anything.

"We had to leave early and it took twenty minutes before they could convince me to open my eyes. Mom felt so guilty for frightening me with one of her childhood favorites, so they took me out for ice cream. We ate *ice cream* for dinner." I can't help but smile at the memory. "Again, we sat around a table in a little ice cream shop and just talked and laughed." We were just a family. "I can still see my mother's face as Dad pushed his ice cream cone into her nose. He'd offered her a bite, but overshot, and it went up both her nostrils. I giggled until my sides hurt.

"Afterward we played at a park. They didn't sit on a bench and watch me like the other parents there. They played right beside me. I fell asleep on the drive home." Closing my eyes I remember the moment. I see it in my mind and since I promised to be honest and to share, I say it out loud. "I woke when the car stopped, but I pretended to still be sleeping. I kept my eyes shut tight and he picked me up." My stupid voice cracks with emotion. "He carried me to bed that night. I didn't want to leave the safety of his arms." I wipe at the wetness on my cheeks.

"In the morning, I woke up and was laying between them. He'd carried me to *their* bed and I'd slept the whole night unknowingly between my parents. I knew they'd put me there to protect me from E.T., just in case. And I felt like the luckiest girl in the entire world."

Wiping at more falling tears, the silence feels thick, like the air has turned to smog around us.

"So," he says, filling the quiet. "I take it you never went to Disneyland?"

Laughing, I tug on the ends of my hair. It's strange telling someone something so intimate this way. It didn't just come up through circumstances, like when I told him about Mom's illness. I thought this out. Liam had specifically asked for this and here it was. "No, I did."

His expression is soft as he nods one curt nod. "Thanks for being honest," he says. "Sounds like a good day."

Biting my inner cheek, I nod back. "So," I say, needing the thickness thinned out with our words, "question number two?"

"You're sure?"

"I am." I've come this far.

"Okay, then on the opposite side of the spectrum what would be your worst day?"

My breath shakes as I exhale. I've had a lot of bad days these past years, more than I care to think about. I narrow my eyes and look at him, a sigh leaving my chest. "I'll have to get back to you on that." But I don't need to think, I know exactly which day it is. I just don't have the courage to share it right now.

13

A ROYAL BLUE DRESS

I can't stop thinking about the nurse at home with Mom while we play in Casper. This isn't right. It's the whole reason Phoebe came to live with us so we wouldn't have to hire out a nurse.

"Shouldn't we wear the same shirt?" Sonia asks Phoebe.

"Honey, do you really want to wear something your boyfriend is wearing? Ick." Phoebe makes a face to show how much she detests the idea, and yet somehow she's still beautiful. "Seriously, be a girl. Being a girl is so much more fun than being a boy. It's cute, and pink, and sexy. And better." Phoebe holds up a short black feathered skirt attached to a white silk blouse. "I'm pretty sure Brice wouldn't look good in this," she says to Sonia, "but you on the other hand... Besides, white and white, it matches. Good enough, anyway. Let everyone else show up in matching flannel. You girls are going to look like you should be out for cocktails in New York City." Her eyes sparkle like emeralds with the idea. Phoebe might be the luckiest woman alive. How did she finagle an adequate nurse on such short notice? She also knows how I feel about Errica, as well as how Errica feels about me. She told me Errica wouldn't be coming on this trip, and even though Chelsea invited her, this day and time were just about the only ones Errica couldn't make work.

Grabbing my arm, Chelsea pulls me until I bump into her. "I love your aunt. Lll—uuv. Is she really from New York?"

Nodding, I muscle through a smile for Chelsea, my head still with my mother. "Originally San Antonio, but she moves a lot. She's in New York, now. Well, before she came to be with us."

"So cool."

I nod. She is cool. "She's a journalist there. Big time. For the Times." Phoebe is so easy to brag about. "They love her so much they're letting her write from Wyoming, while she stays with us." Everyone loves Phoebe. What's not to love about Miss Amazing?

And if I could get my mind away from home, away from Mom, I'm sure I would be having the time of my life, too. Shopping with *friends* and Phoebe. The only thing that would make this better would be Mom joining us.

Holding the dress up to her neck, Sonia looks in the mirror.

Phoebe is looking too. She winks at Sonia. "Try it on."

Sighing, Sonia holds up the price tag. Her red curls cascading down her back. "It's a hundred dollars. I have fifty." Sonia's lips turn up though, always the optimist. "We keep hunting."

Tapping her finger to the side of her full lips, Phoebe continues to look at Sonia in the mirror. "Hmm… but I'm thinking, my fifty and your fifty make up—what? A hundred? Try. It. On."

So, she does. We all do. Phoebe hands Chelsea a dress and then one to me too. I'm not sure how she does it, we don't have her New York options, but somehow she manages to find just what we all need. Chelsea's yellow dress flares at the skirt, the thick navy belt making me think of Doris Day, but when she tries it on, it looks fantastic.

The royal blue dress she's picks for me seems plain at first sight, with its cap sleeves, oval neckline, and just-above-the-knee length.

But it's form fitting and clings to my body like a tailor made it to match my figure type and eye color. No one says anything as I exit the dressing room. I feel silly, barefoot and ponytail.

"Thankful," Chelsea says, her voice hushed. "It's gorgeous."

"*You're* gorgeous." Sonia beams at me.

Looking in the mirror I can't quite stop the silly grin that creeps onto my face. My eyes stand out and my body... well I have one, and it isn't terrible. I almost wish Errica *were* here. She'd hate this. But then, that's kind of awful of me. I regret the conceited thought the minute I have it. Pressing my lips together, I'm glad I didn't say it out loud. I look at myself in the mirror again and see Phoebe behind me. Winking, she rocks on her heels and I can almost hear her *I told you so.*

"IT'S FRIDAY," LIAM SAYS, A GRAVEL TONE TO HIS VOICE.

Nodding, I feel my eyes widen. I know why he says it, but I don't admit to it. "Yep."

Squirming in his seat a bit, he sits up straighter and moves his dark hair out of his eyes. His eyes dark, but not black, stare at me. "Is our deal off then?"

Holding to my own wrist, I feel my pulse quicken. I want to pretend I don't know what he's talking about, but that would just make me a jerk. And I don't want to be a jerk. "No, it's not off," I say, sitting across from him at our lunch table. "I didn't realize I had a time limit."

"You don't." He sits straighter. "Do you have an answer then?"

Shaking my head, I don't meet his eyes. The table has a crusted lunch room surprise stuck to one corner, and I stare at it. "Not yet." The blood in my body feels cold with the lie. But I'm not sure I can share my worst day. Saying it out loud means claiming it, admitting to it, feeling it—again.

"Okay, so you want to come by the diner tonight—"

Looking up, I meet his eyes. "I can't," I say, feeling the sting of guilt. "Sorry. Chelsea and I are getting ready for the dance."

"Oh, right." A quiet growl escapes Liam's throat. "You need four hours, huh?"

"Apparently, I do. Phoebe is helping me. We're getting started right after school. If I look like Bozo the clown, drag me out, will you?" Shooting for humor, I laugh, hoping he'll join me.

"I'm not going," he says, no trace of laughter.

"Maybe you should," I say. "There's no rule that says you have to come with a date. Just come. Meet us there."

"Chelsea would love that, wouldn't she?" he cracks a small grin, which makes me think he's considering it just to torment her.

And really, what would I do if he showed up? Chances are high that Marc isn't a huge Liam fan. And I already know how Chelsea feels, somewhere between hatred and terror. So, if he came, what would I do, spend my night running back and forth? My date and my friend being angry every time I left?

"I don't do dances," he says, shoving his hands beneath the table.

"See you tomorrow then?" I ask, and he nods. I try to summon a smile for him, but it's subdued with my irrational guilt.

"I DON'T SEE WHY THIS IS NECESSARY." I FIDGET IN THE CHAIR Phoebe has me all but strapped down to.

"They're highlights, Thankful, not a tattoo." She yanks on my hair.

"Ow," I yell, expecting the yank to hurt. It doesn't, but my brain tells me it should have.

"Stop being a baby. My little girl is all caught up in a love triangle and I want to make sure she's a hottie-pa-tottie," she gets the words out with a foil strip hanging from her mouth.

"I am not in a love triangle!" I say, trying to look at her. She yanks my hair again until I face forward.

"Sure you are." Phoebe sighs like the idea is actually a good thing.

"It's possible," I say with a forced chuckle, "that Marc and I would need to have an actual conversation and that Liam and I would have to be more than friends for a love triangle to exist. I don't know, call me crazy, I'm just saying—"

"Oh, there's a whole lot more than friendship going on with you and The Face."

"Phoebe!" I fidget with the hair strands on my shoulders and puff out my cheeks at her nickname for Liam. *The Face.*

Spinning my chair around so she's no longer staring at the back of my head, she peers down at me. "There is." Her eyes go wide. "In fact, if Mr. Face doesn't show up tonight, I'll dye my hair purple."

Turning me back around, she starts in with the foils and the hair dye again. I swallow and I'm sure she can hear the gulp in my throat. I can't imagine anyone liking me *that* way. Plain-Jane Thankful couldn't attract the loneliest of souls. But, Phoebe's put the idea in my head... the impossible idea. It fills my stomach with butterflies, and my heart with palpitations. Like Liam always seems to do, only turned up to high.

Still, the idea... Phoebe's beautiful hair... Glancing up at her, I picture her with violet locks and I try to remember the last time Phoebe was wrong about something.

14

THE GIRL CHOOSES THE BOY

Isn't he supposed to get me punch… or something? In all the movies Mom and I watch the boy always offers the girl punch. Marc Bailey has not left my side, my physical person, since we walked through Glenrock High's doors. He's been touching me in some way ever since he and Kent picked up Chelsea and me. Arm on my arm, leg against my leg, hand on my wrist… something… and I am starting to feel like a claustrophobic stuffed into a dumbwaiter.

"Where's the punch?" I yell at Chelsea over the roar of the music. If Marc won't offer me any, I'll get him some.

"The what?" Chelsea cups her ear.

Looking around, I see there isn't a refreshments table. There's nothing, certainly no punch. Kent leads Chelsea onto the dance floor again and she waves goodbye to me, a smile plastered to her face.

The bathroom!

Yes!

Thank heavens for *his* and *hers*.

"I'm gonna find a bathroom," I yell to Marc. His shoulders are moving to the music as his arm rubs against mine.

"Yeah, okay," he says, looking down at me. He bears his teeth in a toothy grin every time he looks at me. I'm starting to think Phoebe did too good of a job picking out my dress and dying my hair. I'm not sure what Chelsea was thinking when she explained in detail how "hot" Marc Bailey is. He's not bad, cute even... but then again, Chelsea's probably never seen Liam smile. Still, it isn't his average cuteness that's turning me off. How hypocritical would that be? No, it's more than that. I feel fake standing next to him, pretending I like him, when I don't even know him. I suppose that's what people do on a date, get to know each other. And I should be giving this more effort... My heart speeds with dread at the thought.

The bathroom!

I exhale a sigh, a breath I didn't know I'd been holding, and start for the nearest restroom.

Holding onto my wrist, Marc follows after me. I stop and look back at him. Clearing my throat, I say, "I don't think you can come in."

"Oh." He laughs. "Yeah. Guess not."

Pleased, I nod, and start my exit again. But Marc is still clutching my wrist.

Holding up my chained hand, I shake it. "I promise not to get lost."

"Right, okay. I'll be right here," he says, and I picture glue on the bottom of his shoes holding him in place.

"Great." Copying his toothy grin, I pull my hand from his.

There's no one in the bathroom, so I feel free to begin my pacing. Back and forth I pass by the six stalls in the long room, glancing at my blonder, curvier self every now and then in the elongated mirror that stretches across the wall.

I'm new to dating, but is this it? Zero interesting conversations and a leash? We hadn't even danced yet, besides Marc's shoulders gyrating against mine. Sadie Hawkins… was I supposed to ask him to dance, too? Ugh, what had Chelsea gotten me into? She and Kent had been nuzzling on the dance floor for the last hour and a half while I… I was being walked like a dog.

Patting my sweating forehead with a dry paper towel, I try not to ruin all Phoebe's hard work. Looking at my sparkling eyes and pink lips, I think she did a pretty good job. I've never looked so glamorous. I didn't grow the right curves overnight, but somehow this dress Phoebe chose for me makes it look like I did.

Okay, if we aren't going to talk, then I'll ask him to dance. I can do that, right? Maybe a fast song. He'll have no reason to attach himself to me and I can try to recall Phoebe's moves the other night when we popped in Mom's old mix CD.

Pulling off Phoebe's black four-inch heels, I give myself a couple more paces without the pinching shoes. I take a deep breath. *I can do this. It's just a boy. It's just one night. It's just a dance.* Slipping back into my shoes, I walk out of the bathroom. Continuing my mantra, I think to myself: *It's just a*—Liam!

"Liam!" I whisper over the bass drumming in the air. "What are you doing here?"

He's just outside the bathroom entrance and I pull on his black T-shirt until he steps inside.

Clearing his throat, I can see the discomfort filling him.

But I don't care.

He said he wouldn't be caught dead at a school dance. So, why did he come?

His chest bumps into mine as we huddle in the corner of the girl's restroom. I'm still clutching his shirt and I feel ten degrees warmer with Liam standing so close. "What are you doing here?"

"What'd you do to your hair?" His eyes rove over the highlights Phoebe added to my dark blonde.

"You can't be in here!" I yell my whisper at him, my make-up threatening to sweat right off of me.

His brown eyes widen. "You're the one who pulled me in." The deepness of his voice bounces off the ceramic walls of the girl's bathroom.

Taking his hand, I feel the warmth that Liam gives off fill my insides. I pull him from the bathroom, bumping into a couple of girls as we walk out the doorless opening. "Ooph!" I grunt. "Uh, sorry."

The two laugh, their heads together in whispers.

Walking to the corner of the large commons room, the music quiets a little. At least I don't need to scream my question. "What are you doing here, Liam?" I ask a third time.

His hand in mine tightens and he shrugs.

"Are you keeping tabs on me?" I ask, irritated at his lack of answers. "I'm a big girl. I don't need—"

"T!" I hear the yell across the room.

"—you," I whisper to Liam, "or Phoebe or—"

"T!" the low voice hollers again. "Where'd you go?" Marc appears at our right. "Gregor?" His eyes skirt down to my hand in Liam's.

He snatches up my other hand. "Get your own date, Gregor." His words spit at Liam, like he's below us in some way. Pulling me, like he's done all night, Marc attempts to drag me away.

Liam's clasp goes tighter and I'm tugged in both directions.

"Hey!" I'm so not in a mood to play tug-o-war. "Wait. We were talking, Marc. Give me a—"

Marc looks back, but he doesn't stop walking. He pulls and my hand yanks away from Liam's.

"Minute." I plant my heels, trying to keep in place. "Whoa! Just give me a minute!"

"Thankful." Marc stops and, for a second just the fact that he's used my given name makes me believe he's listening to me. His free hand comes up to my cheek and he holds my face in his hand. It's weird. His touch isn't warm like Liam's. His hands are cold, like ice cubes on my cheek, and it makes me shiver. I don't know where his affection has come from. Marc and I have no reason to be having a… moment.

With his face lowering toward mine and his fish lips puckered outward, I turn my head. I don't want his kiss. I don't know why he thinks I would. But before his lips can even land on my cheek, Liam's fist collides with the side of Marc's face. Stepping back, I watch his ear and cheek jiggle in slow motion. The crunch from the hit mixes with Marc's grunts. Stumbling over, he holds onto his face.

Gaping at Liam, his chest rises and falls in an ominous, angry manner. I'm surprised when steam doesn't exit his nostrils. Liam holds his hand out to me. Call me crazy- I take it. Running away from the crowd, from my date bleeding on the ground, from the booming music, I don't look back.

I choose Liam.

15

MY WORST DAY

"You punched him?" I say, guilt filling my insides at the image of Marc alone and bleeding. "He does absolutely nothing to you and you punch him. Do you often punch people for no reason at all?" A voice in the back of my mind reminds me that I'm the one who left. I may be blaming Liam, but I left Marc behind, not Liam.

An incomprehensible murmur-growl leaves Liam.

Jogging just behind him, my hand still in his, I let out my own growl. "You are unbelievable! Why did I leave with you?"

Stopping, he turns around. The beat of the distant music drumming in our ears. "Do you want to go back?"

I don't. I would much rather be with Liam than Marc, or even Chelsea. But I'm confused at the violence. "I'm not going back," I say. "I just think hitting him was a tad ridiculous. He—"

"The guy's a jerk, Thankful." His forehead wrinkles as he speaks.

"He wasn't a jerk." I'm grateful he slows his pace and we're walking. I need to take my shoes off. We turn down an empty, dim hallway. "He was a little… touchy, but he wasn't a jerk."

Liam shakes his free hand, I'm guessing still stinging with the hit. A purplish bruise already forming on his knuckles. "You hardly know him. He tried to kiss you," Liam says like it's the end of our discussion. And in a way he's right, but I don't want him to be. And I don't think he is completely.

"Okay, sure, but I had my head turned. I was letting him know his affection wasn't wanted."

"Yeah…" he says, and I hear his teeth grind together. "Pretty sure he needed a stronger message."

Opening my mouth to speak, I stop. Swallowing, I decide on, "He was polite." Liam's hold on my hand tightens. "He opened my door for me." We turn a corner and a light flickers at the end of the deserted hallway. "Oh, crap." Stopping, I take my hand from Liam's and pull my phone from its tucked away spot inside the top of my dress. The trick Phoebe showed me. "I better text Chelsea. She's probably freaking."

Oh crap. Oh crap. Oh crap. I'm in so much trouble.

ME: HEY, I LEFT EARLY. MARC GOT A LITTLE HANDSY AND I DECIDED TO SKIP OUT ON THE REST OF THE NIGHT. SORRY. HOPE YOU HAVE FUN WITH KENT!

Shooting for airy, light and Liamless, I hit send.

Looking up, I see Liam watching me. "Polite?" He opens and closes his right fist. His tone tells me he isn't laughing at my description. He definitely isn't agreeing.

"Okay." I shrug, my guilt must be the only reason I am so dead set on defending Marc. "He was boring and dull. He smiled too much." Although, since when have I not liked smiles? Since Liam almost never gives them out? "His touchy-feely thing wasn't welcome and he was cold."

"Cold?"

"Literally cold. Every time he touched me I shivered." I shudder like I have the chills just thinking about it. "But he wasn't rude."

"Come on," he says, shaking his head at me. Picking up my hand again, he doesn't bother hiding his black eyes.

"Where are we going?" I know these halls are off limits during the dance. Liam knows that too, he just doesn't have my aversion to rule breaking. The path turns a corner and the small dead-end hall has art work all over its walls. We're next to the art room, where students' past work has been framed and hung up to remember.

There's a bench at the end of the hall. Liam leads me there and I sit. There's plenty of room, but he sits right next to me. I look at the wall in front of us, the space covered from ceiling to floor in painting, drawing, and chalk work. *Liam...* dark, secretive... figures he'd be an artist type.

"So," I say after a minute of silence. "Do you have anything hanging here?"

Looking at me, his brows furrow. "Me?"

Maybe that's a secret too. I wait for him to answer, our hands knotted together between us.

"No," he says and then a low, humorous chuckle escapes his throat. "Uh, I like the bench."

"Oh." I cross my legs. "I just— Ah... I like it too. It's very—"

"It's remote." Folding his arms over his chest, he lets go of my hand and I feel somewhat empty without his.

I sigh and my shoulders slump a little, tired of arguing with him. I look from my shoes to the hem of my dress. My legs look longer than they are with the four-inch heel. *Liam. What are you thinking?*

Bringing his foot up, he sets his ankle onto his knee and faces me. "So," Liam says, a pro at changing the subject. "Your worst day... I know you know."

Taking his right hand in mine, I look at the white and purple blotch starting to deepen across his knuckles. I brush my fingers over the bruise, just a touch, so I won't hurt him.

"I was eleven," I say and my voice already breaks. "I knew there had been tension at home for a couple of weeks. Mom and Dad didn't usually argue, but it wasn't totally unheard of. They were quiet arguments. Ones I couldn't hear." Silence filled my home instead of conversation and laughter. "But I still knew they were happening. I knew something was different. And then one day they weren't so quiet. My mom had this old standing lamp that belonged to my grandma. The shade was glass and looked like windows from an old church." I move my hands to explain the pyramid shape. "Mom was on the phone, standing in the doorway between the living room and the kitchen. Dad stood across from her, leaning on the wall next to the lamp. I was reading a book on the couch, but I could see them both. I could see how they didn't meet each other's eyes and how Dad's hands twisted until they were white with stress. Mom said goodbye into the receiver and took the phone from her ear. I looked up from *Anne of Green Gables* just in time to see her nod at Dad. Screaming, I don't remember what, he hit Mom's lamp, knocking it to the ground and shattering the shade into a million unfixable pieces."

Liam listens without interrupting. His bruised hand squeezes around my own.

"Mom and I scrambled to the broken pieces of glass and Dad walked out of the room. He was packing. I didn't realize that as I sat there cutting my fingers on sharp, unfixable lamp remains, he was packing to leave us. Forever."

Clearing my throat and staring at Liam's fist, I continue on. "Finally, Mom got out the broom and dustpan and scooped up all the shards and threw them away. I sat on my knees, crying over my grandmother's lamp, not realizing the worst was yet to come. I was so worried about a broken lamp; I didn't even realize my family was broken.

"Dad came back in with suitcases in his hands. The cry that left my mother was like an animal in the wild dying. She cried out, not caring who heard. 'No, Jared. No, Jared. No, Jared.' She said it again and again. Then he told her, 'You lied to me. You knew it was a possibility, you knew this was coming and you never told me'."

"Her illness," Liam says.

Nodding, I say, "I didn't know what they were talking about then. He looked at me… " I cup my hand over my mouth to stop my own sob. "He gave me a full ten-second glance before turning to go. He didn't say anything. And though I hoped, a part of me knew he wouldn't be back. The worst part," I say, looking Liam in the eye. If anyone in this world can hear this, it's him. I don't know why, but he won't judge me for it and so I tell him. "The worst part is that as I cried and yelled for him to stay, I wondered if something so awful was coming, something that chased him away from us, then why wasn't he taking me with him. If this big bad monster was coming and it was all her fault, then why wouldn't he take me?"

I let that hang in the air for a minute. I've never said those words out loud. Yes, it's horrible that he left us because Mom tested positive for Huntington's. Yes, it's awful that our happy little family came to an abrupt halt because she kept her fear inside and he couldn't handle it. But what horrifies me the most, what makes this my worst day, is that for a short time I wanted to go with him.

"Why didn't he take you?" Liam asks as if he were wondering the same thing I had all those years ago, and in some way that comforts me.

"Because," I say, looking ahead at the wall in front of us. I breathe out a puff of air and let go of his hand to hide mine in my lap. "There's a chance I'll have it too."

Wrapping an arm around my shoulders, Liam pulls me closer to him. Laying my head against his chest we sit there in the dim quiet. No words can help. No words will make what he did or what she kept from him or what I felt go away. And I'm glad that he doesn't try to erase it all by speaking.

"So, how was your first high school dance?" he asks after we've sat in silence a while.

"You mean before you showed up and punched my date. Right?"

"Uh, yeah."

"Well, it would have been better if we'd *danced*, I guess."

He sits straighter, and my body shifts under his. I sit up from my slumped position against him. Clearing his throat, he says, "I can dance."

I bite my lip and look at him, my eyes roving over his beautiful face staring back at me. My heart begins the Kentucky Derby and I hold my hands together at my chest. Maybe Phoebe's right. Maybe I *do* like Liam that way. And even crazier, maybe he likes me back. The realization makes my breath catch in my throat. For once I'm not irritated with her always being right.

He stands, and though he doesn't look entirely happy or even comfortable, he holds his hand out to me. I watch the black overtake his eyes as my hand slides into his. I'm one question away from knowing his truth. One.

We're too far away to hear anything but a low hum from the dance music, but Liam holds my waist with one hand and my right hand with his other. There's none of this arms about the neck swaying stuff that Chelsea and Kent have done all night.

He rocks me around the small hallway, our feet moving in unison even with our lack of a beat present.

"You…" he says, his voice shaky, and I can't help but think that nervous is a new look for Liam. A good look. "You look beautiful."

"Oh," I say, my face flushing. I can feel the warmth springing into my cheeks and I pray this hallway is too dim for him to notice. I'm not Phoebe gorgeous or Chelsea beautiful—I'm just me, Thankful. I tell myself to say thank you. Just accept the compliment. "Phoebe did my hair." I shrug.

He stares down at me, his dark eyes roving from my eyes to my lips.

"I mean, tha—"

His arm around my back tightens, pulling me closer and cutting off my sentence. He leans toward me, beautiful Liam, leans in to *me*. Our swaying stops and both his hands fall to my waist as our lips meet. With my arms around his neck, I close my eyes and pull him closer. His lips move with mine as we offer one soft kiss after another.

Coming up for air, he presses his forehead to mine and I open my eyes. He grins and my heart palpitates. I want the kissing to start all over again. But I have to ask the question at the back of my mind. I have to. "Don't you want to know how great my chance is, to get sick, I mean?" He's met my mother. He's seen what could possibly be me one day.

He doesn't answer, but his eyes pinch into almonds as he stares at me.

"Fifty-fifty," I say. "I can be tested, but—" I begin, knowing my ramblings are about to start, but he cuts me off with another kiss and I gladly take it.

16

KISS ME KATE PANCAKES

Sliding his fingers through mine, my hand tingles and warms at his touch. Liam's staring at me from his spot in the driver's seat. We're in Pop's car, the tiny, yellow, foreign thing looks like something Phoebe should be driving. "Does this mean my lunch sitting privileges have been bumped up to four times a week?"

I laugh because I don't know what else to do. I feel like I'm in someone else's world or maybe like I'm reading one of Mom's chick-lits and it's just starting to get sappy. That's the kind of stupid smile I know won't leave my face.

"Is that a no?" he asks and he offers me a grin. That's cheating, and I think he knows it.

"It isn't a no," I say, even with his treachery. "It's a maybe." I can't resist him this minute. I don't care that I have no clue how to make four days a week work. The girls would freak. And I don't want to lose the girls.

"Hmm." He grunts and his eyebrows rise. His smile disappears, but he isn't angry.

Biting my freshly kissed lip, I look behind me, at my house. "I should go. Phoebe said midnight, it's five past. I—"

"I know." He nods.

With my fingers on the door handle, I pull and open the exit.

"But, uh, question number three," he says, keeping me in place.

Turning back, I face him. "Yeah?" And just like that, I don't care if I'm late. I'm so close to Liam's truth. And now, with the sensation of his lips on mine, I want that truth even more.

He clears his throat and the urgency in his voice relaxes. "Favorite food?"

"You're serious?"

His eyes widen, his inaudible answer.

"Food? You want to know about food?" Wrinkling my brow, I close the door and stare at him, one hundred percent suspicious. We start with the two most intimate days of my life. Two days that wring my heart out like a drenched cloth, and now he wants to know about food? "What's the catch?"

His throat rumbles with his laugh and he pushes his dark hair out of his eyes. He's beautiful. Too beautiful. "No catch," he says. "I've been watching you eat peanut butter sandwiches and corn chips for two months. I really want to know if that's what you like or—"

"Oh." My face flushes, embarrassed. I'm boring. I know it. Phoebe knows it—as much as she tries to convince me otherwise. And I suspect Liam knows it. But for whatever reason these more-than-friend feelings I have for Liam, and realizing that he may like me too, makes me want to hide my boring from him... oh, you know, only *forever*.

How could I have thought I was such an open book? I'm just a dull, soft bound, large print, very few chapters book, with a few non-decodable symbols. Complicated, but not interesting.

I have been *me* all this time. And it's *me* he kissed. I bite my cheek and keep telling myself that. But—"Did you kiss me because of this dress?" This dress is Phoebe. It's *so* Phoebe. He kissed me on a night that Phoebe dressed me and dolled me up. He kissed me on a night when I look very different than normal.

Liam looks over my dress, from neck to knee. My pink face burns I can only imagine how red under his scrutiny. His lips pull into a crooked grin when he's done and I want to yank out my highlights and throw on my sweats. The muscle in his arm tightens as he stretches it out, holding onto the headrest behind me. "Did you kiss me because of my T-shirt?"

The faded *Guns and Roses* logo across the black shirt makes me laugh for whatever reason, perhaps hysteria. "No."

"So, why did you?"

Gulping my swallow, I wish I hadn't brought this up. "You... you didn't answer me."

Nodding and staring, he says, "Okay, no, I did not kiss you because of a dress." The air in the car gets warm and I feel like I'm in a sauna. "But for the record, I like the dress." Watching me, he waits for my answer.

"Okay, then." I'm nervous to say the words out loud. *I like you. I like you a lot. I like you more than I realized.* "Um, hamburgers. Plain-Jane, nothing but lettuce on it, hamburgers. I know, boring. But that's it, my favorite food." I don't answer his *other* question and I know he won't let that fly. So, before getting out of the car, I lean over to him and place a quick kiss on his lips, just to let him know I like him and I don't regret it. Somehow it's easier than saying the words. I'm hoping its answer enough.

Mom's eyes are open wide when I walk inside. Phoebe slumps in my spot in Grandpa's chair, asleep. But Mom looks over a book and by the way her eyes rove over the page, I can tell she isn't reading any of it.

"Momma," I whisper. "Why are you still up?"

She looks at me but doesn't answer. Her eyes don't register.

Taking the book from her hands, I set it onto her TV tray. "Come on," I say, pulling the blanket up around her shoulders. Sitting next to her, I rub my hand on her brow. "I kissed a boy, Mom."

Again she looks at me, questions in her eyes. Maybe she wants details, I think, and the thought warms my insides. She would have, before.

"Me, your little Thankful. Can you believe it?" I look at the ground and attempt to hold back my silly grin.

"I-I have a daughter called Thankful."

I meet her glassy eyes. I rub her brow again. "That's me, Mom," I say, managing to hold back the tears. The lump in my throat aches.

"And-and my husband, J-J-Jared."

She hasn't said his name in—I can't remember how long.

"Jar-Jar-Jared. Thankful." She says it like she's calculating. "Jared loves Thankful."

Yeah, Jared loves Thankful enough to leave her. Jared loves Thankful so much he left her to care for his wife all alone. Jared loves Thankful and Sally a *whole* lot, the sarcastic thought comes automatically. I'm not eleven years old anymore. I have no hope for him coming back. I only hope I'll stop missing him. Then, one day I'll stop wanting him to.

"Awww," I yawn. "What smells so good?"

"These!" Phoebe beams, much too bright-eyed and bushy-tailed. Then again, it's ten in the morning and she could have gone to bed at a decent hour. Pointing to a stack of pancakes, she says, "These are *Kiss Me Kate* pancakes, because *someone* got kissed last night."

My tired eyes pop open. How did she— "You are…" I shake my head. "How do you—"

"You talk in your sleep, pumpkin." Skipping over to me, she kisses both my cheeks. "So… tell me how it happened! Chelsea was pretty right about this Marc guy then, huh?"

I'm not sure how my face looks. I don't feel different, except for maybe a stupid blush. Darn my cheeks. But Phoebe takes one look at me and gasps.

"It wasn't Marc, was it?" Snapping my side with the dish towel in her hand, she smirks. "You little player."

"Oh my goodness, please stop calling me that. I don't even know Marc. It isn't like that." Mom and Phoebe are so different when it comes to men and family. Most teenagers would lean toward the carefree, fun Aunt Phoebs. But my mother would have taken my father for the rest of her life over anything else. Knowing that has made all the difference when I think about my future. I suppose with the outcome I should run from what Mom wanted, from what Mom had and lost in the end. But it was really great when we had it. And I'm grateful she didn't run. I'm grateful she's braver than him. Besides, I am the furthest thing from a *player*, Liam being my one and only kiss.

"Huh! It was The Face, wasn't it?" Phoebe dances on her toes. "He showed up! What'd he do? Come on, give your aunt some details!" Stomping her foot, Phoebe groans. "Thankful, while I am here I have to live vicariously through you. My love life is on official hold. I'm not in the city. I'm not digging up juicy stories. I don't even have a reason to wear my *Louboutin's* while I'm here! Besides, being devoted to one man is like being devoted to one pair of shoes. I love my *Louboutin's*, but I don't want to wear them on my morning jog." She waves her hand at me. "Tell tell, girl. Don't leave anything out."

Laughing, I touch my lips. Comparing men to shoes—so Phoebe. Maybe I should set her up with Pops. "Fine," I say. "Yes, he showed up, there was punching and running and kissing. Good enough?"

"Not even close!" She squeals and grabs me by the hand. Pulling me into a kitchen chair, she sets her kissing pancakes in front of me and sits beside me, her bare legs crossed.

The pancakes are cold by the time Phoebe allows me to eat.

17

OWN IT

Doris Day sings about falling in love and dances across the TV screen. I sit on the floor in front of Mom. She's watching, but her meds are making her all zoned out today. She doesn't even flinch when there's a knock on the door.

I can see through the window that Chelsea waits outside. *Crap.* I'm in trouble. I plaster on a smile that I'm hoping says- *I didn't kiss Liam last night.*

"Hey." She waves with both hands, beaming.

Okay… maybe I'm not in trouble.

Standing on the porch, she rocks back and forth on her heels. "I tried texting—"

"Oh, sorry, phone's dead." My hands flail about with guilt.

Pursing her lips together, she stares at the floor of my front entryway. "You're mad, aren't you?"

"Ah—"

"I knew you would be. It's just we were there dancing, and then we left… I didn't even think. I was just in the moment, you know? You get it, right? I didn't *mean* to ditch you. I just—"

"You left?" I furrow my brows, making sure I heard her right.

"You had Marc, I figured—"

"You left me?" I don't want her angry with me… and yet irrational, hypocritical annoyance stirs inside of me.

Her chest heaves up and down with her exasperated sigh. "T, I was not intending to leave you there. It just sort of happened."

Wow, at least I texted her. Wait, my irritation dissipates. "Didn't you get my text?"

Shaking her head, she says, "No, but remember, my phone has been on the fritz. I get some, but not all."

I didn't know, but then I'm only there for half the girl-time conversations. And with her wondering eyes and apologetic tone, I'm guessing she has no idea that I ditched her first. And that I have no reason for annoyance. "Oh."

Throwing her head back, she closes her eyes and wails. "Don't be mad. Errica's already pissed and I can't—"

"No, it's okay. I'm not mad." And I'm not. I'm only ridiculous for a moment, it's passed now.

Her shoulders rise and fall with her breath. "Really? Oh, good. You're the best. I have so much to tell you about last night. Oh. My. Gosh. You will not believe it, but I gotta go now. Linda asked me to get milk from the store. She'll freak if I have her credit card for more than half an hour. As if there's any place to shop here." She rolls her eyes.

Laughing, I wave goodbye as she trots off the porch step.

"Thankful. Thankful. Thankful," Phoebe says in her *it's time for a life lesson* tone.

Spinning around, I face her. "What?"

"Do you really think Rizzo there—" She waves her hand toward Chelsea's speeding car. "Isn't going to find out about Liam showing up? On Monday, Marc's face alone will tell her something went amiss."

Copying Chelsea, I roll my eyes at her. When did she show up anyway? How long did she listen to us? "I'll figure it out," I say, walking past her.

"Thankful, you need to stop letting those girls tell you what's okay and what isn't. You like Liam. Own it. Tell them. Don't play their games. Stop the his and hers table thing. Make them see what you see or get rid of them."

Did I tell her about the table swapping schedule? Ugh. I *don't* play their games. If I did, I wouldn't even be talking to Liam. Staring at her, I don't say anything. She's not there sitting in my freak shoes every day. She's not whispered about and stared at and—

"Stop caring about what those people think. You're better than that."

18

TRUTH DAY

In the past few weeks I've researched my own explanations for Liam's eyes. Google has given me a few theories, but not truth. My Google options include: near death, on drugs, and embarrassment, though none of those resulted in complete iris blackouts. Liam is *not* on drugs, no way. He doesn't get embarrassed. Angry, sure. Uncomfortable, yeah. But embarrassed? Nope. And I'm pretty sure I would have realized by now if he were at death's door.

But today my guessing stops. Today is truth day. I've answered my three questions, painfully so. Now, it's his turn.

My hands shake as I zip up my jeans. I don't know if it's *because* it's truth day or if it's because I haven't seen Liam since we kissed two days ago. Not even a full two days, more like thirty-five hours ago. What if he regrets it? What if the heart pounding, warm, tingling-ness was all in my head? What if our friendship is ruined and we're left with awkward?

Leaving my room, I look for Phoebe. "How do I look?"

Pursing her lips, her light brown eyes seem to sparkle. Running a strand of my hair through her fingers, she says, "You're gonna kill it."

Shaking my head at her, I can't stop the smile that comes. I'm me. And I'm grateful for that. Yes, I have a few highlights. Sure, I stole the strawberry daiquiri lip gloss Phoebe bought herself the other day, but I'm still me. I haven't changed my wardrobe or had plastic surgery. I'm me. It's just now, well, I just want to be *more* than Plain-Jane Thankful. I want to be special, because he is.

Phoebe squints her eyes at me. "First official date."

I nod. I know what she means—*with Liam*. We've hung out a dozen times, but this… it's different.

"Your mother would tell you no kissing until at least the third date, but I guess you've already broken that rule. So—"

"Phoebe!" I shove her shoulder and she laughs. But she's accomplished her goal. The tension leaves me and I grin at her, a little mortified, but the thought of kissing Liam gives my lips their own brain. They turn up, swelling my cheeks without my permission, admitting to everything she says.

With her hands on her hips, she stands next to me. "Don't do anything I wouldn't do," she says, watching me slip on my shoes.

It's my turn to laugh. What an absurd idea. "I'm pretty sure that won't be a problem."

"Have fun." Her eyes follow me around the room. "Hey, you said his dad is single, right?"

"Phoebe!"

"Hey, if he has a face like Liam's—"

"Goodbye!" Grabbing the boat's keys, I hurry out the door.

Driving to the diner, I think about Phoebe's last sentence. Liam has Troy's eyes, but that's about it. His face must be more like his mother's. We've never talked about her. I wonder if I could get three questions of my own from my… *boyfriend*. The word sounds strange. Mostly, *Thankful's* boyfriend sounds odd. I didn't know if I'd ever put those two words together. Even now—it isn't like he's officially mine… but I feel possessive already with the idea that he is. When did that happen? Wasn't I on a date with someone else just thirty-something hours ago?

The diner has a closed sign on the outside and all the blinds are drawn. Liam mentioned they weren't open on Sundays, but his text from Troy's phone assured me the door would be unlocked.

Walking inside, a bell jingles from the top of the door. I've never noticed it before, but I've never walked into the diner when it's been dark and silent, either. The lights are off. The noonday sunshine streaming in through the front door and windows light the space. I *can* smell food, though.

The nervousness in my chest quickens. I was never uneasy when Liam and I were just hanging out. Why should I be now? I press my lips together and the strawberry daiquiri lip gloss reminds me why. I never wore lip gloss when we were just hanging out. This is something more.

The swinging kitchen door opens and Liam's head pops out. "You're here," he says and he sounds so happy.

Nodding, I try to force away my anxiety.

Leaving the kitchen, he wipes his hands on the white stained apron tied about his waist. Walking past me, he locks the front door and checks to make sure the closed sign faces outward. Taking me by the hand, he leads me toward the kitchen. Pins and needles prick my fingers and I try to remind myself that Liam has held my hand many times before.

There's a stainless steel counter with empty soup tubs and coffee pots on it. Silverware rolled in paper napkins sit off to the side next to a large steel refrigerator. There's a glassless window above the counter; smoke and steam waft through its opening to where I stand. The savory aroma drifts down to me.

"One minute," Liam says, leaving me to stand at the counter. Rounding the corner, he's on the opposite side of the window. Spatula in his hand, he flips the hidden food on his grill.

Wanting to watch him, I follow his path into the cooks' station. I *was* right. Liam is artistic, only with food. I watch as he flips the meat, its color a mixture of reds and browns. He squirts the grill with a spray bottle and presses down on the round slab with his spatula. He sets a metal bowl overtop the meat before looking at me. His hair waves back, gelled to stay out of his face while cooking. He looks different than normal. I can see all of his face as the bright lights shine down upon him. He looks utterly delighted. And yet, he still looks like Liam. If *they* could see him like this, *they'd* stop their silly curse talk... and I'd have a lot more competition.

Maybe I'm glad he's dark and hidden and thought to be cursed. I get him all to myself that way. It's a selfish thought, one I don't even mean. There's a reason I defend Liam, because no one should be thought of that way. No one should be treated like he's treated. Especially someone as wonderful as Liam.

"Can I help?" I ask after watching him for a few minutes.

"Sure," he says, peeking over at me. "There's lettuce on the counter. Do you mind washing it? And maybe grab a couple Cokes?"

Smiling, I nod.

Minutes later he sets two plates on the counter next to my washed lettuce leafs. He lifts the toasted hamburger buns and adds lettuce to each of the fat burgers. Hamburgers—he's made me a hamburger.

Carrying our drinks, I follow him past the cooks' station door and into a small lounge. There's an old brown couch, a dinged up coffee table, and a small television set sitting across from the couch on a TV tray. Liam sets the plates with our food onto the table and takes the drinks from me.

"Hungry?" he asks, setting our drinks down too.

I had been. Now I'm just nervous. But it does look good and it smells fantastic. I nod again, not able to muster any words. He takes my hand, walking me around the coffee table where we sit on the old couch.

"You okay?" His forehead wrinkles with the question.

"Yeah," I say and I try to laugh. It comes out more like a forced wheeze.

His brows furrow and he looks at me, not buying it.

Closing my eyes, a shaky breath leaves my throat. "I'm just feeling a little off. Maybe the word 'date' makes me anxious."

"Were you anxious Friday?" The tone in his voice has gone from soft to irritated with the question.

I had nerves Friday too, but it wasn't like this. It was more discomfort… "Not exactly. But then, I don't like Marc." The words bring on my blush.

Liam's lips form a forced flat line, like he's trying not to smile. But I wish he would, maybe it would calm me down. "Maybe it isn't the word 'date.' Maybe it's what comes after the date."

More blood rushes to my face. I'm certain my cheeks are a betraying red. Denying I thought about our kiss on more than one occasion would be a lie.

Before I can respond, Liam scoots right next to me on the couch. His right hand crosses his body to reach me; he cups my cheek, and I turn, looking at him. "Yes," he says, with my move-ment. His eyes rove over my face like he's figuring something. Just inches away, I watch his mouth move. "Just… like… that—"

My heart pounding, I close the small gap he's left between us, pressing my lips to his.

He returns the kiss and then pulls back, his nose brushing mine. "Better?" A light I've never noticed before radiates from his eyes.

"Mm-hmm," I say, and I am.

We eat and I'm amazed. It's by far the best burger I've ever had. With my stomach full and regular ol' Liam beside me, tension stops threatening to rip apart my body. My skin and chest still go skydiving when he touches me, but that's not so bad or abnormal.

"All right, we've eaten, should we get down to it?" I ask, impatient for his story now that my nerves are behaving.

"All business, huh?"

"Hey, you said three questions for my one. And I answered three." Insanely honest.

Laughing, Liam gathers our plates and cups and sets them on the ground next to the couch. Propping his legs up onto the coffee table, he leans back.

I lean back too. He doesn't say anything. I bring my legs up and fold them in. Facing him, I reach for his hand. I watch his pupils engulf his irises and then return to normal.

Bringing my hand up to his lips, he kisses the inside of my palm. I exhale at his touch and wait for him to speak.

"I know what they all say about me," he says, and his voice sounds almost sad.

Heat rises into my cheeks. He is more isolated than I am. At least I have found *some* acceptance. Even Marc agreed to go to the dance with me. They've known Liam so much longer and still no one has given him a chance. No wonder Liam resorted to punching. I'd like to punch someone myself.

He sighs, and the ray I saw earlier leaves him. "And, they're right."

Shaking my head, I just look at him. How can he be so unkind to himself? He can be gruff and confusing and dark, but that's *because* no one's given him a chance. I did, and I've seen kindness, love, and light in abundance.

"It's true." His brown eyes peer into mine. "Thankful, I'm cursed."

19

THE CURSE

"How can you say that?" My tone holds no sympathy. My pulse quickens in that uncomfortable way when I'm about to approach confrontation. "You, of all people... conforming to what they believe?" I grind my teeth, not wanting to look at him. Facing forward, I cross my arms.

"Thankful, I—"

"What does that even mean? *Cursed?*" I throw my hands up, only to tuck them back under my armpits. I won't let him grab my hand and cloud my thought process. "I mean, what day are we living in? This isn't the Stone Age, Liam."

"Yes, but—"

"*Cursed.*" Shaking my head, I try to keep my anger from filling my eyes with tears. Liam cursed? I will not cry over something so ridiculous.

Liam's growl rumbles low, but I still hear him. "Done?"

Keeping quiet, I let my silence answer. Why is he being so stupid? Wasn't it supposed to be truth day? And he is just being... stupid. *Cursed!*

"I can see you're not." A low, wispy sigh leaves him.

I don't know what my face gives away. I can't remember the last time I felt so angry.

Shoving his shoulder, I say, "Well, you are being an idiot."

He grabs my hand, freed from its armpit prison, and his eyes flood with blackness. The darkness standing out against the white sclera.

"That," I say, pointing at his face with my other hand, "that right there is what you're supposed to be telling me about."

"Thankful." His tone is raspy again and his sigh impatient. "I'm trying to."

Stopping my inner rant, I look at him, confused. "Okay then. Talk."

He keeps my hand in his and clears his throat. The pulse in his wrist quickens against my skin. "We're called The Knowing." Running the back of his finger down the side of my cheek, his eyes go dark again.

I sit at attention, his every word like needed oxygen.

"Human contact turns our irises black. It's our sign."

Every inch of my skin pricks with his words. I keep my mouth shut. He is so serious. He can't be serious though... *The Knowing...*

Inching closer to me, his fingers tighten around mine, like he's trying to keep me in place, to keep me from running. "The Knowing have existed for thousands of years. We touch, we see, we know. Whether we want to or not, we know."

I keep my eyes on his, waiting for a sign of humor, waiting for the fear filling my chest to leave. I'm not afraid of him but the idea —*cursed...*

"We have no choice in the matter," he says, his voice steady and low. "The curse is inherited, passed from parent to child. Any human contact, skin on skin, and we see. Our eyes go dark to the world, but inside, we see. We feel. I don't want to know these things. I didn't choose this, but then most people wouldn't choose to be cursed."

Trying very hard to remember that none of this can be true, I ask, "You know? Know what?"

"The worst," he says, and his eyes fall to our tangled hands. "I see the worst thing that will happen to someone in their day. If I touch them again, twice in one day, I will see another event from the next twenty-four hours. My head is filled with the worst." His free hand rubs his temple like his head aches.

But he's touching me, right now. In fact, he's *always* touching me. Masochist? Wait, I'm not buying any of this... right?

"I see it. I feel it... I hate it." His eyes bore into mine as he stabs the words: "I. Am. Cursed."

I don't know what to say. This is insane. Does he think I believe him? And being with *me*, well, wouldn't that kill him? My worst is never just a hangnail or a test gone wrong. It isn't typical teenage drama.

"And the last few years I've been, well, sort of miserable." He softens his face, but it only makes him look sad and my thoughts return to masochism. "And then you came along, like an angel, here to save me."

Taking a deep breath, I let it fall and breathe in again. "Liam," I say. "I don't—I mean... my life, well, there's *a lot* of bad. How... How is that—"

Twisting, he faces me, his free hand on my shoulder runs up and down my arm. "I'm not sure how, but with you, I see the *best*. I see the best part of your day, the happiest moment you'll have. I see myself making you laugh with a joke or making you float with a kiss."

The blood runs to my cheeks and I bat my eyes, looking anywhere but at his face. My legs have gone numb, and now seems to be a good time to try and walk off the painful pricks and pins.

Standing, I steady myself with a hand on his shoulder. Releasing myself from his grasp, I walk across the room.

"Thankful—" he says, standing.

"You're saying you can touch me and know what's going to happen in my future?"

"Just a little bit." He holds up his thumb and forefinger to show me an inch in length. He says it like it should make the idea better. "I know it's weird." He walks over to where I stand next to the old TV.

"It's crazy," I say. If what he's saying holds any truth... I'm mortified.

"I know. But I swear it's real."

Pacing in the little room, I wring my hands together.

He watches me and says, "I saw our first kiss the night before it happened. I saw us arguing at my lunch table that first day you came over. I saw the red A on top of your essay, *The Thankful Mother*. You still haven't let me read it, by the way."

I've stopped and I'm staring at him. He's scaring the sanity right out of me because he's so entirely believable... and I *might* believe him. How can I believe him?

"And today?"

He knows what I mean. "The kiss... on the couch," he says and his lips curve upward.

I think about what he said just before he kissed me, as he took my cheek in his hands: "Just... like... that..." It makes some sense now, I suppose. "Wait," I say, looking at him and my hands start to shake. "Do you kiss me because that's what you see I want –" The thought makes me want to vomit. To be someone's pity kiss.

"No, no," he says, stepping over to me. "I can't see what *could* happen or what someone wants to happen, I see what *will* happen. Believe me." The tone of his voice has gone hard. "I can't change what I see, not even when I want to."

"This is so... whoa... this is a lot to wrap my brain around." I hold the sides of my head, trying to compute all this words. I mean, why *would* I even believe this?

"But you believe me, right?" He pulls my hands from my head and laces our fingers together.

And the thing that scares me the most is, I think I do.

20

A MARATHON

"What do you see now?"

"Again?" he says, looking at his watch.

"Yes, again." I squeeze his hand tighter than necessary.

A small laugh falls from his chest.

"More kissing?" I shake his hand from mine and cover my face.

"I can't help how happy my lips make you."

I can never, *ever* touch him again. "What about my mother?" I say, trying to forget how humiliated I am. "Tell me something about my mother." I poke his hand.

"Thankful," he says through a rumble in his throat. "I'm not a crystal ball. I told you. It doesn't work that way. I have no choice in what I see." Taking my poking finger, he enfolds my hand in both of his. "Come here." He guides me over and sits back onto the couch.

I sit next to him and he scoots close until his side touches mine. I lean my head against his shoulder. This is crazy.

"I saw her once," he says, and I adjust my gaze upward.

"You did?" I know it's crazy, I know it's unbelievable, but I also want to know what he has to say.

"Yeah." Peering down at me, his lips brush my forehead.

I could stay here all night. Liam's heart beating next to my side, his clean-cottony scent in the air, warmed by his embrace and the promise of a future kiss.

"What'd you see?"

"Movies. You on the floor, your mom on the couch, but her eyes were watching, she was smiling. She seemed…"

There. She was there, a good day.

"She looked like you."

It's a very general description, but I do remember a day like that, not long ago. And it *was* the best part of my day. Mom being mom. Us being us.

I look up at Liam's jaw line, his chin, his throat. I want to kiss that throat. I am becoming obsessed with Liam and lips and—I sit up, giving myself some space. You can't run a marathon in sixty seconds… We can't go from friends to me wanting my lips on Liam's throat in thirty-something hours.

I need more than two inches of space. I may not *want* more, but I need more. I let out a shaky breath and pick up Liam's right hand. Twisting his wrist, I look at his watch. The time doesn't matter. I do it for show. "I should go."

Nodding, he slides his fingers through mine. "Okay. Are you… you're okay? With this? The curse, I mean?"

I wish he wouldn't call it that. I don't know what *this* is exactly. I don't know how I feel. I don't even know if I'm a believer, but I do know he believes. I can see truth all over him. I see it in his eyes, hear it in his voice, feel it in his touch.

"I'm… *fine.*" I squeeze his fingers. "Trying to wrap my brain around it all, but you and me, we're fine."

Still holding my hand, he stands. Liam walks me past the kitchen and into the front of the restaurant. The sky has gone dark.

Unlocking the front door, he opens it, holding it ajar with his body. Placing his hand on my back, he offers me a smile. "Sit with me tomorrow?"

It isn't his turn and he knows it. I nod anyway.

Getting into the boat, I realize I will not tell anyone about this. Not the girls, not Phoebe, not even Mom. Liam didn't ask me to keep it a secret, but I can't imagine he wants me telling the world, either. No, this is *his* and, true or not, he's trusted me with it.

A QUIET WAILING FLOODS MY EARS WHEN I PULL UP TO THE HOUSE.

Oh no.

Jumping from the vehicle, I run inside. Running past the empty living room and into the kitchen, I duck my head just as a plate whizzes by me. It shatters against the wall.

"Sally!" Phoebe yells. "Stop it!"

"Where is he?" Mom screams, and throws a ceramic mug toward Phoebe.

Covering her head, Phoebe bats at the mug with her hand. It smashes into a dozen pieces all over the kitchen floor.

"Mom!" I holler her name, and she looks at me.

"Do you know?" she asks me, her face red. Standing by the open dishwasher, she has plenty of ammunition.

"Who—"

"Jared," Phoebe says to me. "Honey, Jared isn't here." Her voice becomes sugary when she turns back to Mom, but then her tone lowers to just above a whisper and with disgust she adds, "The jack—"

"Don't say his name!" Mom screeches and, though her mind isn't right, I am surprised at her strength. Her words are strong and so is her arm.

"Momma," I say, inching toward her. "Dad left, remember?"

She swings a coffee mug my direction and it hits me in the face, cutting open the skin just below my left eye. Mom gasps at the blood that pours out. Rushing over, Phoebe stands behind her. Wrapping her arms around Mom's body, she holds down her limbs.

"Shh, shh," Phoebe hushes as Mom struggles against her grasp. "He'll be back soon. He's gone to get you ice cream and blueberries, your favorite." She sways back and forth with her, and Mom settles with her words. "Isn't he a sweetheart, bringing you your favorite?"

Mom's head falls back against Phoebe's chest and she whimpers. Sweat drips from her forehead and her nightgown is drenched down to her navel.

"Come on," Phoebe says. "Let's go change and you can wait for him on the couch."

I let Phoebe take her. I clean up the glass pieces and scrub at the smears of blood on the floor. In the bathroom I wash my face and inspect my cut. It's sure to bruise. I butterfly the wound and stare at my pale face. Breathing out a sigh, I know Liam won't be seeing this moment. Changing out of my red stained shirt and blue jeans, I put on my pj pants. My throat is swollen and achy, but I hold back my tears. They can come later tonight.

"So," Phoebe says, standing in my bedroom door frame. "How'd it go?"

I ignore the question. The answer's too complicated anyway. "Why'd you tell her that?"

"What?"

Crossing my arms over my chest, I grind my teeth together. "Why did you tell her my dad was coming back?"

"Oh, that." Her hands land on her hips, and her navel peeks out overtop her cut-off sweats. "It's what she wanted to hear."

"It's a lie!" I bark the remark.

"Yes, Thankful, it is. We both know that and if Sally's mind were coherent right now, she'd know that and she wouldn't be asking for the—" She stops, knowing I don't like her calling him derogatory names, even if she's right. "How's your eye?"

Touching the butterfly bandage, I shake my head a little. "It's nothing."

"She didn't mean—"

"I know." She never means it.

"Okay, then. I'm gonna make sure she's settled." Phoebe reaches for my hand and squeezes my fingers before leaving.

I shut the door after she's out of sight. Lying on my bed that hasn't been slept in for months, I pick up my phone. I want to text Liam. I don't want to call. I don't want him to hear the shake in my voice. But he doesn't have a phone. Troy told me I could text his mobile anytime for Liam, that they both used it. But what do even I say? *Hi, I know you didn't see it coming, but my night really sucked...* Even still, I want to...

ME: FOR LIAM.

I start official, so Troy will know it's for Liam, but I still don't know what to type next. I *officially* ask for Troy to give his phone over to Liam and now...

ME: HEY.
LIAM: HI.

Holding my head in my hands, I moan. What was I expecting? Part of me thinks it would be easier if he just knew. If he *could* see the worst, I wouldn't have to say a thing and he could understand. I don't have the energy to explain myself. I toss my phone onto the night stand, but it dings again, before I can draw my hand back.

LIAM: YOU OKAY?
ME: YEAH.

LIAM: YOU DIDN'T GET A KISS GOODNIGHT.

Just half a dozen throughout the date... Smiling, I feel my cheeks warm with my blush and I hope he deletes our messages before giving his phone back to Troy.

ME: NO, I DIDN'T.

I'm not sure if my flirtation translates. For one, I'm not very good at flirting and through text... ugh, it's impossible.

LIAM: WE CAN FIX THAT TOMORROW.

How is he so good at flirting and through a text message? Still, I laugh at the note. The tension in my body and mind seems to settle, and sure, maybe my pillow will be soaked tonight, but tomorrow I'll get a kiss from Liam.

I might be running a marathon in sixty seconds, but right now, I don't even care.

21

MR. AUGUST

"Wow, Chels." I walk into school with Chelsea after a twenty-minute long story about Kent and the dance. "I'm glad you and Kent had such a good time."

"It was amazing. I don't know if you can understand…" She looks off, her expression dreamy, clutching her books to her chest with one hand. Pushing her black-rimmed glasses up on her face, she sighs. She's so busy swooning over her date that she hasn't noticed my eye, or maybe my make-up job covered the bruise better than I thought. "But then maybe… what are the odds?" Leaning over to me, she whispers, "Did someone else get kissed?"

"Well," I say, trying to laugh. "Ah…"

"You did! I knew Marc was the right choice, he—"

Errica's loud laugh behind us interrupts her. "Or not."

We both turn and stare at her, but of course she only responds to Chelsea.

"Rumor has it, Marc Bailey left the dance alone, and bleeding."

Crossing her arms like she's just discovered the secret to unexplainable crop circles, she sets her glare on me.

Scrunching her face, Chelsea looks at me. "Thankful?"

"Yeah, well…" I laugh, trying to make it seem like it's not that big of a deal. I wish I were better at this. I told Phoebe I wasn't ashamed of Liam and I'm not. She's right. I need to just be honest. I can't be as unkind to him as they have been. Even if it means more whispers and rumors—now, from the people I call friends. "Liam showed up. Marc was kind of being a jerk—" Yes, I see the irony in those words after defending him to Liam. Blowing a raspberry, I toss my head. "Which led to some punching." I bite my cheek. "Remember I said I had texted you? Well, yeah, it was kind of a crazy night."

"Who punched who?" Chelsea narrows her eyes on me.

"Hmm?"

"Who did the punching?" she says, stopping in front of our classroom door.

"Oh." I twist my hands together, my defenses already on guard. "Well, see—"

"Ahem."

We turn at the noise. Marc and Kent stand behind us, waiting for us to move. The crack in Marc's lip is crusted over with blood, proclaiming Liam's guilt. The night of the dance I could see a bruise forming, but now—ick. The reddish purple blotch spreads across Marc's jaw and down his chin. He crosses his arms over his wide chest. The one fist I can see turns white in its clenched state. He glares at me, his eyes small slits that seem to say they are contemplating paybacks, right here, right now.

Chelsea's eyes go wide at the sight of him. Regardless of his friend's state, Kent gives Chelsea a smile and a cool "hey". At which Chelsea seems to lose her concern over Marc altogether.

"Out of the way, loser," Marc says, his slit eyes still boring into me. His baritone voice comes out so loud, everyone around us can hear him.

Chelsea looks away from Kent to scowl at Marc.

I stare at the ground, my eyes blurring with the tiles on the floor. He needs to get out his anger, hide his humiliation with it, and he *is* the one who got punched. I can at least give him that. Right?

"Hey!" The yell comes from down the hall.

Looking up from my cowering position, I see him. All four of us-Chelsea, Kent, Marc, and I peer down the hall at the yeller. Liam.

"Get away from her." Liam strides over to stand beside me.

Marc's face turns red and his eyes follow Liam's arm down to his bandaged hand. "You want a fair fight this time, Gregor?"

Before Liam can respond or I can interject, Mr. August grabs each boy by the arm. I never saw the principal coming, too distracted by the yelling and growling in front of me. Liam closes his eyes and his head bows to the ground with the touch from the older man. To anyone else he looks angry at being caught, but I know what he's hiding.

"My office, now." Mr. August's lips turn up with an unhappy snarl. "Miss Tenys, join us."

"Yes, sir," I say and follow after the three of them, Mr. August still clutching the two boys.

I sit in the chair between Marc and Liam and across from Mr. August. The man's forehead and receding hairline have turned a blotchy red. "Fighting? In my school? Unacceptable, gentlemen."

"Gregor started this," Marc says. "He took me out at the dance, for no reason."

Raising my shaky hand up and then down, I say, "Well, actually —ah, sir—"

"Yes, Miss Tenys?"

"Liam was trying to defend me. True, hitting isn't the best way to—"

"Is this true, Mr. Bailey?" Mr. August asks, his eyes focus on my butterfly bandage.

"No!" Marc's face pulls back until it's wrinkled with disgust and his hands grip the chair arms.

"Well, yes." I look at Marc, but I try to keep any malice from my expression. A part of me still feels bad for him, as well as guilty for leaving him. "You were attempting to kiss me when I clearly didn't want to be kissed."

"Hey, I—" Marc starts with Liam's snarl.

"Okay, okay!" Mr. August rakes his hand through what's left of his hair and holds his palms out like stop signs. "Romeo," he says, looking at Marc. "Mr. Knight in Shining Armor." He turns his gaze to Liam. "Enough! Got it? There will be no other warnings. If I see the two of you so much as glaring at the other, there will be suspensions."

Staring at Mr. August, both boys nod.

"Great. Now, leave." Mr. August waves his hands at us. "First period. Go!"

Marc stomps off, but Liam and I dawdle down the hall. He picks up my hand and walks me toward Mr. Hunt's class, even though I know his first hour lies in the opposite direction.

"You okay?" He peeks at me.

"Yeah, fine."

"Your eye—"

My hand instinctively covers my butterfly bandage and I flinch a little where I touch the bruise. "I'm all right. Mr. August is the one whose day started out horrible. I've never seen the principal look so stressed."

"Yeah, well, his day is only going to get worse."

Stopping, I face Liam. "Wait. What'd you see?"

"The mail," he says. "Divorce papers."

Sighing, I blow out a puff of air. "Poor Mr. August."

Nodding, he looks at me and rubs his thumb over my bandage. "You gonna tell me what happened?"

Shaking my head, I tap my foot on the tiled ground. "It's not a big deal. Bad night. That's all."

"That's why you texted?"

"I just needed to end my day with something non-awful." I squeeze his hand.

"And I'm non-awful?"

Blushing, I purse my lips before saying, "Yeah, you're incredibly non-awful."

Bringing his hands down to my waist, he wraps his arms around me and hugs me close and tight. And it's as if any gloom that even considered coming near me melts away when he's holding me.

***

"It was Liam, wasn't it?" Chelsea leans over, her face close to mine, but her body still in her desk.

"What was?" I say, looking at Mr. Hunt. He's grading and we're supposed to be reading.

"The guy who kissed you. It was Liam, wasn't it?"

I want to tell her it's none of her business, I want to keep all of that perfection secret and safe and private. But she's my friend. Aren't we supposed to tell each other these things? And I'm *not* trying to hide him or deny how I feel. "Yes." I keep my voice steady. "It was."

"So, did you get hurt," she says, pointing to my eye, "before or after he decided to kiss you?"

"Chels." I grip the edge of the desk and stare wide eyed at her. "You know, there are a lot of hard things in my life. Not one can be blamed on Liam. They were there long before I knew him. And my eye has nothing to do with him. Just an accident." I should have known she'd start blaming him for, well, everything.

Blowing out a sigh, she lowers her already whispered voice. "So, are you two like together *together,* now?"

Turning in my seat, I face her. This is a moment. A moment where I can be weak and give excuses and look regretful and make her happy, or a moment when I risk my friendship for truth. Giving myself five seconds to mull that over, I open my mouth. "He isn't cursed, Chels. He's a good person who has been ostracized by an entire school. It's not his fault Errica lost her mother's necklace or Sonia flunked her biology final. And it isn't his fault your cousin passed away."

Her jaw clenches. "But he—"

"So, he happened to be around. He is not a curse." My lashes flutter, and I peer over at her. "Bad things happen on days you don't see Liam, too. Bad things just happen. And yes, we are together now."

She bites her lip until I'm afraid she's drawn blood and stares at me, her eyes narrowed.

"Ladies," Mr. Hunt says, and we both move back into our forward facing positions.

Glancing from my open book to Chelsea, I'm not sure things will ever be the same. But I knew the possible consequences when I opened my mouth.

I SIT ACROSS FROM LIAM AT LUNCH. NOTHING OUT OF THE ordinary, except that now I know his secret. "I think we should follow him." I bite down on my thumbnail.

"Who?" Liam opens his brown paper sack and pulls a plastic container filled with a mystery salad inside.

"Mr. August."

"Why?" Looking up from his lunch, his brows furrow.

"Because," is the only answer I give. "After school. We'll follow him. Do you think it'll be after school? Do you see a time—"

A growl escapes his throat, but I'm not afraid of him. "Yes, it'll be after school."

"So, you do know when."

Shaking his head, he closes his eyes, trying to be patient with me. "No, Thankful, I don't see a date or a time, but it happens within a twenty-four hour period and he wasn't at the school. With someone like you, who I touch more than anyone else, I'll just see the next best thing within that twenty-four hour period." He crosses his arms and sits back, watching me. "Our lives aren't laid out for us, they aren't a mathematical problem that will always end with the same result. We make choices, and those choices often determine the good and bad in our lives. Some choices, like eating, or other definite routine things will without question happen, but different choices determine different outcomes. You're still free to choose. Our paths change when our minds change, when we make a choice. I won't see what will happen days, months or a year from now—not even with you. There are too many decisions, too many factors, too many choices to make in between now and then."

Mulling over what he's said, I rub my temples. "So, even if you saw my worst moments, you wouldn't see—you couldn't tell me when I'll lose her." I'm not sure when my quest for Mr. August turned into my dark curiosity about Mom.

He reaches across the table and takes my hand. "Not with much notice, no."

I'd be lying if I said I hadn't thought about this since the moment he confessed. And in truth, I wish Liam could tell me. How many times have I run out the door to shed tears, to allow myself to lose it now that Phoebe is here? Before she came, I didn't allow it. Sure, I felt like a balloon with too much air, ready to pop, but I didn't run away. If I knew when... If I knew where... would I change what I do? Would I bother going to school and spend all my free time with Liam? Or would I sit by her side until the last second? Not caring if she called me names or threw tantrums. If I knew when, if I knew where, I wouldn't allow myself to step out and collect myself. Because I have to be there, I have to be with her when the end comes.

Blinking back the oncoming tears, I look at him. The back of his fingers brush my cheek and his irises flood with black. "Mr. August," I say, holding myself together and getting back to why I brought all this up.

"Thankful," his kind voice whispers my name, "part of my curse draws me to the people I touch. To the ones I know will be suffering. I see it in my mind, feel the pain in my chest. I've worked hard not to allow myself to witness it play out."

"But—"

Licking his lips, he says, "It's like a pull, an addiction that won't leave my head, and I hate it. I don't want it."

"I know," I whisper the words. I don't want to hurt him, but I want to go. I *need* to go. Almost as if it's pulling me, too.

His chest falls with his sigh. "You really want to see this? It won't be pretty."

It's sick, and I realize that. Still, I lick my lips. "I have to."

Rubbing his hand across his chin, his eyes lock on mine. "Aw, Thankful." His hand rakes through his dark hair and a small rumble escapes his throat. "Okay. Just this once."

22

THANK YOU

Sitting in Pop's little yellow car, I feel like we are the worst people to be on a stake out. We stand out in this thing, parked across the street from Mr. August's house, like we're begging to get caught.

"Stop squirming and just talk to me." Liam pats my leg.

"It's just, this car, it's like we're sitting in a giant lemon. We should have brought the boat." Looking past him, I see Mr. August's driveway. He isn't home yet. We've been here for half an hour. How long do principals stay at school? I have a hundred questions in my head, but there's one I'm not willing to speak out loud: Is this really going to happen? I believe Liam... and yet how can I not doubt? It's all so strange.

"Here." Liam takes my chin in his hand and forces me face him. "Ask me a question."

"A what?" I say, my eyes still diverted toward the little brown house. "Hey! Hey!" I slap Liam's shoulder. "He's home." I hush the words and feel a rush of adrenalin pump through my body.

Before Mr. August can get out of the car, the mail truck has pulled up beside his home. The mailman's hand reaches out, holding an envelope with a green seal.

"Certified mail." Liam's lips pull down in a frown. "Poor guy."

Leaning over Liam, I stare at Mr. August. He drops his briefcase to the ground. It falls over haphazardly. With a shaky hand, Mr. August reaches for the envelope. The mailman hands him a clipboard and Mr. August signs for the post.

The mail truck drives away and I puff out the breath I've been holding. Opening the envelope, Mr. August pulls just a smidgen of the paper from its sleeve. Stumbling back until his backside hits his vehicle, he slides down the side of his car until he's sitting on the ground.

Gasping, I cover my mouth. It happened. It really happened. The man is on the ground. I can't sit and just watch this. I can't stake out. I can't! Opening my side door, I exit the car and start across the street.

"Thankful!" Liam whispers, but with the force it gives off, he might as well be shouting.

Stopping mid-street, I look back.

His eyes are wide. "What are you—"

"Ah…" I shrug, face forward, and continue over.

The envelope lies on the ground. Mr. August holds his head in his hands, his bald spot reflecting the sunlight where his combed over hair doesn't quite hit.

Clearing my throat, I speak, "Mr. August?"

His head pops up and he wipes at his face before looking at me. "Miss Tenys?" Squinting in the sun, he holds up a hand to see me better. "What are you doing here?"

"I—I—I was just... I was just here. And I saw you and I—" I bob my head, stuttering. "Are you okay? Can I do anything?"

Sighing, his eyes stare past me. "Mr. Gregor?"

Looking back, I see Liam standing right behind me.

"August." Liam's greeting is curt. His fists clench at his sides and his forehead furrows with wrinkles.

Knocking the back of his head against his car, Mr. August closes his eyes. "Please," he says in a gravely voice, "run along."

"What can we do?" I squat down next to him.

Shaking his head, he puffs out his cheeks, still not daring to open his eyes. "Go." He moans.

Pursing my lips, I look back at Liam. We can't just leave him.

Mr. August doesn't hear the low rumble of Liam's growl. He isn't pleased... with me or the situation, but still, he says, "Let's get you up. Get you inside."

Mr. August doesn't move. His face has fallen toward the ground, defeated.

"Thankful," Liam says, nodding toward the briefcase and fallen envelope.

I pick them up.

Bending down, he pulls Mr. August's arm around his neck and, in one swift movement, lifts him to a standing position.

Liam walks Mr. August to his front door, while Mr. August's feet drag behind. I follow after them. Liam pulls on the unlocked door and I hurry to hold it open. He hauls our principal inside. This has to be the most bizarre thing I've ever been involved with.

Setting Mr. August onto a white and pink flowered couch, Liam stands straight, his breathing heavy. Lace curtains drape down behind him and a television atop a doily covered table sits across from the zombified man.

I set the briefcase and envelope on the floor beside the couch. Looking at one another, our eyes both question. What now?

"You get him a drink. I'll turn the TV on."

I nod and wander through the nearest doorway to find the kitchen. The small room screams *female,* from more lace curtains to the potted flowers atop the table. Mr. August's wife has left him and it's obvious it wasn't part of his plan. I've never seen a man so distraught before. I fill a clear glass with water from the tap and hurry back into the living room. "How is he?"

"He's starting to mumble," Liam says over the noise of the football game on the television. His arms are crossed and he stares at Mr. August as if studying a confusing work of art.

"I did everything she asked," Mr. August says to himself. "Everything, besides hair plugs. And she *still* left."

Liam's eyes dart to the glass in my hand. "That's the strongest you could find?"

"I... Well, I didn't look for anything else. I mean—" I set the glass in front of Mr. August. Sitting next to him, I lay my hand on his. "Mr. August? Can I get you anything to eat?" He makes no sign that he's even heard me.

I glance up with Liam's movement. He disappears into the kitchen. Patting Mr. August's hand, I watch his glossed over eyes. Maybe he needs a doctor.

"Here," Liam says, back in the living room, both his hands filled. He hands me an open bag of potato chips and I set it in Mr. August's lap, like I'm prepping a mannequin.

Using the coffee table, Liam cracks open the bottle of beer he's brought out and sets it on the table in front of us. "Let's go."

Squeezing my eyes shut, I'm not sure I can leave, not with Mr. August this unstable. Will he eat dinner? Will he make it to school tomorrow? "Ah—"

"Come on." Liam nods at me. "He doesn't want us around. He needs to be alone."

"But..."

Mr. August stares at the television set and takes a swig from the bottle Liam brought him.

"Mr. August?" I say, and he turns his head to look at me. "It's going to be okay. It will. I promise."

He turns back to the TV with no response at my words.

Sighing, I let Liam take my hand and walk me to the door. I

watch Mr. August all the way outside, until Liam shuts it and I can't see him anymore. "Do you think he'll be okay?"

"You promised he would."

Biting my lip, I squeeze Liam's hand. What if he isn't okay? What if he never ever gets over it? "Was that wrong?"

Opening the passenger door, Liam stands in front of me. His hand blankets between my neck and shoulder and black overcomes his eyes for the next half dozen heartbeats. "I love—I love that you told him that. He needed someone to say it, even if he won't be okay for a long time. You did good, Tenys," he says, like we're on the same baseball team.

Scrunching my eyebrows at him, I hope he's right. "Yeah?"

"Yeah."

"And you're okay? Not too terrible?"

He doesn't answer right away. Maybe I've asked the wrong question. How much pain have I caused him? He experiences the worst of someone's day in a vision and then I make him see the live show. I expect an angry growl to escape him, but instead he pulls me in for a hug. "Not *too* terrible." His lips tickle my ear lobe. "Not with you."

"You too?" I ask, seeing Liam in the school's office the following day. My anxious nerves worsen seeing him. *Mr. August.* Why else would we both be called to the office? *Crap.* Maybe facing Mr. August during his worst moment wasn't such a good idea. We'd made him angry, hurt his pride and now we were going to pay. Detention for the rest of the year... what will I tell Phoebe? There had to be a way to get out of this. We weren't *trying* to humiliate him.

The muscles in Liam's arm bulge with the tightness of his crossed arms. He nods at my question. He's had more experience in this. He's already come to the conclusion, the reality that I'm just now getting to. There's a reason people don't like Liam... bad things happen, and he's the one there, the one they blame.

Great. Let's add angry boyfriend to the list of things going wrong today.

Mr. August opens his office door from the inside. "Miss Tenys. Mr. Gregor. Come in, please." He looks no different than he had a week ago, like nothing came in the mail and no one broke his heart.

I start to follow him, but stop with a tug on my wrist. Liam has taken my hand. We made this mess together, even if it was my idea. It looks as if we'll face it united.

I'm not sure that I deserve as much, seeing how I dragged Liam into this. Still, I squeeze his hand, thankful he's there, even if he's mad.

We don't bother sitting, and Mr. August doesn't offer us a chair. We stand in front of his desk and, unlike yesterday, he closes the door.

Clearing his throat, he rubs his hand once over the bareness of his head. The normalcy I noticed before has gone. "I'm sorry you had to see... that display yesterday." He licks his lips and his eyes stare at his desk, not meeting ours. "I'd appreciate your discretion though."

We're not in trouble? He's worried about gossip? "Of course," I say, looking at Liam. "We'd never say anything, Mr. August." And we wouldn't. It had never crossed my mind to spread poor Mr. August's bad news around the school.

Giving half a sad grin, he nods. "You may go."

Before I can open the door, Principal August clears his throat again. "Mr. Gregor."

We both turn to see him watching us.

"Thank you." His hands slide into the pockets of his khaki slacks. "For getting me inside. There would be plenty going around town had you not."

Staring at our principal, Liam nods, but I feel the pressure from his grip increase.

The secretary hands us passes back to class. With our palms glued together, we walk into the empty hallway.

"Breakfast?" Liam's right eyebrow lifts with the question.

"Liam!"

Grinning, he pulls me along.

"Lunch." I halt and force him to pause with me.

Liam laughs and it's almost enough to make me reconsider skipping class with him. "Okay," he says, smiling at me. "Thankful."

"Yes?"

"I've never had anyone thank me before... *because* of the curse. It was..."

"Nice," I finish for him, tugging on the front of his gray T-shirt.

"Yeah. It was." Pulling my hand until we're closer together, he wraps his arms around me. I keep my face forward, breathing him in with our embrace. Chills run from my head to my toes when his mouth brushes my earlobe. "Thank you for that."

23

FOR ME

"**S**o, you're just leaving?" I follow Phoebe around the living room as she gathers her things, my heart racing a mile a minute. How did I let this happen? How did I let us get so dependent on her?

"Of course not," she says, stopping to stare at me. "Thankful, you know me better than that. I will be back by the end of the week and the nurse will be here during the day. If it weren't an emergency…"

She dropped everything and came here for us. She loves us. She wouldn't just—But how can she do this? How can she leave us for *work*? She said she could write from Wyoming. She said she would be here when we needed her. We need her. Now. And she's leaving?

Frowning at my silence, she continues gathering her belongings. "If this weren't important, I wouldn't go. I am not abandoning you, Thankful." Dropping her armful of gadgets, power cords and car keys hit the ground. "Look at me," she says with her hands on my shoulders. "We're family. You and Sally are all I have. I *will* be back by the end of the week."

I nod and try to hold back the tears. We were *his* family too... *We'll be okay. We'll be okay. We'll be okay.* Breathe.

Still holding onto me, she stoops just a little to peer into my eyes. "Blood is thicker than water, Thankful. I wouldn't leave if I didn't know you'd be okay. I wouldn't leave if I couldn't come back. You'll be fine." Pulling me close, she rubs my back. "Sally will be fine."

"So, she's gone?" Chelsea says, and though I know she's listening to me, her eyes keep diverting to the back of the room where Kent sits.

"Just for the week. She said she'll be back, it's just—"

Giving me her full eye contact, she smacks her desk with the palm of her hand. "It's *Phoebe*, T." She says her name with such vigor, it makes me ill. "She wouldn't go if it weren't important. Phoebe's your—"

"Yeah," I say, cutting her off. "I know." Geez. She's as smitten with Phoebe as Mr. Hunt.

"So," Chelsea purses her lips and crosses her arms, "you sitting with us today? We only saw you once last week."

Narrowing my eyes at her, I fidget in my seat and channel my inner Phoebe. "Do you really want me to?"

Dropping her jaw, she spouts an offended gasp. "Of course, you're just always—"

"Okay, then. Liam and I will meet you in the cafeteria."

"Li—"

"All right people," Mr. Hunt's loud voice booms over Chelsea's horror. "Open up your books."

This isn't going to make Liam any happier than Chelsea, but I'm tired of being split in two. And it's time. These two need to get along.

"THIS ISN'T GOING TO WORK." LIAM RAKES HIS HAIR OUT OF HIS eyes. "They don't want me there."

"You mean *you* don't want to be there." Sure, both statements are facts. But I've prepped. I told Sonia and even Kent that Liam and I might stop by. They're all prepared. I've asked them all to be nice. No one rejoiced at the idea, but Chelsea was the only one who I thought might pop a vein.

"Tomato, tomahto. What's wrong with what we do now?"

My head rocks back until I stare at the white ceiling. "Come on. Please." Taking his hand, I hold it with both of mine and look at him. "For me."

His cheeks puff out with air until he releases it all with a blow. "That's unfair."

Reaching up on my toes, I kiss the corner of his mouth.

"You know what you're doing, don't you?"

Dropping back down onto the heels of my feet, I bite my lip. I don't though. This whole relationship thing is one big guess for me. "Yeah. I'm asking my—you—my…" What do I call him? My close-friend-type-person? "I'm asking you to do this for me."

"Argh." Taking my hand, he laces his fingers with mine. "Let's go."

I laugh, and follow Liam into the cafeteria. He leads me over to where Chelsea and the girls eat. Kent sits opposite of Chelsea. My stomach turns with nerves. This shouldn't be so scary. I prepped!

The chatter at the table stops at our approach.

Errica ignores us.

Sonia offers a small, fake smile.

Chelsea tries, it seems, not to grimace.

The booming silence has Kent turning around to see us. "Oh, uh, hey, Thankful."

"Hi." I wave. "You guys all know Liam?" *Of course they all know Liam.*

"Sure, I mean we've never actually been introduced," Kent says, and my opinion of him doubles with the comment. He speaks like a normal human being. He looks at Liam like a normal human being. He's the only one trying.

Kent holds out his hand to shake Liam's and I swear a hush falls over the surrounding tables. But instead of taking it, Liam lifts our knotted fists and shrugs.

I grin, bearing all my teeth, but I can't take the fake thing from my face. Trying to laugh, I say, "Okay, then, Liam, meet my friend Kent." I knew Kent as well as Liam did, hardly at all, but he earned the friend title by not cringing or punching at the sight of Liam. "Kent, meet my... my... Liam."

"Her boyfriend," Liam says, looking at Kent.

Pins and needles prick at my skin. Sure, I'd used the word in my head, but never out loud. It's just a word. A silly title. But it means something to me. Chelsea's face turns a strawberry-red. The word means something to her, too.

"Pftt." Puffing air through her lips, Errica stands, hands on hips. "You can all sit here and *pretend*, but I'm out." She glares at me before turning her back on us.

"Look at that, a seat opened up," Liam says, dispelling the silence that Errica left us with.

Kent laughs and we walk around to the other side of the table. Sliding in, I sit by Chelsea, giving Liam the end seat next to me.

My eyes dart from one person to the next. The quiet at the table thickens and I'm not sure how to break it. I force a smile at Sonia and bite my inner cheek.

"So, the holidays are coming." Sonia clasps her hands together. "What's everyone doing for Thanksgiving?" She winks at me. *Trying.*

"Headed to my grandparents in Dubois," Kent says, stuffing a french fry into his mouth.

Licking my lips, I add my two cents to the charity chat. We have to start somewhere, right? "We're staying home. Just me, Mom, and Phoebe."

"California," Chelsea gives her one-word answer, looking only at Sonia.

Liam's quiet. He stares at the exit like he'd like to run for it. Squeezing his hand in mine, I try to bring him some comfort. *Show them. You are fun and normal and wonderful... Show them!*

"Ah, Liam?" Sonia taps Liam's free hand sitting on the table. And it isn't lost on me, how much effort she's giving this. I'm not sure she knows what that means to me or how I now view our friendship. "Thanksgiving? Do you have plans?"

Turning his head even farther away from us, he bows to the ground for an awkward four seconds before looking at Sonia. "I'm not going anywhere."

"How about you, Sonia?" I clutch Liam's hand, knowing the blackness my touch has caused is long gone, as long as I *keep* touching him. But the vision Sonia gave him has just left.

24

RED ON RED

Tapping his forefinger on the edge of the table, Liam stares past me into space.

I push one of the drinks Pops brought out for us toward him. "Hey," I say, waving my hand in front of him. "What is it?"

Shaking his head, a straight brown lock falls across one of his eyes. "Sorry."

"You're so distracted. Is this about today? Was it really so awful? I mean—"

"Yeah, Thankful." He looks at me and his brows furrow. "It is about today. There's a reason I sit alone. There's a reason I stay away from people."

My throat stings with pain. I want to cry at his harshness. Taking a sip from the Coke in front of me, I keep my eyelids low, hoping the tears won't fall. I don't trust myself to speak.

Sighing, he rakes both hands through his hair. "I know you meant well. But I see these things and feel these things and they don't just leave. They linger and then I'm stuck wondering why I'm cursed to see, but never change, awful things."

"Wait. You saw something bad? Like *bad* bad." I ask, not caring about the crack in my voice.

Rubbing his hands over his tired eyes, he nods.

"Liam," I say, the weakness in my voice gone. "What is it?"

"Sonia—"

"Sonia!" I think of her efforts today. Of the friend she became to me today. Taking his wrists in my hands, I tug at his arms. "Liam! Tell me."

"Ahh, Thankful." Liam puffs out my name in a heavy breath. "She falls, off her bike. I think she needs stitches. Nothing too life threatening. Just a lot of blood."

Gasping, I cover my mouth. *Sonia.* "Come on." Sliding off the café bench, I pull Liam's wrist until he's standing. "We can't sit here and do nothing."

"We can't stop it." Closing his eyes, some of the darkness, the meanness, that has clouded Liam for so many years returns.

Crossing my arms, I glare at him. I'm not arguing over this.

"I've tried." He shrugs, any anger he felt before diminishing. Dejection filling the space.

"Well, we can at least help her." I reach for him again and pull on his hand, making him follow after me.

Getting into the boat, Liam sits beside me—less than thrilled at yet another Knowing adventure. Spinning the wheel, I turn the car around and we drive toward Sonia's house. "What if we took her bike?"

"Then she'd borrow her brother's, something. We can't stop it."

Nodding, the nerves dance inside me. *Sweet Sonia.* Pulling up to her house, I lay my hand on Liam's knee. "Wait here."

"Hello, Meg," I say when the house door opens. I've only met Sonia's mom once before.

"Thankful." She wipes her hands on a dish cloth. "Sonia isn't here, sweetie. She just biked to Brice's house."

The news still hits me in the gut, the supernatural of it all is such a shock. I don't know that I'll ever get used to Liam's ability. "Thanks," I manage to get out.

Cranking the car into reverse, I glance over to Liam. "She's already left."

"When?" He glances in the side view mirror as if to spot her nearby.

"I don't know," I say, taking off down the road.

"Thankful." Liam lays his hand on my shoulder. "Then it could be over and done. You don't even know—"

"Are you saying if it were me you saw crashing and bleeding, you'd just let it happen? Just let it be?" I take a hard right, jerking Liam over closer to me.

"No," he says, his hands on the dash. "But we can't stop this. I've told you that."

"So?" I glance over at him. "If it were me what would you do?"

Resting his head back against the seat, he sighs.

"That's what I thought." I turn the wheel. "Well, Sonia's my friend." A better friend than I realized.

And suddenly, there she is.

Sonia's already on the ground, her bike three feet from her body. I hit the brakes and jerk the car into park. Leaping from the boat, I'm unsure if Liam follows behind me. Hurrying to her side, I kneel down. "Sonia!"

She lifts her head and the blood runs down her face like a faucet.

"Ohh." My voice shakes and I jerk back a little. She looks like a scene from a zombie movie.

"Here," Liam says. So he did follow me. He bends down on the other side of her, his jacket in his hands. He rolls it up until its folded small and thick. He lays the makeshift bandage onto Sonia's head.

On her hands and knees, Sonia's body shakes as she looks from me to Liam. "T?" She tries to stand, but falls backwards onto her butt.

Wrapping an arm around her shoulders, I squeeze. "Yeah, it's me. Hey, stay still, you're pretty wobbly."

Liam readjusts the jacket on her head. Blood soaks into his gray coat and seeps into her bright red hair. The mixing of reds disturbs my stomach.

"That's a lot of blood." Liam shifts the jacket again to face a clean, new section. "She needs a doctor."

Sonia's head tilts up at him, her eyebrows knit together.

"Here, hold this." Liam nods to his jacket atop Sonia's head. "I'll get her up and to the car."

Liam drives while I sit in the back with Sonia. "What day is it, Sonia?" He glances at us in the rearview mirror.

"Ah… Monday?" She leans her head against the seat of the car.

I follow his lead. She could have a concussion. "Where were you going? Sonia?" I wiggle her shoulder, keeping her awake.

"Going?" she says, both her hands over my one, holding Liam's cotton jacket in place. "Um… ouch, my head hurts."

"I know. Do you remember what happened?"

Closing her eyes, she licks her lips, her forehead wrinkling. "I… I was biking… The curb… I didn't—"

"Okay. It's okay."

"We're here." Liam parks the car and together we walk a groggy Sonia into the Urgent Care Clinic.

Her bloody face and hair, plus the wadded jacket around her head gets us right back into a patient room. A doctor enters in less than two minutes.

"I better call her mom." I step out of the room, leaving Liam and Sonia with Dr. Jacobs.

I pace back and forth in the hallway, talking to Meg. "She's going to be fine." Even as I promise the words, my stomach turns with the image of all Sonia's blood, in her hair, down her face, on her shirt.

Sneaking back into the room, my eyes dart to Liam, sitting beside Sonia, holding her hand. Her face is washed clean of the bloodstains, but her cheeks now streak with tears.

Liam stands when he sees me, but Sonia still clutches to his hand. I offer him a smile and he sits back down. His face contorts with worry and discomfort all in one. His eyes widen and I walk over to relieve him.

Dr. Jacobs has the razor out. My stomach plummets at the sight. *Sonia's beautiful hair.* Her grip on Liam turns two-handed. She isn't letting go, and I don't want to make her. I sit beside him and rub her arm.

"It'll be okay, Sonia," I say, wondering if I know any other comforting words. It's all I could say to Principal August, too.

More tears stream down her rosy cheeks. She whimpers while the doctor cuts away a section of red curls on top of her head. He shaves around the cut and I move my gaze away. I can't watch. More than blood attempts to spill out of the deep cut.

The door to the room creaks open and Sonia's mom steps inside. Meg takes my place, but Sonia won't let go of Liam. I stand back while Dr. Jacobs sews her up and gives her mother instructions for the sutures and slight concussion she's sustained.

"How bad is it?" Sonia touches the hair around her cut once the doctor has left.

"It's fine, not bad at all," Meg says, smiling down at her daughter. "You've got so much hair, honey, and it's on top of your head, hardly noticeable!"

"Thankful?" Sonia says and I walk over, standing behind Meg and Liam.

"She's right." I nod, trying to be encouraging, and wonder how

Sonia would look in a hat. "You'll just need to part your hair differently."

Finally, she gives the smallest of grins. But then, as if startled, she says, "Oh." Looking at her hands white and tight around Liam's, she loosens her grip. "Um, sorry." Opening her fingers wide, she stretches her hands, moving them to her lap.

Scooting his chair back, it bumps into me. Liam rises. "Don't worry about it." Moving behind his chair, he stands next to me and takes my hand.

"I'll check on you tomorrow." I pat her arm and resist staring at her head.

Holding to Liam's hand, we walk outside. The fresh, crisp air feels good after the sweat and blood from Sonia and the doctor's office. My heart starts to settle and that's when I realize it's been racing. I take a deep breath and look at Liam. "Thank you."

He nods. "Let's go get her bike."

"Okay."

Walking over to the driver's side, he opens the door for me, but I don't get inside.

Facing him, I hold both his hands. "You were good in there." He was and he needs to know it, because he doesn't, I'm sure of it. I know it wasn't easy for him, but again, like with Mr. August, he did well.

His eyes narrow and he stares at me. "It... it was strange."

Laughing, I sigh and lean against the open door. "You know, I thought you were wrong before, about being cursed."

He shakes his head. "But now—"

"And now, I know you're wrong." Letting go of his hands, I wrap my arms around his waist. "Liam, you have a gift."

25

THE STORY OF SIA WESTCOTT

Troy sets another Coke in front of me. I'm starting to become addicted.

"Dad," Liam says, sitting beside me in the diner booth. "Tell her. She can't quit school."

"I wouldn't be quitting." I draw circle after circle with my finger on the tabletop. "It's an online program."

"Thankful, you can't quit your one and only year of public schooling. You aren't even halfway through."

"I know, but Phoebe's work called her away again. Mom's been with a nurse more now than ever, and I hate it. She needs one of us with her and this—" It's been less than a week, but the second time Phoebe has left now. And its already made everything I thought I liked about public school go right out the window. The whole reason for Phoebe to work from Glenrock was so that Mom wouldn't be stuck home with a stranger. If Phoebe can't be there, then I should be.

"This isn't what your mother would want, Thankful. She wanted you in school." Troy wipes his hands on a clean dishcloth.

"Yes, but—"

"No buts. I'm no Reader." He guffaws at the word *reader*. "But this is where she wants you. This is where you should stay." Troy eyes me like a parent lecturing his child.

Liam's squeeze on my hand increases. It seems to say he knows where *he* wants me.

"Reader?" I don't understand his reference. I know he has a point, but can Mom make those kinds of choices right now? And Phoebe is gone *again*! The second time this month already. She's promised to be back for Thanksgiving.

Troy narrows his gaze and leans across the table, his tone a whisper, though we're the only ones in the diner. "Li has never told you about Readers?"

"Dad—" Liam says in a low, threatening voice that would make anyone other than his father think twice. Inching somehow closer to me, I feel his body go rigid.

"Liam." He snaps his fingers at his son, silencing him. "You can't bring her into our world and not give her the warnings. You can't tell the beginning of a story and never the middle or the end. You can't give her yin without—"

"I get it." Liam's brows furrow at Troy and I want to tell him it's not respectful to growl at his father.

"Readers." Troy's face seems to darken with the name. "They are the opposite of us. We see what will come. They hear all around them. They know your thoughts without your consent. They manipulate and twist your own thinking until it has become theirs. They use those in power to direct and control certain matters. Readers. They are the servants of Beelzebub."

Whoa. Beelzebub? Eccentric Troy means business. His brown eyes stare at me without blinking.

"Mind readers?" I look to Liam for support. Knowing was difficult enough to grasp, I'm not sure my mind can comprehend another paranormal people. "And we don't like them?"

Liam's lips turn up in a small peace-offering grin. He knows it's a lot for me to take in. "Yes, mind readers. They use our kind to know what they can't. The future."

"But it's not as if you see everything."

"No," Troy says, his hands spreading out onto the tabletop. His long fingers gather and he points to the counter, stressing his position. "But we see enough for them to use, to be in the right place, at the right time, to manipulate what will be. Wars have been waged because of Readers using what we know."

A chill runs down my back, and it isn't at all like when Liam touches me, or brushes his lips against mine. It's fear. I can sense it in Troy's tone, in Liam inching closer, though his side touches every bit of mine. They are both afraid of these things, these *Readers*. The knowledge is sure to give me nightmares, faceless monsters who manipulate my thoughts to get me to do their evil bidding.

The phone rings and I startle with the noise.

Troy walks away to answer the café's receiver.

I peer at Liam. "Is it really that scary?" Troy has left me on edge.

His brows knit together. "Yes. It is."

Elbowing him in the side, my voice goes squeaky. "And you never thought to tell me about them?" I'm with Troy on this one, maybe I should be made aware of the whole story and not just half.

"Thankful." His fingers press the spot where I hit. "You've lived seventeen years without knowing. How would it have helped? Besides, Readers haven't been in this part of the country for decades. There aren't enough people of consequence to manipulate. Who in Glenrock would a Reader need to control?" His eyebrows rise, trying to convince me. "They aren't trying to take over the least populated state in the country. They're more into swaying one political party in the direction that best serves them."

I guess he has a point. "Well, for history purposes then."

"Oh—kay," his throat rumbles, "I'm sorry."

"You want history," Troy says, hanging up the receiver and walking back to us.

"Dad…" Liam snarls the word. But with one glare from his father he's quiet.

"History is important, Li. It makes certain we do not repeat ourselves. The mistakes of the past will only stay in the past if we teach." Troy grabs a chair from a middle table and sets it at the end of our booth. "It began with the Rule. The Rule is the leading power source of the Readers. There may be some who do not practice mind manipulation, but they are rare, if not nonexistent. The Rule are at the top of the hierarchy in the Reader world. They lead and others follow. There are Reader groups all over the world, but they all report to the Rule.

"The Rule began in the '60s with a man named Harris Lloyd. Lloyd, a Reader, recruited other Readers until they were strong and many. When they discovered the Knowing and found they too could be manipulated, they were almost unstoppable."

I shiver with Troy's words, but stay quiet.

"There was one family, the Westcotts. Lloyd and his men had 'recruited' their entire Knowing family, from granddaughter to grandmother. They all worked under the Rule's decree. Some of them understood that their minds were not safe, that they were used as puppets. Those particular individuals either learned to be quiet or they were exterminated."

"Killed?"

"On the spot. Yes. The Rule does not show mercy for those who rebel against them, even a rebellion from those who have been forced to work for them.

"Lloyd worked closely with the Westcott's youngest daughter. She was of the right age and state of mind to work for the man. She acted as his assistant for whichever company he dissected at the time. There are too many to know which. She did as he asked and, happily for him, she showed him many visions that produced successful manipulations over other businessmen."

Troy lowers his head and his voice, his eyes darkening on their own, without the contact of another human being. "One night after a great success, Lloyd manipulated the girl, Sia, into bed, his reward. That was the beginning of a long affair. After a year Harris Lloyd realized he'd fallen in love with a Knowing, the cursed. To his people, the scum of the earth. He could act as though he didn't love her, he could hide the lie they lived and he did, for a while, until Sia became pregnant. And then Harris knew he could not hide anymore."

Entwining his fingers, Troy rests them on the table in front of him. "Sia loved Harris in return and she begged him to go to his council, to speak with them, to plead with them. She wanted her family freed and Harris for her husband. He told her he wanted the same, though his emotions were mixed. He did want Sia, but he also wanted to rule. Still, he did as she asked, mostly. He went to his council, a board of twelve men and told them he loved the Knowing, Sia. He loved her and his seed grew in her belly. However, he did not plead for her people. He knew that would be the quickest way to dethrone himself from the empire he'd worked so hard to build. His council listened; they heard the horrific truth that Lloyd lay before them. They asked his permission to speak to Sia. Lloyd gave consent and the following day she was brought to the council meeting room. Twelve Rule council members picked and pried and dissected their way through Sia Westcott's mind. Like a leash guiding her brain they led her down a path Sia had never in her life thought to walk. A path her faith, her family, her own personal conviction would never have consented to, all while Harris watched."

"She joined them." My body goes rigid, listening to Troy's tale. This is history. It's done, and yet I find myself pleading in my head for Harris to do what is right, to take Sia and his child away from the Rule.

"No, Thankful, she did not."

My shoulders relax with relief.

"Before the night had ended Sia Westcott hung herself. She took her life and murdered her unborn child."

I cover my mouth and muffle the cry that leaves my throat. I have a picture of Sia in my mind: long black hair, slender and pretty, a smile that lights the room. Although I've been given no description of her, my mind has made one up. And now Sia's long hair and slender neck hang from a rope, her expression a blank, dead stare.

"The council had convinced Sia that she was an evil being, a cursed being, and her child being Knowing and Reader combined would be born a devil."

"But Harris loved her, how could he sit there and say nothing?"

"He loved his power more. When the deed was done, he sat at the head of his council, their leader still, and thanked them for removing the distraction."

Tears prick my eyes as I stare at the speckled table top.

"Lesson over," Liam says, his voice stern.

Troy clears his throat and in my peripheral I see him nod. He looks in my direction, but doesn't speak. Turning, he leaves, walking through the swinging kitchen door.

"I'm sorry," Liam squeezes my hand. "He gets worked up and then there's no bringing him down. It's an awful story. It's—"

"But it's true?"

Liam's throat bobs with his swallow. "Yes. It is. And it's only one of many awful stories."

"Are you saying that every major crisis in my history book has occurred because of these people, these Readers? They've infiltrated our government and our religion and our—" I'm panting and thankful when Liam interrupts me.

"It's not quite that encompassing. Yes, many historical events have been the cause of Reader manipulation, but not all. People still have their opinions and some are just plain crazy without Reading or Knowing. And Readers don't produce like the Knowing. The Knowing are born with the curse. It's a dominant trait. If either parent is Knowing their child has no chance." He says it like a warning. What he means is *his* children, if he were to have any, would all be cursed. "Readers pass their gift onto *one* of their children. The child of their choice. Once they do, it leaves them."

It doesn't escape me how he refers to the Readers, the monsters Troy just described as having a *gift,* while his ability is always a curse. Will I ever convince him otherwise? "One per family," I say, concerning Readers and the change in direction has calmed my racing pulse.

"Right. Unless both parents are gifted, then they each pass on the trait. But if a Reader dies before the gift is passed on, it's gone. Their family loses the gift."

"Why do you do that?" The words tumble out before I can stop them. His morbid, self-deprecating claim makes me angry. How can he not see himself as more than a curse?

Shrugging, his forehead wrinkles. "What?"

"Twice now, you've said Readers have a gift. They're the bad guys, but they have a *gift?* And then you—you're good, you've helped others, but you're cursed?"

"Two people, Thankful. *We've* helped two people. And if it weren't for you I wouldn't have touched those people or been in those places. You're the one—"

Turning in our booth, I face him as best I can. "No," I say, smacking the table. "You. You got Mr. August into his house, and you sat there holding Sonia's hand while the doctor shaved her scalp and sewed her up. You. Not me. You."

"Thankful—"

"Stop acting like you can't walk when you can fly."

He stares at me, his brows raised, his lips pursed, like I'm a child. Sure, my analogy may be a little dramatic, a little superhero-childish, but he doesn't see himself right. He doesn't see his *gift*.

My eyes well with tears too easily. I'd leave the booth if he weren't blocking me in. Staring at the table, a tear falls on the speckled counter.

"Thankful," he says, in a low rumbly whisper.

Where did these dumb tears come from? "I know I'm acting stupid."

"No."

"I don't know why I'm crying. It's childish. It's just that story and I—"

Holding a hand to my cheek, he forces my gaze up to him. "You aren't acting stupid; human and overconfident in me, but not stupid." His eyes turn to slits. "I don't want to disappoint you."

Shaking my head in his hold, I say, "You won't." How could he?

26

THE PLAGUE HAS STIPULATIONS

"Sonia!" My heart flutters at the sight of my friend. "You're back!"

"Oh, T, thank you so much. What would I have done if—"

"You have thanked me a hundred times." And she had. Between her accident and the two times I went to visit her, she had spent half her time thanking me, for nothing.

"Yeah." Biting her lip, her fingers press at her newly side-parted hair.

"It looks good. Maybe you'll never go back to the middle."

She laughs. "I guess it could be worse, right?"

"Always." I think about Mom home with the nurse. Guilt punches me in the gut, that's *worse*. She's not the same with the nurse. It's like there's never a good day. How can I be here at school when Phoebe is gone and Mom is home with a stranger? Phoebe said she'd be back; she didn't want me missing school for her three or four day absence. And she did come back, for one day, and then she had to leave again. She's promised to be home tomorrow. But I hope she won't have to leave again. We need her. She makes our lives easier, no... *better*, she makes our lives better. Maybe I should tell her that more.

"So," Sonia says, looking past me. "Is Liam here today?"

"Yeah, I think he's in English now." We sit down in our usual desks near the back.

"Have you guys still been eating at our table?"

"Ah, no, we haven't again. I think it's a lot for everyone to handle." And I'd already put Liam through a lot this month.

She nods and holds her hand to her head.

"Hey, are you okay?" I reach out, brushing her arm.

"Yeah," she says, shaking her head. "Just a headache. I get them sometimes."

I watch her, wishing Liam were to here to make sure a headache will be all she faces today.

I SIT ACROSS FROM LIAM IN THE LUNCHROOM; HE'S GIVING ME THE latest on Pop's online dating experience. "But he's not going to meet her, right?"

"She lives across the country and she's half his age. I'm pretty sure Dad will lock him in his room if he mentions a face to face meeting."

I laugh and wonder, did he see this today, making me laugh during lunch. I don't ask him what he sees. There are too many touches. And I don't want to know anymore. He's proof that good will come, and at this point, that's all I need.

"Uh, hey, guys." Sonia stands beside our table, hands behind her back. "Would you mind if I joined you?"

Looking over to Liam, he stares back at me, not bothering to hide his shock, though it isn't anger or repulsion. So, I turn back to Sonia. "Sit." I move my chair closer to Liam, making space for her.

Standing up, Liam grabs a free chair from the table next to us and sets it down for Sonia. She sits and the lively lunch room feels like a funeral, somber and quiet and watching. I don't understand. Our classmates didn't go silent when I approached Liam and only a few surrounding tables hushed for a brief moment when Liam and I went to Chelsea's table, but with Sonia's joining us I can hear the breath of everyone around me. In the silence, I can feel eyes upon eyes watching our backs.

Within seconds Liam excuses himself from the table.

My eyes dart to Sonia. "Ah… I'm gonna—"

"Yeah." Her hands wring together in her lap. "Go, ahead."

"Hey!" I yell out in the hall. This feels like a moment, a pivotal, important turning point and he's abandoning it. He doesn't like the attention. What I don't understand is why he's even getting it. Everyone ignores Liam, unless he's too close or accidentally touches a person.

He doesn't answer me or stop walking.

"I don't get it." I move my feet faster down the hall, trying to catch up to Liam. "That didn't happen when I sat with you the first time or any time. That didn't happen last week when we approached them. What—"

"I'm seventeen, Thankful. Eighteen next month, and no one since middle school has purposely come near me. I'm like the plague."

"I did." Didn't I just say that? Am I no one? Geez, he's fast.

"Yes, but you…"

"What?" My breathing heavy, I reach out and yank his hand, bringing him to a stop down a deserted dead-end near the gym.

"You were already—"

"An outcast, right. My own plague. I get it." I let go of his hand and look at the ground. I know this isn't about me, but I can't help the punch I feel at the implication, even if he didn't say it, even if he doesn't believe it. And maybe the stress of the nurse and Mom and

Phoebe has me all wound up because I so easily find offense at the idea he's thought of me this way, that he's inferring that our classmates have thought of me this way. I know it's unfair of me, I know it, but that knowledge doesn't make it go away. Is it the law that to some extent every high school student has to care what their peers think of them? I don't want to and yet on some stupid level, I do. And apparently so does Liam.

"I didn't say that," he says, and I can feel his eyes staring at me.

"You didn't need to." I heard the whispers before I ever met Liam.

"I was going to say *new*. You were already someone everyone was curious about, sure, but everyone knew you didn't know me. Sonia, who they've all known for years, Sonia who believes in my curse, she knows the magnitude of her actions, you couldn't have."

It doesn't matter… it doesn't change his point, being that the school thought I didn't know better. But I did. Chelsea had made certain I did. Errica had warned me. And that matters to me. I want him to know that. I did know and I still came. I still wanted to know him. I didn't judge him because of them. And I realize I'm not upset because of what the school may or may not have thought of me. I want Liam to know that despite what everyone said, I wanted to know him.

27

YOU SKIP, I SKIP

"I know this is hard to understand, but I am not being selfish here." Phoebe's voice sounds strained and unsure over the phone. "I don't have a choice."

"Or you'll lose your job." I know that's a big deal, but it feels like a miniature, tiny gnat that just needs to be swatted away, while the enormous, deadly spider waits in the corner to pounce on us here at home.

Her long pause reveals that she *won't* lose her job. She isn't here when she said she would be, and what is at stake?

"Phoebe?" Her name comes out louder than I intended. But I'm not eleven anymore. When *he* left I was a child, innocent and naïve and, I'm not anymore. I deserve to know why Mom is sitting home with a stranger every day.

"Thankful, sweetie, don't read too much into this. Believe me. Have faith in me. I wouldn't be here if it weren't important. We'll do Thanksgiving two days late. I promise." There's a noise in the background like a car door slamming shut. "Gotta go. Love you."

"B—" The click of the phone hanging up doesn't give me a lot of hope. Whether I deserve to know or not—it doesn't matter. I'm not finding out, not today anyway.

Maybe I'm being the selfish one. Phoebe left her life for us. She'd been here almost four months before she went home. She has a life, a life she left. A life she misses, a life that's been put on hold, friends she hasn't seen in months, men she's yet to woo—a life. I know that. She has a right to visit her own life. I tell myself that story again and again without success at convincing myself that she's where she needs to be.

She should be here.

I stare at the phone in my hand, at the top corner, the time. It's early, but I'll still be late for school at this rate. Opening my phone, I text Chelsea. I'm glad her cell is fixed. I don't want her to hear the tremor in my voice.

ME: RUNNING BEHIND. I'LL DRIVE MYSELF TODAY.

The stress in my head makes it ache. Getting up from the kitchen table, I walk into the living room where Mom sleeps. Her even breaths make her chest rise and fall in steady movements. And then I pick my phone back up.

"Hi, Neeta?" I lick my lips. "Yes, it's Thankful. I won't need you to come take care of Mom today." I listen to her question and the lie leaves my lips so much easier than it should. "No, Phoebe isn't home. She should be soon, in the next day or two. She said I could take off for Thanksgiving break early to be with Mom."

"See you," the older nurse says and though I like Neeta, I hope I never see her again, ever.

THE DISHES ARE DONE, THE BILLS ARE PAID, MOM'S FED AND NOW taking a nap, and it's only nine in the morning. I sigh and sit on the floor in front of her, laying my head back against the couch. Switching on the TV, my brain zoning out, I flip through the channels.

A rap on the front room window jolts me upright. Spinning to face the glass behind us, I see Liam peeking in. My chest falls with relief. Jogging to the front entrance, I huff out a breath. I open the door and glance out into the cold.

"What are you doing?" I watch him trudge through the newly fallen snow, from the window to the front door. November had flipped a switch in our little town. The bitter cold seemed to come out of nowhere. But then it did every year.

"You weren't at school."

"Yeah." I shake my head. It was stupid of me to think he wouldn't worry. "I'm sorry. I would have called, if I could." Liam never took Troy's phone to school and since he didn't have his own... I felt awful for making him worry and even worse, he walked to my house in this cold.

Standing in the entryway, Liam shakes the snow from his hair and rubs his hands together.

"Liam, what are you thinking? It's ten degrees out there."

He looks at me, his face scrutinizing. "You aren't sick."

Pressing my lips together, I shake my head.

He nods and his brows lose their furrow. Shrugging he says, "You skip, I skip," and walks into my front room.

"Wait!" I grab his hand. It's like ice and causes a chill to run down my body. His eyes go black and I wait for the irises to return before continuing. "Liam, you can't miss school because of me. I can't let you do that. This is my—"

"Ah..." He cuts me off and stares past me like he sees something there and nods. "Yep, pretty sure you can. And," his voice hushes to a whisper, "it'll probably be the best part of your day."

I fold my lips in, one on top of the other, trying to keep my laugh inside.

"Is your mom okay?" His voice hushes when he sees her on the couch.

Tugging his hand, I pull him into the kitchen. "She's fine. I just couldn't have Neeta taking care of her one more day. Phoebe won't be back until next week. So, I'm doing it. Even if that means I had to tell the nurse Phoebe would be home tomorrow and the school that I'm sick."

He raises his eyebrows, his tongue making tsking noises. "So dishonest, Thankful Tenys."

"I think you're rubbing off on me."

He sits on a kitchen chair, smiling his Liam smile that makes my insides go all mushy. If only he knew what I'd agree to just to see that smile... Dipping his hand into Mom's decorative Mexican bowl atop the table, he pulls a grape from its vine and pops it into his mouth. I sit across from him and watch him down the entire bunch, and for once Liam Gregor reminds me of an average teenage boy.

"So, Thanksgiving." Liam clears his throat. He sounds uncomfortable even saying the word.

"You don't like it?" Three whole extra days away from Glenrock High, it should be one of his favorite days of the year. Getting up from the table, I grab another bunch of grapes from the refrigerator. I wash them and fill up the bowl with hot peppers painted on the front. Setting it in front of Liam, I take my seat again.

"I like it." He sets his hands on the table, ignoring the bowl I've slid in front of him. "I want you to come over."

"Oh." Now I feel uncomfortable. Thanksgiving with Troy and Pops, sure it might not be traditional for me, but it's not even that. Mom *couldn't* come. I'd have to hire the nurse. And I sort of just swore to never see her again...

"We could do it at night, so she's asleep," Liam says and if I didn't know better, I'd think he were a Reader. "I know you don't want to leave her, but at night—"

"It doesn't matter what time of day it is. She can't be left alone."

I bite the inside of my cheek. And the guilt of leaving her with a stranger about consumes me. "I can't leave her. I'm done with the nurse. I just—"

"Okay, I just thought—wait, what if I come to you?" He plucks a grape from the bowl and rolls it between his thumb and finger. "My Aunt Nora's coming. She bakes like twenty pies, I could steal one away. You could—"

"You have an aunt?" It's a stupid question. I have an aunt, most people have at least one aunt, but still I'm surprised. I've only ever thought of Liam's family as Troy, Pops, and Liam. And his mom of course, but the only thing I know about her is that she's passed away.

He smirks. "I do. And two cousins. I have an uncle somewhere too, but he took off when he found out what Nora was."

My unasked question *what is she* must show on my face.

"The curse, Thankful. He took off toward Canada after Nora told him. Idiot, does he think the Knowing are banned from crossing the border or something?" Liam pops a grape into his mouth.

"So you have family coming?" Somehow that surprises me more than a man being awful enough to leave his wife over something she has no control of. That, well, that doesn't surprise me at all. "You can't come to me. You need to be with your family, Liam."

"They'll be here all week." He takes my hand, lacing our fingers together. His eyes go black and my stomach flips all at the same time. "I'm not letting you spend Thanksgiving alone."

"I won't be—"

"Not alone, but not together either." He's blunt. And he's right. Most likely Mom won't care or even realize it's a holiday. But I'll know.

I wish Phoebe would come back. I've never attempted a big meal on my own. I'd be the only one to eat it, anyway. Mom's limited diet makes it difficult to feed her anything Thanksgiving-ish. If Phoebe would just come home, we could have a semi-normal holiday. *Phoebe. Please. Come back.*

A groan from the living room bolts me upright. "I'll be back." Patting my hand on his shoulder, it's my way of saying, *stay in the kitchen.*

Her eyes are open and her elbow bent, her body lying on it like she's tried to reposition. "Help. Thankful."

"You want to sit up, Mom?"

She nods, the movement one quick motion. Sliding my hand and arm between her and the couch, I hold her open side with my other hand, and prop her up. Taking the extra pillows from the floor, I squish them between her and the end of the couch. Adjusting her blanket, I kneel in front of her. "Better?"

She nods again.

I rub her hand with my fingers. "Do you need some water?"

"You g-go. You go."

I blink back the oncoming tears. "Momma, Phoebe isn't here. It's just me."

How can she not want me? My head asks the unfair question before I can stop it. She doesn't have a choice how she feels right now. She isn't rational. Her kind heart is more often suppressed than not.

"You g-g-g—"

"Neeta isn't here, either. It's just me. But I can help you. What do you need?" I speak easy, happy, trying to hide my suffocating heart.

She shakes her head, two shakes, it's all she can muster, but it's enough to tell me I've gotten the message wrong, again. "You... go..." She lifts her hand just off the couch, her finger pointing out.

I turn around, still crouched on the floor in front of her. Liam stands in the doorway, watching us. "You want *Liam* to go?"

She shakes her head again, her breathing uneven. She's getting irritated with me.

"Do you want Thankful to come to my house for Thanksgiving?" Liam stands behind me, his hands shoved into his pockets. He was supposed to stay in the kitchen.

Mom's body relaxes. Her head lies back against the couch and her breaths are heavy, like she's just done a ruthless workout. Her long skinny fingers find mine and she covers my hand with hers, a physical love she can't always show these days.

Liam understood her.

I look up at him, a thank you in my expression, but he's watching her. He doesn't see me. "You got it," I say. "She must have been listening to us."

His neck cranes down to see me. His hand reaches for my face. Caressing my cheek with the tips of his fingers is enough to make his eyes go dark. "So, you'll come?"

Darting my eyes from Liam to Mom, I shrug. Does she want me to go to get rid of me? Or is she trying to show me love, a kindness that's so difficult for her to muster nowadays? I don't know. I bite my lip, staring up at Liam, unsure how I could refuse such a gift. "Maybe."

28

MORTIFICATO

How can I do this? How can I go have *Thanksgiving* without her? It's five o'clock, Mom's already down for the night. She had a good day. I tried to make our traditional *what are you thankful for* list. She only listened, but she never broke down today. She never yelled at me. That's something to be thankful for.

I stand in front of the bathroom mirror, combing through my highlights. I stole a black pencil skirt and deep orange blouse from Phoebe's pile of clothes in Mom's room. I use Phoebe's margarita lip gloss and rub my lips together more times than necessary. Liam will be here any minute and I'm more anxious than ever. I'm leaving Mom again. I swallowed my pride and called *that* nurse. *And* I'm meeting his family, a family I didn't even know existed. What will they think of me? I shouldn't care by now, with everyone in town having an opinion on me, but I do. I can't help it. It's Liam, it's his family.

The doorbell rings and Neeta calls my name. "Thankful." The older woman has the door open before I step out of the bathroom.

Her short, white hair stands to spikes with the cold breeze gusting inside. "Get in here," she says to Liam, waving her hands like crazy. "If I catch my death—" She trails off glaring at him.

"Hi." I ignore Neeta's unfriendliness. I'm not the only one who's cleaned up for the holiday. Liam's trimmed his hair, though it's still falling into his eyes, probably from the wind. He's in jeans I've never seen before, no grease stains and no holes. His white button-up shirt wrinkles under his jacket, but I can see the top button undone, and a skinny black tie falling loosely around his neck.

"Ready?" he asks and I can see that Neeta's staring makes him uncomfortable.

I nod, not feeling ready at all, but I've done my hair and applied my lip gloss, and that's what he means. "I'll be home in two hours," I tell Neeta.

"Take your time, dearie." Neeta's tone does a complete one-eighty when she addresses me. "My kids were here all week. They left an hour ago." She turns to Mom, not bothering to lower her voice. "And Sally won't make a peep. Don't worry about us." Leaning in, she doesn't hide the peeking glare she gives to Liam. "But come back as *soon* as you need."

"Thanks, Neeta." I don't know that Neeta would have been my first choice, but Phoebe brought her in special, said she's worked with a dozen Huntington's patients. She's frank and loud and seemingly judgmental, but I suppose if she's the best nurse for Mom I can put up with her.

I slide into my coat and slip my arm through Liam's. He doesn't even have to hide his eyes from Neeta with no skin contact. Walking out to Pop's little yellow car, the wind takes my breath away. Liam opens the passenger door for me and I hurry inside.

He slides into the driver's seat and looks over at me before starting the car. "I don't think she likes me." His mouth breaks into a grin and I laugh. He doesn't care whether Neeta or anyone likes him and I love that about him.

"Well, I do." I force my hands between my legs, squeezing the tremors out of them between my knees. Liam doesn't make me nervous, but everything else about tonight does.

Leaning over the car's console, he cups my cheek. "I'm glad."

I meet him the rest of the way, wondering what he's seen. Closing the inch gap that's left, he kisses me. And with Liam's lips on mine, it's easy to forget my anxiety.

Pulling back, he closes his eyes, like it's painful to stop. He tilts his head against the back of his seat and sighs. "We need to go before Nora gets impatient and makes the gravy without me." Narrowing his eyes, he lowers his voice like it's a family secret. "You don't want to eat Nora's gravy."

The lights in the diner are on and there are more bodies inside than I've ever seen at one time.

We get out of the car and I shake out my hands, trying to get rid of the jumpiness. Liam laces his fingers with mine and gives them an encouraging squeeze. We walk in and the chatter quiets down. Six people, four strangers, turn and stare at me.

Liam's eyes widen towards Troy.

"Ah, hello, welcome!" Troy shouts, winking at me.

Liam clears his throat. "Everyone," he says and his hand tightens around mine, "this is Thankful."

The woman with auburn hair to her shoulders looks me over. Her lips turn upward, the men next to her just stare.

"Thankful, these are my cousins." Liam points toward the two boys. "Franko." He motions to the tall guy with curly black hair. He must be just older than us. He reminds me of a younger Pops. "And Anthony." Anthony's curls are less pronounced than his brother's and the color shades somewhere between his mother's auburn and his brother's black. It's almost iridescent. I bet in the sun it's a different color than under the diner's lights. Anthony's younger than Liam and I. I'd guess he's around twelve or thirteen.

Both of them mutter a hello, Anthony looking at me as if I were an alien.

A man stands next to the boys. He's older than Troy, I would guess. His brown hair and long nose look nothing like the boys next to him—and Liam had said his uncle ran off. "This is Jackson, ah, a friend. And my aunt, Nora."

Nora's friendlier than the men. She steps forward, her auburn bob bouncing with her steps. "Hello, Thankful." She smiles and the mole next to her lip moves with the gesture. "It's lovely to meet you." She holds out her hand and I give her my empty palm.

Nora's eyes blacken and she gasps, her grip on my hand tightening. Pulling my hand from her clasp, I fold it into my stomach. I hadn't even thought of what it would mean to touch her. The curse. I hadn't thought of what she'd see or the private things she'd know once our hands met.

Pops doesn't like me enough to touch me and Troy always does his best to keep his hands to himself. He says me knowing about the curse makes it feel like an invasion of my privacy. Only Liam has ever seen my future, what would undoubtedly happen to me, the best of my day.

The blue in Nora's eyes return and widen with shock. She looks from Liam to me. "You weren't kidding," she says, looking behind her to Troy. "You've *never* touched her?"

Troy shakes his head, though he looks at me as if he's proud of me. As if I've accomplished the impossible, though I've done nothing.

Liam's nostrils flair and he blows a puff air from his mouth. "Nora." He growls her name.

She moves her stare to Liam, like a dagger. "You don't even know what you have here. I've never in my life touched a *Mortificato*." With the strange word on her lips she studies me.

"Mortif—um, what? What is that?" I say, feeling goosebumps all over my body under Nora's scrutiny. Nora doesn't answer, she just moves to the left to see another side of me. I turn around and face Liam, so that I can't see her eyes watching me like a scientist, ready to dissect.

"Nora," Troy says, and I've never heard his tone so unforgiving. "Thankful is Liam's guest. Behave or remove yourself."

"Nora. *Figlia* come." Pop's gruff voice overrides anything Troy might be saying, even if they have the same meaning. "Come here."

"Yes, Papa."

I don't see Nora walk away, but I hear her steps on the diner's linoleum, along with Troy and the others. They busy themselves with chatter and work.

Liam holds my hands and looks at me as if he thinks I will break with Nora's words. "I'm sorry, Thankful. She isn't usually—"

"What did she mean? That word…"

"*Mortificato.*" He holds my hands together at his chest and leans his head close enough to peck my lips. "It means *crestfallen.* It means your life is mortifying. It means life is so bad that the Knowing see the good that will come instead of the bad."

He's honest and he's right. My life can feel devastating. My life *is* devastating, I suppose, which explains my mutation to the Knowing. Still, it's strange hearing an actual explanation of why I am so different to them. But it's the name Nora's given me, *Mortificato,* that makes my blood run cold.

29

THE L WORD

Franko and I push together tables until there's enough room for the eight of us to sit together. Liam cooks in the back.

"So, where do you live?" I ask him, trying to make conversation. Maybe it will help him to stop staring. Even among Knowing I am an anomaly.

Franko's eyes crease with happiness and he looks not only like Pops, but like Liam, too. "I'm going to school in Boston."

"Really? The big city, huh?" I push chairs under the tables until there are eight of them.

"Yep, Mom hates that. The Readers will get me, she's sure of it." He grins again and I'm surprised at how lighthearted he speaks of Readers. I've only ever heard Liam and Troy talk about them and it gave me chills. He stands next to a pushed in seat, looking at our small accomplishment.

Behind him, Nora smacks the back of his head. "They *will* and you will break your momma's heart for not listening and getting yourself killed."

"Momma—" he starts, but Nora cuts him off with a glare.

Rounding the tables, she stands next to me. She lifts her hand, flat and hovering, a tremor making it unsteady. She sets it on my bare arm. She sucks in a breath with her vision and then lets it out shaky and slow. "Thankful, dear, put this tablecloth on?"

Watching her black eyes, I nod, rather than rip my arm away from her. Clearing my throat, I find my voice. "Sure."

Her hand pats my skin and she walks away, her long, green skirt swaying side to side like a bell. She could have handed the cloth to Franko, but she walked around the tables to touch me. Our contact wasn't an accidental brush. She set her hand on my bare skin deliberately. My skin pricks with goose bumps at the invasion. Just like the Reader talk.

Walking around to my side, Franko takes the white, lace cloth from my hand and unfolds it. "Don't mind her. She's just never met someone like you."

Right, Mortificato. Biting my lip, I take one end of the tablecloth, shaking out the wrinkles with Franko. We lay it on top of the three pushed-together tables. "And what about him?" I nod toward his brother Anthony, who hasn't stopped staring at me.

"Don't mind him, either. He's never met anyone who knew our secret and didn't go running."

My heart softens at the thought. "Your dad," I say, though I meant it to just be a thought.

Franko's brows raise high on his head. "Yep."

"I'm sorry." I shake my head and stare at the table. "I shouldn't have said that, I mean— "

Shrugging, he pats my shoulder, careful to stay on the fabric of my short-sleeved shirt. "It's the truth. I keep telling Anthony there are people out there like you. He hasn't believed me yet. Maybe now he will."

Crossing my arms, I risk another peek towards Anthony. "My dad ran off too."

"See," he says, pointing at me. "Some people are just like that.

They run. You don't have to be cursed to turn someone into a coward. You could be—"

"Dying," I finish for him.

Franko's eyes narrow. I don't know how much he knows about me, but his mouth forms a flat, sad line and he doesn't ask any questions. I can't look at the pity right now.

"I'm going to see if I can help Liam." I can see Nora and Anthony watching me still or maybe it's all in my conceited head. Either way, I bolt for the kitchen that will hide me behind closed doors.

"Whoa!" Troy shouts when we almost collide. "Thankful, you're in a hurry?"

"Oh, yeah. Well, no. Just coming back to see Liam."

Leaning in, his hand cups his mouth and nose sideways as if to tell me a secret. "And to escape the family, I think."

Forcing a laugh, I nibble at the loose skin on my bottom lip. "Maybe just a little."

"Nora is intense and melodramatic. Well, she is *my* sister. But she'll get better, I promise. Mostly she's jealous."

"Jealous?" Would she like to trade lives with me? She can become the *Mortificato*.

"Sure. He points towards the open kitchen window where Liam's working, a beat in his movements with his earbuds in and his music loud enough that even Troy and I can hear the hum of it. "You *know* that Liam is cursed. You *know* the big bad secret and you're still here. You still love him."

I hiccup at the word *love* and cover my mouth. My eyes dart back to Liam. Did he hear that? I didn't say that. But Liam moves to the music, his head still down with his work.

Troy doesn't notice my anxiety attack happening. He laces his own fingers together, as if one hand is Liam and the other is me. "You're together, open and honest. Nora's never had that. Sure, Jackson is here and he knows, but he knows because he too is a Knowing. He isn't someone she would have chosen otherwise."

"Jackson and Nora..." Right, let's shift the subject a bit. "I didn't know—"

"Oh sure, they share the same bed. Love, that they don't share." His hands fall to his sides. "She'll get over you. She did with Elsa and she will with you."

"Elsa," I say, my interest peaked. "Liam's mom. She wasn't a Knowing like you?"

"No! Oh, heavens no." He laughs like I've made a joke, but I don't see what's funny. "She didn't know about the curse until we'd been married two years."

"Two years!"

His eyes widen, but he's still smiling. "I know! Boy was I in trouble that weekend."

A weekend. Elsa Gregor forgave her husband and accepted the truth in a *weekend*, while Nora's husband ran away from his children, away from his wife. Still, I grin at his laughter, he's so light-hearted about it all. "Liam doesn't talk about her." I dare another peek at him. I don't want to get into trouble.

"It's very hard. Lots of good memories, and yet, lots of bad ones too. It's harder for him than for me. And if I were him, well, let's say his feelings, his muteness, it's understandable." His hand moves to the swinging door. He's ready to leave, but I can't let him. Until this minute I've heard almost nothing about Elsa Gregor.

Grabbing his arm, I stop him from pushing the door open. Troy's brown eyes smother in blackness, but he keeps them open, taking in a deep breath through his nose. "Wait. Please," I say and I hate how I sound like I'm begging. "Why? What happened?"

Covering my hand that still sits on his arm, Troy cocks his head to the side. He stares at me, his expression soft and pleasant at whatever he's just seen. "You'll have to ask him that." Troy squeezes my hand, removing my fingers with care. As long as we don't break contact, he'll only have the one vision. He looks at my hand in his. "You are a good girl, Thankful."

I'm ready to cry and I don't know why. Is it because Liam's father has shown me more fatherly love in one night than I've had in six years? Is it because I feel so desperate to know more about Elsa? It feels important to me, to understand her and her relationship with Liam. Is it because Nora has given me a nickname, one worse than *untouched*?

Dropping my fingers, Troy pinches his hand into a fist at his side. "Dinner will be soon."

I nod and a tear falls from my right eye. I swat it away like an uninvited guest and turn for the cook's station. I walk up the one step and enter the doorless entry.

Looking up from the salad he's tossing, Liam sees me and pulls the earbuds from his ears. "Hey."

"Can I help?" I look at his face, his thick hair, his dark eyes, the stubble from where he shaved a week ago. He has a small scar on the side of his jaw I've never asked about. And I can't help but think of what Troy said. *Love.* Can you love someone at seventeen? I mean be *in love* when you're so young and so inexperienced? My heart races with the thought and I feel the urge to kiss the mark on Liam's jaw. It's long since healed, but I don't care.

"It's ready. Can you help me carry it all out?" He wipes his hands on the white apron about his waist and his expert fingers untie the laces from behind his back. Tossing it to an empty spot on the counter, he picks up a bowl of stuffing and sets it in my hands. He's different than I've ever seen him. He loves to cook, but I already knew that. Before, I thought he loathed Thanksgiving and I didn't understand why. Now I realize that I couldn't have been more wrong. He *loves* Thanksgiving. He loves the break and the food and his family. This is a Liam that no one at Glenrock High has ever seen.

Smiling, I set the bowl of stuffing back in its spot on the

counter. He's holding the salad he just finished tossing and questioning me with his stare. My steady hand cups his cheek and my thumb runs over the soft skin of the scar. Standing taller on my toes, I kiss the mark. The bowl in Liam's hands falls onto the cook's floor, green leafs spilling everywhere. I look down at the mess that's my fault, ready to apologize and clean. His hand on the back of my neck stops me, pulling me close to him, so that my stomach touches his. His lips engross mine, but it isn't soft and gentle like the peck I gave to his healed wound. It's urgent. It's needful. It speaks. His lips are moist, moving with mine and they tell me he needs me. Not because I'm the first person at school to talk to him, not because I'm a *Mortificato*, but because I'm Thankful and he's Liam.

Our movements slow until we stand there, holding each other. *Seventeen*. How can you put an age stipulation on love? How can you put any limitations on love? How can someone be too old or too young or too inexperienced?—At least when it's right. If this isn't love, I don't think I'll ever know what is.

I lick my lips, my face burning where his sharp whiskers rubbed against me. "Oh! Your salad." I bend down, picking up lettuce leafs and tomato slices. "I'm sorry, Liam."

He's on his knees too. He rights the bowl and fills it with the now dirty salad remains. "No one will miss a green salad." Leaning toward me, he pecks my lips once more. "At least it wasn't the stuffing."

I laugh and toss the greens inside my fists into his bowl.

"So," he says, his brow in its usual furrow. "How's it going out there?"

"Umm... Franko's nice." I sit up, straightening my back and sigh. "It's strange, Liam. All of those people could see my future. With a simple touch, they could know things about me that have yet to happen. Your aunt probably witnessed this very moment an hour before it occurred. It's—"

"A little unsettling."

"Yeah." I bite my lip. Liam loves these people. I hope I haven't offended him, but then I can't imagine ever offending him.

Liam and I finish bringing out the food, placing it around the pretty white china and matching silverware. I've never seen either at the diner before. Troy stands at the head of the table, the big golden turkey in front of him, ready to carve.

Taking my hand, Liam seats me between him and Franko, and all the way across the table from Nora. The family has turned their attention to Troy who smiles around the table at each of us, winking when he gets to me. My face flushes pink, remembering how I grabbed his arm and begged him to talk to me and how he saw some small piece of my near future.

"Family," Troy says, "friends," he looks at me and then Jackson. "Today we are thankful. Thankful to be together. Thankful for the food on our plates. Thankful for those new to our table."

Pops nods, his full, gray hair flopping with the motion. He sits between Nora and Troy. The collar of his green plaid shirt opens at the top and curly, white chest hairs peek out, trying to escape the confines of his shirt. "Let's eat!"

Anthony sits across from me. He stares at his plate, then me, then back again. Looking down at my plate, my blonde tips, curled for this evening, touch the tabletop. The highlights Phoebe added are still a vibrant gold.

There's chatter around the table as the food passes from right to left. Jackson's telling Pops and Troy a story that Nora's clearly already heard, but her face lights up with each peak moment. I shovel a bite of mashed potatoes into my mouth, plain, no gravy, sighing inside at how good they are. I have underestimated Liam's skills.

"Anthony," Liam says, his fork hovering. Starting a conversation isn't his forte, but then he's surrounded by family not Glenrock High students. "Thankful's best subject is science."

My cheeks warm up until I'm certain they must be a rosy red.

"What class are you in?" Anthony asks, speaking to me for the first time.

"This year," I say, looking across at him. "Physics."

"She's brilliant." Liam says, and it sounds strange in his voice. He's trying to get Anthony and me to talk. I can see that, but I've never heard him brag about my schooling before. Still, the words are sincere.

I can't help the laugh that bubbles from my lips. "I'm not *brilliant*." I smirk at him, shoving his shoulder with mine.

"You are." His brows furrow, not in aggravation, but humor. "She is," he says, turning back to Anthony. "Her favorite is biology."

Sitting straighter, Anthony looks at me with new life in his eyes. "Biology!"

I bite the inside of my cheek and nod.

"I'm trying to prove that Knowing isn't supernatural. I think there's something in our genetic code that makes us different, a dominant gene that we pass on to our children. I think if we could study the genetics of it, our DNA, compare and test, I think we could mutate the code before conception and cure the curse."

"Really?" I'm no longer playing Liam's get-to-know-you game. This kid is interesting. He's smart. "How old are you, Anthony?"

"Thirteen." He smiles, the Gregor cousins have more in common than Knowing. Did they get those grins from Pops? "I really think there's a cure though, but I don't have any test subjects... or equipment... it's not as if I can use it for my science fair project and ask my teachers to use their inadequate tools."

Franko, Liam, and I laugh, and Anthony breaks into a grin as if he meant to be funny.

"Ain't that the truth," Franko says, his hand raises to high-five his little brother's comedic moment. Their hands smack together before they turn back to their full plates.

I giggle, relaxed and enjoying myself more than I should. But then—"Your eyes," I say, pointing from Franko to Anthony, "your eyes didn't go black, you didn't—" I turn to Liam. "They didn't *see* anything."

His eyes are tender when he looks at me, whenever he looks at me. "Knowing don't see other Knowing."

"Thank goodness." Franko chuckles again.

"So," peering at me, Anthony's forehead wrinkles. He lays his arms across one another on the tabletop, his dress shirt sleeves folded up to his elbows. "You *really* know."

I gaze around at my seven Knowing dinner companions. "I really do."

30

FOR THE LOVE OF PIE

The sink turns into a mountain of dishes, due to Phoebe's Thanksgiving spectacle she's calling dinner. Her things are strewn all over the house after being back less than twenty-four hours. She's dramatic and crazy and unpredictable. And back.

She's back. I'm so grateful she's home.

She lays on the floor, her flat stomach pooching out just over the elastic of her leggings. "Ohhh." She moans, closing her eyes and holding her head in her hands. "I'm going to burst. My insides will soon be my outsides."

"I told you to stop eating after your second plate." I sit in front of the couch, next to a sleeping Mom, and watch the Phoebe drama in front of me. "Why did you buy an eighteen pounder anyway? They sell turkey breasts that would have fed the two of us for a couple days."

Her groaning stops and she sits up, her long legs still stretched out. Her red hair falls down her back in a cascade of curls. "A turkey breast? Thankful, this is Thanksgiving, we don't insult it with a turkey *breast*!"

But it isn't Thanksgiving, it's two days after Thanksgiving and Phoebe made a feast that could have fed a dozen people. We will be eating turkey for a month.

She rolls her eyes at me, still annoyed that I'd even suggest a turkey breast. "Besides, the guy at the market gave it to me." She bounces her eyebrows and flashes her teeth in a fabulous Phoebe grin. "Are you sure Liam's bringing the pie?"

"Yes!" I throw my head back and laugh. "I thought you were about to burst."

"I might," she says, holding onto her gut. "But it's *pie*, there's always room for pie."

I laugh. My heart swells with the thought once more, *she's back*. I blow out a small breath I didn't even know I'd been holding. Leaping from my spot on the floor, I tackle her in a hug.

"Omph!" She falls back to the ground and I fall with her, my arms around her neck. "I missed you too." She squeaks the words through my strangulation.

I let go of her and we lay on our backs staring up at the popcorn ceiling in my living room. I don't want her to leave again. I don't want her to feel like there's another life waiting for her. *This* is her life. We are her life. "I moved Mom's things from her closet into the storage shed. Just the things she isn't using."

"Yeah?" she says, twisting her head around to look at me. Her hair fans over the tan carpet, her legs bent, her green leggings stretching thin. "How come?"

"You've been here for months and your things are in the living room or the bathroom or still in a suitcase, that's silly. You sleep in there, use the closet." *Stay.*

"Sure, okay. Thanks." She looks back up to the ceiling and takes my hand, giving it a squeeze. "So, Thanksgiving with The Face, huh? That sounds *serious*."

Laughing, I don't look at her, afraid my face will give something away. Troy said with nonchalance that I loved his son and I didn't dispute it. I couldn't. But I was still in shock over something I had yet to declare. "It was pretty laid back."

Phoebe flips to her side, resting her head in her hand propped up by her elbow. "I doubt that. You're holding out on me." She purses her lips, waiting.

"*Really*, it was." I ignore her stares, finding dot-to-dot pictures in the specks on the ceiling.

"Then why is your face a lovely shade of raspberry?"

Both my hands jerk to my face, my palms flat on my cheeks. I didn't feel the blush coming on, but she sees it. "It was nice, okay. That's it."

Reaching for the throw pillow sitting in Grandpa's old recliner, she swings her arm around and hits me with it. "Was there more smooching? Goll, for not being oh-so-touchy, this guy is a kissy face."

This time I feel the heat in my cheeks.

She hits me again with the throw pillow. "What have I told you? I have to live through you right now, so you have to give up the goods!" Her gold-brown eyes widen. "Always, *always* kiss and tell!"

Snatching the pillow from her hands, I hold it to my chest. I bite my lip. This isn't something I talk about with my girlfriends. And it might be nice. "Yes, okay, there was more kissing. And it was… kind of… amazing." I say each word slow, still deciding if I'm ready to divulge.

"Yeah? Yeah?" She shakes my shoulder. "And?"

"We were back in the kitchen." I roll to my side, facing her. Holding my bottom lip between my teeth, I stare at her, waiting for her to tell me I'm a silly, little, innocent girl.

"And?" She shakes me again.

"It was kind of *passionate*—" I wait again for my more experi-

enced, sophisticated aunt to laugh at my seventeen year-old version
of passion. But she looks as exhilarated as I feel. "He dropped this
bowl with lettuce and tomatoes to hold me and—" I stop and roll to
my back. This feels too private, but I see the scene in my head and
it makes me almost lightheaded.

"Ooo, ooo!" Phoebe sings. "Rolling around in the hay or in this
case the lettuce leaves."

"We were not rolling around," I say, my insides stretching like a
rubber band ready to snap in two.

But Phoebe doesn't hear a word I've said. "I made out once in a
pile of spaghetti noodles. He thrust me up right on the stove top."
Her hands mime out the motion. "Pots and noodles and marinara
everywhere, it got a little messy." She closes her eyes and swoons at
the memory. "And once in a fridge, you know just the fridge door,
but still." She shivers, staring up again, trying to visualize her past.
"But never a bed of lettuce…" She cocks her head, staring at the
white ceiling and I cringe, knowing she's trying to visualize me and
Liam now. "Lettuce… not so cold at least, and less messy. No marinara to wash off, that's a plus."

I cover my face. This is horrifying.

Sitting up, she pulls at my hands glued to my front. "Come on!
It's a good story. It's a *sexy* story. You just need to—" She stops
talking with the ring of the doorbell.

No! "Phoebe! Be good. Please be good. Don't you dare mention
kissing or marinara or—"

Using me as leverage, she pushes herself up. "Chill out." She
kisses the top of my head. "Hmm…" She smacks her mouth, licking
her lips. "You taste like that purple cabbage they put in those store
bought—"

"Phoebe!"

"Salads!" She laughs, ruffling my hair and hurrying to the door.

"Phoebe!" I yell her name again, running after her. Leaping, I
jump onto her back, my hair a scrambled nest in front of my face.

She opens the door and I slide down her back, just in time for Liam and Franko to witness my little spectacle. I brush my hair back and comb through it a couple times between my fingers. "Liam!" I say, trying to stand somewhat in front of Phoebe, but she's draped an arm around my waist, keeping me level with her.

Liam's mouth twists into a crooked smile. "Hi," he says, a pie in his hands.

Franko holds the other one.

"Oooh!" Phoebe points to Liam. "One for Thankful." And then to Franko. "And one for me."

I elbow her side, but she just ignores me.

A moan from the living room has my senses heightened and my worries over Phoebe gone. *Mom.*

"Hello, there," Phoebe says, staring at Franko.

I bite the inside of my cheek and look at Liam. "I need to—"

"Yeah," he says, nodding. "Go."

I hurry into the living room, the entryway and the people in it removed, but only a few feet away from us. "Mom," I say, but her blank glare stares ahead at the black television. Her right arm twitches over and over, but her eyes don't move from the TV.

"Thankful?" Phoebe yells, checking in with me, before she asks Liam and his cousin into the room.

I don't answer her, not just yet. "Mom." I crouch next to Mom's side and whisper the words. "Do you need something? Water?" She doesn't answer me, she twitches and stares. I turn the TV on. She might as well have something to see.

Peeking her head through the doorway, Phoebe gives me a questioning thumbs up. I nod, out of breath from my short jog into the living room, or maybe just the thought of Mom losing it with Liam and Franko here has worn me out. Still holding their pies, but coatless now, they follow Phoebe into the living room. My arms prick with nerves at Franko meeting my mother. I don't like people meeting her, judging her, staring at her. She's a person with a sickness no different than cancer or Alzheimer's, not a parade float.

But Franko doesn't act surprised at Mom's statue-like form lying on the couch, staring into space. "Mom, this is Liam's cousin, Franko," I say, watching her, knowing she won't react, but going through the motion of it all anyway.

Franko doesn't say anything, but he looks pleasantly at Mom and then me.

"*Franko*," Phoebe says rolling the *r* in some fake accent I can't identify. She looks at Liam's cousin, who is an inch taller than Liam, with the same dark eyes and full lips, his hair just a shade darker with short curls, like he's her dessert. She's so tired of living vicariously through her boring niece, and Franko might as well be a tasty treat delivered to her door.

I want to smack her. She still has making out in marinara on the brain, and I need to smack it out of her thirty-four-year-old head. I clear my throat, trying to get her to stop staring, but Franko has started staring back. His expression smolders, like she's on the menu as well. My eyes wide, I look at Liam. Is he seeing this? There's no way he's okay with this. I *hate* this. But he's staring at Mom, his glare soft, but intense.

Twirling her finger through a red curl, Phoebe peers at Franko. She runs her hand down her neck until her ring finger hooks onto her shirt. "Mmm." She bites her lip. "I would *love* some of that pie."

"Phoebe!" A low hiss escapes my lips, but no one in the rooms seems to notice.

Phoebe hooks her arm through Franko's to lead him into the kitchen. They jolt to a stop and I know that with Phoebe's bare arm on Franko's, he sees the worst moment of her day, which for Phoebe might be a hangnail.

Franko's quick to take the hand of the arm that Phoebe's laced through his. Bending, he kisses her knuckles. "Lovely to meet you," he says, his black eyes hidden from Phoebe's view.

Liam breaks away from Mom, and we both watch Phoebe. Her face contorts with narrowed eyes, a quizzical brow and her mouth in a flat line, though it *cannot* be the first time a man has kissed Phoebe's hand. Franko stands up, his brown eyes back to normal.

Phoebe laughs, but it's fake, and I can't imagine why she isn't swooning over the attention. "Shall we?" Her arm stays linked through Franko's and together they walk into the kitchen.

Crisis averted, I stand alone in the living room with Liam. "I'm sorry. She—"

"Don't worry about it," he says, grinning at me. "It happens. Most of us know how to avoid being caught. I'm the worst at it. Franko's pretty good. He's more social than the rest of us though. He's had more practice."

"No." I shake my head. "I mean, I'm sorry about *Phoebe*. She all but threw herself at your cousin." I bite my lip, embarrassed.

Shrugging, he puts a hand on my cheek, his thumb caressing my cheek bone. "That also happens a lot... to Franko, anyway."

An airy chuckle leaves me and I lean into this hold.

He's balancing the blueberry pie in one hand and stretches it out toward me. I take the pie and he pulls back both of his hands. "I just —I wanted to—" Bending down next to Mom, he takes her hand in his own. "Hello, Sally."

Mom's eyes skirt from the TV to Liam's face. I crouch next to him. His eyes go dark, but he doesn't bother closing them. Mom watches him, her eyes on his, her head tilting to the side in study.

"Momma, you remember Liam?"

She doesn't answer me.

"Are you hungry?"

No answer.

Sighing, I stand. Liam takes another second before he's stands up beside me. "Phoebe's going to burn something. Sally isn't going to like it."

I bite the inside of my cheek and stare at him, remembering my conviction that stipulations couldn't be placed on love. Yes, I may be inexperienced and only seventeen, Liam eighteen tomorrow, but everything I've ever felt or thought I felt... this, well, this is so much more. "Thanks for the heads up."

He laces our fingers and I lead him into the kitchen, too preoccupied with his wonderfulness to remember that Phoebe is there, attempting to seduce his cousin.

31

THE PARTY PLANNING COMMITTEE

P hoebe holds the metal fork in her mouth, Franko attached to the handle. "Mmm." She hums her way off the fork, her eyes closed.

Watching the spectacle from the kitchen door, I grit my teeth, holding in a scream. If Liam could see the worst part of my day, I am certain this would be it.

"Franko," Liam says, his voice like a drill sergeant. His hold on my hand tightens. "Time to go."

Phoebe's eyes pop open and her bottom lip pouts out. "But you just got here."

I grip the blueberry pie tin with both of my hands. Walking over to the table, I drop it between them. Franko's hand skitters out of the way. Phoebe glares at me, but I glare right back. She isn't going to have her *fun* with Liam's cousin. "Nice to see you again, Franko. Have a good trip home."

"Oh." His eyes find mine and they seem to shine. "I think I'm staying another week."

"Another week?" Liam's dark brows knit together. "Your plane leaves tomorrow. You're headed for Casper tonight."

"And miss your birthday party, coz? Nah." Franko's gaze turns to Phoebe and I'm pretty sure it isn't Liam's birthday that's keeping him in Glenrock.

Phoebe's hands are under her chin, her smile angelic. Her long hair falls over her bare shoulders and I can't help but think she looks a decade younger than her thirty-four years.

"Party?" Liam almost growls the word. "Why in the—" He clears his throat. "Why would I have a party? I've never in my life had a party. I'm not starting now."

"Because," Phoebe reaches out and shakes Liam's wrist. He faces me, but habit still shuts his eyes. "Eighteen is a big deal! You have to have a party. Franko and I are planning it."

"Phoebe, he doesn't want one." I don't wait for a response. I pull her up by her arm and drag her behind me. "Can I speak to you, please?"

Mom's still watching TV, oblivious that we've entered the room. "What?" Phoebe shakes herself from my grasp.

"Don't do this."

Leaning back, her hands fly to her hips. "What?"

"Flirt with Franko. Plan a party. Don't. Just stop. This is my life, not yours." My cheeks are red with anger. She opens her mouth to speak, but I'm not done. "You're eleven years older than he is! He's twenty-three! Stop making a fool of yourself!"

Her eyes pinch into slits and her hands squeeze her waist. "I have never in my life made of a fool of myself. The party was Franko's idea and it's a good one. Liam doesn't want it? Well, he never wanted a girlfriend either, but that seems to have worked out pretty well for him. You both need to try new things. You could step outside your comfort zone from time to time." She spins for the door, her hair flaring out. Stopping, she looks over her shoulder at me. "And as for my age, Thankful, you know better than to put *stipulations* on matters of the heart."

I'm out of breath, like I just ran a 5K. She's just so...*Phoebe!*

"I don't understand why you *have* to go. I just got home!" Phoebe lies on my bed in her gray pajama pants, staring at the ceiling fan, still and dusty.

"It's his birthday." I run another layer of mascara over my eyelashes and peer back at my blue eyes blinking in the mirror.

"But we're throwing him a party."

"Right, a party he doesn't want, this *Friday,* that you and Franko decided he needed *yesterday*. We planned to do something tonight, on his actual birthday, more than a week ago." Of all people, shouldn't Phoebe get that? She loves Liam's beautiful face, and she loves that he likes me. She's usually giddy about it all. In fact, I'm surprised she isn't dressing me for this occasion.

"You make me sound like an overbearing mother. I just thought it would be fun."

"You just thought it would be a good excuse to see Franko every day and party with him on Friday."

Phoebe bounces her eyebrows. "Well, yes, that too. Franko is more *pleasing* than Liam, isn't he? I mean his disposition alone—"

"Phoebe, why? Why would you say that? Stop it." I smack her foot.

She sits up on her elbow, propping her head up with her hand, her long hair falling over her arm. "Sorry! It's not my fault Liam is grumpy and rude and his cousin isn't."

"Weren't you the one who referred to him as dark and mysterious?" I attempt Phoebe's raspy voice. I pull Phoebe's sheer black blouse over my head and tank top. And what's with the Liam hate?

Sitting up, she crosses her ankles. "Did I say you could borrow that?"

"I thought 'your closet was my closet', and I should 'learn how to *wear* my clothes to accentuate my body'." I run my fingers through my hair and wonder what happened to Phoebe on her last business trip to make her so ornery. Maybe it isn't Liam hate, it's Phoebe anxiety.

"Right. Right." She shuts her eyes and takes a deep breath. "I'm sorry. Just stressed. I need to de-stress myself. You have fun tonight, sweetie." Standing, she's just a couple inches taller than me. Kissing my forehead, she wraps her arms around me. "I only want for you what you're so deserving of."

I squeeze her back. Liam's more than I deserve. And non-stressed Phoebe would see that. I'm about as plain as it gets and he's anything but. Still, I love that as hopeless as I am, Phoebe never sees it that way. She always makes me out for more than I am. I don't have Chelsea's beauty or Sonia's sweetness. I don't even have Errica's confidence. I'm not gifted like Liam. I'm plain and uncoordinated and—

"Spectacular." Pulling back, she peers at me.

I narrow my eyes in question.

"You look spectacular."

I bite my lip, trying to keep from smiling. I look okay, not terrible. Not how Phoebe would look in the black blouse and gray skinny jeans.

"So, what'd you get him?" Her eyebrows bounce up and down, her sun-kissed, freckled face so beautiful without anything to make it up.

Clearing my throat, I tell a half truth. "An apron."

Phoebe laughs, running her hands down my long sheer sleeves. "You are more amazing than you know."

My eyebrow quirks. An apron? Amazing? Glenrock has lowered Phoebe's standards.

Pulling on my coat, I kiss Mom goodbye. I grab the boat's keys and open the front door. The blue in the sky won't last long. The sun will go down soon and the pretty sapphire will turn to black. Darkness comes so early this time of year. The air stings my face, and I suck in a freezing breath.

Phoebe trots over to the door before I can pull it closed. She wraps her arms around my shoulders and pulls me in for a hug. "Have fun my amazing girl."

32

BETTER THAN NORMAL

The smell of spices fills the air when I enter the diner. I rub my nose, the strong scent making it tickle. Holding to the box with Liam's apron inside, I turn the lock on the diner door, knowing it's only open for me. Pops sits at the counter, but everyone else must be in the back.

He nods at my entrance but doesn't say anything. His button-up flannel shirt as usual opens at the top, his curly chest hairs spilling out. His round belly folds over his khaki pants.

"Hello, Pops." One day I'll get used to the older man disliking me because of my gender. *Women are not to be trusted.* Ignoring his silent greeting, I head to the back.

The fumes are even stronger back by the kitchen. Liam and Troy are in the cooking station together, standing side by side. I've never looked at them this way. Liam's smiling while he works and Troy, spatula in hand, does the same. They look more alike now than I've ever realized, Troy just a thirty-year older version of Liam. Steam or smoke, I'm not sure which, rises from the grill top and Liam looks up with the smolder. His eyes crease with his grin as he sees me. The gesture gives my insides an electric jolt. Leaving the cook's station, he rounds the corner, his stained apron around his middle.

"Hey." Reaching for my hand, he kisses my cheek.

"Are you cooking? It's *your* birthday." I should have offered to help.

Waving a metal spatula out toward me, Troy laughs from the open window where he works. "He's cooking for you!"

"What?" I feel the blush in my cheeks. "What are you—"

Holding onto my fingers, our hands at our sides, he says, "Dad made my favorite, spicy New Orleans shrimp, which I'm pretty sure would not be your favorite."

More blood rushes to my cheeks. Plain-Jane Thankful, he's right. "You don't need to make anything different for me. I can eat whatever you eat."

"You can, but you're not going to." Kissing my cheek again, he trots around the corner and back up the step to the cook's station, his head appearing next to Troy's in the open window.

Pops guffaws when he sees my plate. It's what Liam's eating without the Sriracha and chili sauce. My shrimp, noodles, and bread are plain, the way I like them, while his—and everyone else's, is covered what looks to be a thin, spicy sauce.

We sit at a booth, Pops and Troy on one side, Liam and I on the other, and Franko pulls up a chair at the end. We laugh and talk and I follow most of what they're saying. There's a few family jokes I don't get, but I like hearing them. I like watching Liam in his most comfortable of comfort zones.

"The top of his class and—" Pops holds out his fingers, listing off Franko's achievements for us.

Liam's fork hovers with his last bite in midair. "And the most handsome, we know," Liam says, suppressing his chuckle.

Franko laughs. I've never had a sibling or even a cousin, so I don't know if it makes Liam feel less, but it doesn't seem to bother him. He looks as proud as Pops. And Pops would probably brag about him, too, if he weren't dating a *Morificato*.

"The next *Chancellor!*" Troy bellows, slapping his leg.

Pops' long, wiry brows rise on top of his head. "He could be."

"All right!" Franko rubs his hands together. "Did you hear that? You're eating dinner with the next Chancellor of the Knowing."

Pops waves off Franko's nonchalance and mumbles something in Italian.

"What's that?" I nibble on a piece of shrimp Liam breaded and fried up for me.

"Ahh..." Troy sighs at the end of his chuckle. His eyes water from laughing, and he dabs them with his napkin. "The Chancellor is the organized leader of the Knowing. It's not a government. We aren't taxed and we don't have rules of whom we can tell or where we can live. It's more like keeping records, keeping track—"

"Protection," Pops says.

Troy nods once, then bobs his head to the side like there's more to it though. More than he wants to explain over a birthday dinner. "The Chancellor and his board keep records of us, but of Readers as well. See, Thankful, we are organized. We vote in our leader, we make our own choices, where Readers are more like... like the mob. They live in families made up of power and fear. Groups that tell their people where to go, who to manipulate, and who to kill. Many are famous for their cruelty. The Chancellor and his board stay informed, they keep *us* informed. They have eyes on them the best they can—to protect our people from being used and—"

"Yes!" Liam says, his hand on my knee beneath the table. "And Franko will be the most handsome Chancellor yet."

Franko's laugh booms through the empty room, his face and grin light, airy, and unafraid. We join him and the serious turn in our conversation dissolves.

"Now, what about cake?" Liam asks, changing the subject.

Troy brings over the white, coconut covered, three layered cake. He lights it up, we sing, and Liam blows out the eighteen lit candles. It's all very *normal*, for a not so normal family. Troy cuts the cake and hands each of us a paper plate with a prism shaped slice of coconut cream cake.

"Did you make this?" I whisper to Liam, though no one else would have heard me with Pops, Troy, and Franko talking and laughing.

"Nah," Liam says. "Dad's the baker."

Troy's eyes flutter from Pops to me. He winks at me and turns back to Pops, defending his point about the Brazilian *futbol* club.

Pops shakes his head, not buying whatever Troy's trying to sell. "No team could ever be as unbeatable as the 1938 Italiano boys!" Pops slaps his hand against the table, his word final.

"*Pelé, Papa!*"

I giggle watching Troy's fists punch the air.

Liam ignores their argument and brushes a piece of my hair behind my ear, his hand lingering on my cheek and his irises black as coal. He smiles and the sounds and people around me seem to disappear. His hand slides from my cheek and intertwines with mine on the seat of the booth.

"Gifts!" Franko says, hopping up from his seat at the end of the booth and tearing my eyes from Liam. "I've got somewhere to be, so let's do it." No doubt he's meeting Phoebe later to "party plan." Maybe I'll let the air out of his tires.

Troy moves our empty dessert dishes to the table behind him. He picks up the serving plate with the remaining cake. A few white flakes fall from their frosting bed with his movement, and he walks it over to the bar's counter.

Franko sets the small stack of gifts in the empty space the cake has left and rubs his hands together. "Mine first," he says, handing

Liam the largest of the pile. The messy wrap job isn't in a box and looks lumpy.

Liam shakes it, but no sound emerges from the blob. He rips open the blue and silver striped paper and a red Boston University sweatshirt falls into his lap, something I could never imagine Liam wearing.

"Hint, hint." Franko bounces his dark, perfectly shaped eyebrows.

Pops nods, pleased with the gift Liam will never use and Troy starts laughing. "No, no, no," Troy says, pulling the sweatshirt out of Liam's hands and holding it up to look at the insignia. "Boston is much too far away for my Li." He tosses it to the booth behind us and it slides from the red seat to the green-and-white tiled floor.

Franko reaches for it and slips it over his head. "Hey, this is quality BU bookstore material." He chuckles, his grin wide, and straightens out the sweatshirt over the blue polo shirt he's wearing.

"Thankful?" Troy holds up the thin flat box I've wrapped in plain white freezer paper.

Sitting up straighter, I nod. "Yeah, that's mine." I bite my lip, nervous. My face flushes with heat, and I try to remember why my gift *isn't* stupid. I remember Phoebe's laughter and it doesn't help my case. But it's only part of his gift, the part I'm willing to give him in front of his family. I try to remember the last time I gave someone other than Mom and Phoebe a present and I can't. I'm sure the reality would be my father and, before him, Errica at some childhood birthday party.

Liam's fingers slide beneath the tape, and he pulls the box from its wrapping paper cocoon. He lifts the lid and pulls the black cotton fabric from its box.

I nibble at the loose skin on my lip, wishing I had acted as if I'd brought nothing at all. "It's an apron." I shake my head, wanting to toss it away like Troy did Franko's sweatshirt. "I made it. I just thought it wouldn't show as many stains and—"

Liam's lips part into a grin and his eyes stay on the black apron he's holding up. "It's perfect." It smells like the fabric softener I used when I washed the material, and I can see a crease in the material where I didn't iron enough. The line of stitches down the left side curves cockeyed just a touch. It's certainly not *perfect*. Swiveling his head to face me, he kisses my cheek. "Thanks."

"Okay, next!" Pops yells, moving right along. He picks up and shakes the remaining small box. It makes a small thudding noise.

"From me and Pops," Troy says, taking the little white box out of Pop's wrinkled hands and handing it out to Liam.

The box isn't wrapped. Liam pulls off the top and a single key sits inside. His eyes widen. "Really?"

"For around town," Troy says, his head bobbing side to side. "You can drive Thankful to school every now and then for a change."

"For college!" Pop's fist hits the table.

"I don't know." Franko shrugs, the collar on his shirt sticks out over the BU sweatshirt and brushes against his jaw. "I saw the *beater*. I don't think it will make it to Boston." His serious eyes crease as he smiles, laughing at his own joke.

Pops glares at him.

Liam's mouth curves into a crooked grin at the word "beater." "Where is it?"

Troy slides out of the booth and Pops follows him. "Come on," Troy says, waving his hand. He wiggles like a little boy on Christmas day, bouncing on the balls of his feet. "Bring your key."

We follow Troy through the kitchen, past the cook's station and the small lounge and out the back door. A small trailer with cream colored siding and orange shutters sits behind the diner. Liam's home. An old two door car with a long hood and a fresh skiff of snow on its surface sits parked next to the trailer. In true Liam fashion, the car is black, except for the rusty grey passenger side door.

It's so cold and none of us grabbed our coats. I shiver, running my hands over my arms.

"It's not perfect, but it's in good shape." Troy says, walking over to the vehicle and laying his hand on the roof. He taps the metal.

"She's a 1986 Monte Carlo." Pops crosses his arms over his chest and kicks at one of the tires. "There's-a nothing wrong with her."

"Ahh—" Troy tilts his head. "It's won't be the prettiest car in the lot, but it will run well."

Liam runs his hand along the hood and over to the gray colored door, making tracks in the little snow blanketing the car. He peers over at me, a look of pure giddiness in his eyes.

"I like it," I say, keeping my teeth from chattering. "It's got character."

For the first time in the months that I've known him, Pops looks at me without a trace of annoyance. "*Sì,* character." He shoves his wrinkled brown hands into his pockets. "Take her for a spin, Li."

I don't know if he means "her" the car, or "her" me, but Liam doesn't take two seconds before waving me over. "Thankful, come on."

I jog to catch up and Liam opens the passenger door for me. The gray door sticks, not being the car's original, but Liam tugs it open and I climb inside. I run my hand along the seat; cracked, black vinyl with a worn, red, velvet strip down the middle. I turn to investigate the back, it matches the front: a bench that could fit three skinny adults with the same black and red, only not quite as worn. It smells like a mixture of must and vanilla. An air freshener dangles from the rearview mirror, *vanilla* flavored. A lighter shade of black wraps around the steering wheel, bearing evidence of sitting in the sun. The radio has round dials and a tape deck. It may be more than thirty years old, but it's clean, and not in terrible condition. And it's Liam's.

Liam climbs in beside me and turns the key in the ignition. The engine roars to life. Rolling down the automatic window, he waves goodbye to the three standing there watching us.

I find the heater dial and turn it up to high. Warm air rushes in from the vents along with a dusty cigar scent.

Liam pulls onto the main road and rolls up his window. "I can't believe they did this." He's still grinning.

"You *are* eighteen." I stare at him behind the wheel. He's happy and normal—by anyone's standards. Only he isn't, not really. He's so much better than normal.

Liam takes a gravel road and drives a few minutes more before pulling off to the side, there's nothing but land in front of or behind us.

"Pops is pretty excited about college, huh?"

"Yeah." Liam puts the beater in park and unbuckles his seat belt. He stares out the front windshield at the hills in front of us. "He never had the chance. It's pretty important to him." He turns in his seat to look at me. "What about you?"

"Me? And college?"

He nods his strong jaw in one movement.

"I don't know. I'm sure I'll go, one day." I don't think about college. It can wait, but Mom can't. Half the time I feel like finishing high school wastes what little time we have left. No, college isn't something I'll even consider until… later.

He nods again, this time a double movement, seeming to under-stand my unsaid reasons. "I don't really know what I'm doing either. One day," he says, and I can't help but wonder if I'm to blame for his uncertainty. I know Pops will blame me.

I don't want to be the reason, and I want him to go. At the same time, I shrivel inside at the thought of him leaving. Before I can be unselfish though, before I can join with Pops and demand that he go somewhere, anywhere, he leans across the console, his hand on my neck. His breaths are short and warm and we arch toward each other so that I feel the warmth from his breathing on my cheeks. His lips mold to mine and it's like he's leaving today and we won't see each other for months. We have to make it count. We have to make it last.

He pulls away and I'm breathless, my side aching from the gearshift hitting against my hip, but I don't care. I want his lips back where they belong, on mine.

"Thanks for the gift," he says.

"Oh," I say, remembering, "I have something else." I clear my throat and sit my back against the beater's seat.

His eyebrow quirks upward.

"Just something small." I dig into my jeans pocket, slouching in the car to fit my hand into the tight opening. I pull the leather rope from my pocket and hold the charm in my hand. "It's kind of silly. It's just, ah, so it's an Italian euro." I hold up the small copper coin attached to the leather cord, showing him the side that reads *one euro*. "Italian, to represent you—your heritage." I clear my throat and fidget in my seat, feeling like an idiot as I explain my reasoning. "And then," I flip to the other side, showing the strange building, "this is the Castle del Monte, I looked that up." I put my finger under the date on the coin. "And this is my birth year, to represent me." I pierced a small hole in the coin, placed a little metal ring through it and hung it from the leather cord. "You can hang it in your car or from your keys." Holding the leather string, I whip the coin from side to side, my heart pounding and nervous. "Or you can toss it in a drawer." I laugh, my breath shaky and quick.

Taking my wrist, he stops the coin from flopping and takes it away from me. Pinching it between his fingers, he holds it up to his face to see it better. His hand tightens around it until it's tucked tight in his fist, the leather strings hanging out, pinched between the folds of his fingers.

"My parents went to Italy before I was born. They brought back all kinds of things and they kept some of the coins and bills. Later, when I was in elementary school, they gave me a few things… it isn't worth anything. I just thought—"

"I love it," he says, staring at me. His free hand finds the back of my neck again. His brows furrow, his eyes darken and he almost looks… miserable. "I—I love you, Thankful."

33

FIGHT

Liam picks me up for school and, I'm pretty sure it's the fact that he told me he loves me and I said nothing in return that's causing my inside to scramble. He didn't seem to care that I didn't return the gesture even though I've thought it a hundred times since my conversation with Troy. I did smother him with another kiss, so maybe he took that as affirmation. Or maybe he forgot what he'd been saying altogether. Either way, my heart still races when I tug open the beater's gray door.

"Hey," he says. His brown leather jacket that looks old enough to belong to Pops is zipped up, his black T-shirt just peeking out.

"Hi." I smile and hope that it looks real. It has to be the dumbest problem anyone on the planet has ever had. I love him, he loves me, but I missed my chance to say it back. And now, well, now that moment is gone and I can't quite say it. And why, I have no idea.

He leans over to peck my lips, and the Italian euro slips from beneath the ribbed collar of his black T-shirt. The leather cord peeks out just a touch, tied around his throat. And though I made the cord just long enough for him to wear, I never thought he would.

I cup my hand around his cheek, my fingertips brushing his dark hair and pull his face close again. His eyes close and his mouth moves with mine. I break our connection and his eyes flutter open. My head screams: *say it!* But I don't. At least my nerves have died.

Holding my hand, Liam walks me to class. Chelsea waits by the door, rolling her eyes when she sees us.

Biting my lip, I let go of him. "Bye."

His eyes skirt to Chelsea, like he doesn't trust her, even though it's him no one trusts. Chelsea's just another Glenrock Higher. Still, he doesn't hover, he walks away.

"Remember when life was normal and Liam grouched at anyone who touched him?" Chelsea looks bored with her own conversation starter. "Remember that first day you met him, when I barely touched him and we all thought he'd rip my head off?" She sighs.

It's my turn to roll my eyes. I follow her into Mr. Hunt's class.

"Those were the good ol' days."

"Good?" I say. "Those were the psychotic days when everyone thought he was cursed."

"Thankful, I love you." She pushes up her black rimmed glasses with the back of her hand. "But that's the one thing that hasn't changed."

"WHAT DID TROY SAY?" I SIT ACROSS FROM LIAM AT LUNCH, THE room loud and chaotic. I can't help but think of what Chelsea said. Is it true? Liam's come so far, we both have. Do people really still think he's cursed? Sonia doesn't. I'm sure of it. Between her efforts and mine, I guess I thought people had come around.

"He doesn't care that my birthday was yesterday, he thinks it's a great idea."

"He doesn't care that you don't want a party? Or that Phoebe and Franko are snuggling up like two ridiculous…"

"Teenagers?" he finishes for me.

"They're different than us," I say, defending my concern.

"Of course they are. They're *Phoebe*. And *Franko*. They will both have moved on possibly before this *party* even happens." He squeezes his hands together and I don't understand how a party can upset him so much, but Phoebe and Franko nuzzling does nothing to his anger management issues.

"Party?" Sonia stands behind Liam, holding onto Brice's hand. Brice looks uncomfortable being in the same country as Liam, let alone at the same lunch table. Nope, Sonia and I haven't even come close to abolishing the rumors over Liam. "Are you guys throwing a party?"

"Ah, not exactly." I look at Liam, unsure of what to say. Phoebe told me to find bodies, which in Phoebe language means guests. Troy got on board and Franko stayed solely for the event, at least that's what he's saying. Wouldn't it be better if the bodies were people who liked Liam? People who didn't call him cursed behind his back. At least Sonia fits that category. "Liam's cousin is planning a party for him. His birthday—"

"For you?" Sonia's frizzy red curls bounce as she takes the empty seat beside Liam.

A low groan escapes Liam's throat. It's not Sonia's presence that brings it on, but the fact that I'm extending an invitation.

"Uh, yeah, for him." I lick my lips, knowing I'm digging my own grave. "It's Friday night, at Liam's café." My eyes skitter to Brice who's standing behind Sonia. "Bring a date."

"Sounds great." Sonia stands, linking arms with Brice, who looks anything *but* happy.

"Will you tell Kent?" I ask before they leave. Chelsea's still seeing her date from the dance, so that will include her. So, I suppose maybe a few will be there who call Liam cursed, but at least Kent's been nice to Liam. *Who else?* I ignore another growl from Liam. Maybe Phoebe's right. Maybe we do need to step out of our "just-the-two-of-us" comfort zone. And maybe a few guests at a party will shout the opposite of *cursed,* and prove to Chelsea that Liam isn't the evil monster she has him made out to be.

"You bet," Sonia says. Waving goodbye, she heads over to where Chelsea, Kent, and Errica sit. I watch her hands wave and her mouth move. Soon Kent nods and Chelsea grimaces. Errica stands and leaves.

"What are you doing?" Liam takes my hand, claiming my gaze. His eyes are dark and his mouth sits in a flat line.

"What? Franko and Phoebe said to get bodies." I purposely throw Franko's name out there first. I don't want all of this party business on Phoebe's head, even if it is her fault.

Leaning forward, a lock of his dark hair falls into his eyes. He runs his empty hand through his hair, combing back the sprig. The motion brings his leather cord and euro to the surface. "If we don't invite anyone, then it's *you* and *me*. That's what I like. That's what I *want*. But then, does it matter?"

"To me? Yes. To Phoebe? To Franko? I doubt it." I try to laugh. Squeezing his fingers laced with mine, I shrug. "Maybe it won't be so bad. It could even be fun. Having friends isn't so terrible, Liam. Besides, think of the good you've done. You aren't cursed, despite what you or anyone says. I've seen you with those who need help. You know what to do. You're—"

"Okay, okay." He hushes me with a glare. "But keep it small. Ease me in, okay?"

"Sure." My lips twitch, at least he's trying. "Anyone else you want to—"

"No. Kent and Sonia. That's it."

I giggle at Liam's horrified expression. I can't imagine any other eighteen-year-old on the planet finding a party so miserable. "I have to talk to Mr. Hunt. It's about my missing work over Thanksgiving break."

"Right. I forgot. You're a skipper now."

My skin tightens with guilt at the word *skipper*. I glower and my eyes widen with the expression. "I did not skip! I just—"

Liam's face softens and his lips part into a grin with his low Liam chuckle escaping. "I enjoy the face you make when I accuse you of being less than an impeccable student."

I can't help but smile with his expression so tender and happy. That's *my* Liam, the one I need, the one I... more than like. Standing, I attempt to frown at him, but it's a poor effort. "I'll see you in government."

"I'm coming with you," he says, shaking his head.

I furrow my brows and push down on his shoulders. "Eat. I can make it on my own. Besides, you make Mr. Hunt nervous. I'll see you later."

He blinks and stays put, but his content Liam face is gone.

Walking through the double doors the noise from the cafeteria dies as I step into the quiet hallway.

"What? The guard dog left you all alone?" Errica leans against a set of lockers. Standing straight, she skips ahead to keep stride with me.

Ignoring her snarky remark, I keep pace down the deserted hall.

She pulls my arm, yanking me to a halt, and I face her.

"What do you want, Errica?" Talking to her just makes me tired. I don't have the patience for it—or her.

"Do you really think anyone will come to this *party*? You think this will make him accepted?" She rolls her eyes, making her seem surly and childish. "You think it'll make *you* accepted? You both still—"

"You aren't invited," I say, starting down the hall again. I don't need this. "I asked Sonia to invite Kent, not you."

"Like I'd ever go." Her head rolls back with a laugh. "You may have fooled Sonia, but—"

I can't stand it anymore. I can't stand her or the lies or the manipulation. I can't stand that we were once friends, that she ignores truths all around her, that her highest priority is her status quo. I can't stand to even look at her. Her highlights have grown out so that there's a line across her head with dishwater-brown growing from her scalp. Her brown eyes are dull and sad. And as angry as I feel, I also feel so much pity for someone so smug and so cruel they have no room for kindness. Stopping my feet, I hold up my hand in front of her face, and stop her from finishing her sentence. "Were you always like this?"

Her pink cheeks pale. She knows it's coming, the unspoken truth we've both ignored the past three months.

Staring into her dull amber eyes, I wonder where the young Errica went. Or maybe she was always this mean and I was too lonely to realize it. "When we were seven years old, you fell off my bicycle. You skinned both your knees and cried for twenty minutes, while *my* mother, the woman you've never even asked me about, held you, wiped your tears, and cleaned your wounds. You wrapped your arms around her neck and you told her you loved her. That you *loved* her, Errica! Was that just another lie? Another line for your *background* check?"

If possible, her face pales even more. Her brown eyes glisten with moisture. And I know she knows what I'm talking about. She hasn't forgotten a thing.

"You were always selfish, Errica, but when did you become so callous?"

The pale in her cheeks turns to red. Though she doesn't speak, her wet eyes, red face, and clenched fists scream anger—not remorse. Her hands spring up and before I know it, she's hit me, a hand on my shoulders, shoving so hard that I fall and hit the ground.

"Oomph." My head knocks against the lockers behind me and my hands instinctively pull up around my face, waiting for another blow.

"Errica Cowan!" The yell comes from clear down the hall. My hands still block my view, but I hear the drumming feet of someone running. "My office. Now!"

Opening my fingers, I see Principal August standing over me and Errica's back huffing down the hallway toward the main office. The man has impeccable timing.

"Thankful," Mr. August says, his long comb-over strands stand up on his head from the jog down the hall. "Are you all right?"

"Ah, yeah."

He holds a hand out to me and I take it, letting him help me to my feet. "Let's walk down to the nurse."

"Oh, no. I'm okay. Really." I rub the back of my head.

"I think we should have you checked out." He takes my elbow, guiding me.

I wait for the twenty questions. When Liam and Marc Bailey even barked at each other Mr. August nearly suspended the two of them. Technically, I suppose I was just in a fight. One more thing to add to the list of things Thankful isn't good at. I hadn't even realized a fight was brewing, at least not one with our hands. Still, the questions don't come.

"I'll call your guardian, or do you want to?"

"Oh, please. Don't do that. We don't need to call Phoebe." I stop walking and look at him, pleading.

His hand pats my back, starting me down the hall once more. "You aren't in trouble, Thankful. I want to let her know you've been hurt."

I bite my lip. "Mr. August, I really feel okay." Swallowing, I shut my eyes, a silent plead. "If you have Phoebe come here for me, she'll have to leave my mom."

His brows knit together and he nods, knowing my home situation from Phoebe's visit at the beginning of the year. "Okay. Then the nurse will double check. And if you need something—"

"I promise I'll let you know."

He nods, appeased with my vow. I'm still not sure why I'm not being interrogated, but I'll take it.

34

ANOTHER PHOEBE SUITOR

I sit alone in the nurse's office, an ice pack on my head, missing my next class, missing my meeting with Mr. Hunt. Other than a headache I'm fine, but Mrs. Bird insisted I sit for a few minutes. She's worried I have a concussion. I don't. But I sit here just the same. Laying my head back on the pillow she's left me, I close my eyes and sigh.

"I can't leave you alone for even a minute, can I?"

Jolting up, I open my eyes. "Liam. What are you doing here?"

Despite how playful his words seem, his dark face and rigid stance tell me this isn't a joking matter. Muscles bulge from his forearms with his tight cross. "August came and got me."

"Really?" It surprises me that Principal August would track down Liam to tell him. At least he kept his word and didn't call Phoebe. "I'm fine." I shake my head and it makes my eyeballs sting. "Just a little bump."

"Errica… *hit*… you?" The words come out slow, and his tone matches the way he looks now, livid.

Standing too quickly, I sway, which doesn't help the point I'm trying to make. "I'm fine," I say, pulling his arm out of its stiff fold until I can grasp his hand. "We had a conversation. She didn't like it. But I'm okay." I pull him until he's sitting beside me and I can lay my head against his shoulder. Already, I feel better.

"You aren't going to let me *talk* her, are you?"

"Of course not."

"Well, then, I'm talking to August about arranging all our classes together."

"No." I sit up, staring at him. He's still so angry, it seeps from his essence. "I don't need a bodyguard. I made her mad. She overreacted. I won't give her the satisfaction of being afraid of her when I'm not."

A rumble leaves Liam's throat, but he doesn't argue with me. "How'd you make her mad?"

I bite my cheek to keep from grinning. It felt good to get the truth off my chest, even if it was to the only person who already knew it, even if Sonia and Chelsea still don't have a clue. "I dug up some old skeletons, that's all."

I DON'T MENTION THE SO-CALLED FIGHT TO PHOEBE, THOUGH THE entire school had learned of it by the end of the day and she's bound to find out. I was never more grateful to have one less class period than everyone else than I am today.

Chelsea had even asked me what I'd done to Errica.

"Nothing!" I'd told her.

"I've never seen her act that way before."

She was grumpy and not as concerned for me as I thought she'd be. I think she's mad about the party. Sonia said Kent was excited, but I knew how Chelsea would feel about it.

There's no reason for me to worry Phoebe, though. My headache is gone, and I don't need sexy-mother-hen making another appearance at school to take care of me. I can defend myself. Besides, Errica wouldn't do it again. Her style was more back-biting than actual physical contact.

"Okay, so I'm thinking black balloons. I know that's an over-the-hill color, but Liam doesn't strike me as a red or blue kind of a guy." Phoebe walks into the living room, a notebook and pen in hand.

I purse my lips. "I don't think Liam is a *balloon* kind of a guy." If she goes all Phoebe on this thing Liam may never talk to me again.

"Please!" She tosses the notebook into my lap. "It's a party. Balloons might be a bit cheesy, but they say *party*. And we need to teach Liam to party." She looks down at her phone, distracted even though she's the one talking.

"Fine. Whatever you want. Black balloons, streamers. This is your chance." I'll take the punishment. "You may never get another one."

Her brows furrow as she stares at the little screen. Nodding, she offers a weak, "Yep." Slipping into her coat, her eyes don't leave her phone.

"Phoebs. What's up?" I point at her coat. Where's she going?

"Oh." She looks at me. "Ah, I need to make a work call. You think party food. Okay? I'll be back."

"You're leaving the house to make a work call?" *Don't leave us again.*

"Thankful, I've been inside all day. I need the air. I'll be back in a few minutes."

A few minutes turns into an hour. When Phoebe's Jeep pulls up in front of the house a black Ranger truck pulls up behind her. I can't see the lone man in the truck, only a shadow of a figure that tells me it's a man.

I stand in the window, the off-white lace curtain covering part of my face and view. Watching Phoebe jump from her vehicle, she takes a large pizza box from the passenger seat. She runs inside and I pull back from the curtains. I stare at her statue figure standing in the living room. She's acting strange, even for Phoebe.

"Pizza," she says, opening the lid. She walks back to the kitchen and I follow her. Tossing the box onto the table, she takes out a slice. "I think we should eat pizza at the party."

"Where've you been? Who's outside?" A shiver runs down my back. I don't know why I feel so scared. Maybe because when *he* left, he gave no signs that it was coming. I can't read any of Phoebe's signs, so what am I supposed to think.

"Agh." She nibbles on her pizza, like there isn't a man outside waiting in front of our house, but like she has all the time in the world. "*That* is a long story."

"Phoebe!" I pull on her hand, forcing the pizza from her lips. She's scaring me.

"Sweetie, chill out." She tosses the half eaten slice back into the box. "It's nothing to get your panties in a bunch over. Just an old suitor."

"Suitor?"

"Yeah," she flails her hand about, then sucks off a dab of marinara from her thumb, "you know, a *gentleman caller?*"

"You have a *gentleman caller* from *Glenrock?*"

Jutting her head back, she stares at me like I've gone mad. "Of course not!"

"But the truck, his license plate—"

"Oh, Thankful, it's a rental. He flew in. Listen, do not get your tender feelings all worked up over this. It's a *guy*." She's says it like they're wishing pennies in a fountain—too many to count and not worth our time. "One I am no longer interested in. One that came here on a whim. The end. I'm sending him packing. Okay? Okay." She claps her hands, brushing them together like the job's already done. "Whatever you do, don't tell Franko about him."

"Franko? Why?"

"I don't need my new beau getting all upset over my old beau. You know?"

Franko, her new beau? They met days ago.

Maybe this visitor is a good thing. Phoebe doesn't seem to be going anywhere and maybe this man will get her mind *off* of Franko. She *needs* to get her mind off of Franko. Maybe sparks will fly and she'll realize what a horrible idea she and Franko together would be or forget about him altogether. Just another penny in that fountain, right? "Can I meet him?"

"No. And zip your lips. Eat, I'm getting rid of him."

"What's his name?" Walking back into the living room, I peek out of the curtains again. I try to discern more details from the dark shadow, but it's difficult.

Phoebe follows after me. "Thankful, argh, back it up. Be cool. Do not stare out the window at the man obsessed with your hot auntie. That's not okay. Back into the kitchen." She zips her coat back up and points a finger at me, "Go! Now!"

I backtrack, but laugh as I do so. It isn't like Phoebe to be so nervous around a man—she's always so in charge. Maybe this guy has more of a pull on her than she's letting on. Maybe he really will get her mind and her hormones off of cousin Franko.

35

INVASION

I push open the door to the diner, ignoring the closed sign, and step onto the green and white tiles. I shake the cold chill from my body, feeling the warmth of the large room.

"We should be cancelling this stupid party tonight! We should be investigating or doing something," Liam yells at Troy. He's wearing his black apron, and he doesn't look like he's ready to go to school.

"Calm down." Troy wipes off the already shining counter, ignoring the un-Liam-like tantrum. "You know the drill, Li, we act *normal*. We act like nothing is happening, we call the Chancellor and we don't touch anyone—*anyone*." He glances past Liam and forces a grin for me.

"But, Thankful—" Liam turns and sees me. "*Thankful*, you're here."

"Yeah, remember, my turn to drive today." I scan the bright room from Liam to Troy. "What's going on?"

"Nothing," Liam says so fast it's unbelievable. He's by my side, holding my hand, no matter that I just heard Troy tell him not to touch anyone today, for whatever reason.

"Troy?" I know he won't lie to me.

"Readers." He growls the word. "Pops saw them at the Quickie-Mart." He scrubs the white speckled countertop with quick back and forth motions, though I don't see anything on it.

"Readers?" There's a tremor in my voice that I can't keep away. "How... how do you know? I mean they don't have any physical signs, like you." I look at Liam and realize I'm shaking. Why am *I* so scared? They can't hurt me or use me. I'm nothing. I'm no one of influence. I'm no Knowing to steal away for information.

But Liam is...

And the shaking gets worse, from my hand in his, to my arms, and then my insides start to jolt.

If they knew about the curse, if they knew what he could do, they'd come for him. They wouldn't think twice about taking him from his home, his family, his life. From me.

"No," Troy says, throwing the clean cloth onto the lower counter beneath the bar. "But there are some so cruel, they are known for what they've done, for their high ranking in the Rule."

A *high ranking* Reader... in Glenrock? How is that even possible?

"Maybe Pops was mistaken." I squeeze Liam's hand. "Or maybe they're just passing through. I mean Interstate 25 is just—"

"Maybe." Troy doesn't look convinced. He sits on a red vinyl stool, covering his eyes with his hands. "You aren't going to let go of her, are you?" he says, lifting his eyes to Liam.

Liam stares at his father, his death glare, a silent *no*.

Blowing a sigh from his chest, Troy crosses his arms. "Then I suppose you'll both have to stay here today. Let's hope they leave soon."

"Stay here?" My shaking stops on the outside. I can't skip class again. I still have three days of makeup work to do. Phoebe would kill me. And I don't understand—"Why?"

"Thankful, we *can* control our thoughts," Troy says, his eyes darting from me to Liam.

I feel like a Reader, the way he looks at Liam as if he's saying, *you know better, you know the rules, you know the drill, let go of her.*

"But we cannot control what we see. If we could, none of us would have this curse. If a Reader were in the same room as you, let the Heavens and Spirits forbid, and Liam touched you, they would know immediately that a Knowing was near. And it wouldn't take much to figure out whom." Standing, his fingers squeeze the countertop until the tan of his skin turns white. "No. If you cannot keep your hands to yourself for twenty-four hours, Liam, then you will stay here, back at the trailer."

"But, I—" I turn to Liam who's squeezing my hand as if it might be ripped away. "I need to go. You stay."

Liam shakes his head again, his throat rumbling low and animal like.

Bringing my hand up to his neck, I tuck my fingertips beneath the collar of his black T-shirt, feeling the warmth of his skin. "Troy's right." He needs to stay. I am the only person Liam touches. I need to go. "It's too dangerous for you. But I'm—"

"I said, no."

I am the only one endangering him. Without me, Liam doesn't touch another soul and no Reader is any the wiser. He's just another eighteen-year-old boy at Glenrock High. I know we need to separate, but I don't know how to convince him to even loosen his grip on me.

Glancing back at Troy, I bite my lip. Troy nods at me, maybe understanding my thought process, and exits through the swinging kitchen door.

"Liam," I say, holding his neck with one hand and wrapping an arm around his waist with my other.

He holds me closer, his eyes boring into mine. "No."

"Who am I?" I give my head a slight shake, but I don't break eye contact. "I am no one."

His brows furrow with my words and he opens his mouth to speak—

"No one to them. I'm fine. I'm safe."

"You don't understand—"

"I do," I say. "I'm the one person who could put you in harm's way."

"That's not true. There are always accidents, things I can't control. What about that first day of school, when Chelsea ran into me?"

I brush a piece of dark hair from his forehead. "You wouldn't let that happen. You'll stay inside your house or the diner. This is what we need to do today. Tomorrow, if they're still here, we'll regroup, come up with a better plan. I'll even let you change your schedule to follow me around all day." I try to laugh. I push all my nerves and fear deep down into my gut and force myself to access only love, concern, and selflessness. "I'm not in danger, Liam." I smile for effect.

He closes the gap between us, pressing his lips against mine.

I feel a whack shoot from Liam's head to my head before I hear or see anyone. Separating, Pops stands there, his hands at his side, but I know he's just walloped Liam in the back of the head. I felt it.

"What part of 'don't touch anyone' don't-a you understand?"

Liam glares at his grandfather, and I want to scold him for it. Pops may not like me, but this won't help. Respect your elders and all. "But—"

"No," he says, waving his hands like an umpire striking someone out. "No buts. More than anyone this rule applies to *her*." He points at me without looking at me.

"I agree." I step back from Liam, letting go of him and brushing his hands off of me. His face burns red and I wait for the steam to shoot from his ears. "Stay here. Stay safe. I'll go to school and if I even think of you, I'll start singing the *Cheers* theme song in my head."

Pops spares a glance my direction, his furry eyebrows knit together.

"Ah, it's an old TV show." I bite the inside of my cheek. "You know—" I sing, "*sometimes you want to go where everybody knows your name*—no? Oh. Well, it's a good one." I shrug, feeling stupid as I try to explain myself to Pops, but the plan does make me feel better. It slows the shaking inside. If Liam stays home, away from being tempted to touch me, and I'm away from him singing theme songs in my head, we'll be fine. Right? The Readers can go, they have to. There's nothing here for them, and then we can get back to normal.

"*Sí*. I know that one." Pops nods, humming the chorus from the song.

"But the party—" I agree with Liam, it should be cancelled.

"Is on!" Franko pushes the swinging door open. Troy follows him out and they stand behind the lunch counter.

"Have you all gone crazy?" Liam yells, and I can see that he wants to run back over to me, but he doesn't. "This isn't happening!"

"It is," Troy says, wiping a glass clean of water spots with a white dishrag. "Pops has called the Chancellor's secretary. We'll know more tonight. But they know of no reason for Readers to be here. No one is in a perilous situation. Not yet. We're just being safe. *Normal* is safe. It may be normal for you to skip out on school now and then, but it isn't for Thankful. There'll be questions, phone calls, things she'd need to explain to her aunt, and she's right. You two being separated is safer."

Liam's face deepens its beet color. "But tonight—"

"Tonight is a private party with guests you've known for years. The doors will be closed, the shop locked. Normal, not suspicious." He lets out a sigh and looks from me back to Liam. "And that way you can have time with Thankful, time that we won't have to justify or worry over."

Pops snorts, crossing his arms over his red and tan flannel shirt. He agrees with Liam... it should be cancelled. Only Pops would add that I should travel to Canada until he proclaims crisis averted... or maybe forever.

"They're just people," Franko says, raising his eyebrows. "We don't even know—"

"Stupid boy!" Spittle flies from Pop's lips. "It's Byron Kobe and he's-a brought Payne Shultz."

"The albino?" Franko asks, not caring that Pops just insulted him. He sounds more fascinated than scared.

"Sì." Pops grits his teeth together, stomping around the bar and pulling Franko toward him by the fistful of shirt he's grabbed. "The albino." Dragging him to the side of the room, he shoves him into a booth. "Sit here while the grownups talk."

"Pops!" Franko yells, jumping to his feet.

Pop's crazed face scares me and I stumble back toward Liam, maneuvering at the last minute so not to touch him. Pops points his finger so close to Franko's nose, the boy falls back into his seat. "Until you are-a smart enough to have fear, you will sit in the corner like the child you are, while we make decisions to keep-a you safe."

Standing, Franko punches the wall behind him, leaving a mark on his fist and the light green paint. "I am not a child, *old man*! I refuse to live in ancient days. We're all people. We *can* live together. We *can* be peaceful—but someone has to be tolerant enough to try!" Lumbering for the door, he shakes his hand, bleeding from the punch. Twisting the lock to unlatch the door, he pushes it open, stepping out into the wind and snow.

"Peace! Hah." Troy cackles, taking his cloth and clomping to the other side of the room to wipe the blood from the diner wall. "That was *so* peaceful."

Pops holds his head in his hands and whimpers something in Italian.

I stare at Liam, trying to speak with my eyes. *Please. Listen. Please stay safe.*

He swallows hard, his Adam's apple bobbing. "All right, Pops. What do you want us to do?"

36

THE PLAN

S itting next to Liam at the bar, I feel semi-proud and semi-
terrified that Pops has decided to go with *my* plan. What do
I know? I wrap a straw wrapper around my finger until the
tip turns a light shade of blue.

"If you can control your mind and your thoughts you will be
fine." He stands over me, looking at me more now than he ever has.
I watch the wrinkles around his mouth and eyes move with his
expression and words. "Can you?"

"Yes." To keep Liam safe, I can. I will be singing the *Cheers*
theme song all day.

"If at any time your thoughts stray from school or the TV jingle,
you are to come home sick. Understand?" My eyes wander to his
whiskered chin, the gray matches the squares on his flannel shirt.

"I do. I can do this."

"You can." His confidence gives me a small glimmer of hope
that Pops might start to like me. "Why would a high ranking Reader
go to a high school, anyway?" He shrugs his shoulders and, as

afraid as he was before, he seems calm and collected now that we have a plan.

His confidence doesn't help me though. I instantly have an answer to his question. *Liam*, that's why. I glance at Liam who does not look happy, at all. His face is dark and glowering, worse than the first day I met him. He's ripping my small leftovers of a straw wrapper into confetti shreds.

Pops sighs, running his wrinkled hand through his full, gray hair. "We have the advantage, *bambini*. They don't know we are here. No Reader has *ever* known that. They are here, *sì*, for something, but it *isn't* us." He puts a hand on Liam's shoulder. "Your *ragazza* will be fine, *nipote*."

Liam walks me to the door, holding my hand, not caring that Pops will scold him the second I'm gone.

Its better this way, he'll be safer the less I'm around. "No big deal. This kind of thing must happen all the time. Right?" As harmless as a fire drill.

His eyes rove over my face before saying, "No. It doesn't. Known Readers traveled through here only once in the past that I know of, before I was born."

I bite my lip, okay, not *all* the time, then. "But everything ended up okay back then, right?" Just say yes.

He doesn't answer. He sets his hands on my hips over top of my heavy coat. I'm not sure he's going to let me leave.

"Liam, the only thing they'd want from me is you. Troy's right. I'll be normal and everything will be fine." If I don't think about him or his gift, they'll have no reason to even look at me, let alone question or interrogate me… who needs interrogation when you can read minds? "There's only danger when we're together." That sentence sounds so wrong.

And he agrees. "Then why does everything inside me say there's only danger when we're apart?"

I MENTALLY SING THE *CHEERS* THEME SONG AS I WALK THROUGH THE halls of Glenrock High. It's strange how exposed I feel without Liam next to me.

"No psycho boyfriend stalking you to class today?" Chelsea raises an eyebrow above the line of her glasses. Man, she's been ornery the past few days.

Troy prepared me for this. People may ask me about Liam, but as long as I think of Liam, just Liam, and not his gift, it would still be *normal*. "He's home. If Phoebe is going to make him go through the torture of a birthday party he thought he'd rest up to endure it." I force a laugh with the lie and sing in my head. ...*and they're always glad you came*—

Stopping in the hall, people bustle by us. "Wait, he doesn't even want the party?"

"Well, no. You know Liam—er, okay maybe you don't, not really, or you wouldn't scowl like that every time I said his name, but he isn't big on parties. You *do* know Phoebe, she was kind of insistent about it." Pulling on her sleeve, we start to walk again.

"Phoebe's planning? Maybe it won't be terrible."

"So, you and Kent, how are things?" I change the subject, trying to keep my head clear, though I'm pretty sure an albino and his brute friend would stick out like a sore thumb in these halls. Still, I don't take any chances—*normal*.

The ice melts from her expression and she gushes over Kent for the next ten minutes.

We sit across from Sonia and Brice at our lunch table. Errica isn't there yet. Sonia's holding out her fingers, listing off names to me. "Me, Brice, Kent, Chelsea... who else?"

"Ah, Liam, his cousin Franko, Phoebe, and me. That's it."

"Eight of us? Huh, eight people does not a party make." Sonia scrunches her face and scratches her head, her red curls staying neatly in place.

"Sure it does," I say, my turkey (no mayo, no mustard) sandwich hovers in front of my face.

"Nah, now ten, ten would work, but eight? I mean we aren't children whose moms allow us to invite as many people as our new age, you know?" She pops a chip into her mouth. "Don't worry about it. I'll get a few more."

"You really don't need to. Besides, I'm not sure how much food Phoebe is preparing. We don't want to run out." The lie to sweet Sonia tastes bad in my mouth; between Phoebe and Troy, half the school could come and be fed. "And no gifts. He doesn't want anything."

"No problem." Chelsea mutters something else under her breath and only stops when she shoves a french fry between her lips.

"Well, I already bought him something." Sonia gathers up her garbage and shoves it into her brown paper bag.

"You did?" Brice and I say together.

She swivels her head from Brice to me. "Yes, he's my friend *and* it's his birthday."

Chelsea snorts and Brice's face has turned a pink bubble gum sort of color.

"What'd you get him, T?"

"Ah—" and I can't. I refuse to tell my peers about the cheesy gift I gave to Liam or the way my heart speeds up every time it peeks out from under one of his T-shirts. That will stay ours, alone. "I didn't," I say. "Like I said, he doesn't want anything."

"Wha— No, T, you have to. He's your *boyfriend*." Taking a strawberry from Brice's tray, Sonia waves her hand. "No worries, we have time. We'll go shopping after school."

"Um..." I let the air fall from my chest. "Okay."

I SIT NEXT TO SONIA IN THE BOAT, MY PHONE TO MY EAR. "HEY, Phoebs. I'm going shopping with Sonia. I'll be home late."

"Shopping?" she says through the receiver. "Here? What for?"

Biting my lip, I smile at Sonia, trying not to think of the pile of lies I've told today. I don't like lying and today I've done more than my fair share. *Sure, Liam stayed home for no reason. Nope, I didn't get him a gift.* Why not—*he's going to love that Sonia invited ten more guests!* "A gift for Liam, you know... Since. I. Never. Got. Him. One."

"You never... oh, whatever. Okay, don't be long. I need your help rolling pigs in a blanket."

"Great," I say through my clenched teeth. Acting *normal* has never been so stressful.

We wander the aisles of Super Foods, Sonia scanning up and down each shelf. "T, I need to say thank you, or apologize. I'm not sure which."

"What do you mean?"

"Well, Liam. So many years... So many times... He's been ostracized and I've been a part of it. There were just so many coincidences. So many times he'd be there when something would happen or even things he'd say when we were little. It just felt too strange not to be wrong, not to be... evil. And now, now I just feel foolish and cruel. Like we've been the evil ones, spreading rumors, seeing things that weren't there, treating him like he has a disease. He's been alone for so long. I'm honestly glad he has you."

I swallow and the motion hurts my swelled throat. Blinking back tears, I bite my bottom lip. "Me too."

She winks. "So, what does he like?" She runs her finger along a middle shelf with fishing equipment. "Something personal would be best."

"Music... sports..." Cooking, though I don't say it out loud. I'm not sure he'd want me to.

"You." She laughs. "Seriously, T, I've never seen anyone look at anyone the way Liam looks at you."

Heat rises to my cheeks and I chew on my lip. "Really?"

"Really." She almost laughs at my uncertainty. "I take it back, maybe the way my grandpa looks at my grandma. That might be a fair comparison." Her green eyes glisten with her words. She links her arm through mine. "And they've been married fifty years! My parents divorced when I was ten—"

"I was eleven," I say, connecting with Sonia in a way I hadn't realized I would before.

"Brice was sixteen when his parents finally stopped arguing and gave up living together. They're still married, but they've been separated for two years. The way my granddad looks at my grandma, that is something special. Something that lasts."

My eyes fill with tears at her words. *Something that lasts* and that's how Liam looks at me? Ugh, I can't even get out the words "I love you."

"That's it!" She turns down the busy aisle of Thanksgiving clearance items. Paper turkeys are seventy-five percent off. Wow, what a gift! Sonia reaches for a shelf crammed with things from the past holiday and holds something secret to her chest, covered by her flat hands. "We both agree, he likes *you*." Holding out the object, she beams.

Her fingers fold around the five-by-seven picture frame, the wooden casing carved with small script. I take it from her hand and read: *thankful thankful thankful...* over and over again, covering the entire frame. I laugh, but I don't hate it and it's seventy-five percent off, right in my budget.

Walking out to the car, I swing the plastic bag at my side. "Thanks, Sonia, this was a good idea."

She squints at me, her nose wrinkling with the expression.

"You know, I—" Stopping mid-sentence, I stare at the truck parked next to the boat. It's black with tinted windows and I recognize the license plate. Phoebe's old flame stayed in town? She said she was getting rid of him. The side windows are rolled down, even though it's bitter outside. The man in the driver's seat has short curly, brown hair and a mustache that takes up entirely too much of his face. There isn't an albino sitting next to him, so I don't feel the fear that I should- today of all days- at the sight of a stranger.

He's scrolling through his phone, but looks up when Sonia opens her car door. "Excuse me, miss? Oh girls?"

I'm more curious than anything. This man doesn't look like what I think should be Phoebe's type. Then again, if it's male, Phoebe will more often than not swoon. "Yes?" I ask, approaching his truck.

"I'm looking for Deer Trail Road—"

Sonia laughs and comes around to stand beside me. "This is a small town; it's not that difficult. Just visiting?"

"Yeah, here to see an old friend." He smiles, and his mustache doesn't look as terrible as I thought before. Maybe he would be Phoebe's type.

"Uh—I think you know my aunt," I say.

He looks taken aback and his eyebrows raise in question.

"Phoebe. Phoebe Morgan. I saw you in front of our house the other day."

He chuckles, but his face turns a bright shade of pink, like he's embarrassed for being caught. "Yeah. That wasn't a very successful visit."

"So, you two used to—"

His brown eyes go wide and he presses his lips together, nodding. "I'm Ellis." Holding his hand through the open window I shake it. Ellis' warm hand is strong inside my skinny chilled grasp. "It's crazy seeing Phoebe in a place this deserted. She likes the busy life, you know?"

The crazy, romantic, wild, city life: yep. I grin. "I know."

Sonia's grin deepens, catching on. "Well, Ellis, you came this far. You shouldn't give up. We're having a party for a friend of ours tonight. Phoebe will be there. You should come."

I elbow her in the ribs. "Oh, ah, I don't think that's the best idea." I can't see Pops being down with a stranger coming to the party. Phoebe's ex showing up out of nowhere, the same week as the Readers and then to Liam's birthday party of all places... nope, Ellis might not make it out alive. "Sorry, it's kind of a private party. No offense."

Ellis shakes his head. "Don't worry about it."

By the time he pulls away, I've decided I like Ellis's mustache. Why shouldn't Phoebe give him another chance?

Starting up the boat, I check in my rearview mirror. There's a rusty-gold car with a longer hood than the boat's and two men sitting inside it parked in the space behind us. They don't get out to go inside, but the car doesn't move from the lot, either. Tugging the gear shift into drive, I watch in the rearview mirror. The sun glares off of the snow and into the mirror, playing tricks on me... like the passenger could be a ghost. The white of his skin and hair...

A chill runs down my back and I break my gaze in the mirror. Glancing at Sonia, she holds the frame I bought up to her face for inspection. Facing forward, I start singing. "*Making your way in the world today takes everything you've got...*

37
_____

ALWAYS

I want to speed to Liam's. I want to run into the diner and lock the door and never look back. But I don't. I hold myself together pretty well, not letting my nerves or fear show until Sonia has exited the boat and disappeared behind her home's front door.

Staying still too long feels unsafe, so before a second has passed I'm back in gear and heading down Sonia's street, my eyes peer more on the rearview mirror than out the front. I keep waiting for the gold Chrysler to pull around the corner and tail me, the ghost-like figure in the passenger seat.

I can't go to Liam; it isn't time for the party. There could still be customers at the diner and Phoebe needs me to roll pigs in a blanket. Pigs in blankets… it sounds so trivial with the looming danger, but since I can't tell anyone other than the people who already know, and Troy is certain they must be passing through, I head home.

I squeeze the steering wheel again and again. My knuckles turn white and then pink with the movement. Pulling up to the house again, I don't feel like taking my time. I grab my bag from Super Foods and run into the house, slamming the front door shut. I turn the lock and it sticks. It's never used so it takes me a few seconds to get it to turn over.

"Thankful?"

"One minute!" I yell, though I shouldn't with Mom asleep in the living room. I hurry into my room and shut the door. I fall onto my bed, but I feel so exposed just lying there staring up at the ceiling. Standing, I circle the small room, trying to catch my breath. I consider hiding myself in the closet for ten cowardly minutes, but I'm afraid the confined space wouldn't help. I need to do something. I need to stay busy, but I'm not quite ready to venture out and roll pigs in a blanket with Phoebe. She's too perceptive when it comes to me. She'll know I'm off.

I pull open the second drawer of my old desk. It was Mom's desk before mine. The one she used at college. The old, chipped wood could use a refinishing, but I love it. The deep drawers have a miniature shelving unit built in at the back. The second drawer pulls down when I open it, the front edge touching the ground with the weight of what's inside. I pull out the pictures one by one. And it works... my mind is totally distracted, my breathing even normal.

I flip through picture after picture... "Argh. I hate this one... And this one." Why haven't Liam and I ever taken a picture together—then I could put that in the frame. Sonia suggested a picture of me and I can't find one. "Didn't I ever take a professional picture after age ten?" The last portrait of me alone was taken the same time as our last family picture, the year before Dad left. The rest are snapshots, none of which I want to put in a frame for Liam to display. Maybe this frame wasn't a good idea.

I sit on my purple shag carpet, my legs spread, flinging one picture away at a time.

Phoebe taps on my door, but before I can give permission she opens it and peeks her head inside. She scans left to right at my mess. "Where's my slave labor? I'm up to my eyeballs in hot dogs."

I don't look up at her, I just keep flinging picture after picture. "I thought you were going to go with pizza. 'Easy breezy,' remember?" I say using her words.

"What are you doing in here?" She opens the door wider and a picture collides with the door knob.

"I am the most un-photogenic person alive, Phoebe! Look at this!" I hold a picture out to her.

She takes the two-year-old picture from my hands. "Well, honey, your eyes are closed."

"Yeah, so? The rest are just as bad." I hold up a stack and flip through, tossing them to the ground one at a time. "This one I'm not smiling. This one I am, but it looks like I just ate something sour. This one, look at my hair, do I really look like that?" I hold it up to her and she takes it, examining my bad hair day. "I can't put any of these in a frame for Liam. He'll decide he's made a huge mistake and break up with me."

Phoebe sits on a pile of pictures, her bare legs crossed, setting herself in front of me on the floor. "That's a load of—"

"I was never in school until now!" I don't know why, with so many other things to worry about today, I feel panicked over a picture, maybe it's my way of getting the anxiety out. "So, I don't have the option of four years of school portrait pictures. Even this year, we couldn't afford to buy a stupid picture package. Besides, what would I do with pictures of myself? Except now when I—"

"Whoa." Phoebe closes her eyes and shakes her head all dramatic. "Why does Liam need a picture of you, anyway? What? He doesn't see you in person enough? You practically live at that diner."

I drop the rest of the pictures in my grasp and press my fists into the carpet at my sides. "No I don't. That's not true. I'm here. I'm here for her. I…" I am, but I'm gone too. I've left my house more in the last three months than ever before, and if I'm being honest with myself, it's not just school. I spend a lot of time with Liam, at *that* diner. The guilt I have for my absence and the need I have to be with him play tug-o-war with heart.

"Oh, geez, Thankful." She rolls her head back. "It was just a question. Give The Face a picture. He'll love it."

I huff out an impatient breath. "That's easy for you to say." I point at her in her tank top and cut off shorts, even though it's freezing out. Her eyes are bright, her freckles sprayed perfectly along her cheeks and nose, her hair pulled up into a messy bun on top of her head that looks just right on Phoebe. "I don't look like you."

Phoebe looks down at herself and laughs.

Squeezing the frame, I stare at the sea of pictures on my floor. "Sonia talked me into this stupid frame and now I'm supposed to fill it. I don't have a picture of Liam and me together and all of these are just—"

"So don't fill it. Take a picture of the two of you tonight and tell him it's for the frame."

I sigh, staring at her. I breathe easier now. Phoebe... she always knows the answer. How does she do that? It never occurred to me to take a picture, to fill it later. Will I ever, *ever* be like that? Most likely not. But at least I have her in my corner, even if that corner includes unwanted parties and inappropriate flirting.

She laughs again, her hand cupping my face. "You look like I just cured the common cold. Come on, let's roll up some pigs."

I SPIN THE LAST OF THE HOTDOGS UP IN A CRESCENT ROLL. "YOU DO remember this is a small affair, right?" We just rolled a hundred pigs in blankets.

"Boys like to eat, Thankful. Haven't you noticed?" Phoebe sways her hips to the Mexican music playing in the background.

We cover the three industrial-sized cookie sheets with aluminum foil and stick them on the back porch. There isn't room for the pans in the fridge and they'll stay plenty cold outside. I told Phoebe I'd go early and bake them at the diner. They'll stay warm that way… and I would get to see Liam before everyone else arrives.

"All right," Phoebe says, eyeing me like a crescent roll in need of molding around a hot dog. "Hair and clothes time." She bounces her eyebrows and drags me into her room. Mom's old closet is stuffed with Phoebe's clothes, unshuttably stuffed.

Sitting on Mom's bed, I watch Phoebe rummage through her clothes. "Were you and Mom close? As kids, I mean?"

"Sure," she says without looking back at me. She uses her body to hold back a bundle of blouses and dresses, reaching in the back for something. "I mean she was still her, I was still me. We haven't changed that much, just a little older and wiser. Sally was always nicer than I am. But we were both smart and liked to have fun."

"When did you know there was a chance you'd have Huntington's?"

She yanks out a thin, stringy, little red thing. I'm not sure if it's a dress or a shirt. She holds it to her chest, her breathing heavy with all her efforts to reach the article I have no intention of wearing. Her back leans against the clothes budding from the closet. "Ah…" She walks over to the bed and sits next to me. "When Dad started with the symptoms. Your grandma and grandpa sat us down then and told us what was happening. They didn't waste time telling us we could have it too."

"How old were you? Were you scared? Did you ever, you know, get checked out?" I stare at her face, waiting to see if I've crossed a line, but I don't know how you could with Phoebe.

She runs a hand over her forehead, sweating with all the exertion of retrieving the dress-shirt I'll never be brave enough to put on or sexy enough to pull off. "I was ten, so that means Sally would have been… fourteen."

"Did it scare you?" I ask again. We've never talked about this and I've always wanted to. Today of all days it's the perfect distraction.

"Yeah." Her brown-gold eyes stare into mine. "Of course it did. I'm not superhuman, Thankful."

Maybe not. But she's a million times braver than I am.

She purses her lips, her eyes narrowing. She has something to say, but she doesn't. "What was the last question?"

"Did you ever get tested?" I bite the inside of my cheek, feeling like I'm opening her up and dissecting her. "You know, to see if you have it too?" It's a question for myself. It's a question I've suppressed, but never gotten rid of.

"I did not. I'm happy. I'm living. I'm fulfilled." Each word is more pronounced than the last. "I don't need a test to tell me I'm going to be okay. I'm better than okay." And her conviction almost commands that I never get tested, either.

Nodding, I stare at my hands, thankful Phoebe and I share the same blood. Maybe I'll grow some of her spirit, as well. Smiling, I look up at her. "I'm not wearing that."

"Pah!" She throws the slinky garment in my face. "This is for me!"

I laugh. That makes much more sense.

"And Thankful," she says, pulling the red dress off of my head. "Don't ever be afraid to ask me a question. I will always be here for you. I will always answer you. *Always*."

38

LITTLE BLACK DRESS

"No, Momma—don't!"

She throws the TV remote at Neeta's head. The old gal ducks, covering her gray, spiky hair with her hands. She comes up puffing, her face red and angry.

Mom's sweaty, blonde hair sticks to her cheeks, her backside drenched with sweat and possibly urine. "Out!" She screams, standing next to the couch. Neither Phoebe nor I saw her get up.

"Sally! Sally!" Phoebe yells. Her red strappy dress shows bare skin on her arms and legs and stomach. It's short already, but shrinks even shorter when she wraps her arms around Mom's body, pinning her down. "Neeta, get in the other room!"

I hurry over and together we sit her back onto the couch. "It's wet," I say, and we've done this so many times, we don't count or plan, we just stand her up again. "She'll need to bathe."

"Yep." Phoebe walks her toward the bathroom.

Mom's gone quiet with Neeta out of sight. Her head lulls to the side, resting against Phoebe's perfect up-do. I knew Neeta wasn't working. I dismiss the thought though. It wasn't that long ago Mom threw a coffee mug at me. It isn't Neeta, it's Mom. And it's the disease.

I clear the bedding on the couch and scrub the cushions the best I can. They're wet, and won't be dry in time for Mom to lay back down again, so I flip them over like I have so many times before.

Neeta's behind me with fresh sheets and blankets. "I've got this, honey."

"Thanks, Neeta." I straighten out the glittery dress Phoebe's loaning me, the one I talked her down to. At least this one has straps.

I walk back to the bathroom. Phoebe sits in her New York ensemble on the toilet, looking insanely out of place. Mom's in the tub, her bones seem to protrude through her skin more than they did the last time I bathed her. She's lost more weight. But she's calm. Her chest rises and falls with even breaths. Her head lays back, lulling to the side, resting against the porcelain of the tub, and her eyes are closed.

"So much for going early, huh?" I laugh so that I won't cry. And truly not because I won't be early getting my alone time with Liam, and not because my dress is wet and my amazing Phoebe-made curls mussed, but because my angel mother just wet herself and tried to kill the nurse. "I'll call Liam, let him know we won't be coming."

"Uh-uh-uh." Phoebe stops stroking Mom's brow with a wash-cloth and holds her hand out to me. "Go. You're going and you're going now."

"But—"

"I'll stay."

"You're sure?" I ask, remembering what Phoebe said about my practically living at the diner. "Because when she's like this, I'd rather be—"

"I know, sweetie." She reaches up to pat my cheek. "No mother has ever been as lucky as Sally."

I drop my eyes, sniffling back the tears. It isn't true, but it makes me hope that what I do for her at least counts for something; my sincere love, my real grief, my insane desire for her happiness counts in somebody's books.

"No, I'm serious." Standing, she lifts my head with a tip of my chin. "You think Sally and I helped take care of Dad the way you take care of your momma?"

I stare at her, waiting to hear the answer, though she's set it up so I already know.

She shakes her head. "We didn't. Not even your angel mother." She wraps me into a hug. "I'm sorry my humor made you question yourself before. You are the best, Thankful. I wish you could see what I see, know what I know. I've never exaggerated your greatness." Leaning back, she looks me in the eyes and wipes the tears from my cheeks. "I'm here now and that means you don't have to constantly sacrifice. Your burden is shared."

I don't say anything. I just stare at her, wondering how she always says the right thing and feeling crazy for ever worrying she wouldn't come back to us. Even if I'll never be who she believes I am.

Holding my face in her hands, she says, "Get in my closet. Change out of your wet clothes. Head over. We'll be okay."

THE BLACK DRESS FROM PHOEBE'S CLOSET COVERS MORE SKIN THAN any other I could find. But it's short and I'm certain my thighs will be frostbitten before the night ends. I combed through my curls and applied more mascara. After Mom's fiasco, I'm only an hour later than I said I'd be. Still, today of all days, I know Liam will be worried. Worried and forbidden to come look for me.

I leave the uncooked pigs in a blanket in the back of the boat and knock on the diner's door. It's unusually locked, but it doesn't surprise me today. My legs are bare except for the knee-length black boots Phoebe insisted I put on when she saw which dress I'd chosen. The heels are high, but I didn't have time to argue with her. My coat hits my waistline. So, my bare mid-thigh to knee turns to ice.

Liam's dark visage softens with relief when he sees me outside the glass door. He runs over, twisting the lock, pushing it open and yanking me inside by the hand. "What happened?" he says, pulling me against him.

"I'm so sorry. I didn't mean to worry you. I, ah…" I drop my head. "Bad day. Mom wasn't too happy to see nurse Neeta and in the commotion I forgot to text you."

His mouth forms a flat line, a sorrowful line, and his warm hand cups my cheek, his thumb tracing below my eye. "I'm sorry, Thankful. Is Phoebe—"

"She's staying with Mom. I needed to see you and—" Before I can finish his mouth presses against mine. He knows exactly what I mean.

Troy clears his throat in the background and I force Liam to separate from me. I touch my fingers to my lips, and look over Liam's shoulder. "Hello, Troy."

"Good to see you, Thankful."

The diner doesn't look much different except the middle tables have all been removed and a handful of balloons have been scattered on the floor, taking the tables place. White twinkling lights are strung on the walls around the room.

"Phoebe and Franko apparently thought I would like to *dance* for my eighteenth birthday," Liam says, following my gaze about the room. "So, we've cleared some space and it took them three days this week to make up a playlist." His flat tone speaks volumes. Nothing about this amuses him. I can only imagine what those three days entailed. Maybe Phoebe staying home tonight and Franko leaving for college tomorrow isn't such a bad thing.

Walking to the bar, I hold Liam's hand. Why does it feel like forever since I've done so? How can that even make sense? I've known him less than four months. How can such a short acquaintance make such a big gaping hole of an absence when we aren't together? My list of people I *have* to have in my life is short: Mom, Phoebe, and now Liam. Even Chelsea and Sonia are in a completely different category, not the *have to have like air* category, but the *grateful for friends* category. I'm not sure when the formulating part of my brain put everyone into a pie graph, but it did.

"Did you hear from the Chancellor?" I ask Troy, watching Franko blow up more black balloons.

"We did. Readers have no reason to be in this area. We don't know why they're here, which means it's probably a fluke. They won't be here long."

I sigh and the breath comes out shaky. "That's good."

"Good and confusing." Liam shoves his empty hand into his pocket. "I've never heard the word *fluke* used before when talking about *Readers*."

Troy holds the long knife in his hand still. "Right, me either. But we have to hope it's a first." Looking at the pile of carrots on the counter, he starts to cut them into strips once more. "What do we do? We ask ourselves what we know. We know the California Readers have been working on loosening the reins on abortion laws in that area, making it easier to accomplish. The Washington D.C. group has been trying to pass laws to make all illegal immigrants pay back taxes. More specifically, the New York Rule, Byron and Payne's group, have been working on getting Francis Lent voted into the senate. The New York seat, let's see, that's just a couple *thousand* miles away from where they are now."

I nod. Their just normal things that normal people want or don't want. The difference is that Readers use manipulation, force, lies, and even murder to gain the power to get the things they want.

Almost sounds like your average politician, but I know better. It's not the same.

"Why is that?" Liam asks through his teeth.

Troy shakes his head. The one answer he doesn't have. Scooping his pile of carrots, he arranges them on a platter next to the neatly sliced celery sticks. "We know they *shouldn't* be here. That has to give us hope, Li."

Franko tosses another balloon onto the empty floor of the dining room. He taps his cheeks, red from blowing up half a room full. "How'd you do today, Thankful? Any trouble?"

"No, no trouble." I shake my head and grind my teeth, remembering the ghost in the gold car behind me. I don't mention it, though. Liam is already tense, and nothing happened, nothing we don't already know. They're here. And I am still a no one to them. I didn't give anything away. Hours later, I'm not even sure if my memory is accurate.

"And Phoebe will be here when—"

"Ah, she won't be. Sorry." I bite my lip and offer Franko a fake sad-courtesy smile. "Emergency at home."

His eyes skirt to the ground. Looking up, his lips part into a large grin. Franko is too optimistic to be depressed for long. He shrugs. "Maybe later."

Tilting my head, I scratch at my neck, more nervous than needful. "Maybe... Oh, um, Franko, there's three pans of pigs in a blanket in the back of my car. Do you mind?"

"Nah, I got it." He lets go of the half-filled balloon, sending it flying about the room all on its own. "My favorite," he whispers on his way past us. Of course they're *Franko's* favorite. Not Liam's. Franko's.

"The cake is in the back," Troy says. It's strange to me how easily we all shift from the big bad Readers to party supplies. "And—"

"And we're not singing, or blowing out candles, or playing pin the tail on the donkey." Liam runs a hand through his hair. "This is a diner, we do food. We'll set the food out. They can eat, they can dance. And then, they leave."

"You really hate the idea of friends coming over to celebrate with you?" Troy looks sad, almost defeated, as if the fact means he's failed in some way.

"Yes, I do. Most of these people are *not* my friends, for one. And this is stupid. It's dangerous. If we were truly having a *normal* evening, it would be me and Thankful and no risks being taken." His hold on my hand tightens.

"Normal for whom?" Troy says, his face red, but he looks more angry than melancholy over Liam's unhappiness.

"For me. Normal for *me*, Dad. Normal for Liam Gregor's birthday."

Pops walks through the swinging kitchen door. "Ah—*nipote*, shut up. What's done is done." His strong hand pats Liam on the neck. He grabs a newspaper from the countertop and turns back for the kitchen. "*Buona notte.*"

"Night, Pops," Liam says.

Turning around, I lean my back against the counter, keeping Liam close to my side.

Franko props the front door open with his foot and slides himself and the large tray in his hands inside. He sets it on one of the booth tables that sit against the wall. "Thankful, I found this." He tosses the wrapped picture frame over to me and thankfully Liam catches better than I do. Turning around, he goes out for another pan.

"What's this?" Liam twists the package in his hands.

"Another gift." I chew the loose skin on my lip, I can't lie to him. "It was Sonia's idea. I told her I hadn't gotten you anything so that no one else would. And this is the result."

He nods without asking why I'd do such a thing. Being more private than I am, he already understands my efforts.

Franko sets the last tray down and locks the diner door before hauling all three to the back. I should offer to help him, but I can't seem to leave Liam's side—and Liam isn't offering, no doubt because it's Franko's fault he has to endure such an evening.

The minute hand on the clock on the diner wall moves to the twelve. Its eight o'clock and like magic, there's a knock at the locked diner door. Sonia and company. Franko hurries over from the kitchen entrance and opens the door, taking their coats like he's the butler. Sonia has on the dress Phoebe helped her pick out for the dance that feels like a lifetime ago. Beside her, Brice looks more comfortable than I thought he would. He's much more casual than Sonia, jeans and a T-shirt, his hair in its usual brown swish on top of his head.

Franko locks the door behind them and Brice's head jerks around, their movements reminding me of a teenage thriller movie. They're locked in. Sonia doesn't seem to notice. She walks over to where Liam and I stand. "Matching? *Cute.*" She eyes my short black dress. It may be sleeveless, but at least there aren't gaping holes in the sides and stomach. Seeing Sonia in her dance dress makes me wish I'd worn my navy one. Liam likes that one. The first time he kissed me I wore that dress.

But... *Matching?*

I hadn't realized that. Liam is in his black dress shirt. We do match, but it isn't on purpose. I ignore her comment. I don't know how to respond, anyway. Instead I send a small wave to Brice behind her. "Hey, Brice."

"Hey," he says, nodding toward Liam and me and then looking out into space again.

Gazing past us to the bar, Sonia spots the gift we bought for Liam. "Is that—"

"Uh-huh," I say, biting the inside of my cheek. "Liam's gift."

"Oh good, you didn't open it without me!" She's holding a gift of her own. "Here, mine first." She hands Liam the square box wrapped in balloon-covered paper.

I watch as their fingers graze and Liam turns around to the counter, hiding his face and setting Sonia's gift next to mine.

Sonia sits on the barstool next to the one Liam stands in front of.

"Thanks, Sonia. You *really* didn't have to." After a second, he faces her, a small grin on his lips.

"Open it!" She pushes the box closer to Liam.

"Ah, okay." Liam stops the box with his hand and peeks back at the glass door, but no one else has shown up yet. I can almost see the relief wash over him. He rips the paper from the box and lifts the lid. He pulls a gray T-shirt out, the name of a band I've never heard of before plastered on the front. "Nice. Thanks, Sonia."

Clapping her hands, she points to the box. "There's more."

Holding up the wallet-sized first aid kit, Liam's brows furrow in confusion.

I sit on his opposite side and laugh when I see what Sonia's given him. "A first aid kit," I say like it's obvious. It should be.

"You know," Sonia says, her smile ear to ear, "for the next time you stop to save someone."

He tries to return the gesture, but it's nowhere near normal. He's uncomfortable with so much attention and I'm afraid it's only going to get worse.

"Now Thankful's!" Sonia doesn't wait for me to pass my newest gift to Liam. She does it for me.

Liam peers over at me, his expression instantly softer. He tears off the paper and pulls the frame out. My cheeks warm at seeing my name written a hundred times on the wooden casing. It feels a little presumptuous of me…

"No picture?" Sonia's brows sag, her mouth already in a pout.

"No. I want you to take a picture of Liam and me tonight, one he can put in the frame." My coat is draped along the stool next to me. I pull my phone from its pocket and hand it to her.

"Perfect!"

Liam stiffens as she points the camera towards us. Moving, I stand in front of him. It feels so normal to take his hands and wrap them around my middle. He doesn't need much of a guide before we fall into a natural, but posed, stance. I smile, hoping he does too. The flash from my camera phone goes off twice before Franko opens the glass door.

A small sea of people file into the diner, talking and laughing and handing Franko their coats. Liam's body goes rigid next to mine and any feeling of normalcy vanishes like a disappearing magic act.

39

THE TRUTH ABOUT ELSA

"These people must *really* like Sonia," Liam whispers in my year.

We stand to the side while most of the others are in the middle dancing. There are maybe twenty-five people in Liam's little diner, the most I've ever seen.

"Because no one is here for me." The words aren't said with pity. In fact, it's almost relief that fills his voice with the knowledge. And I know what else he's thinking: they're all here *despite* him.

I don't say anything, because he's right. Sonia and Kent are here for Liam and that's it. I haven't even convinced Liam that Kent *actually* likes him. It doesn't help that a scowling Chelsea won't leave Kent's side, not even to come say hello to me. Then again, Kent hasn't been over to see Liam. So, it's no wonder his counter reads that two are here for him: me and Sonia.

The lights are low and balloons float about the floor as people walk through the sea of them. Franko is running the music and trying not to sulk since Phoebe hasn't shown up. I knew she wouldn't, not with Mom's breakdown. She sounded exhausted when I called to check on Mom, anyway. I'd wager she's already in her pajamas.

Standing next to the lunch bar, I lean into the crevice of Liam's side, tired of watching other people dance. "Want some cake?" I don't mean for the words to come out with a sigh, but my chest is full of air and my shoulders rock with the breath. I shouldn't be bored standing against a wall, not when I'm with Liam. And I'm not *unhappy*, but the place is so crowded with bodies and it's so loud, I can't even talk to Liam. Everyone keeps their distance from us, like they're still pretending Liam doesn't exist, even though this is his birthday and his diner. Well, except for Sonia, who tried to talk Liam into dancing with her once. It didn't work, and I thought Brice's eyes would pop out of his head when she offered.

His arm around me tightens and his mouth presses against my ear. "Come on." The words tickle the side of my face. He slides his hand from my waist to my wrist, lacing his fingers with mine. We walk over to where Troy has sliced and set the cake out on little white paper plates, both of us picking one up. He doesn't let go of his hold on me, leading me through the kitchen's swinging doors. The music's still loud, but turns muffled when the door swings closed. We pass the cook's station and the small lounge where Pops and Troy are eating pigs in a blanket and playing cards.

"Hey," Troy hollers as Liam walks right by, "how's it going out there?"

Backstepping, we stand in the doorway of the lounge, cake in hand. "Just peachy," Liam says, raising his eyebrows at his father.

I nudge him with my side. "It's nice, Troy. Everyone seems to be having fun."

Liam pulls my hand, heading toward the back door once more.

"Where are you two—"

"Bye, Dad!"

We walk out the back doors and the music almost dies out with the distance and barriers. The beater sits parked next to his house trailer. It's cold, but the wind has slowed down. At least I can catch my breath.

"So, can I ask?" Troy wasn't allowed to. I hold my cake plate steady so not to send it toppling over to the gravel, snow covered ground. "Where are we going?"

"Home, alone."

"But Troy said we shouldn't—"

"I already cleared this with Troy," he glances back at me, still in the lead, "my rule loving friend. He said we could walk from the diner to the trailer together." His lips part in a half smile.

I've only ever been inside the diner. We never hang out at Liam's house. It's my house or the café. My pulse quickens. He turns the knob and I don't know what I expect of Liam's home, but it's nothing out of the ordinary. A small living room with brown carpet and brown walls; there's a doorway to the kitchen and another to a hall, but Liam doesn't offer a tour. There's an orange couch against the back wall and a long book shelf to the side. We sit in green cushioned spinning chairs that look like they're from the 1970s. They're set adjacent to the front door, next to a large front window with sheer curtains that gives us the back of the diner for a view. There's a small wooden end table between us, and Liam sets his cake on it.

We're alone. Finally, alone. I should tell him about the gold Chrysler, about the ghost-man sitting in its passenger seat. But for the first time all day I'm not nervous and I don't even know if what I saw was right or *them*. Even if I am right, I don't want to talk about it. I don't want to bring back the nerves or see the fear and anger in Liam's eyes. What would we do now, anyway?

"I feel a little guilty," Liam says, pulling my mind away from my afternoon. I let him.

"Guilty?" I set my untouched cake onto the table next to his and spin my chair to face him instead of the window.

"Sonia's worst moment—"

"What did you see?" I sit up straighter, my feet planted, stopping the small movement of the swivel chair. I hadn't thought twice about Sonia's hand brushing Liam's when she passed him her gift. He mostly sees inconsequential things, and when he doesn't, he's told me before now.

"Nothing bloody or broken. Don't stress. It's just, well, it looks as if her worst moment of the day is my fault. She's going to spend a portion of the party searching for you, through the diner and outside around it." He wiggles his fingers through the hole in the knee of his jeans. "As much as I hate to admit it, I don't... dislike Sonia."

I laugh at how cryptic Liam makes having a friend sound. "I'm so glad you 'don't dislike' her," I say, mocking his evasive tone.

"I don't. She's... nice." It sounds more like a question than an answer. "Still, I'm too selfish to make sure she finds you."

Chuckling, I smirk, and look past Liam. The bookshelf covers the short wall, wall to wall, ceiling to floor. It's cluttered with books and magazines and pictures. I stand and walk over to the sun-scorched black shelving unit, running my finger along a row of hardbound books, their binding tattered and fading. I stop at my real interest, the photos. Picking up the framed picture, I chew on my lip. It's young Liam, his brown eyes as dark as ever, and his dark chocolate hair long and unruly. He's standing in front of two people, Troy and Elsa. Troy looks so much younger, though this picture is only a dozen years old. Maybe that's normal aging for twelve or so years, or maybe it's what the death of your soul mate does to you. Elsa's clinging to Troy's hand and she has Liam's dark, protruding eyes.

It feels like it's the perfect moment to ask about Elsa. I couldn't have planned it better. We're alone in the home where she raised him, and I'm staring at her beautiful face. But then Liam's hands pull the picture from mine and he sets it back onto the shelf, not even glancing at the people in the photograph. He moves his hands around my waist and mine find the nape of his neck and the bump from the leather cord. We're swaying, like we're dancing, but once again there's no music.

"I missed you today," I say, looking up at him.

Closing the gap between us, he stops moving. Burying his head in my neck and shoulder, his arms around me tighten. My hands fist in his hair and I know, this is it, my best moment today. I can feel his heart beating against me and we stay there for a long time, not swaying, not speaking. Just reunited, after one long day.

We hold each other until I'm certain he's holding me up, my legs wobbly on Phoebe's high-heeled boots. I feel his lips brush below my ear and he loosens his grip around me. Standing straight, he leads me back over to the green swivel chairs. The worn crushed velvet must have belonged to Pops and a teenage Troy.

Liam clears his throat. "I missed you, too." It's been so long since I said so, I forgot he hadn't replied.

Laughing, I feign surprise. "I never would have guessed." My insides are a puddle of warmness. Strange, with how miserable this day started out. Liam has a way of making me feel like the world needs me, like it wouldn't be the same without me. The planets would shift, the stars wouldn't align, nothing would be right.

He laughs too, his knee bumping into mine. Picking up his cake, he shoves a bite of the coconut cream into his mouth.

I rest my cake on my bare knees, the bend abnormally high due to the stupid boots I'm wearing. I take a bite of Troy's new masterpiece and make a mental note; I want this one for my birthday. I take another bite before setting my plate back on the table. I lick my lips and run my fingers along the corners of my mouth. "I like the family picture," I say bobbing my head over to the book shelf.

Liam nods, focusing on his cake.

"Your mother was beautiful."

Another nod. "Do you need a drink?" He stands up, walking past me to the kitchen doorway.

I follow him through the door. The lights are off in the kitchen and with one window and only the half-moon shining through, I can just make out his features. The room's small, but I can't define any real details, just the normal counter, table, appliances… Liam stands at the sink, filling two clear glasses with tap water.

"Why don't you talk about her?" I ask, leaning against the counter that I think looks like fake wood grain, but it's not quite clear in the dark.

He doesn't say anything. He finishes filling the cups and hands one to me. I set it on the counter behind me and take his empty hand. "Liam," I say and, though I don't mean to, it comes out a whisper.

Meeting my eyes, he shrugs. "It's hard. I don't like to."

So many things Liam doesn't like that I've forced upon him now… I should start tallying. I remember what Troy said about Elsa's death, that it was harder for Liam than anyone else. Why though? Because he was her child? Because he had no siblings to share his grief with? But that isn't how Troy made it sound. It was something more.

In my thoughtful state, neither of us speaks and finally Liam sighs. "Thankful." His hand cups my cheek. "I've loved two girls in my life."

My heart speeds and I almost wish I hadn't asked.

"You. And the other, I had to watch her *last* worst moment. Dad was out of town and Mom just hugged me goodbye before school. I walked away from her knowing what was coming, and having no idea what to do. It about killed me." His dark brows knit together, his hands in fists at his sides. "It about kills me to talk about her, to think about her, to remember what I saw and felt and couldn't stop. I can't—"

For the first time since Nora told me what I was, I am so grateful to be a *Mortificato,* to know he will never see that moment for me. To know I will never inflict that kind of pain on him. She didn't just die, he watched her die, felt her die before it ever happened. Tears cloud my vision and I cut him off, pressing my mouth to his. I don't want to be the reason this hurts him again, the reason it hurts him right now. So, I shut him up and kiss him until I can't breathe.

A faint slamming stops me and Liam pulls away, winded. Past the walls of the trailer we both hear voices and walk out to the living room's front window.

Franko stands out on the pavement in front of Phoebe—*Phoebe.* I don't understand why Phoebe is here… *Mom? Something must be wrong. Why else would Phoebe have left her?* Franko's back faces Phoebe and he's talking. I can hear him through the thin walls, though I don't know what he's saying. I'm ready to bolt for the front door when I see them.

Readers.

The tall man's white hair ruffles in the breeze, and his unusually pale face focuses on Phoebe. The man next to him could be his opposite with long, straight, black hair and skin that's darker than Liam's.

My heart quickens and I look at Liam. The blood has drained from his face, and he's almost as white as the albino.

"Your phone?" His voice is low, his tone urgent.

I shake my head. "It's in my coat pocket. In the diner." This stupid, pocketless dress! I always have my phone on me. What if Mom had needed me? What if she *does* need me? Why else would Phoebe be here?

He exhales and the breath comes out shaky. Liam doesn't even have a phone and there isn't one in the trailer.

The dark man, Byron, Pops had called him, yells something and pulls a gun from his pocket. Franko's arms fly out in front of

Phoebe whose eyes are wide, staring at the pistol pointed toward them both.

Liam moves to the front door. "Stay here."

A cry falls from my chest. I can't. I can't stay. I can't let him leave. I can't watch and do nothing. I shake my head, my gaze falling from Liam back to the window. I gasp in a breath. Payne, the ghost-man, the man I *did* see earlier today, watches me.

40

ONE NOTHING

His pale gray eyes stare into mine. Not the eyes of a ghost though, even with the night sky and lighting from the moon and street lamps. I can see he's just a man. A man with white, blowing hair, whose white face without pigment is stark against his pink, cold cheeks and next to his black jacket. His hand grips a revolver that doesn't waver from its aim—Franko and Phoebe.

My mind still circles my mother… why else would Phoebe be here? How am I supposed to get to her?

Blinking, I dart my eyes toward Liam, my body frozen and rigid with fear. I can't stay in here now. I don't want to. I don't want to leave Liam, but I need to get to Mom. And Phoebe, how do I explain any of this to her? How do any of us escape?

Liam reaches out for my hand, knowing I can't stay hidden inside anymore. "It'll be okay," he says, his mouth twitching with the lie. My hand slides into his, his normal warmth goes cold and clammy. He twists the knob on the trailer's front door and we step outside.

The night air hits our skin hard and cold. My teeth rattle against each other. Snow scatters across the gravel between the diner and the trailer, with more threatening to fall from the sky. A quiet hum of music leaks through the walls of the diner. The music has been turned up, erasing all hope that Troy would hear my scream. I'm not sure what Troy and eighty-one-year-old Pops would do against two guns, anyhow.

"That's right, princess, no calling for help today," Byron says in a New York accent. His stout body bulks with muscle. He waves his revolver at us, motioning for us to hurry down the steps and stand next to our friends. His words catch me off guard, but of course he can hear my thoughts. I try to remember the theme song to *Cheers*, but not one word comes into my mind. It's too clouded with fear. Not that it would help us now, anyway.

"A couple more Knowing rats hiding out in the cold." Payne's smooth voice sings out low and accentless. He cocks his head to the side, his long, slender body leaning like a tree bending in the wind. His eyes, wide and focused, bore into Liam. "Or *not*," he says, stepping in front of us. He's still staring at Liam as if he could peel off his skin layer by layer and know everything about him.

We stand a yard away from Franko and Phoebe. Franko's hands still stretch out protectively in front of a quiet Phoebe. Liam's hand sweats in mine, and he pulls me close to his side.

"Nope," Byron says, chuckling. "One Knowing, one nothing."

"Simmer down," Payne says to Liam, though he hasn't opened his mouth yet. "She knows your secret, huh, rat? Yet she doesn't squeal and run from the vermin that you are?" He moves forward until he's inches away from us. He talks about me, but he doesn't look at me, only Liam.

Liam doesn't answer him, at least not that I can hear.

"Why haven't you reported your location?"

Liam's teeth grind, never losing eye contact with Payne. When he opens his mouth to speak, he looks as though he's eaten something rotten. "That's your law, not ours."

"But it's ours that matters." Byron laughs again, the loud, ugly noise filling the empty space around us. Payne doesn't join in. He looks annoyed, but I'm not sure if he's irritated with Liam or Byron.

I peer over my shoulder at Phoebe. She can't be following any of this. She must be scared senseless. I am and at least I know what's happening, somewhat. Then again, maybe it's better she doesn't. Maybe her ignorance will keep her safe.

My mind conjures Sia Westcott's body swinging from a rope. None of us is safe.

Byron laughs at his joke again or maybe my thoughts. No one has spoken for at least a minute, but then I suppose that doesn't matter for Byron and Payne. They could be in private discussion and none of us would know any better.

Between the cold and fear, my body starts to shake. *Liam, Mom, Phoebe… how can I save everyone?* What's happening at home? I don't know what to do for myself let alone—

"Could you *please*," Payne says, placing himself in front of me. He pinches the skin on my chin, the gun tight in his other fist still pointing at Franko. "Shut up."

I fold my lips inward, though it doesn't matter, I haven't used them. I can feel Liam twitch beside me and then his hand comes up fast and hard, batting Payne's fingers away from my face. Payne's empty hand tightens into a fist, the cold air and rushing blood making his face without pigmentation appear even more red. But the blow doesn't come. He stops himself, his head jutting toward Franko and Phoebe. He backs up, his feet sliding through the snow on the dirty ground.

Byron side steps to the Gold Chrysler parked behind the beater. "Get in," he says to Liam and me, whipping his gun toward the back door. His head jerks to Franko and Phoebe. "And you two. Get in."

"We want peace. We can live in peace," Franko pleads, his arms slapping to his sides. "You don't have to do this."

Byron and Payne ignore him. None of us attempts to move toward the Chrysler.

"Ah, not you." Byron points the gun at me and I flinch. "You stay."

"No." Payne doesn't look at Byron. "She goes."

"Ah…" Byron moans, staring at Payne.

"She goes!" Payne shouts, still not looking at his partner. He looks at Liam, the wrinkles around his eyes creasing. Payne lifts the gun, running the barrel along Liam's temple and jaw. "That's very brave of you," he says, though his tone doesn't match his words. He's mocking Liam. "So selfless." He shoves the barrel against Liam's neck and tears seep from my eyes. "But does she know you have this darker side? Does she know what you're capable of? What you'd do to another person, if you had to? Do you think she'd love you if she did?"

A growl rumbles from Liam's throat.

"Really?" Payne says, his brows rising like he's amused at whatever Liam's thinking. He drops the gun from Liam's throat. He still doesn't look at me, and his body jerks so fast, without warning I'm yanked away from Liam's side. Payne's cold hand runs from my bare shoulder to my forearm. "How about now?" He pulls me against him, forcing the gun hard and cold to my temple. "How about now?" he screams a second time.

"No!" Phoebe yells, finding her voice for the first time tonight, her tone a command. But Phoebe's demands mean nothing to them. These men won't fall at her feet like Mr. Hunt or Ellis, her ex.

The tears stream now as I picture Mom and Liam and Phoebe, and leaving them all. I'm going to die and I haven't even told Liam how I feel.

"Very touching," Payne says to me. "You'll live at least another

hour if you get in the car. And more important to you, so will they."
His head nods to the others.

They will live. I don't know for how long, but longer than if I
stay. I can't feel my face or my toes, but I back my unsteady feet
away from the barrel of the gun and toward the Chrysler.

"Thankful," Liam says to stop me. Through my watery, blurry
vision, I can just make out his hand reaching for me in the darkness.

"Is that her *name*?" Byron's hand flings to his forehead and he
laughs. "I was so confused." His dark face wrinkles, his lips parting
into a grin. Byron is the muscle of this duo.

Payne opens the door to the back seat of the Chrysler and I
climb inside without looking back at Liam. What choice do I have?
Payne pulls something from a bag in the back seat and snatches my
hands. He wraps the zip tie around my two wrists and binds them
together until the plastic cuts into my skin.

The car is running and hot air rushes over my frozen limbs. I
shake despite the warmth thawing my body. My nose wrinkles with
the inhalation of pipe tobacco and sweat. In seconds, Liam
squeezes in beside me. His hands, already tied together, reach for
my face.

"I—I'm sorry. I couldn't let them—"

He shakes his head and I stop talking and lean against him.

Byron shoves Franko's head into the car and he squishes in
beside Liam. "This isn't how it has to be, guys." Franko holds up
his bound wrists. "Come on, I—" Byron slams the door shut,
quieting Franko.

"They aren't interested in peace, Franko." Liam's back presses
against his cousin and he sounds as if this whole thing could be
Franko's fault, all because he believes in co-habitation, peace
between Readers and Knowing.

Why can't Franko be right?

"But then what?" Franko twists his neck to look at Liam.

I don't know, and either Liam doesn't or he isn't saying. But from the little I know, when have Readers ever been interested in anything but power?

I think about Pops and Troy in the minutes or hours to come. They'll wonder where we've all gone, they'll assume the worst, and they'll be right. Sonia will search for me tonight not because of Liam, but because of Byron and Payne. And Mom... what will Mom do when I never come home? When Phoebe doesn't return? When she's stuck with Neeta until Neeta turns her over to the state.

"What's taking so long?" Franko says, peeking out the dark windows of the Chrysler. "Where's Phoebe?"

"Phoebe!" I say, jolting upright. They said they wouldn't hurt us. No, he said he wouldn't kill us yet. My young, beautiful aunt entices men like other women can't, what if... if they've hurt her, forced themselves on her—"Phoebe!" I scream again.

The driver's door opens and Payne's pale face and white head bolt inside. "Shut her up."

Byron opens his door too and a bound Phoebe climbs inside.

"Phoebe, are you okay?" It's my fault she's here.

"I'm fine, sweetie. So is your mom." She sneaks a quick look back at me.

Our captors stand outside the open car doors in a silent mind-reading conversation.

"But then—" I shake my head. It aches with cold and fear and built up tears I haven't yet shed.

"Franko." Her head twists to see me from the front seat. She closes her eyes and sounds ashamed of the truth. "Sally fell asleep and I came to see Franko."

"Franko?" I say, trading in my guilt for revulsion. Why should I be disgusted? I came to see Liam. But then, I am seventeen and have known Liam for months. She's infatuated and missing her old, free life. Mom will be alone tonight, possibly forever, because Phoebe can't keep her hormones in check. I suck a deep breath through my nose, my lungs filling with the smell of tobacco and man-dirt. I need to be grateful Mom is all right. Fighting with Phoebe *now* won't help any of us.

Byron and Payne climb into their seats, both of them rubbing shoulders with Phoebe. Their doors slam shut at the same time and Payne looks back at us from the passenger seat. "Close your eyes," he says. "Anyone opens their eyes before I say they can and I shoot the blonde in the kneecap."

I cover my knees with my hands. I shut my eyes and bury my face into Liam's side. Why didn't I tell Liam I saw them today? Why didn't I shut down this party? Phoebe would be home, maybe nuzzling with Franko, but safe. Mom wouldn't be alone.

We are going to die... We're driving to our death. But worse, I know they won't kill Liam. They'll use him, manipulate him, treat him like a science experiment until his spirit withers and dies. Phoebe and I are dead. Liam and Franko... their fate is much worse. Like poor Sia Westcott, they will be used until no longer needed.

What have I done?

41

I HEAR YOU

"**G**reat news, little girl, you get to keep both of your knees today." Payne's voice fills the silence after an hour, maybe less, and the car jerks to a stop.

"Does that mean we get to open our eyes now?" Franko asks, no more pleading for peace in his voice. I wonder if he's changed his mind about Readers now. It's a stupid thought, a childish *I told you so* thought, one I know the Readers can hear, and one that doesn't help anyone.

"Yes, you can open them." Payne doesn't even snicker.

I blink, adjusting my eyes to the darkness around us. I look out the side window and see nothing but space, black space. I can't tell where the land ends and the sky begins.

Liam taps my leg and I face forward. A dim light floats in the distance, until my night vision makes out the small cabin surrounding the light. There's a truck parked yards away from us, but I can't tell its color amongst the darkness.

Payne opens his door and crisp, stinging air cuts into the Chrysler. I shiver and wonder why Byron parked so far away.

There's nowhere else to go. Unless they plan on nailing us to the frozen ground and leaving us here, they must be taking us to the cabin.

The digital clock on the radio reads just after midnight before Byron turns the car off. "Out," he says, opening his door.

Up front, Phoebe scoots her way out after Payne.

I sit in the warmth of the Chrysler, terrified. "Liam," I whisper, watching Franko exit the car. I can feel tremors spread through my body.

His hands reach up to my face. Dried blood coats his zip tie. He's been fighting it, trying to free himself, without any luck. His hands held together rub against my jaw. His eyes are dark and scared. "I won't let them hurt you," he says. "I can see you asleep in your bed. It's going to be okay."

He can see me. He can see me! My heart flutters harder, praying he isn't lying to me.

"I don't know how, but sometime in the next twenty-four hours, you'll be there in your bed. They can't read us outside their own boundaries, their own parameters, so don't think about it." We're left alone in the car, does that mean they haven't seen the vision he's just had? Is that what he's telling me? The walls of this vehicle block their gift?

But the small sense of relief I feel in my gut vanishes. Why would my best moment be alone in my bed? Shouldn't it be with Liam? It's always with Liam. My breathing becomes panting and the tears start to leak from my eyes. "In my bed?"

He nods and attempts a smile, but it isn't his, not his real one.

"But you aren't there?"

Blinking, his gaze drops from my eyes to my lap, Phoebe's dress bunches and twists around my legs. He shakes his head and a sob falls from my chest, one I can't control. I cover my mouth with my bound hands as more sobs break through my lips.

"Out!" Payne yells, feet away from the vehicle with the rest.

"Shh." Liam hushes. But he isn't asking me to be quiet; it's a soothing sound, like one would make to a baby to bring them comfort. I breathe in through my nose, out through my mouth and try to quiet myself. I don't want to make Payne mad.

The snow crunches outside of the car and Phoebe pokes her head inside. "Come on, guys, they mean it."

Mean what? I don't know. I didn't hear any threat, besides the last one to shoot out my kneecaps. Let them. I don't want to leave this car. I don't want my next best moment.

I want Liam.

"Come on, honey," Phoebe says again. Her normally perfect mascara runs and her freckled face strains in a way I've never seen before. She sighs, tired, and steps back to give us room to exit.

Leaning in, Liam kisses my lips, fast and hard. His bound hands take mine and he backs out of the car, pulling me along with him. I shake my head. I don't want to go. We can't go with them. *He* can't go.

But he pulls my hands until my heeled boots hit the ground. My legs sting with the bitter breeze. Shaking, I stand. Liam keeps hold of my hand and pulls me along like a saddled mule who doesn't want to go. We pass Phoebe and my eyes lock with hers, my head turning to keep her in my vision and screaming an apology that won't reach my lips. She may have come to see Franko tonight, but she wouldn't even know him if it weren't for me. She wouldn't be here if it weren't for me.

Phoebe falls in place, walking at my other side. She inclines her head, looking past me. "There's a reason he continues to threaten Thankful," she says, talking to Liam. "He sees how protective we all are of her."

"So, you want me to act unprotective?" Liam scoffs at his own words. "It doesn't matter what he sees. It doesn't matter what he hears."

"Then change what you're thinking, but stop putting my niece in danger." She stomps past us to stand near Franko.

She has no idea how truthful her statement is. Not about Liam putting me in danger. He can't be blamed for that. But about changing our thoughts, that's where she's right. It's too late, though. We've all given ourselves away with our unvoiced feelings. It won't matter how non-caring she acts, Payne knows her mind.

Payne leads us, with Byron in the rear. I expect jokes or threats to leave the brawny man who isn't the brains of this couple, but nothing comes. He's as quiet as we are. Payne stops and unlatches a wooden fence I hadn't noticed before in the dark. No wonder he parked so far away from the house. The old slotted fence has huge gaps between each piece of wood. It wouldn't keep any type of animal or human out or in, but the fence line gives the little cabin a massive enclosed yard.

We walk through the gate, our feet sinking into the snow. I can't feel my toes or fingers or legs or even my tremors anymore. My head pushes my body forward. Byron shuts the gate behind us and the light in the cabin window grows brighter and closer.

Payne twists the knob on the door and it opens without trouble. Someone must be inside, someone turned that light on, but I don't know if they're expecting us.

The six of us shuffle inside. There's an old couch against the far wall, a small table next to a miniaturized kitchen on the other side of the room, and a roaring fire in the corner giving off the light we saw. But there is no person in the front room. My body aches from the sudden warmth and starts to thaw.

"Sit," Payne says. The gun back in his hand, he points to the couch with the barrel.

The four of us walk to the other side of the small room and sit on the old tattered couch. Its green, stringy material showing the cushion beneath it.

"I hate this place," Byron says aloud. "It's old and cheap and the food is—"

"Shut up." Payne sets his revolver on the table across the room and glares at Byron.

Byron's lips mash into one. His dark straight hair falls past his shoulders onto his Columbia coat zipped to his chin. His eyes flutter towards Payne, who doesn't return the glance. There's an alpha here, and it's not Byron.

Twisting his head, Byron looks at me, reading my thought. His eyes resemble an animal, ready to rip apart anything that offends him. I look down at my hands tied together, wishing my brain would stop talking.

Byron's gaze leaves me and I peek up at our surroundings. There are two other doors within the walls of the small combo front room of the cabin, one closed, and one slightly ajar. The open door doesn't allow any space to see what's inside the dark room though. I look around the room for a telephone, any type of communication device. But I don't see one and it only takes seconds before I remember; now they know I'm looking. They must not care, because they both ignore me, in silent conversation.

I watch as Payne's facial expressions change, but no words escape his mouth. He's angry. Byron looks like an enormous child who's landed himself in trouble. He peeks over at us, his eyes coming to Phoebe who watches back.

The silent room, thick with tension, feels so strange and then Payne erupts. "Rahh!" The roar rips through his teeth, and he shoves Byron in the chest.

Byron could break Payne like a twig, but he takes the hit and his eyes dart to Phoebe again. I look at her too, but she stares out at the pair, quiet and confused like the rest of us.

Payne shakes his head and opens the mini fridge, pulling out a long neck bottle out. Using the table, he pops off the cap and takes a swig. "I'll be back. Anyone moves, shoot the blonde."

Byron's eyes widen. I don't understand his sudden uncertainty, but he gapes from Payne to us, the gun in his hand and his eyes landing again on Phoebe, though I'm the one Payne told him to shoot. The more Byron looks at her, the more I worry. I can't go home without Liam *and* Phoebe.

He wants her, there's no other explanation.

Payne opens the closed door in the cabin to a dark room and shuts it behind him. A light shines from beneath the door, but no sound escapes.

I'm so tired. My mind becomes a puddle of confusion and fear. I lean back, but we're so squished on the couch that I lean on Liam. I can't watch Byron stare at Phoebe anymore, but before I can close my eyes, his eerie glance darts to me. I turn my head, laying it against Liam's chest, and I feel his lips brush my forehead. I stare to the side, at Franko and Phoebe. Franko holds his head in his hands and Phoebe sits straight and forward. I stare at her mouth, her full lips in a straight, unhappy line. Her cheeks are pink with blood and chill. I follow her freckles up to her eyes, her mascara dried and crusty around them. She stares at Byron like she's studying him, and I pray she won't do anything stupid. Trying to seduce a Reader won't help us.

Once again I'm asking myself how I can save everyone, even though I know I can't. I can't change what Liam sees. We make choices and decisions that lead to our best and our worst, and the choices I've made this night have already ensured I'll end up home, in my bed. Alone.

The door to the mystery room inside the cabin opens, but it isn't Payne who comes out. It's *Ellis.* "Ellis?" I say and Byron raises his gun with my silence broken.

His brown curls are mussed from sleep and his hand falls on top of Byron's gun, lowering its aim to the floor. The way Byron lets him tells me there's more to Ellis than I realized. Byron and Payne weren't the only Readers invading Glenrock. Ellis is a Reader.

Phoebe's brows knit together. "Ellis, what are you doing here?"

"I could ask you the same thing," he says, running his hand through his hair.

"You know him?" Liam cranks his neck to look at me, the muscles in his eyes and forehead bulge questioningly.

"Ah, sort of. I *met* him today," I whisper back, though the volume of my words is pointless.

"Me?" Phoebe says, raising her voice. "I was dragged from a private party out into the cold and dead of night to this—this place."

My aunt, the brilliant and beautiful, the *never ending* flirt, had a relationship with a *Reader*? Of course she did, she's that irresistible. *Every man wants Phoebe and Phoebe wants every man*, I say in my head as sarcastically as I can. I say it for Ellis and Byron, to let them know what twits they both are. Did my boyfriend really get found out over a lover's quarrel?

"Ah, ex-lover," Ellis says to me. "And we mean you no harm. Truly."

Franko's head perks up from the ball he's rolled himself into. His face is rosy red like the rest of ours, but I suspect, like me, he's let a few tears fall. I don't blame him. Still, his desire for peace brightens with the slightest glimmer of hope feeding it.

"Is that right?" Liam says, holding up his wrists covered in blood-crusted shackles.

Ellis smooths his mustache with his fingers, a breath falling from his chest. "Cut his tie," he says to Byron.

My heart flutters with hope like Franko's. Pointless, stupid hope. Liam's vision... What reason would I have not to see Liam for twenty-four hours?

Byron pulls a knife from his pocket and flips open the blade, but after one step, he stops, changing his mind with an unspoken command. I peer past Ellis for Payne, but I can't find him. Perhaps Liam's wrong and, Byron *can* hear commands through the walls of the cabin.

"Byron," Ellis says, and there is authority in his kind voice.

A shaky breath leaves Byron's chest and he looks from Ellis to us—no, to Phoebe. "Ma'am?"

Phoebe's eyes skirt to the ground.

"I'm sorry ma'am, I just... I don't..."

Phoebe glances for half a second my way before lifting her bound hands in the air. Byron scampers over and scores the knife through her zip tie.

Blinking, I watch her, my heart pounding with confusion.

Standing, Phoebe rubs her wrists with her fingers. "Byron," she says, and his name doesn't sound foreign on her lips like I know it should.

Byron's head jerks upward, like a soldier jolting to command. "Yes, ma'am?"

"You are an idiot." Her hand flies up to Byron's face, slapping hard against his cheek. The zip tie is wrapped around her hand, its protruding knot scratching a bloody scrape along Byron's cheek.

Phoebe pushes past Byron to stand next to Ellis.

Byron rubs his face; his eyes narrow in angry slits. "You know it's difficult for me when you converse inwardly and outwardly at the same time. I can't—"

"Shut up, Byron." Phoebe rubs her head like she has a headache, like his impossible words are annoying her.

Phoebe, *my* Phoebe, *conversing inwardly and outwardly*? What does he mean? What does *that* mean? How—*what* is she? "Answer me!" I stand up and scream at her.

She rubs her hands together and walks toward me.

I can't stop shaking and the tears stream down my face. *No. Not Phoebe. This isn't happening. This isn't real.* I glance at her and peer back to the floor. *She can hear me, she can read me. Phoebe.* I wipe my wet face, and look up from the ground. All those nights... all those times Phoebe knew just what to say, just how to help, when Mom fevered, when I felt so small, when my anger silently kindled, she knew anyway. *Is it possible? She can hear me?*

Her gentle hands wipe away more tears from my cheeks.

Answer me! I scream in my head again.

"Yes," she says, her hand cupping my face. "I hear you."

42

AND THEN THE WORLD CHANGED

I t's a trick, a horrible Reader trick. A way to manipulate me, a way to use me, a way to get into my head and—

"It isn't a trick." Phoebe's hands hold a drink Ellis has poured her. She stands next to the table across from us. And for the first time I realize she isn't wearing her party dress. Of course, she couldn't after Mom's outburst. Her tan raincoat lays over her tight jeans, her brown boots come up to her knees. She sips from the mug and hands the steaming cup over to Byron. "It's truth."

"Truth." Liam scoffs next to me. "That's what Readers do. They lie and lie and lie and then offer a tiny morsel of truth and think you should kiss their feet for it."

My head pounds. I turn and look at Liam. This is Phoebe he's talking about. His words are like a foreign language. One I can't make sense of.

There's so much hatred in his eyes, more anger and malice than I've ever seen. More than when Marc tried to kiss me, more than when Errica hit me, more than before we were together and it seemed the whole world was against him.

So much hatred—for *Phoebe*. I don't know how I feel… confusion… denial, but *hate*? I could never hate her.

Phoebe smiles at me, hearing my thoughts. And that fact helps me to make sense of the confusion. Of how I feel. *Invaded.* So very invaded… infiltrated, violated, infringed upon, lied to, abused—

"Okay!" Phoebe holds up her hands, her eyes wide and her joyous expression gone. "Okay, I get it."

"Oh, but I'm not done." My hands shake and I stand to face her. "Angry. Very, very angry." And if I'm being honest, I'm angrier with myself than anyone else. It wasn't Phoebe that led Liam to his doom, it was *me*. I brought Phoebe into his life. I introduced them and gave him confidence in me. And I truly never meant to give anything away.

Phoebe's head hangs to the floor, like she's tired of listening to me. "You didn't, Thankful. Does that help your conscience? How in the world you didn't, I'll never know, but you can be assured you weren't the one to give up *Liam*," she says his name like it leaves a bad taste in her mouth. "Somehow you never thought about the curse when I was around. He never touched me or you in my presence. Believe me, had I known, I *never* would have allowed you to get so close to him."

Liam's lip curls into a snarl.

"Liam is right about one thing though, Readers and Knowing, we've never liked each other." Phoebe's eyes shift and the malice she held for Liam leaves her face. Sighing, she stares at Franko and folds her arms. "No, it was Franko's touch that told me the truth. And he's right, too. We *should* be able to get along."

I turn to look at Franko for the first time since Phoebe's been outed. He's no longer in his fetus ball. He's sitting up, staring at Phoebe with as much adoration as ever. How can that be?

"Franko?" Phoebe says and her mouth, her tone, it's so beautiful. The words come out with kindness and clarity, like music, and so very believable. "I know this is confusing. I know this seems impossible, but I do *like* you."

Ellis's eyes flicker to Phoebe's face and then back to the floor in his quiet, invisible stance.

Liam's throat rumbles and I can only imagine the screaming happening inside his head, but Phoebe's crafted her skill well. She never wavers from Franko's face; she never gives any implication that there are four other people in the room whose thoughts she can discern.

"Would you mind if I spoke with my niece alone?"

Franko shakes his head.

"There's a bedroom, through here. You could wait for me. I'll explain." She points to the closed door Payne went through. "Or you can go. You aren't a prisoner here."

"Not a prisoner?" Liam says, holding up his bound hands, his voice booming.

Ignoring him all together, Phoebe strides over to Franko and pulls a knife from her back jeans pocket. Franko flinches, but doesn't retreat. Bending to one knee Phoebe takes Franko's hands in hers. She runs the fingers of her empty hand through his and then pulls the blade through the zip tie holding Franko's hands together. "It's your choice." She says the words like she didn't just walk past Liam still bound, like she didn't hear him cry out a contradiction. "Either way, we're both out of hiding," she says, her eyes glued to the blackness that has overcome his.

Holding his wrists, he rubs away the pain from the ties. Straightening his head and his gaze, Franko looks into Phoebe's eyes. "I'll wait."

She lays a hand on his cheek and smiles, watching as his irises go black again. My stomach churns because I don't believe the beautiful grin. For the first time in my life I don't believe Phoebe, and not because she's professing more faith in me than I know is humanly feasible. But because now I know, she lies. She is capable of lying in a way I didn't think possible.

Franko stands and strides over, glancing back at Phoebe.

"Payne won't hurt you."

Franko nods and walks through the door to where our other captor waits.

"Thankful Tenys." With her hands on her hips Phoebe speaks like a stern mother. "I am *not* a liar. You have always known who I am. That hasn't changed."

I choke on my tears. "Everything has changed!"

"No," she says, reaching out for me, but I step to the side, bumping into a standing Liam. "Now you—" Tears on her own face, Phoebe quiets when the door to the bedroom opens again.

Payne exits the room and Phoebe's long legs stride over to him. A yell rips from her chest and her knee shoots up, jarring him in the groin. Payne hunches over and Phoebe catches him. With her arm against his throat, she pushes Payne against the cabin wall. "I told you to get out of here!"

Pressing myself closer to Liam's side, I'm afraid—of *Phoebe*.

Payne wheezes through her hold and Phoebe lets go, dropping the tall man to the ground. "And yet you sent me into the *bedroom*."

"So?" Phoebe yells over him. "Jump out the window, cut a hole in the wall. I don't care how you accomplish the task! When I tell you to leave the premises, you do it!"

"Yes...*ma'am*." Payne growls. His white hands rub his pale throat.

"I told you to leave the girl at the diner!" Phoebe screams, forgetting that the rest of us are watching her. She spins her body and kicks Payne in the side like she should be wearing a black belt.

Coughing, he falls to the floor. Holding his hands at his side, he protects his body. "I was following proto—"

"You follow me!" She kicks him again. Ellis and Byron stand behind her, watching without any attempt to help Payne. "Me!" She pulls him up by his jacket collar. Payne stands and, even hunched in pain, he's taller than she is. "You held a gun to my niece's head! My *family*, Payne!"

His voice garbles, but he still speaks, he still defends himself. "The law says—"

Whipping her knife from her back pocket once more, Phoebe holds the point to Payne's neck. "On this mission, I *am* the law."

Covering my mouth with my hands, I shut my eyes. I can't watch this. I can't watch *Phoebe* do this. *Stop! Stop, Phoebe!* I beg in my head. I hear a shaky sigh come from Phoebe and I open my eyes to slits.

The point of Phoebe's knife, in her expert grip, pushes into Payne's neck until he groans and blood drips from the wound. I can see through my slit vision that it isn't deep. Still, the red on Payne's pigmentless skin startles me and my stomach turns again.

"Come near my family again," Phoebe hisses, her face right next to his, "and I'll drive this knife clear through without a second thought." She pushes him back to the ground and he covers his wound with his white hand.

"Phoebe!" I yell, squeezing my eyes shut. "How can you do this and tell me nothing has changed?" Falling back onto the couch I push my fist into my eyelids and sob. I want to erase this night. I want the world to be right again.

I see taco nights, Phoebe dancing, lying on the floor and talking until it's long past midnight. I see Phoebe being there and saving me when I couldn't have been more alone and then the memories vanish, replaced with a picture of Phoebe holding her knife next to a neck too tan to be Payne's. Tan and smooth, with a leather cord wrapped around it; I know whose neck it is before I see his face. Liam.

It's all in my head. But it's a nightmare that could too easily be a reality. I feel like I'm going to be sick. I jump to my feet and

Phoebe's face turns pale with worry. She points to the second door, the one open a crack, and I scamper over to it.

Opening the door, I see a small bathroom and I kneel next to the toilet. My hands, still bound together, I lift the lid and my tears fall into the basin. I gag and heave, but nothing leaves my stomach. The light from the living room grows brighter as the door opens again. I glance back to see Phoebe standing there.

"I wouldn't do that," she whispers, talking about my daydream nightmare.

I look back in the bowl and shake my head. "I don't believe you anymore."

Kneeling next to me, she takes my hands, soft and gentle in hers. Pulling the knife through my tie, she cuts me loose and sets the knife on the ground. Brushing a hair from my face, she tucks it behind my ear. "I love you, Thankful." She wraps her arms around me and I don't pull away. I lay my head against her shoulder and sob.

I love you. I think in my head, but I see her beautiful face in my mind—her beautiful, deceitful, *reading* face. I see her with the knife, I see her beating Payne, I see her charming Franko, and I know she sees it too.

43

ONE LAST

Pushing away from Phoebe, my eyes have cried dry and my stomach has settled. I'm not going to wake up from this. Blinking, I stare at her. Phoebe's eyes are red and swollen from crying with me. She looks distraught. Which doesn't mean much to me at this moment.

Her head falls at my thought, but I don't say anything to console her. I don't have any words of comfort. Getting up, my legs are stiff and painful from kneeling on the hard bathroom floor for I don't know how long.

Rigid, I limp from the bathroom. My legs with pins and needles adjust to weight and movement again. Liam waits by the bathroom door, Byron at his side. His gun gripped in his hand. I don't waste a glance on Byron. Liam's dark hair feathers into his eyes and, though his normal angry face is ever present, there's a newness in his wide eyes that I'm unsure of at first. Fear. Stress, maybe.

With my hands free, I reach for him, but stop. What if he doesn't want me? What if he's angry with me? Or worse, what if he blames me?

I do.

Despite what Phoebe said about Franko, Liam wouldn't be in this mess if it weren't for me. And he doesn't reach out for me.

"Are you okay?" he asks, his voice barely above a whisper. Still, I know everyone around us has heard him.

I nod, but I'm not even in the same room as *okay*. I look past him at Byron and Ellis and feel Phoebe's presence behind me. Readers. *Everywhere*. At least Payne has disappeared. "Are you?"

"I've..." His eyes dart from mine to Phoebe behind me. "Been better."

"Ellis," Phoebe says, her voice all business again. "Take Thankful home."

Ellis sighs and pulls at the tie on his grey sweatpants. "Let me change," he says, and Phoebe doesn't argue with him. He disappears into the room where Franko waits.

I clear my throat and dig for courage. It's Phoebe. I can find my courage with Phoebe, I can find my courage for *him*. "Thankful *and* Liam."

Byron shakes his head, but doesn't speak.

I ignore him, he isn't in charge here. My *aunt* is. "Ellis will take Thankful *and* Liam home, now."

Running her hand over her brow, Phoebe sighs. "Byron, go help Ellis find his pants."

"Ma'am?" Byron's dark eyebrows knit together.

She doesn't say anymore, but she darts a glare Byron's way and he scuttles off toward the bedroom. "Thankful," she says, her voice low and her eyes on my feet. "He can't leave. I'm sorry."

"He can!" I shout. "You're the *law* here." I repeat her words and stand in front of him. He may not want me anymore, but at least I can give it my all to protect him. "Tell them to take him home and they will."

"Believe me, honey, when I tell you it doesn't work that way."

"It works however you say it works!"

"Thankful—" Liam tugs at my dress, but it's small. I don't feel his touch at all. I've led him to this disaster and now before I leave him he gets to watch me throw a tantrum.

But I don't know what else to do. "Do it!" I scream at her.

"I can't!" And I wish so much she at least appeared remorseful with the words. "But I can give you *something*." Phoebe licks her full lips and her teeth grind together. *Something* she doesn't want to give. She walks back over to the small table and picks up her mug that's no longer steaming. Sipping it once, she sets it back down. Raising her head she looks pointedly at me and then Liam. "She hasn't changed her mind," she says, the words coming out taut. "And," she looks at me, "he doesn't blame you." Clearing her throat, she crosses her arms and darts to the front door of the cabin. "You leave in five minutes, Thankful." Charging out the door, she slams it closed behind her.

Liam and I are left alone in the small cabin living room. Alone, but not. Phoebe stands out front, Ellis and Byron in the only other room with a window. There's nowhere to hide, nowhere to run. Her gift is moving us past our uncertainties and giving us five minutes without anyone to read our minds as we say goodbye.

It's the worst gift ever and yet I'm grateful to have it.

Facing Liam, I don't waste time. I don't have any to waste. Wrapping my arms around his neck, I pull him close; his hands tied together press between our middles. "How can you not blame me?" I say into his neck.

His head careens back and his eyes rove over my face. "You aren't guilty. If it weren't for this curse—"

Closing my eyes, I shake my head. "*You* aren't guilty! You didn't kidnap anyone or tie my hands together or stab Payne. You didn't ask for—"

"Okay," he says, bringing his hands up and brushing a hair from my eyes. "Neither of us is guilty."

The clock on the wall behind us ticks like its volume has been turned up. My chest grows heavy with the sound. Five minutes.

They're going to *keep* Liam.

My mind races with what ifs and my heart may burst from my chest. All I can do is look at him, while he stares back at me. I don't tell him I love him like I should. I don't kiss him goodbye, because I can't do it, knowing it will be the last time I'll feel his lips on mine. I can't do anything but breathe, and even that feels like a small feat.

Ellis steps out of the bedroom, fully dressed, his hair combed to the side. His brows knit together when he looks at us. "Time to go," he says like he hates the chore Phoebe's assigned him.

"No. No, no, no." My head shakes and the weight in my chest turns to panic. "I'll stay! I can stay!"

Liam shakes his head.

"You can't stay, Thankful. And you know you won't," Ellis says, his hands in his pockets.

"I will!" But even with the declaration I think of Mom. If I stay what will happen to her?

"You won't. Liam's already told you that." Ellis walks to the cabin door, holding it open for me.

Ellis is right. Liam had told me that. One of us must have given up that secret with our thoughts. Asleep in my bed, that's where he saw me, right? Though I can't remember the last time I slept in my bed. Shouldn't he see me asleep in my grandfather's chair next to Mom? My head quivers side to side and the tear ducts I thought had run dry spill more moisture from my eyes.

Ellis holds his hand out, as if I'll willingly take it. "You know you can't change it."

He's right. I can't. And I'd rather Liam's last image of me not be one of kicking and screaming as Ellis drags me out the door. Throwing my arms around Liam's neck, I pull him as close as I can.

On instinct I whisper my thought in his ear. "I'll get you out of here."

Rocking back, he peers like he's trying to memorize my face. "Don't worry about me. Stay safe."

I press my mouth to his, despite the fact that I don't want to remember one last kiss. I just want to have a hundred kisses, a thousand touches, a million heart beats in my head, to keep safe, to keep close, to keep mine, forever. I don't want *one* last, one that will be the only I can remember, but the thoughts come too late. My mouth already presses to his. One last is what I'm getting. One last is what I'll remember. The endearment feels wrong though, our lips are hard, unbreathing, and broken apart before it's barely begun.

"Go," Liam says, his lips still touching mine. And I do.

44

DO YOU KNOW HOW ANNOYING
THAT IS?

I sit in the cab of Ellis's truck, watching out the window. Byron offered him a gun, but he wouldn't take it. So, he handed him a bag for my head to keep me blind, but Ellis doesn't use it. It sits on the bench of the truck between us.

It's so dark anyway. I don't know that it would make much of a difference. Maybe Ellis knows that.

"Actually, I don't care for riding without sight. I thought maybe you were the same. Just a courtesy." Ellis stares out the front windshield, one hand on the wheel, one reaches into a bag on the cab floor between us. "Water?" He holds out a bottle of water and sets in on the seat next to me.

I don't take the bottle or say anything. What does he want? A thank you? I watch out the window, seeing nothing, my tears spilling, pretending he hasn't opened his mouth. My mind tries to wrap around the betrayal and loss tonight has brought, but it can't. It's impossible.

"Sorry, it's sort of a habit, answering unasked questions." He glances my way, but I pretend not to see him in my peripheral.

I adjust myself so that I can't see him at all.

"It's a long drive back into town. Well, a long drive for silence. Do you mind if I turn on the radio?"

I don't answer him. I don't care what he does. Would it matter if I did anyway? Has anything I wanted tonight mattered to them?

He turns the music on. The country tune plays low in the cab. I don't recognize the song and I can't make out any of the words with the volume turned down so low. But I do realize I gave him confirmation with my thoughts. *Nothing* stays private with Readers. *Nothing* remains sacred. You can't keep anything to yourself. You can't even rebel with the silent treatment.

"Ah… you learn," Ellis says. "You gain control of your thoughts. When you get good at it, you can unconsciously make sure your mind only roams free when no one else is around. Others can learn as well. Well, it's harder for Knowing, but other people who aren't gifted or cursed. My father for instance, he wasn't a Reader, but he learned how to control his thoughts so that I never knew what my Christmas gifts were until I opened them Christmas morning like the rest of the world."

Why is he telling me this? I don't care.

"But Knowing, they feel things more intently than the rest of us and then of course they can't control what they see. They can never hide those things."

It's why they're so valuable to you. I'm so angry, can't he feel how angry I am? I take the cold bottle still lying next to me and break open the cap, taking a swig of the crisp water.

"Exactly," Ellis says and the sensation of never hearing my own voice, but having my comments and questions acknowledged and answered makes my head spin.

Screwing the lid back on, I set the bottle back down, hating that I accepted his offering. *It's why you take away their rights, privileges, and lives. Because you're greedy and narcissistic. Because you care about no one other than yourself and your cause.*

"I can see why you'd view it that way. But we are trying to make the world a better place."

Sure you are, by sacrificing one Knowing at a time. I turn, staring out the front window. I want to see Ellis in my peripheral vision. I want to see him squirm. I want to see him feel uncomfortable. And he does look slightly shamed. But how can you trust anything from a Reader. He knows I want to see him looking guilty, so he does.

"I really don't like this part of the job. I do know what you're thinking, Thankful. But I'm still my own person. You can't lump all of us together in one category just because we have the same gift."

"No," I say, facing him. "I can lump you all in the same category because none of you tried to stop this night from happening. None of you said—yeah, let's keep the innocent teenagers out of it. None of you cared enough to do anything, but benefit your own."

"I didn't agree to this night. Notice I wasn't there." His hands twist the steering wheel. "When Phoebe talked about bringing Franko in, I was skeptical. I didn't feel right about it, but she didn't say anything about you or Liam. And by the way she reacted to Payne, sounds like she hadn't planned on the 'innocent teenagers' either."

I turn back to the side window, hiding my face from Ellis, watching the blackness speed by. I wonder if that's true, that he didn't agree to what happened tonight. He wasn't there. In fact, he was in bed.

"Exactly."

Holding my chin high, my nostrils flair with my breath. *Do you have any idea how annoying that is?*

"Ah, I'm not sure if you want me to answer or not... Um, yeah, I do. Sorry. Like I said, habit."

Rotating in my seat again, I look at Ellis. "If you didn't want this to happen tonight, prove it. Go back for Liam."

Ellis glances over at me again. "It isn't that easy."

"Sure it is. Franko chose to stay, let him," I say, though the words sound cruel and harsh. "But Liam didn't. He doesn't want to be there." What would I say to Nora if she were waiting for me at the diner and asked where her son was, why I hadn't begged for him? What will I tell Pops and Troy?

"I'm not in charge here. There's a hierarchy. A line of command and the punishment for—"

"Excuses!" I press my fists into the seat of the truck. "Those are just stupid excuses. If you wanted to save Liam, you could." *I don't want to talk anymore. Don't say anything else to me unless you plan to turn this truck around.* I lay my head against the window pane and close my heavy eyelids. Sleep feels like a drug, one that I'm in desperate need of. One that will take me away from Readers and Phoebe and truth—the horrid truths of this night.

45

RATS

I wake in my bed, still dressed in Phoebe's little black dress. My boots have been removed and a blanket draped over me. But I have no memory of falling asleep.

Sleep. Dreamless sleep.

It took me away, allowing me to think of nothing and no one. I can't help but realize the relief that it was, the best part of my next few future hours and the few already past, as Liam saw. Though it's hard to believe I didn't wake when someone, most likely Ellis, carried me in. I've never been so out of it my entire life.

The sun shines in the wrong part of the sky. Did I sleep so long?

"He probably drugged you."

My head spins and I scan over to my bedroom doorway in one slow motion, keeping myself steady with a hold on the blankets beneath me. Though I'm lying down, the spinning room can't knock me over. "Neeta? Drugged?" I sigh. "The water..."

"I told your aunt." Neeta says, coming into the room and picking up the boots that are sprawled across the floor. "I didn't trust that Gregor boy. Not for one little minute. The rat." She folds the black boots under her arm. "You can't trust anyone who knows things about others that have yet to happen. It's just not right. Of course, I didn't know at the time he was Knowing, but I knew something was off."

I squint in the sun. Trying to make sense of what Neeta says, of what Neeta knows. "You're a Reader?" I close my eyes, somehow unable to be surprised or even panicked.

"Of course I'm a Reader." She clicks her tongue, like I've asked something ridiculous. "And you may not be a Reader, but you, like your mother, have Reader blood. We take care of our own."

Reader blood? The thought makes my stomach turn.

Neeta sneers and waves away my thought. "Get up. I've got dinner ready."

I wait for Neeta to leave before standing. I hold to the bedpost, the room still carouseling around me. Breathing, I stand, waiting for things to slow down. They do, but still, I walk to shut my door as if I'm on water. Peeling off my dress, I pull on my robe and head to the bathroom.

I should be afraid of Neeta. I should be pulling Mom through the front door and escaping in the boat. But I'm *home*. As fuzzy as my head still is, that I understand. There are no guns, no knives, no threats here, at least none that I can see, only an overbearing nurse who knows more than I'd like her to.

I turn on the shower and strip off my robe. A million different distant fears go off in my brain. Where is Liam? What are they doing to him? I need to call Troy, though I don't know what either of us can do. I promised Liam I'd get him out of there, but how? Will I ever see Phoebe again? Do I want to? I push away all of the fears and questions from my brain, things I can't possibly begin to work out. A twenty-minute thoughtless shower feels deserved. Even if I've just woken from hours and hours of dreamless sleep. I need to be conscious and thoughtless. I step into the water, letting it wash over my sticky face and stiff body.

I stand until the stream runs cold and I'm shivering. My teeth chatter and my hands wobble as I reach for the faucet handle. All the good the hot water has done me vanishes.

I dry my body and pull on yesterday's bulky sweats still lying on the bathroom floor. Not bothering to dry or comb through my hair, I exit the bathroom.

I don't know how to fix this.

I don't know what to do.

I need to know… I need *information*.

"Neeta?" I say, stepping into the hallway. I'm happy the space doesn't spin. Walking out to the living room, I see Mom, on the couch, her head propped on a pillow and her eyes zoning out on the TV. *Mom*. I was so afraid I wouldn't see her again and yet my dizzy, distracted self didn't run out to greet her. "Momma?" I say, kneeling at her side.

She ignores me, her eyes looking through me.

"Oh." Neeta walks in with a basket of laundry. "She's been like that all afternoon."

That's right, *information*, knowledge. The sight of Neeta reminds me of my goal. I'm going to learn what I can.

"Knowledge is a good thing. It's important."

I jolt, remembering of course that Neeta hears my thoughts like words from my mouth. I speak before my thoughts can betray me. "How does that work? When you're pretending for someone who doesn't know your secret, I mean. How don't you accidentally answer their thoughts?"

"Well," Neeta says, her gray hair spikes on top of her head and her blue eyes have dulled from what I imagine they once were. She pulls out one of my T-shirts and folds it with nice neat lines. "They sound a bit different. Your thoughts make you sound like you're talking inside of a cave or a tunnel. There's not an echo exactly, but it's like the sound waves are bouncing off the walls in the room."

"Doesn't it get confusing? Hearing so many voices at once?"

"No more confusing than when you're in the school lunch room and everyone speaks to their particular parties at once. Do you try to listen to every word being spoken?" She doesn't wait for me to answer. "Of course not, you listen to what you *want* to hear."

"But when you touch a Knowing—"

Neeta stops folding, her hands fall into the basket on her lap and she looks over at me. "Now, that is entirely different. That's the one time when our gift isn't a one dimensional sense. We see what they see. We hear what they hear. We feel what they feel, and if they've touched us, we see, hear, and feel our own future. Our worst. Or another's worst, of course, if they've touched someone else." She shakes her head. "*That* is something else, something horrific. Them rats are tormented creatures. Bedeviled."

Crossing my legs, I sit up straighter, out of Mom's view of the television. Grinding my teeth, I try to keep my thoughts mild and speak before they give me away. "Why... why do you call them that? They have a name, Knowing. Payne did that too, he called them rats."

Neeta's brows quirk upward like she's confused at what I'm saying. "Because that's what they are."

I bite my lip and somehow I don't even allow my thoughts to call Neeta a dirty name. She's talking about Liam, *my* Liam. "So you say," I can't keep the disdain from my tone. "But I still don't understand."

"Have you heard of the Murray house in Ashland, New Jersey?"

I shake my head. Listening and trying my best not to think, to only hear and learn.

"James Murray—"

"The author from the 1800's?" I had heard of him. He wrote dozens of books. I'd read one, but they were all pretty morbid. Still, for his time, he was a bit of a pioneer.

"Yes," she says, setting the basket down and smiling. She seems pleased I know of James Murray. Maybe Neeta's taste spans in the morbid section. "There was this old abandoned house in Ashland, New Jersey. It was in need of some tender loving care, but still beautiful, at least some felt it could be. Hadn't had owners in years. It was becoming a hazard. Well, a group of do-gooders found out it was the house James Murray grew up in. They held rallies, petitioned the city council, then they spent two years earning funds to eventually refurbish the old place, turn it into a museum for New Jersey authors, something beautiful and historical for the community. The whole town rallied behind it."

I listen, having no idea where this could be going. What does this have to do with—

"I'm getting there," she says, her hands laced together. "When the city council finally allowed the committee inside they found the place infested."

"Infested?"

Neeta nods. "Yes, *rats*. See, Thankful, rats find a place where they can eat and breed and go undetected and they spend their lives gorging and hiding and multiplying."

I feel squeamish with the image of a house full of rats, but I sit and wait for her to continue.

"So, what did they do, Thankful?"

"To the house?"

She nods.

I don't know. "Cleaned it out? Removed the infestation?" They'd done so much work, what's a little more?

"They burned the entire thing to the ground. House, history, rats and all." She snaps her fingers and I blink, watching her. Leaning toward me, Neeta licks her thin lips. "See, Thankful, rats are dirty, filthy creatures, who infect and poison all they touch. A handful of rats are good for the lab; they're tested, tried, experimented with. They give us knowledge, help cure diseases and create medicines. But a *houseful*, those rats are burned to the ground. Destroyed. Because what would anyone do with a houseful of rats? No one wants the house now. No one loves the vermin. They only love themselves and each other."

I bite my bottom lip until the pinch breaks the skin and I taste blood. I try not to scream in my mind or out loud. How does this answer my question?

"It's simple, Thankful," Neeta shakes her head. "They're the rats. Reading is a gift, like a crown passed from father to son, king to prince. Knowing is a *curse*, a disease you contaminate your seed with. Any Knowing, full or half blood, male or female, sends the curse onto their children. They multiply, hide, and infest. But no one needs a thousand lab rats."

"They are *people*." Before their curse, they are people!

"No dear, they're not."

46

BIRTHRIGHT

I check on Mom and return to my room, closing the door so Neeta can't spy on me. *Rats.* She's the vermin. I've had more cruel thoughts in the last twenty-four hours than I have in my entire life.

"Come on, more than you've had for your dad?"

I jolt; holding my hands to my heart. I manage to keep my scream inside.

"*I* didn't abandon you," Phoebe says, leaning against the wall, scrolling through her phone, like nothing happened last night, like she's paying me a social call and she's just reading a message real quick.

"Checking Facebook?" I don't care for once that I can't keep the emotion from my voice like Phoebe. That the sarcasm and anger I feel seep through in my tone.

Dropping her hand, the glow from the screen disappears from her face. "Thankful, you know I don't do social media. Too many stalkers."

Ignoring her attempt at a joke, I curl my hands into fists. "Where's Liam?"

"He's fine. Really. Don't worry about him, honey."

I fold my arms over my chest and lean against my bedroom door. "So, that's it? We're just going to act like nothing happened..." My brain whirls back, trying to remember with my long drugged-out sleep. "Uh, last night?"

"Of course not." She plops herself onto my bed. "We can't erase last night. But now you know. You can ask questions, learn, understand."

"I don't think I want to understand what you do, Phoebe. Besides, you put on quite an act. I'm pretty sure I wasn't supposed to find out." I don't sit next to her like I would have a day ago. I don't move from my spot against the door.

She sighs and runs a hand through her hair. "Well, that's true." Standing, she rests her hands on her hips. "But that isn't my fault. I hated lying to you. But I promised Sally—"

"Wait." I step forward. "Mom knows?"

"Of course your mother knows." Phoebe shakes her head, and I can see the exhaustion in her face. I wonder if she's slept yet. "Our mother was high up in the Rule. We knew who she worked for. It was an honor. And Sally would've..."

"Sally would have what?"

"Well," Phoebe sits again, glancing from me to her folded hands. "Sally's the oldest. She would have been passed the gift."

"Why wasn't she then?" I ask, knowing what that means. I too would have been passed the *gift*.

Phoebe leans back on the bed, staring up at my ceiling fan. "After our dad got sick with Huntington's, Mom had us tested. Both of us. When Sally's test came back positive, Mom passed the gift onto me."

"Wait. Hold it." I cover my face with my hands, my brain on overload. "You said you never wanted to be tested. I asked you that

—" My head jumbles with too much information. I can't even remember *when* I asked her that. "And Mom, Mom found out when I was eleven. She had signs of the disease, was tested, Dad left." It sounded like I blamed her, but I didn't. It was just the timeline of it all. She couldn't help his reaction. She couldn't help her diagnoses.

No disease meant she would have become a Reader. Huntington's or Reading, I didn't know which I'd consider the lesser of the two evils.

"*Really?*" Phoebe sits up, shaking her head at me. "Mom never told Sally that we were tested. She called the doctor's appointment, the tests, just routine exams, but when I was eighteen she fessed up. So, your Mom didn't know until she had her own test done."

I cross my arms and start to pace in the room. "Grandma never told her?"

"No. All she told her was after a lot of deliberation she'd chosen to give the Reading gift to me. Your mother was angry. Though it was your grandmother's choice whom she passed her gift onto, Sally, along with most of the Reader world, felt she'd been denied her birthright. She didn't speak to Grandma again until after she met your father. The jack—, well, he at least helped our family with that."

A jackhammer starts in my ears. I couldn't be hearing this right. This couldn't be right. Mom *wanted* to be a Reader. I run my hands over my head, my hands forming fists around balls of hair.

My mom. My angel mother.

"What have you done with Liam?" I yell, flipping the conversation upside down. But I can't think about Mom and Reading with what I saw happen last night. I can't let the image of a healthy Sally Tenys beating some man for his thoughts and actions come into my brain. I need her to still be *her*.

I need one person in my life to still be *who* they were before yesterday, Huntington's and all. Not a mind reader. Not a mind reader's prisoner. Just who they were when they woke up yesterday.

"Geez, Thankful!" Phoebe throws the pillow from my bed at me. "I am your *family*! Can't you trust me? Can't you trust anything I say? You believe everything that *rat* told you, all the way down to me being evil. *Me*, Thankful! Me!"

"*He* didn't make me believe anything!"

Pushing herself off the bed, Phoebe runs her hands over her face like she's washing away my thoughts. "Oh, right."

"And I don't think you're evil." But I don't think she's good either.

Throwing her fist into the air with my thought, Phoebe points at me. "See?"

"That wasn't him!" I yell back at her. "You're the one who lied! You're the one held a knife to Payne's throat, you're the one who's keeping him!"

"I'm not! Okay?" She bellows the words, but her hands and arms fall to her sides like a defeated animal. "I'm not *anymore*." Turning around, she faces my bedroom window. "Your precious Liam is home."

"What? Why?" I grab a sweatshirt from the floor and throw it over my head. "Now?" My head slips through the sweatshirt hole and my still damp hair flattens against my head. "Don't lie to me, Phoebe! Is he really?"

Turning back, she crosses the room, both of her hands on my upper arms, holding me in place. "He is, Thankful. I won't lie to you again. But you can't go over there."

"I *have* to go over there." I shrug out of her hold. "I can't believe he hasn't come here. How long ago?"

She sighs and the breath that falls from her chest shakes. "I dropped him off just before I came here."

I yank on the doorknob, when her hand pulls on my elbow, stopping me. "Please, Thankful, don't. They're going to hate you. You're the reason their son was identified and forced to the cabin last night." Her head falls. "I'm not trying to be cruel, it's just how they'll see it, and I don't want you to get hurt."

"Liam doesn't blame me." *You're the reason he was taken there, not me.* The thought comes strong with my urgency to get to him, even if I don't completely believe it.

"Fine," she says. "Then I'm coming with you."

47

TRUST

"Why did you let him go?" I ask, sitting in the cab of Phoebe's Jeep.

"Ellis," she says, her eyes steady on the road. "He thought it was a good idea. We don't like to involve our legal people unless absolutely necessary and since he's still in high school…"

Ellis holds the credit for Liam's safety, for him being home tonight. Not Phoebe, Ellis.

"It's not a good idea." She glances at me, defending herself. "It still goes against protocol, he is *eighteen*. High school or not, he's an adult now, and Ellis and I could be killed for his freedom."

"Why then? Why did you listen to Ellis?"

Phoebe shakes her head a little. "Ellis can be very persuasive. Besides, Payne and Byron don't know his age, only Ellis and I. And we aren't telling or thinking about it."

"How did Ellis know?" If Byron and Payne were still in the dark, then who brought Ellis in?

She clears her throat. "I did. Ellis being my ex wasn't exactly a lie."

I nod, waiting for the five-minute drive to come to an end. I'm ready to see Liam.

"I meant what I said, Thankful. I won't lie to you again. I never wanted to, but Sally, well, I couldn't go against her wishes." She stops the car, but doesn't turn it off.

I'm not sure if she thinks this heart-to-heart will continue or end with some type of resolution before I head into the diner, but I won't attempt either. Not now. I'm not sitting here chatting while Liam waits inside.

It's late and the doors are locked, but I can see a light under the kitchen entryway. I pound on the glass, not caring that my frozen, windblown hand stings with the contact.

The kitchen door swings open, and Pops stands in the doorway. His white hair shoots out in disarray and his full gray eyebrows knit together when he sees me. He doesn't move from the kitchen entrance.

He hates me now. He never liked me, but now dislike has turned to hate, resentment, loathing, blame...

Brushing his hands down the side of his plaid shirt lying over his khaki pants, he walks over, slow and steady, his limp more pronounced than normal. He stands on the other side of the glass, his mouth twitching. His eyes look through me, past me, and I know Phoebe stands behind me.

He'll never let me in now. I lift my hand to pound on the glass again, though he stands on just the other side.

"Thankful!" The sound of my name muffles through the glass door, the owner of the voice hidden somewhere behind Pops.

I lean to the side, looking past him and see Troy bounding over to the diner door. He nudges his father out of the way and twists the lock. Pulling it open, he reaches for me, plucking me in by my hand. Troy, who's hardly touched me since we first met months ago, pulls me into a hug. He wraps his arms around me, like he's had a son *and* a daughter in danger. I hug him back, my chest lurching with silent sobs.

Lugging back, he wipes the tears from my face. "You're okay?"

I nod, my head still in his hold.

The bell to the diner dings and Phoebe comes through the door.

"Why are you here?" Pops spits the words at Phoebe, but I notice how he's standing a great distance from me as well.

"I am here for her protection," Phoebe says, her hands behind her back and her raincoat completely unruffled.

"She needs no protection. She is safe here." Troy's arm wraps around me, tucking me at his side.

Phoebe stays silent. She knows that Troy means what he says. But she also knows Pop's thoughts and he looks as if he could hurt me without thinking twice. Still, I'm not afraid. If Pops were to hurt me, it would be for his grandsons, one who is lost to him.

"Where is Liam?" I ask Troy.

"Changing, at the house. I'll let him know—"

"Could I?" I need to be alone with him. I need to be away from the rest of them.

He nods and kisses my forehead, letting me go from his clutches. I don't care what he's seen, I'm so happy to have him welcome me back. I'm so grateful for his forgiveness and kindness, that he doesn't look at me the way Pops does.

I hurry through the kitchen door, flying past the cook's station and the lounge. I yank the back door open, out of breath already with my small plight.

Liam stands there, his hair wet and his cheeks pink from the crisp air. His eyes widen, surprised at the sight of me.

"Liam." Like a silent prayer, I say his name. Charging out the door, though there's only a couple feet between us, I slam into him. I wrap my arms around his neck and my feet swing off the ground. Squeezing him, I attempt pulling him closer to me, though I don't know how that's possible. He crushes me back until it's hard to breathe, but I don't say so, I don't want him to let go. Ever.

He's here. He's back. He's exactly who he should be and exactly who I need.

I kiss his neck and cry into his dark T-shirt. *I love you, Liam.* I wish I could speak. I wish he could hear me. But when I try to say the words out loud, a small sob escapes my mouth.

"You're okay. You're okay." He hushes the words in my ear.

But that's not why I'm crying. *He's okay.*

I lift my head and meet him eye to eye. My gaze roves over his face, hardly believing we're together again. Twenty-four of the longest hours of my life, twenty-four hours ago I was certain I'd never see him again. I just knew we'd had our last kiss, our last goodbye. I was never so thankful to be wrong.

Leaning my head down, I peck his lips, forgetting the hard awkward kiss we shared last night. He sets my feet back on the ground. I rub the nape of his neck, not wanting to let go. Liam's hand comes up to my cheek, wiping away the moisture there. His wrist is scabbed and swollen. I unlock my hold on his neck and take his hand and wrist in mine.

"They look infected," I say, my first sentence to Liam, the first thing I can utter. I hold his hands in mine, but I don't touch the wounds.

"Pops is taking care of me." He doesn't look at his hands, only my face.

"You're home." The words squeak from my mouth and my crying begins again. I cover my mouth with my hand and try to drown out the sobs.

"Shhh," he says, towing me into his chest once more.

"I didn't think I'd—"

"I know." He leans his head against mine and speaks into my damp hair. "Me either."

Liam holds me a few minutes more and then we walk back

through the kitchen, though it feels too soon. I want to live on a deserted island, one only Liam and I can find, one where there aren't angry family members ready to rip each other apart in the other room.

The voices from the dining room grow louder and I dread seeing the others all the more. Liam is with me. I've found my happy place. From now on, I won't make him sit or speak or touch another soul again as long we live. He's happy with just the two of us and now, I am too.

The hollers grow. I look at Liam and he puffs out his cheeks.

"Phoebe's here, and I'm pretty sure Pops will never forgive me."

He gives one curt nod, and tows me through the dining room door. All three of them are yelling and I can't quite make out what anyone says. Liam keeps hold of my left hand and pulls me along with him behind the bar. Reaching for a metal malt cup, he bangs it against the hard counter top until the noise rises above the yelling and they all stop.

"Thankful, time to go." Phoebe stands at the door, her tone indisputable.

"*Sì*," Pops says, his face a bright red. He looks as though he may have a heart attack if Phoebe the Reader doesn't leave his home soon.

"Thankful does not have to go anywhere." Troy looks from Pops to Phoebe, informing them both. "You," he says, pointing at Phoebe, "are the only one not welcome here. You cannot steal our children in the night and then think all will be forgiven when you bring two-thirds back."

"Broken and bruised!" Pops stomps and points towards Liam.

"His wounds are his own fault. I didn't touch him." Phoebe glares at Pops before turning on Troy. "And Thankful is *not* yours. You stay away from—"

"You're the only one here who's hurt her!" Troy steps towards her, his finger stabbing her direction. "You stay away—"

"Stop it!" Liam yells, letting go of me and coming out from behind the counter. "We aren't going anywhere," he says to Phoebe. "And no matter what she may be, Phoebe is Thankful's family, Dad. No one can send her away from Thankful, but Thankful."

They are quiet, and then, both of them look at me. I walk out from behind the counter, and stand next to Liam. I lace my fingers with his. In the strangest way, I've never felt so wanted, so loved. "Things cannot go back to normal. I know that. And what's been done horrifies me. The truth *horrifies* me. But Liam is right, Phoebe's my family. And I can't let go of that, yet."

Pops snorts, refusing to look at me.

"Pops," I say, trying to be brave. "There is Reader in my blood, I get it, but I am *not* a Reader. I do not condone what's been done and if Phoebe threatens your family again, I will no longer be able to look at her, I—"

"Again? What about now? What about Franko? What about my *nipote*?"

Phoebe sighs. "I told you old man—"

"He agreed to stay," Liam says, but I can tell it pains him to do so. "I was there. I heard it come out of his own mouth, Pops."

"Out of his deceived, manipulated, mind-twisted mouth!"

"He's always had a softness for Readers," Troy says, his tone sad. "You know that, Pops. You confronted him about it over Thanksgiving. You heard—"

"Rah!" Throwing his hands in the air, Pops storms from the dining room through the kitchen door. It slams open with his shove, hitting the wall behind it hard.

"Time to go," Phoebe says, peering at me.

"No." I blow a breath through my lips. "I'm not asking you to leave town. I'm not disowning you." I don't know what to do with her. "But I don't follow your rules anymore. I don't jump just because you've said I should. I'll go when I'm ready. I'm not."

Phoebe's chin circles, a sign she's grinding her teeth. She can read my mind. She knows I mean every single word. I won't be bullied. "Fine." She folds her arms. "Maybe I'll stay too."

Troy runs his hand through his hair. He doesn't like this, but he's staying out of it. *"Oh buon, Dio aiutami…"*

Liam turns his head, staring at me in the silence. His hand squeezes mine as the awkward minutes drag on.

One minute… two minutes, three… quiet, stubborn, silent minutes.

"Oh, yes! La-la-la." Troy holds up a finger, signaling he needs one second, his mutterings breaking the awkward silence. He jaunts over to the bar and, leaning on the counter, he reaches over to the work counter on the opposite side of him. "Thankful, I found this taped on the front door this morning." Hurrying back over, he holds out a white envelope with my name on it.

"For me?" I look at Liam who shrugs. He wasn't here this morning.

"Sonia?" he says, reminding me that our mutual friend had an awful evening because of our disappearing act.

I nod. It's better than my guess. I take the envelope from Troy's hands and glance towards Phoebe. I don't need to be a Reader to see that she hates being here, but she refuses to leave. She's here to protect me, even if I don't need protection. Trust builds brick upon brick and our trust has been hit with a boulder. Rebuilding that, if possible, will take time, a lot of time. I glance at her with the thought, but she sighs, chewing on her cheek and staring at the tiled floor.

Slipping my finger through the envelope tab, I break the seal and pull out the lined notebook paper. Unfolding the creases, I look at the signature at the end of the note. My heart rate quickens and I flip the envelope around to look at my name again, to look at the handwriting.

My breath in my throat accelerates and I blink over and over again, trying to take in the name, the signature. Looking up from the envelope, Phoebe's head has shot to attention, hearing the name in my mind. Her eyes dart through me, waiting for me to read.

I do. And again my eyes fall on Phoebe.

I don't understand.

Liam's eyes narrow and he shifts from me to Phoebe. "What? What is it?"

I let the shaky breath fall from my chest and stare at my aunt. "It's a warning."

"A warning?" Liam's arm wraps protectively around me, his hand resting on my waist.

"From… my *dad*."

Liam's hold on me tightens.

"He says…" I stare at Phoebe, knowing she's already heard the note in my head. "He says I can't trust you." Shaking out another breath, I look up at Liam, watching me. "Or you."

ACKNOWLEDGMENTS

I feel so much gratitude for the people who have helped me to bring this story to book form. I could not have done it alone, and I cannot express enough thanks for the time and effort put into my creation by others. I am insanely blessed with wonderful people in my life.

So, thank you, Heavenly Father, for loving me enough to bless me with more than I deserve, like wonderful people in my life, and the gift of opportunity.

To my beta readers, who are much more than beta readers, but sweet friends who read this book in its first stages of life and gave me hope that it could be something special. Thank you. Fara, Kim, Heidi, and Samantha, your input, your excitement, your love for the people I've made up is what makes me want to write more and more. I'm so grateful for your honest input; it always makes the story better. Sam, thank you for reading round one *and* two! And for entertaining FaceTime edits. Your input is more valuable than you know, and I'm really grateful! And a special thanks to Kim who helped me title this book! She read chapter one, had an idea and didn't even realize how brilliant she is or how perfect the idea was! I did though. Thank you, friend!

To Maggie Dallen, my editor. Thank you for being thorough and thoughtful and honest. It was such a pleasure to work with you.

To Eric, thank you so much for helping proof this book. You don't hold back and I love that. When I asked you to do this, I thought I was double checking everything with your English and grammar knowledge... what I didn't realize was how beneficial your insights and thoughts would be. I so appreciate you taking the time to do this and to do it right.

To Heidi. It's hard to know how to thank someone who you will never really, truly be able to thank *enough*. You have read this book almost as many times as I have. You love Liam possibly more than I do. You believe in me probably more than you should. Thank you for proofing again and again and again. You want it to be right and so you read and check and study and proof—which I so appreciate. You understand commas like I understand chocolate. It's a gift that I don't have, and I feel so reliant on someone else to make it right. Thank you for being that person. Thank you for caring enough to do it so well. Also, thank you for working your skills on my cover. I asked you again and again to switch things up and you so kindly did it, wanting it to be perfect. I love you dearly, and I am so thankful for you investing so much time and effort into me and my work.

To my dad. I love you, Dad. I am so grateful for your kind, giving nature. I hope I got a little of that. I am grateful for your belief that I could go another direction with this book and make it work. Thank you for loving me and for believing in me and for always being there.

To my beautiful mother. There are so many things I wish I could share with you, my books just being one of them. I can hear in my mind how proud you'd be of my little accomplishments. You'd make them feel so much grander than they are. You always made everything better. Thank you for loving me so fiercely on earth that

I still feel that love and compassion and care from heaven. I love you, Momma.

Thank you to my dear siblings, Becky, Kris, and Greg. I am so grateful for your love and support. I am grateful for your friendship and for the special piece of Mom each of you have inside you. Thank you for always cheering me on.

To Ron and Kathy. Thank you for always supporting and believing in me. Thank you for being so willing to host book signings and sell books at your store. Kathy- it means so much to me whenever you read and tell me how much you enjoyed one of my books. Thank you for loving me by taking time from your busy life to read a book.

To my family: Jeff, Tim, Landon, Seth, and Sydney. You are the best things in my life. My love for our family and each of you individually is inspiration and motivation to write about the greatest thing in the world—*love*. It's because I love you so dearly that writing about love is so precious and important to me. Thank you for being who you are. Thank you for loving me so sweetly. Thank you for being the kind of nerds who tease me about being *the* Jen Atkinson and "mom burns". You make life so much more fun.

And...

As cheesy as it is, I love the characters that I've created. They have practically told me their stories and taught me a load in the process. So...

Olivia, you are brave and true and I needed to be brave and true to myself to give publishing this book in a different way than all my others a shot. It was scary and nerve racking, but right.

Samantha, you had to give something up to find where you needed to be. So did I.

Marcela and Natalie, your friendship is what made you great. It's what made you figure out who you are. It's what helped you to be brave enough to face the world. I could *not* have done this without the help of my friends, old and new.

ALSO BY JEN ATKINSON

LIKE HOME

Knowing Amelia

Roses Don't Have to be Red

About the Author

Jen Atkinson is a born and raised Wyoming girl who believes there is no better place on earth. Jen fills her days raising kids, dating her husband, working with elementary students, and of course, writing. She loves reading a good, clean, love story as well as a young adult dystopian.

Jen lives next to one of Wyoming's many mountains where the wind regularly whips through her hair and bites at her cheeks. Jen's greatest loves are her four children, Tim, Landon, Seth, and Sydney, as well as her husband Jeff. She is the author of women's fictions: *LIKE HOME, Knowing Amelia,* and *Roses Don't Have to be Red.*

Follow Jen on Instagram @jenatkinson_author

For more information

jenatkinsonwrites.blogspot.com
jenatkinson.author@gmail.com

10308144R10177

Made in the USA
Monee, IL
27 August 2019